ENGEL

Corporal Heinz Engel's patrol have orders to survey the jungle around their camp, assessing its threats. They soon find that in the mid-Cretaceous, threats lurk everywhere, and foolish mistakes have bloody consequences. Peril brings out the best in some and acts of cowardice and betrayal from others, which soon leads to disaster, leaving Engel alone to seek vengeance.

ENGEL is set during **REVENGE,** the New World Series Book 2.

STEPHEN LLEWELYN

FOR KEEPS: ROOKSTONE

FOR KEEPS | BOOK 1

***For Sally**
**Thank you for your unwavering commitment,
support and for everything you do.***

The author also wishes to acknowledge:
Mum, Dad and Bill. Thanks to Sally-Marie and Andy Wake, all at Fossil Rock and
The Chapter House for the reads, re-reads, marketing, publishing, IT help and
on, and on, and on...

To my long-suffering friends, thank you for a lifetime of memories and support.
Lastly, and crucially, my sincere thanks to everyone who reads this book and
enjoyed my others. Thank you.

This work of fiction draws inspiration from Chillingham Castle in
Northumberland, one of my favourite places, though any similarity to any
persons alive or dead is purely coincidental.

*No artificial intelligence was used in the writing of this book, only the limited
intelligence of Stephen Llewelyn.*

'Lo, there do I see my father.
Lo, there do I see my mother.
Lo, there do I see my sisters and brothers.
Lo, there do I see the line of my people,
back to the beginning.
Lo, they do call to me.
They bid me take my place among them,
in the halls of Valhalla,
where the brave live forever!'

Taken from the movie *The 13th Warrior* – based on the Michael Crichton's novel, *Eaters of the Dead*. The prayer is inspired by Viking beliefs in courage and its rewards in the afterlife, as recorded through the words of 10th-century Arab explorer, Ahmad Ibn Fadlan. To this day, many believe the ancestors watch over us, and that no matter how badly things go, our people are waiting to catch us when we fall. An evocative and comforting thought in troubled times.

part one

The Interview: part I, August 1994

Immaculately turned out in his tailored suit, silk tie and handmade shoes, the interviewer smiled at the camera. "Hello and welcome, everyone, to *An Evening with Brandon*. I have with me in the studio this evening a man who's been in the news rather a lot recently, and I'm sure will need little introduction. I'm talking, of course, about Gary Stone – Worcestershire-based builder and restorer of all things ancient, and proprietor of For Keeps Ltd. Gary, good evening."

By contrast, the interviewee wore tradesmen's trousers with large pockets at the sides, a branded fleece jacket and work boots – albeit new ones. Rabbit in the headlamps, his return smile was awkward. "Good evening, Brandon. Thanks for having me."

The interviewer raised his smile a notch. "You're most welcome." Whether or not that was true, the ratings he expected the working-class hero to deliver certainly would be. "Gary, the very first thing everyone sitting at home will be dying for me to ask you is, are ghosts real and can you prove it?"

Gary Stone blinked into the camera. "Erm…"

Someone behind the camera waved frantically, urging the builder to look back to Brandon. Gary returned his gaze to the slick suit seated before him.

"So," Brandon prompted, "ghosts – can you offer proof of life after death for our viewers?"

"No."

The interviewer's smile froze.

"But I *know* they exist – though they prefer to be called spirits."

Sixty years earlier...

"What are you doing, darling?"

Sir Henry Grey, first of that name, turned at the sound of his wife's voice. He grinned toothily, shielding his eyes from the brilliant sunshine. "Hello, old girl. You remember Roger, don't you?" He gestured to a tall man wearing a smart pair of crisply ironed cream slacks with a white sweater tied about his neck and shoulders. He held a Kodak Six-16 Junior camera in his hands, about to take a picture, though he was dressed for sports.

Lady Evelyn Grey frowned. "Good lord, is that you, Dodgy? We haven't seen you in an age. What are the pair of you up to out here?"

Sir Henry buffed the single, silver wing that adorned the bonnet of his new Bentley with loving attention. Not quite satisfied, he breathed on the forward-leaning, art deco style 'B' to buff it again. "Just setting up a snapshot of the jolly old Bentley. Dodgy's got a new Box Brownie he wants to try out."

"Steady on, old chap, those things went out with the ark. This is brand new glass – 1934, latest model! Hello, Evey." He leaned forward slightly, so that they could 'miss' each other in the general vicinity of their cheeks. "After this, we're off for tennis. Fancy a set?"

"Hardly," she teased. "Some of us have work to do."

He laughed heartily. "Saving us the embarrassment of a beating, eh?"

Evelyn smirked. "Modesty forbids me, but don't let me stop you boys. And no fighting over who serves! Hear that, Henry? Flip a coin or some such. My dear brother is still limping after last week."

Sir Henry wore a hunted look. His wife always called him Harry; 'Henry' usually meant he was in trouble. "Come on, old love. That was a complete accident. I—" He stopped mid-excuses, interrupted by the roar of an engine.

High above, another trio observed the three below from the dark windows of Rookstone Castle's long gallery. A blond woman, her hair braided into two long plaits, pointed out and down, towards the lane running adjacent to the castle.

"There. That's the tear. I felt it coming – that's why I gathered the three of us here. Didn't you sense it, Edward? Surely you see it?"

Of her two associates, the older male squinted out into the bright sunshine at a vehicle approaching down the lane. "I don't know, Inga. Those contraptions all look alike to me."

"It doesn't matter what it is – it's what it represents." She looked to the youngest member of their triad. "Geoffrey, what do you think? Geoff?"

Geoff paused with his hip flask halfway to his lips. "My brother looks happy, doesn't he?"

Inga and Edward shared a look of sadness. "I meant about the horseless cart out there," she tried again, gently.

Geoff rallied immediately. "I say, goes well, doesn't she, what?" He offered his flask to Edward. "Still, the sun's over the yardarm. Anyone for a snifter?"

Edward accepted the proffered tipple, absently. Without taking his eyes from what was happening outside, he raised his arm to drink.

Inga glared at him until he lowered it and handed back the flask.

Below, Sir Henry was also watching the white, boxy vehicle driving down the lane. Something of an expert on internal combustion and adjacent technologies, he was mystified. "What the devil's that? The engine has a whine to it. Looks like something from one of my son's Flash Gordon comics."

Roger squinted into the sun. "Never heard the likes of it, but she goes like a witch! Surely that's not a van, is it? Can't be..."

The vehicle vanished and Sir Henry shrugged, assuming it had disappeared behind the high walls of the outer courtyard. He returned to posing with his beloved Bentley. "Come on, Dodgy, we're losing the afternoon."

Refocusing on the job in hand, Roger looked through the small viewfinder. "Hold still, old man. You're swaying like a sailor."

"I am not!"

Roger sighed, waiting indolently for Henry to find a pose he was comfortable with. "Right. Three, two, one..."

Click.

From the windows above, hidden in shadows, Inga shook her head with concern. "We haven't seen the last of this."

Edward opened his mouth to ask for further explanation, but when he turned to her, she was gone. His beard twitched, irritably. "I think I'll take that drink now, Geoff. Geoff?" He turned again, but the young man was gone, too. Left alone, Edward rolled his eyes and vanished.

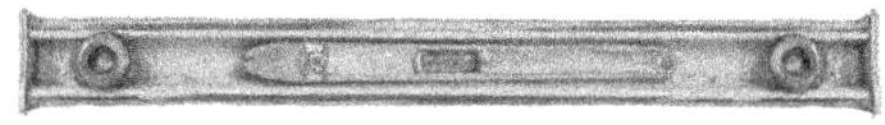

Friday, 29th April 1994

Lunchtime at a proper table, and with warm food, too – a rare treat for Gary. Lunch was usually sandwiches on a dusty building site somewhere, or in his van, hundreds of miles from home. If he was lucky, his squashed butties, wrapped in soulless clingfilm, might even be followed by a chocolate bar – but not today. He pushed his almost-empty plate away with satisfaction and reached for his mug of tea.

Woof!

Startled, he remembered his responsibilities and swerved smoothly away from the drink to pick up his crusts instead. Each liberally soaked in sauce from his baked beans, he passed them to the Parson Russell Terrier bitch waiting expectantly under the table, excitedly thumping her tail against its leg.

Gary was about to pass her the second crust, when he sensed a change in the room's atmosphere and glanced up to see Emma standing arms crossed, shaking her head with disapproval and long-suffering acceptance.

He looked back down to the dog, now drooling on the kitchen floor tiles. "Sorry, Poppy. Mummy's rumbled us."

"Again!" Emma snorted. "You may as well give it to her now. It's not fair to tease – or to blame me for it."

Woof! Poppy agreed.

Gary gave her a secret wink. "But I think we got away with it. Here you go, girl." He watched her devour the second crust before standing to down the remainder of his tea. "Thanks, Em. That was great."

Emma kissed him on the cheek. "I could get used to you working this close to home. Gives me a chance to cook something more than beans on toast."

"You still *did* make beans on toast."

Emma grinned at his confusion. "Only for you. I've got chilli con carne."

"I thought I could smell it," he accused. "I love chilli."

"I know, dear, but it upsets you. Can't send you back to site with a bad tummy, can we? Don't worry," she interrupted his protestations, "I'll save you some for dinner. Here, I refilled your flask with tea." She kissed him again.

Dismissed, Gary sighed, called Poppy, and together, they left the house, the little dog trotting at his side. "Come on, girl. We'd better get back to it, before those lot knock down the wrong wall or brick up the owner's mother-in-law in the new bathroom."

Emma watched Gary's van back off their drive – Poppy jumping and yapping excitedly on the passenger seat. Smiling, she waved them off. When they were out of sight, she puffed out her cheeks and returned to her final checks of the dreaded For Keeps Ltd end-of-year accounts before signing them off.

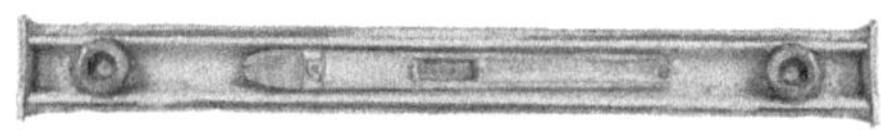

The young man was nervous and excited. Landed Worcestershire gentry, born and bred, Jeremy Horatio Jarvis had nevertheless secured a lowly labouring job with For Keeps Ltd. The opportunity to travel the length and breadth of the British Isles, restoring old, sometimes ancient properties and places, suited Jerry just fine. He hoped to learn a trade, while gaining a measure of independence from his father, who, in turn, hoped the work would make a man of him.

Returning from lunch, Gary Stone pulled up on site and watched Jerry from his van, making sure the new recruit was all right on his first day.

Four separate and distinct reasons fed into his decision to employ the young aristocrat. Firstly, Jerry was exceptionally friendly and likeable. Perhaps, on the face of it, not the sharpest tool in the shed, but Gary had taken to him.

Secondly, reading between the lines of conversations with Jerry, he suspected there might be family problems. His father was Sir Kenneth Hornesby Jarvis, a man well known in the shire for his connections with the government and military institutions – and also for owning half the county. From what Gary could tell, he seemed to have virtually disowned his son for being 'too damnably soft to ever amount to anything'. Jerry wore it lightly, but his story saddened the tough, middle-aged builder, who had no son of his own. It also explained why Jerry leapt at the opportunity to work away much of the time.

Thirdly, despite feeling sorry for him, Gary immediately recognised how the Jarvis name, contacts, and even Jerry's outrageously plummy accent, might carry water with the type of people For Keeps usually worked for. In that regard, some of his other salt-of-the-earth lads often proved *too* salty for the upper crust. However, though obviously a tryer, he suspected the young man's thoroughbred speech might count against him on site with the rest of the team. Gary had had some scruple about that, eventually deciding it would be unfair to discriminate against someone for their accent. That was when his fourth reason struck, more like epiphany than strategy. He simply realised that he could do with a good laugh.

His mind returned to finishing their current project, a small manor, for once, close to his home near Claines. He could hear his younger brother, Jimmy Stone, bellowing at someone for moving his favourite bullnosed chisel.

Someone within the building shouted, "Look out, James-the-Mason's on the warpath again!"

Gary snorted. His brother's nickname was so silly, so obvious, yet it always made him chuckle.

"I say, chaps," Jerry called, plaintively, drawing Gary's attention. "Could I get a hand over here? If I've to move all these bags of cement, it will take me all afternoon before I can get the jolly old mixer going again... Chaps?"

Gary climbed a ladder to the first floor of the scaffolding and leaned over its handrail to direct. Patiently, he called, "Set the mixer up by the sand – over there, by the ton-bags, because they can't be moved. Then take the first two bags of cement over *to* it, get a mix on and then move the rest. Mix it four-to-one, and one of lime, remember? Like I told you." It was then that young Aleksander walked out from under the scaffold beneath him, bare-headed.

Gary's sister, Kim Stone, had led an exciting if complicated life during the late seventies, returning home from Europe one day with Aleksander Kaminski,

Gary's half-Polish nephew. That nepotism was working well for the young labourer – he would have found himself sacked after his first week otherwise. His surname meant 'stone cutter'. A master mason himself, Gary's brother loved that, and Jimmy constantly made the predictable joke about Aleks being a chip off the old block, but Gary hired the boy chiefly to get his sister off his back and fully expected to regret it. As the eldest sibling, he suspected Jimmy and Kim would be the death of him one day. He sighed. "Oi, dick 'ead! Where's your hard hat? Get it on!"

"It's in Jimmy's van," Aleks shouted back, as if that explained everything.

"When you get your head caved in, shall we put that in Jimmy's van as well?"

"Eh?"

Gary sighed again. "If we get fined, thanks to any amateur photographers in the area, working on behalf of the Health and Safety Executive, it's coming out of your wages! Now get your hat and then help Jerry move the cement from that pallet to the mixer, got it?"

"Why've I got to help Jeeves with her bags? I've got my own work to do."

Jeremy Horatio Jarvis sighed, too; he already hated the nickname they had assigned him, just because they thought he was posh.

"*Because,*" Gary replied, sweetly at first, working up, "he needs help. Because your job as a labourer is to do labouring. And because I damned well told you to! Now, come on, shape yourself!"

They heard laughter from inside the building. Someone shouted, "Hobnob's in trouble again, lads!"

Aleks reddened. "Get lost!" he called back, also hating the nickname the lads used to describe his teenaged complexion.

"Never mind them," Gary called down. "Get on with what I told you."

Aleks looked balefully up at his uncle. Pointing a thumb at his own chest and believing himself genuinely hard done by, he answered back, "I work to my pay grade, mate."

Gary was not in the mood. "You'll be working your way down the dole queue in a minute," he bawled, losing his temper at last. "Get moving or get lost!" He turned away and stooped into the building through a window to continue his work. The project was nearly complete. They would soon be on their way to the next, up in the far north of England, which meant he would spend the coming weeks stressing over whether their current customer would cough up honourably for the considerable outlay For Keeps had already made on their behalf – it was always the same.

Collecting his plasterer's bucket, Gary went to the nearest tap and began pouring fresh water. He needed a half-mix of finishing plaster to resurface the small area where he was working, but the water pressure was down. One of the floorboards was already lifted for his plumber to swap the antiquated lead pipe, pinched to a narrow bore, for modern, fifteen-millimetre copper to feed the upper storey. Taking care not to put his foot through the ceiling below, he waited, keeping his eye on the bucket until it filled to about five inches. Glancing down into the dusty detritus within the floor void, he saw a few remnants of old newspapers. It was common for him to find all sorts of broken oddments and tatters of paper under floors; sometimes they provided dating evidence for when that floor was either laid or last lifted. He turned off the tap and reached down, curious as ever to see if the paper would reveal such a date, when something else caught his eye. He knelt for a closer look. Forgetting the newspaper fragments, he removed something even more intriguing, for sticking out of the thick carpet of dust was an old cross.

Turning it over, he blew on it and rubbed it to see what it was. Of dull, tarnished metal, it had a simple design. Unlike a crucifix, each point of the cross was of equal length and etched with simple concentric circles. It looked old.

Distracted, he checked the tap was off again and pocketed the cross to keep it safe for when he next met with the building's owner, though he doubted the item would be worth much.

Gary barely had his first spread of plaster on the wall, when he heard a cry from outside. Giving his finishing trowel a quick wash down – no self-respecting plasterer would under any circumstances leave his trowel dirty – he set it, and his hawk, down on the mortar board[1].

"AAAARGH! HELP! HELP ME!"

"What now?" Gary growled.

The voice sounded like Jerry's. What kind of calamity could the youngsters have possibly caused in the time it had taken him to mix half a bucket of Multi Finish? Making his way back out onto the scaffold, he burst out laughing.

Clearly working hard, Jerry already had several bags of cement moved and the mixer going, but as the powerful little diesel motor drove the large drum round, he had also made the rookie mistake of trying to scrape the sand stuck behind the mixing blades back into the mix with his shovel. Experienced operatives did that all the time, so he had at least been paying attention.

Unfortunately, having never tried before, he got the shovel stuck, too. Gary laughed again; they had all done it. However, Jerry's inexperience led him to hang on rather than let go. He span around the head of the mixer like the guitarist in a glam rock stage show, screaming for his delighted audience, who were already outside to see what all the commotion was about. The other builders collapsed in hysterics at the spectacle and Jerry's cultured cries for help.

Terrified, Jerry hung on, even more afraid to let go.

At the rear of their group, a huge, blond man with a beard like a haystack emerged from the building to stoop under the scaffold, grinning. As mountainous a man as his name suggested, William Manton leaned down to the paint-spattered site radio that blasted a recently deceased American musician's most famous and raucous four-chord progression. Cranking the volume, he sang along.

"*With the shovel out, it's less dangerous – here we are now, entertain us!*"

---

1. A 'hawk' is the hand board used by a plasterer in tandem with their trowel. The tradesman scoops product onto their hawk from a 'mortar board' (sometimes called a 'spot'), which is larger and often set up on a trestle. Anyone confusing a mortar board with the type worn by students collecting their degrees is liable to receive a bad neck.

Soon the whole gang joined in.

"*You look stupid and contagious – here we are now, entertain us! Yeah!*"

In his mid-forties, Gary did not know all the words but doubled up in stitches at the spectacle as he leaned over the handrail. "Swi——" he tried, but the words came out as little more than a wheeze. "Swi——" he tried again. Eventually, he managed, "Aleks – switch it off!"

"What, the radio?"

"God help us. The mixer! Switch off the mixer!"

Barely able to stand for laughing, Aleks complied, hitting the kill switch.

Jerry slumped to the ground, white faced, his hair mussed and full of mortar.

"You alright, Jeeves?" Aleks enquired, disingenuously.

"Jarvis," Jerry muttered, dizzily. "The name is *Jeremy* Jarvis."

"He thinks he's James Bond!" Aleks cackled and pointed.

"Yeah, he hates it stirred," Andy Wilson called, tucking the handle of his plasterer's trowel into his belt, "Though I dunno what *you're* laughing about, Hobnob. You should have told him that would happen."

"Don't call me that!"

William Manton's bushy blond beard swayed as he barked raucous laughter.

"Don't know what you're laughing at, either, *Willy Mammoth!*"

The giant Brummie enjoyed his nickname, so Aleks' jibe bounced off.

While his lads insulted each other and bickered about whose fault it was, Gary climbed back down the ladder and walked over to help Jerry up, trying to suppress his own amusement. "Never mind[2], lad. Every day's a school day. You didn't get any of that lime mix in your eyes, did you?"

"No. I'm fine, honestly. Thank you."

"Good. Stop the mixer if you need to, when scraping down. At the very least, let go of the shovel if you get it stuck. You're lucky it didn't break your arm. Still, you won't do it again, will you?"

The lads carried on laughing and catcalling. Gary knew they were only trying out the new kid, to see if he would fit in and find his place among them. Jerry's real interview had begun, and his reaction would matter.

Gary arrived home that evening to take Poppy for her usual stroll around the village before he showered. Cleaned up and fit to rejoin the human race, he sat down to his promised chilli con carne dinner with Emma and showed her the cross he had found earlier.

"I offered it to the customer, but he wasn't interested – said I could have it, if I wanted it, so here it is." He handed it to his wife. "What do you think?"

---

2. Gary completely missed the significance of those words following the recent song.

Emma took it and wrinkled her nose. "Yak! It's filthy. Don't put that on the dinner table. Why don't you clean it up later? It might be silver... looks old."

"Yes, I looked it up in the finds book I keep in my van." He smiled. "You never know what we might come across, one day."

Emma rolled her eyes and smiled back. "Chance would be a fine thing."

"Yeah, well, anyway, I think it might be Saxon – if it's original, that is."

"Really?"

He nodded. "It's the same shape as the cross on our company logo. What were the chances of that? There's even a hint of the little circles along each arm of the cross. Might be a sign," he added, spookily. "By the way, did you know my family is distantly related to the people we're working for at the moment? Going back a couple of hundred years, of course."

Emma was intrigued. "I didn't realise. *Very* nice manor. I take it your side of the family decided to downscale, did they?"

Gary laughed, ruefully. "That's our excuse, anyway! Back to this cross, though, I think it might be over a thousand years old." He rubbed a twinge in his neck. "I know how it feels."

"Pulled something?"

"It's nothing."

"Need a rub later?"

He smiled again, changing his mind. "Actually, that might help. The pain's unbearable. I just didn't want to worry you."

Emma laughed, lightly. "If that cross cleans up nicely, you should wear it – on a leather string, maybe. Very manly. My very own Viking."

"Yeah, they weren't really known for being Christian, Em – not until later, anyway. They might have pinched this, though. Hope they didn't kill any of my relatives for it!" He grinned, deciding to do as Emma suggested.

Five days later, in the North...
Sir Henry Grey III switched off the radio. The news cycle was full of stories about the grunge star who recently took his own life at the apex of a glittering career. Depressing listening on such a bright day. Of greater moment to Henry was a footnote about the Greys' arrangement with the National Museum coming to an end and the famous Grey Emeralds' return to their family seat – Henry's family home, Rookstone Castle.

He turned to his study's mullioned windows to feel the sun on his face. Situated on the third floor of the west tower, they looked out over the forest and castle grounds. His ancestors had lived there for centuries, give or take a few sidetracks-by-marriage. When his father died two years earlier, Henry inherited all the trappings and honours of owning a medieval castle and estate – along with all the problems and costs associated with owning a medieval castle and estate.

He sighed. This was going to be expensive – a day of strange destiny all round. He shivered, wondering who had just walked right through him. In that place, it might have been anybody – the ancient stone walls had recorded so many lives and memories.

"I hope you're enjoying this," he spoke to the air, though he knew someone was watching him. He shrugged his shoulders uncomfortably, to settle the hairs rising on the back of his neck.

Feeling the need for some human company, he opened the window and craned to look out north and east. Down at the outer gates to the castle grounds, hidden among the deciduous canopies below, he could hear a diesel engine. No. Diesel *engines*. The whine of their turbos was unmistakable as they laboured up the steeply twisting driveway. The men he half-dreaded, half-longed to meet had arrived.

After spending most of the morning poring over a family photo album, he kept returning to the picture of his grandfather standing proudly beside his new 1934 Bentley. He had always loved that photograph, but more than that, the anomaly in the background fascinated him. He closed the album, collecting it from his desk as he made for the door.

The ancient stone staircase was cool, his footsteps ringing as he stomped down to the ground floor and exited from the tower into the castle's central courtyard. It was a beautiful day, just like the one his grandfather had described sixty years earlier. The day that photograph was taken.

Sir Henry passed into the tall, coach-sized entrance that penetrated the castle's mighty walls on their north-west elevation. One of its large oak gates stood half-open, the crack allowing spring sunshine to scythe across the gloomy passageway, lighting the opposite wall. To the right was a small room set within the walls, used by the staff as a ticket office during the seasons when they were open to the public. They needed every penny they could get, these days.

Henry dropped the family album on Albert's desk. His elderly curator and family historian was away that day, welcoming a new grandchild into the world. Henry smiled, sending his dear old friend and retainer positive wishes as he made his way through the open gate to meet the man who, until recently, was known to him simply as 'the builder'.

He took a deep breath and whispered, "Are you watching, Grandpapa?"

He could almost hear the old man's infectious laughter. Despite serving as a captain in both world wars – with all the horrors and loss that entailed – until the day he died, his grandfather remained the jolliest soul Henry ever met, and he had loved him dearly. The polar opposite of his austere father, also Sir Henry, and with whom he carried vanishingly few precious memories. No. If there was someone at his side at that moment, as he strode through his castle gates, he had no doubts it would be Grandpapa Harry.

Two vans pulled up in front of the castle entrance, crunching gravel on the D-shaped turning area. Both were clearly marked with 'For Keeps Ltd' livery along with a Worcestershire telephone number and the strapline 'An Englishman's Castle is His Home'.

Despite their long journey up from the Midlands, the vehicles were immaculately clean – a worthy first impression for a proud tradie. If Henry was any judge, they had taken the trouble to stop off at a car wash before turning up to the site where they would spend the next several weeks. It spoke well of them and their intention as a company, only slightly marred when a third van brought up the rear a few moments later. Obviously late, it was filthy from the motorway and splashed with mud from the lanes.

A stocky man in his mid-to-late forties hopped out of the lead vehicle, stopping only to glare at the late arrival. A little Parson Russell Terrier jumped out behind him, running on proportionally long legs to the lawn in the centre of the driveway to stop and stoop. The man closed his eyes with dread, sighing with relief when she merely emptied her bladder. It could have been worse. "Poppy, back in the van, girl."

After answering an urgent call of nature, the little dog immediately found a stick. As is the way with small dogs, the stick was far too large for her to drag, but that did not stop her from trying. "Come on. Leave that. Back in the van – hup, hup! Good girl. You guard Daddy's tools." He closed the door gently behind her.

Noticing Sir Henry for the first time, his face lit up warmly and he approached, hand outstretched.

The two men met for the first time, for when the builder came to view the project, prior to tendering his quote, groundsman Tom had shown him around. Henry was out of the country on business at the time, leaving his personal secretary, Richard, to deal with the details thereafter. He deliberately kept his distance until the day For Keeps arrived to start work.

The tradesman's reputation and experience with the type of project in question made him an ideal choice, but Henry had other reasons for hiring the man. As he shook the rough, work-hardened hand, Henry could feel a circle closing, and wondered how Gary Stone, proprietor of For Keeps Ltd, would react to the revelation he held in store.

Though Gary saw what lay ahead as just another project, Henry believed it might prove anything but – had carried a sense of inevitability about their meeting for some years. Since 1986, in fact, and like a bolt from history, the moment was now here. Yet, there was no tingle when they shook hands, no *bong* of the clock of doom – there was not even a sudden, spooky gust of wind. Not a single tumbleweed was displaced. There was just a hard-working man standing before him, ready to offer his honest skills and expertise for a price that was probably more than Henry wanted to pay, and less than Gary needed. Sir Henry Grey III was almost disappointed.

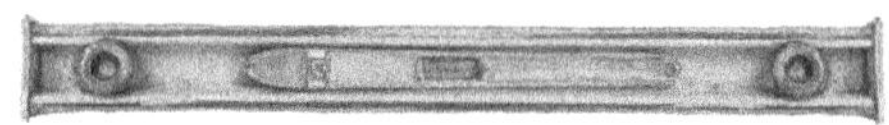

The man was a villain. He owned it. His three companions were similarly disposed, but for now at least, he was their undisputed leader. Barely had he snapped his fingers when a pair of binoculars appeared in his hand.

"Who are they, Ham?" asked his second in command.

Jack Hammer looked through the binoculars and shook his head. "Just a bunch of cowboys[3] . I knew they were coming." As with his reputation, he owned his name, too, and anyone finding it amusing did so at their peril. Known throughout the London underground simply as Hammer, he would never have realised there *was* a North, had it not been for the recent news chatter about the Grey Emeralds – chatter that led to what might euphemistically be called a job offer.

In the world of organised crime, small 'firms' like Hammer's must secure funding, do the job, and make a profit – just like small firms working *within* the law... apart from the profit.

Hammer never did anything without a healthy margin for himself. He never proceeded blindly, either. From his initial research into the gems' provenance, history and value, at the British Library, he had learned two things: one, the Grey Emeralds were not actually grey, and two, he needed them – had contacts, who had contacts, who had contacts on the Continent who would pay any price for them. A chain that pulled both ways, which was why he was there, but it was not the only reason. Upon seeing photographs of the emeralds, he felt a draw that surpassed his usual avarice. He could not quite put his finger on it, but he really did feel a *need* for them.

He returned the binoculars. "Have a butcher's."

Worzel had grown up with Hammer in the sixties, in the East End, his own nickname down to his shaggy hairstyle, worn since the late seventies, now fashionable again in no small part due to the same recently deceased rock star. He, too, enjoyed the moniker bestowed by his peers, though anyone following it with the supplementary 'Gummidge' would find themselves in trouble – fingers had been lost.

He looked through the binoculars as instructed. "There was only meant to be the old geezer and the groundskeeper – once the nob[4] and his family were out of the way. This complicates things, Ham."

"Nah. This can work for us."

Worzel lowered the field glasses to look questioningly at his partner in crime. After a moment's cogitation, a smile spread across his face. "Someone to hold the baby."

---

3. High romance, can-do frontier courage, lone justice and freedom from horizon to horizon across the rolling North American plains – "No taxation without representation!". Like the dragging of a cultural stylus across an old record, *Britain*'s cowboys are either builders of dubious reputation or young males who work on a farm – possible evidence of what happens when access to anything approaching the American Dream is denied.

4. An abbreviation of nobleman and slang term for one of wealth or high social standing. Not to be confused with knob, though such status can often open doors.

Hammer grinned, wickedly, seeing no need to elaborate. His oldest 'known associate' almost always arrived on the same page, though he usually started out a page behind.

Their companions joined them from the van. Neither Scott nor Serj spoke; they merely peered through the six-foot wrought iron railings, along the gap in the forest that led all the way to Rookstone Castle.

The atmosphere in the corridor leading to the cellar beneath Rookstone Castle was dank and treacle thick, the muck ankle deep – though a tideline higher up the walls was evidence of regular, more severe flooding. Gary could already hear complaining at his back. "Shut up and fetch your wellies. You know the drill. Aleks, bring the pump from the van. We need the pipe unwound and an extension lead with a transformer, got it?"

Aleksander wandered off, back along the narrow, damp-smelling vaulted tunnel, chuntering to himself. He was eighteen.

"Electrics aren't up to much, Gaz," Vincent 'Blackout' Barnes commented, his North-Walian accent harsh as he spoke in hushed tones. "Lights keep flickering."

Knowing his electrician's penchant for switching the power off without checking with anyone first, Gary replied, pointedly, "We could do with having them on for a *little* while longer. If that's not too much to ask."

Blackout grinned. "I'll do my best, like."

Regardless, Gary knew the Welshman had a point. It was always dark, damp and cold in old cellars, but this one seemed unnaturally gloomy – like the tired old lightbulbs were losing a war.

"Tell you what, though," Blackout continued, "I've just looked at the fuse box for this part of the castle."

Gary turned to squint in the dim light that barely illuminated the corridor. "Bit of a mess, is it?"

"Needs changing for circuit breakers before we'll be able to sign any of this off, but worse than that, some comedian has replaced one of the fuses on the socket ring main with a lost-head nail, isn'it. That'll never burn out if there's a problem, so don't hit any cables here, boys. You'll be fried like a kipper!"

"Been there before, haven't we, but?" Floating George jibed, his jovial Geordie[5] accent ringing loudly from the vaulted ceiling as he jabbed Blackout Barnes in the ribs.

---

5. Someone from Newcastle in the North East of England. Some say the term extends as far south as the collieries in County Durham, and that the name was coined by the Jacobites in the mid-eighteenth century as lands that were for 'George', Third of England. There are several other theories. What may have begun as an insult is now worn like a badge of honour among some of the proud North East peoples.

Gary gestured for his plumber and electrician to calm their rhetoric as he spotted Sir Henry squeezing down the narrow corridor past his men. "So what do you think, chaps?"

"Shouldn't be a problem, Sir Henry," Gary reassured.

"Just Henry, please," he replied, jovially. "We don't usually worry about that sort of thing here."

Gary nodded. "I take it the skip we ordered arrived?"

"Yes, it's in the outer courtyard. Let me show you the way."

As they walked through labyrinthine corridors towards a small door in the east side of the castle – that Gary surmised was a repurposed sallyport from way back when – Henry explained how his secretary had fought Heritage to a standstill before they finally granted permission to drain the cellar, in line with Gary's proposal. "In the end, we needed a structural engineer to offer evidence that it would benefit the health of the building as a whole. He was able to argue that the cavity drain system you recommended would be kinder to the stone walls than any form of waterproofing slurry."

Gary understood. The system was still relatively new in 1994, so for any organisation calling themselves 'Heritage', it was naturally deemed heresy, if not outright anathema. Of the several projects For Keeps were about to carry out for Sir Henry, draining and clearing the cellar beneath the east tower was the grimmest and would require all their manpower, so Gary wanted it out of the way first.

"Once your men are all set," Henry continued, "perhaps you'd be kind enough to spare me a few minutes? There's something I'd like to show you."

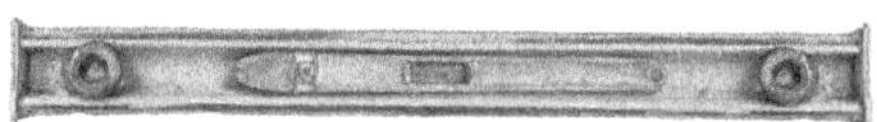

Within the hour, Gary rejoined Sir Henry back at the castle gates. Henry was deep in conversation with another man in the passageway, while bearing on a folder and signing documents.

"And this one, Henry. This is the new finance agreement."

Henry sighed, dutifully applying his signature.

"And if you could just initial these changes, we should be good to go."

Henry complied again, replacing the papers within the folder when he noticed Gary's approach.

"Ah, Gary. Thanks for coming. Won't keep you a tick."

"Sorry if I'm interrupting," the builder apologised awkwardly, standing to the side.

"Not at all, not at all. Just signing my life away. This is my personal secretary, Richard Clarence. I don't believe you've met in person. If you need anything when I'm not around, Richard is fully across the project." Henry smiled, ruefully. "Probably knows more about it than I do."

"Ah, yes, we spoke on the phone a few times after my initial visit. Nice to put a face to the name, sir."

"Likewise," Richard replied with a warm handshake. "Anyway, I'd better get this little lot filed with the bank – they're on a half day, today. Nice to meet you, Gary. I'm sure we'll talk again over the coming weeks. Cheerio."

Henry gave a quick nod goodbye and led Gary into Albert's ticket office. "Please, take a seat. I won't keep you long. Firstly, you need to be aware that we have some rather valuable items coming home to Rookstone tomorrow – you might have heard about them in the news?" Henry paused, gauging Gary's reaction. Sensing none, he pressed on. "Just to put you in the picture, they're being delivered by Secure Nation – in case you encounter any strange vehicles or personnel about the place over the coming days. Actually, we've had all manner of security types here for weeks, setting this up."

"Must have passed me by," Gary confessed. "Did it make the nationals?"

"It did, but as a mere footnote, and not of any broad significance, I'm sure. The items are little more than a collection of wretched family heirlooms, really. They're virtually priceless, of course, which means they're costing me an arm and a leg to keep safe whilst being practically worthless. They've been on display at the National Museum for the last eight years. Which is pretty much how long I've been waiting for you to arrive."

Gary blinked, not sure he understood. "Been a long time in the pipeline, then? This work, I mean."

"No. Sorry, I'm getting ahead of myself."

Gary frowned, still none the wiser. "Hope you don't mind me asking, but why've you brought these valuables home, if they're such a ball ach— I mean, if they're such a problem, like?"

Henry smiled. "Funding ran out. It was an eight-year deal. Museum can no longer afford to keep them safe, either. I'd sell the damned things, but..." He sighed. "Well, that's a whole different story. Don't misunderstand me, I'm proud of our heritage and I want to see them cared for, but this comes at a vast cost we can ill afford these days. Believe it or not, they were originally gifted to my family many centuries ago, so we could raise capital against them. Now, they're just another cost. How things change, eh? I tried to find them a new home, but, well... here we are."

"I take it the security you had in place when those items were here last didn't pass muster today?"

Henry shook his head sardonically. "Insurance chappie nearly had a fit!"

Gary's lip curled into a smile. "Thanks for letting me know." He gestured through the walls towards the east tower, where his men were working. "I'll be sure to keep that lot away from anything delicate. I'd better get back to it. We've a great deal of work in front of us." He made to stand.

"No, wait. Please. There's something else."

Gary sat once more.

Sir Henry fiddled with his collar awkwardly. "This is where it gets a bit weird, I'm afraid."

Gary leaned forward, interest piqued.

Sir Henry opened the family photo album he had brought down from his study, found the page he wanted and span it round so Gary could see it. "What do you make of this?"

The builder leaned forward a little further. The photograph was a time capsule in sepia. Squinting at the details imprisoned within the fading print, Gary checked them against the date and description handwritten in beautifully stylish cursive beneath, the ink also slightly faded with age. His eyebrows shot up in astonishment. "I don't understand?"

"No. Nor, I'm afraid, do I," Henry confessed. "This picture was taken almost exactly sixty years ago. There were fewer trees in the way then. That vintage Bentley was barely a week old, at the time. And yet, in the background, there's clearly a modern Transit van. That would be a month of weird in its own right, but, here..." He handed Gary a magnifying glass from one of Albert's desk drawers. "Look more closely."

"Bloody hell!"

"I know. But there it is. For Keeps. Your logo, jolly old Saxon cross and all. It's how I knew you were coming, you see? Years before this day. Long before the estate hired you. I was always intrigued by this photo as a child. Like my grandfather, I've an interest in vehicles – the old chap was something of an early petrol head." He smiled again. "So when Ford restyled their Transit van to the latest shape in '86, I knew the time was close. The fact that the Grey Emeralds took up their new residence, also in '86, I confess, was completely lost on me at the time, but now..."

Gary looked doubtful. "You think there's a connection between us being here and the return of your family heirlooms?"

Sir Henry shrugged. "Perhaps it's mere coincidence. Some type of foreshadowing through time. Damned if I understand it – and I've been pondering it for years, I promise you. All I can tell you plainly is that I knew both these events would happen, roughly now-ish."

Gary sat back, suddenly wondering if he was being taken for a ride – with one of his own vans, no less. "This photo's been manipulated, or altered in some way, surely? It *has* to be a fake."

"'Fraid not, old chap. That picture's been in our family since 1934. All my life it's been stuck in that album. Until recently, it was a meaningless oddity, lacking any context. Now, I'm not saying that your presence and the return of the emeralds are directly connected, but clearly there's a confluence here."

Perfectly on cue, the spooky gust of wind that failed to materialise at their first meeting chose that moment to blow through Albert's office.

Both men shuddered.

"I don't know what to say," Gary admitted, still not entirely sure whether he was simply being drawn into some sort of elaborate practical joke. He had worked for old money many times – usually lovely, they sometimes had strange little ways. "Is there anything else I should know?" he asked weakly.

"No. The items will arrive tomorrow. They'll be heavily guarded and placed into their new secure environment within the castle." Sir Henry kept the full extent of his security arrangements, and his suspicions, to himself. "We're hoping they will at least be a draw for the tourists. Just maybe, they'll pay for their own upkeep, over time. We'll see."

"Traditionally, castles are good places to store valuables." Gary grinned. "Your ancestors swore by them."

"Quite, but in those days they had a few dozen archers and men-at-arms walking walls ten feet thick – without the elaborate Elizabethan manor house windows, that barely close, cut into every edifice. And don't get me started about the rickety old gate. A fortress, this isn't. Not any more. So housing these things has been a damned expensive inconvenience, I can tell you – with the new alarm system and its direct lines to the region's police headquarters and so on."

Gary nodded, absorbing his points. "We can help you with the gates," he offered.

"You have a good carpenter?"

"Certainly. A tidy lad. Irish. Name's Liam McGeegonnaroghonnaghy. Superb joiner. Lads call him Liam-the-leaver." He shook his head, wryly. "Their banter's not sophisticated."

Sir Henry chuckled. "The world would literally be a broken-down place without them and their kind. Nothing would be fixed and we'd all freeze to death."

Gary accepted the compliment with a nod as he stood. "True enough. Though I'd better get back to it, before they break anything to need fixing. Thanks for the warning – about the security guards and so on."

"No. Thank you. Talking about breaking things – this feels like a broken dream for me. Been waiting for us to have this chat for years. Heaven knows what it all means." Henry stood, too. "Oh, and by the way..."

Gary turned at the door.

"You should probably warn your chaps, they might find some of their gear gets moved around."

"You think Secure Nation might need access to the cellar where we're working?"

"No. Nothing to do with them. This place is haunted as hell. It's a bally nightmare!"

Chapter 2

Sweet Dreams
(Aren't Made of This)

Despite the late start, their first day was going well. Willy Mammoth single-handedly raised one of the enormous flagstones in the cellar floor, so Aleks and Jimmy could dig a sump in which to situate their pump. The free water vanished quickly into the hole, the pump evacuating it via a pipe to drain down the bank outside. A mostly intact stone floor was gradually revealed, slick with the slime and sediment of years.

"Get the shovels and buckets," Gary ordered. "Let's scrape all this crap out."

"To the skip?" asked Jimmy.

"No. The Heritage people already tested for contaminants. We can barrow it out to that patch I showed you, where the customer said we can dump it. It'll be full of nutrients to help the soil."

Across the cellar's far end, some of the flagstones had at one time been roughly broken and replaced with a strip of concrete. Gary knew the castle was employed by the War Office as barracks during the 1940s, and were he to guess, would age the concrete to that period. He turned to his brother. "We have permission to lay a new slab, so that'll need to come out. Can you get the breakers?"

Jimmy nodded. "Come on, Floating George, they're on your van."

"So I'm not doing any pipework today, then?" the Geordie clarified, sourly. "You could at least give me a hand, could you not? I cannae carry all that by myself, man."

"'Course not," Jimmy agreed. "Ask Jeeves[1]. He's standing around." He slapped Floating George on the back. "A bit of labouring is character building, lad. You, of all of us, should be used to digging – the army has more shovels than rifles!"

The plumber rolled his eyes. "Why aye," he agreed, unenthusiastically, ushering Jerry towards the exit. "Come on, bonnie lad. They'll be laughing on the other side of their faces when some idiot goes through a pipe!"

"Erm, chaps... Been meaning to remind you all, my name's Jerry, actually."

"Howay. Come on, Jeeves, man."

Jerry followed Floating George through labyrinthine corridors, back out into the daylight of the outer courtyard. "So, do I understand correctly that you were in the army?"

"Aye. Only for one tour. I got out after the Gulf War."

It was unlikely the plumber knew his family, but Jerry thought it best to be sure. "Never met my father, Sir Kenneth Hornesby Jarvis, did you?"

"Don't think so. Why?"

Suddenly uncomfortable, Jerry deflected with the obvious, "No reason. George, why do they call you Floating George?"

Floating George's shoulders slumped and he stopped. Jerry almost bumped into him as he turned. "I daresay you'll find out soon enough. I *was* Corporal George Robson, of the 21st Engineer Regiment – of the Corps of Royal Engineers, naturally."

Jerry nodded. He knew. His father had him well-drilled, so to speak, for a military career that never happened.

"We were based in Germany for a few years before moving back to Catterick, North Yorkshire." Floating George shrugged. "Knowing I was for leaving, I trained to become a heating engineer there and..."

Curious now, where the tale might be leading, Jerry urged, "And?"

Smiling at the memory, Floating George continued, "I plumbed a new underground command centre, up on the Otterburn Ranges, didn't I?"

Like extracting blood from a stone, Jerry tried again. "And?"

The plumber's cheeks reddened. "I forgot to tighten one of the compression joints, leading behind the display wall to the privy." He laughed, suddenly. "Was like a swimming pool the next morning. I'd never seen my sergeant so angry. Thought I was gonna get court-martialled – or shot! The lads called me Floating George, 'cause I had to go down into it, to switch off the water at the main. Couldn't bring myself to dive, could I? It was bloody freezing, man! I never lived the debacle, or the name, down after that. I was stuck with it, 'til I left like, you know?"

Jerry smiled. "Did that hasten your departure from Her Majesty's Forces, then?"

---

1. No punnery here; Ask Jeeves would not become a household name for another three years.

"Nah. Not really. It was where I made my first big mistake, though. My second one happened a couple of years later when I took the job with Gaz and the For Keeps lads."

"Second mistake?"

"Why aye." Floating George sounded disgusted with himself.

Again, Jerry had to force the information from him. "And that was?"

The plumber looked him in the eye. "Telling those idiots about it! Stuck with it forever now, am I not? Reckon my tombstone will say 'Here lies Floating George, amphibious gift to Britain's enemies'. Let that be a lesson to you, bonnie lad. Don't tell that lot anything. *Anything!* Understand? Right. Now, come on, let's get the breakers before Andy 'Walsall's finest plasterer' Wilson starts using his head to crack the floor."

They laughed and strolled towards the vans.

Later that afternoon, the local merchant's lorry arrived to crane offload materials for the new concrete slab Gary intended to lay in the ancient cellar. His team stored any perishables indoors, leaving the rest of their supplies by the skip in the outer courtyard.

Lifting the stone flags was a massive undertaking. Some were four feet long and up to five inches thick in places. While four of the men stored them in a small chamber at the far end of the entrance tunnel – stacking them on edge to prevent breaking, so they could be relaid in a few days' time – the others took turns working the breakers to smash the concrete into moveable pieces. A deafening, repetitive clatter rang from the stones and vaulted ceilings, loud enough to rattle their teeth as it shook the whole tower above. The stink of the sludgy sediment, built up over decades in stagnant water, was nauseating, but at least the damp, for once, kept the dust down. Everyone wore ear defenders, the lads on the breakers wearing goggles, too. The lighting was dismal, communication almost impossible. Everyone hunkered down and worked hard to get through that stage of the work as quickly as possible.

Gary hated this part of cellar renovation. It could be truly grim. If there were any spirits looking over their shoulders, he hoped they had the sense to vanish. It was bad enough spending days or weeks of one's life in those disgusting conditions, but the idea of spending eternity in such filth was too much to bear. *Soon have it looking a lot better for you, lads.* He stopped and considered. *And lasses, maybe.* The idea of his own wife being forced into a place like that made him shudder. She would have a paroxysm, if she knew what working conditions were often like for them. *Best say nothing and just show her the Polaroids of the finished job.* He smiled, despite the misery of their conditions. It would all be over in a few days, when the new slab went in. Then the magic would begin, as everything came back together.

He looked around. Everyone was grafting for all they were worth, equally desperate to get through that phase. Waiting in the narrow corridor was a figure he did not recognise. He squinted in the dim light, wondering if he was seeing things. Among the clamour and movement in the small space, he stepped around his workers towards the entrance tunnel and almost bumped into Willy. The enormous Brummie almost filled the passage.

"Did you see someone standing here?" Gary cried over the din.

"What?"

"I said, did you see someone standing here?" He pointed to the floor where they stood.

Willy threw a thumb over one shoulder. Clearly, he had not heard Gary's question over the rattle of the breakers and took a guess. "He's gone to the bog, mate – for a dump!"

Gary rolled his eyes, smiling ruefully. "Too much information."

"*What?*"

"It doesn't matter." He shook his head, returning to his task of barrowing the broken concrete. There was certainly something weird about this place. It did not feel especially threatening, just weird. He wrinkled his nose. *God, it stinks down here. It's hard to imagine anything smelling worse.*

Barely had he thought it, when both breakers stopped suddenly. "Oh, crap!" Andy cried out.

Gary lowered the barrow to the floor, daring to slide his ear defenders down around his neck. "What's up?"

"Looks like we've gone through a soil pipe," Jimmy explained. "An old clay one – no surprise. Numpty's gone and smashed it. I told you to be careful, until we knew why the concrete was here!"

Andy rounded on him. "Don't blame me! I'm a master plasterer, not a bloody breakerer! I haven't got X-ray vision!"

"Master plasterer," Jimmy sneered. "Hamster pesterer, more like."

"That's right. Blame me," Andy chuntered to himself. "Honestly, it's a bloody conspiracy!"

"Alright, alright," Gary calmed them, wrinkling his nose. "Call me psychic, but I smuggled some four-inch pipe and couple of flexible clay-to-PVC adapters onto the van. Aleks, go and fetch the grinder, the big one – the nine inch. Floating George! You wanted some plumbing work to do – over here, son. Knock yourself out. We'll neaten the edges with the grinder and..." He tailed off, horror-stricken, for in the sudden silence, they all heard the flush of a nearby toilet.

Several hours later, exhausted, covered in slimy sediment and thoroughly miserable, the team emerged to a fragrant dusk.

Drawing lessons from his army days, when he unwittingly became an expert on overnight flooding, Floating George dropped the pump back into its hole in case further groundwater seeped through the ancient walls while they were in their beds. A float switch would activate it automatically, if needed, so he was happy to leave it plugged into a 110-volt extension cable, hanging from a wicked-looking wrought-iron hook sticking down from the ceiling, dangerously close to head height. He wrapped the cable around the hook and nodded, pleased that the cable would highlight the hook's presence, even in the low light.

Last out of the cellar, he took a deep breath of the fresh air. "Reckon we've all earned a shower and some pub grub[2] – maybe even a shandy or two, like." He looked hopefully to the boss.

A sudden gust of foul-smelling wind blew down the corridor, making them shudder and cover their noses. "Let's get out of here for the night," Gary mumbled, his voice muffled by his sleeve. "You've certainly earned a mixed grill – all of you – I'll grant you that. *First* drink's on me. After that, you can dream on, sunbeam."

"Quadruple Jack Daniels and Coke then, please," Willy Mammoth called.

Gary winked. "Nice try."

It was a beautiful spring evening, and their weariness evaporated as they sucked down lungfuls of fresh air, imagining plates of something hot with a jar on the side, maybe two – Gary was always more generous than he liked to pretend.

Blackout Barnes rubbed his hands together, enthusiastically. "Champion! Mine's a fish and chips and a pint, isn'it!"

Gary smiled back at him. "Sounds great. Been thinking about a mixed grill all day, but you might have twisted my arm."

The castle was closed to the public for the time being, so Sir Henry was able to make the guest suites available for Gary and his workers. It was convenient for them and cheaper for him, the cost of accommodation immediately removed from his bill. It was rare for the men to sleep in the ancient building where they worked. Gary looked back down the vaulted passageway, now thrown into a darkness so complete, he could almost believe it was solid. Puffing out his cheeks, he remembered the figure in the doorway to the cellar and Sir Henry's parting words. *This should be a night to remember.*

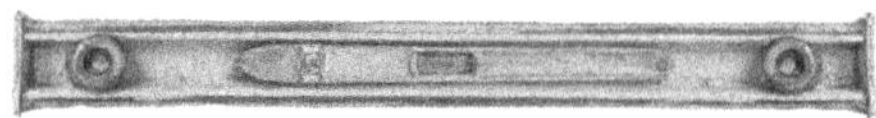

Hammer watched nine workmen and a small dog pile into one of the three vans – three in the front and six in the back, with the dog sitting on the driver's lap[3] . The van roared away down the lane, its early turbo diesel engine whining as Gary floored it in second to climb the rise to the main lane. Headlamps flickered

---

2. A meal at the local public house. Not to be confused with grubby, meaning filthy, although both certainly applied to Floating George's current state. 'Grub' has been recorded slang for food for many centuries in Britain – possibly since the 1300s. New terminology, and positively 'down with the kids', for some of the ghosts who remembered the cellars being constructed in the 1100s. However, the pub as a bespoke building, as we would understand it, did not really come to be until the much later Beerhouse Act of 1830. Some words and concepts change, others do not, so it's small wonder that verbal communication with the beyond was so difficult before EMF meters and Google Translate.

3. It was the nineties.

between the trees in the deepening twilight until it turned away from them, leaving the evening silent but for a gentle rustle of the breeze through the forest. "Right. The staff have left for the night and that bunch o' brickies won't be back 'til kickin' out time, if I'm any judge." He turned to Worzel, who shuddered. "Wassup?"

"Don't like the J-word, Ham."

Hammer snorted. "Leave it out." He beckoned Scott and Serj to him. "The tom's[4] arriving tomorrow, so this will be our last chance to move around with no one caring. His lord and master will be holed up in the west tower with his family, so as long as we're quiet, we're golden, got it?"

His three accomplices nodded. Dressed in black, they all pulled three-hole balaclavas down over their faces, Worzel hoisting a black felt bag over his shoulders. Sticking to the shadows, they left their forest hiding places and ran, one at a time, for the high crenellated wall that enclosed the ornamental gardens butted against the castle's western elevation.

On point, Hammer waited for them to regroup. He glanced around the corner towards the castle entrance. High above, the west tower showed several lights across the second and third storeys[5]. The curtains were left undrawn – after all, anyone prying would need a fifty-foot ladder. However, it was possible to make out the flicker of a television set. Perfect.

He ran to the main entrance, skirting the garden walls and then the castle walls themselves to arrive at the stone steps that led up to the arch-topped panelled doors. They were of immensely heavy oak, but the lock was old – centuries old.

Beckoning Worzel, he stood as close to the doors as possible, completely invisible from the residence above. Scott and Serj waited behind the garden wall for him to call them next.

Worzel took the bag from around his shoulders to retrieve his lockpicks and paused. He turned to his companion and whispered, "Blimey, Ham, I could get my fingers in there. The key must be the size of my jemmy bar."

"Get on with it, then!" Hammer hissed, urgently.

Worzel tried the handle and exhaled with a near-silent chuckle. "It's open, innit." The giant door creaked loudly.

Hammer cringed. "*Shhh!*"

"It ain't my fault," Worzel mouthed, opening it just far enough ajar to squeeze through.

Hammer waved for the others to make their way over.

"I can't believe it was open," Worzel muttered to himself. "What kind of place *is* this?"

---

4. Tom, or tomfoolery, is cockney rhyming slang for jewellery, although the Grey Emeralds were now free and no longer set into brooches.

5. Third and fourth storeys, by US reckoning. To translate, floors are counted: ground, then first, second, third, et cetera, in Britain. So, yes, the description does have its flaws.

"The help-yourself kind. I thought it might be," Hammer admitted. "Those tradies look like they're stayin' 'ere. His nibs upstairs won't want to get up past eleven at night to let a bunch of drunken cowboys in. Tomorrow will be a different story, so come on, we need to find what we're after and get out."

They edged through the large passageway, keeping to the wall, completely hidden in shadow. "Worzel, I want you to practise with that lock, anyway. It should be easier while the doors are open. I want you to have it sussed – it won't be unlocked next time. Serj, keep a look out. Scott, with me."

Hammer's contact and inside man had gone mysteriously silent during the last week – a cause for concern. However, the people funding their project would be less than sympathetic, should he get cold feet and call off the caper they were paying him a huge sum of money to carry out. Always well prepared, Hammer employed someone to take a trip to Northumberland a few days earlier, with a camera. His scout returned to London with photographs of the castle. Unfortunately, it was closed to the public, meaning he could only take external shots, but thinking on his feet, his photographer had managed to buy a guidebook from an old boy with a barrow, weeding the driveway.

Before he went dark, his contact had warned Hammer about the likelihood of builders being on site, so their arrival was no surprise. Indeed, he saw their presence as an opportunity and fully intended to turn it to his advantage. Though he had no knowledge of where the For Keeps team might be working *within* the castle, judging by the look of them, he expected to spot the signs without difficulty. "Come on, Scott. Stay close to the wall and keep 'em peeled."

"What are we looking for?"

"A mess, to begin with."

No one knew Scott's real name. Within their circles, he was simply known as Scott, or The Scot, because he was Scottish. Everyone knew he hated being called Jock and that was good enough for Hammer, who never looked for trouble he did not need. Even Hammer felt on edge around the man. Like most of his associates, Scott had a reputation and was not someone to be teased lightly.

Approaching the east tower, the moonlight revealed a row of arches across the whole south-eastern end of the courtyard. Beneath the arches was an undercroft in total darkness. In front of them rose a large, ornate stone staircase at its centre.

The men slipped beneath the arches into deep shadow. Scott tripped and swore. The clang of metal rang loudly around the ancient courtyard.

They froze, waiting.

Releasing a sigh of relief, Hammer whispered, "What was it?"

"Looks like a crowbar. Nearly broke ma damned leg! How dae they get away with leaving stuff lying around like that?" Despite entering illegally and nefariously, he nevertheless found time to rage against the injustice. Rubbing his shin with his left hand, he reached for the offending object with his right.

"*No!* Wait." Hammer lifted the bar carefully with a gloved hand. "This should do nicely. Looks like we've found where they're working. See what you can find down that passageway. Careful how you pick anything up and don't switch your headtorch on, neither. Not 'til you're well out of sight. And don't lift nothin' valuable. We don't wanna cause a stir."

Scott nodded and disappeared.

He returned in moments, carrying a large, flat-bladed screwdriver that appeared roughly used, more like a chisel. He carried it by its tip. "This any good?"

Hammer nodded and they set off, back to where Worzel and Serj waited by the gates.

A dog barked.

They froze again.

Hammer swore. "Leggit!" he hissed.

Dashing past his companions without a word, he ran as silently as possible through the entrance tunnel and out through the castle's still open main door. Panting, he pressed himself against the door's twin that remained closed and bolted in place. Worzel exited last, closing the door behind him. Thankfully, the creak was not so loud as it had been when they entered.

The dog barked again. "Hopefully, they'll just think one of those headbangers stayed behind. Come on, let's scarper!"

Retracing their steps, they vanished, one by one, into the forest, heading for their getaway vehicle. "That's gotta be the lamest haul in history," Worzel puffed. "A crowbar and a bladdy screwdriver! I hope it was worth it, Ham."

Hammer stopped running. "Shh. What was that?"

"I didn't hear nuffin'."

Scott and Serj caught them up, slowing to a halt. It was almost pitch black under the canopy, but Hammer could just see the glint of Serj's hard stare. From somewhere in Eastern Europe, he almost never spoke. Hammer had no idea what had made him that way – and no interest in finding out.

A sudden, stiff breeze blew through the trees.

Worzel shuddered. "I don't like it here, Ham."

"Shut it! There's someone 'ere with us."

"Ah cannae hear anything," Scott noted. "Damned sure Ah cannae see anything!"

All his instincts told Hammer to keep his torch off while on a job, but he could not stop himself. The flashlight blinded his unsuspecting comrades, so he was the only one to see what stood behind them in the forest. Wits immediately scattered, he swore again, loudly this time, as he belted through the black forest, heading for the road.

Within minutes, they were back at their van and away.

Serj drove.

In the back, Worzel stared at Hammer. Eventually, he pressed, "What was it, Ham? What did you see?"

"Nuffin'. I didn't see nuffin', you hear? Just leave it!"

They travelled in silence to their camp up in the hills. An increasingly nervous silence.

Gary gritted his teeth. It was quarter past eleven, he was the designated driver, and his lads had found the van's radio. Between their drunken roars and belches, interwoven with snippets of Annie Lennox, he was developing a twitch. "You lot had better be up in the morning, otherwise I'll prise you out of bed with a shovel – you get that?"

They may have heard him, may even have understood, but it changed nothing.

After a torturous two-mile drive, he switched off whatever late-night channel they had found before they could crucify the follow-on Bowie track.

Someone in the back was still singing; it sounded like Jerry. Gary snorted, in spite of himself. He doubted the lad ever had occasion to even smell beer before, so obviously the others had shown no mercy. *Somebody's going to be cleaning up sick in the night,* he thought, chuckling to himself as he pulled up in front of the dark, craggy edifice of Rookstone Castle.

In the sunshine, she was a beautiful stately home – though her credentials as a medieval war machine were still much in evidence. However, at night, she was eerily forbidding and absolutely silent.

Someone in the back of the van made ghostly noises that were less than convincing.

Gary pulled on the handbrake. "Whoever's making the concussed pigeon noises, shut up! The customer's got kids here, they'll be asleep. And don't set his dog off, either—"

Before he even finished the sentence, the barking began. Naturally, Poppy woke up in his lap and yapped right back. Gary covered his face with his hands. "There have to be better ways than this to make a living."

His lads disembarked, clambering out of the vehicle and slamming every door at least once. The sliding side door was slammed twice, when Blackout went back to retrieve his forgotten wallet.

"What you need that for?" Andy, pride of Walsall's plastering community, slurred. "You never open it!"

"Shh!" Gary tried to quiet them. Which naturally led to a round of ostentatious shushing as the lager louts tried to help him out.

"If we're not fired first thing, it'll be a miracle. Come on, wind it in now, will you?"

Still shushing and staggering and giggling, they made their way through the castle gate, which creaked open loudly.

Sir Henry's dog sprang into action again. Gary desperately shushed Poppy. Another round of helpful shushing ensued, echoing down the high vaulted entranceway that led through Rookstone's massive walls.

Poppy leapt from his arms and ran to the centre of the courtyard. The moonlight bathed the castle's core in a spooky, silver glow. Spotlit and centre stage, Poppy left a gift on the flagstones.

"Oh, *God!*" Gary hissed. "Of all places, why there?"

The lads' laughter caused Sir Henry's dog to put in further overtime.

"You lot, get in, before we bring the place down." Gary herded them inside, through the ground floor entrance door to the north tower. Before following, he crossed the courtyard, lighting a torch from his pocket.

Disappearing beneath the undercroft, he returned with a shovel and scooped up the evidence. He would have to dispose of it discreetly, in the morning. He certainly would not leave it in the centre of the man's courtyard to discover over his breakfast. He hid the shovel back beneath the undercroft and just inside the adjoining vaulted room, before recrossing the courtyard back towards their digs.

A scraping sound from behind made him freeze. It sounded like someone dragging a leg. Turning slowly, he peered into the blackness under the arches at the southern end of the courtyard and shuddered. That was when he heard the snarl.

Gary slumped. "Poppy! Where the Dickens did you find that in here?"

Poppy reappeared from the shadows into the moonlight, growling and snarling in frustration. Typically blurring the margins between stick and log, she was making a spirited attempt to drag what looked like a small tree across the flagstones.

"I swear, you could find a stick on the moon! Have you no sense of scale? No? Never mind. Come on, girl, leave it there. Time for bed." The last was heartfelt, weariness unmistakable in his voice as he tripped over an uneven paving stone, complaining about employees, dogs and uneven ancient surfaces.

The Interview: part II, August 1994

"We've heard all kinds of outrageous claims about Rookstone Castle in recent months," Brandon pressed. "Are we to believe that you and your workers were actually 'saved' by a bunch of vengeful spirits?" He waggled his fingers in the air to bracket his words, while introducing just the hint of a chuckle before grinning suavely for the camera.

Gary's shoulders slumped. Clearly, the niceties were over, the condescension about to begin. Considering the man opposite owed the sudden boost to his career entirely to Gary's recent nightmare, he would have expected more civility. He answered tautly, "Not vengeful. Not all of them, at least. Bad-tempered, maybe."

Suddenly realising that he was mocking a man who worked with tools and lifted heavy building materials for a living, Brandon cleared his throat and wound his neck in. "I understand your wife, Emma Stone, is writing a book about your recent exploits. Perhaps you'd like to give it a plug?"

Gary nodded. "She is. It's called *For Keeps – Rookstone: A Bally Nightmare* and should be in the shops for December."

Brandon's smile seemed fixed as he tried to ingratiate. "A bally nightmare," he laughed. "A quaint old expression for a quaint old place, and just in time for

Christmas, too. That'll make a nice stocking filler for all our viewers, I'm sure. We'll have to get you on again for the launch."

"By all means, contact my wife's agent," Gary replied, coolly. "We've had so *many* enquiries."

Brandon cleared his throat again, aware that he was losing the initiative. "Now, perhaps you could give us a sneak preview of what's in the book?" He forced another smile, slightly less sure of himself. He hated working with amateurs – so unpredictable. "We'd all *lurve* to hear one of your stories about things that go *bump* in the night."

Gary's lip twitched, the smile never reaching his eyes. "As a matter of fact, I *can* tell you a story about that."

Thursday, May 5th, 1994
Something went bump in the night. Gary groaned. "Oh, what now?" The others shared twin and family suites on the floors below, whereas he shared the top suite only with Poppy – which suited him just fine. He picked up his trusty, work-scratched digital watch from the bedside table, pressing its light button. It read 02:17.

Another bump. He sobbed softly as he reached for the lamp and found the switch. Nothing happened. "Oh, come on!"

Ferreting around for his trousers, he fumbled in the pockets for his small torch again. It lit, but flickered, like there was a bad connection. He breathed out a plume of warm air into a room that was suddenly freezing. Even the recently appropriated Saxon cross about his neck felt icy against his skin.

Gary hissed, softly, "*Poppy?*"

Now was her moment to shine, to jump into action and remind him that, come what may, he was not alone, for she would defend the master she loved, to the death, if necessary.

She snored.

Gary sighed, slapping his torch. "Why is it always me?" Having made his career restoring ancient places, he was no stranger to this sort of thing and knew better than to lightly brush aside Sir Henry's warning. "Look," he grumbled, wearily, "whoever it is, I know what it looks like, but we're not a horde of barbarians... well, mostly... and we're not trashing the place... well, not intentionally. We'll put it all back together, better than before, I promise."

Another bump from the corner of the room.

He sat down heavily on the bed. "OK. That's how it's going to be, is it? You know, builders experience this crap all the time. I'm not impressed, but I'll tell you what would impress me – if you managed to wake that useless lot downstairs, instead of me. Any chance of that? No?"

Thump.

Despite his bravado, the hairs were rising on the back of his neck and arms. "Poppy, wake *up!*" He nudged her little bed with his foot. She snarled, but otherwise refused to stir.

"Some help you are!"

The temperature warmed, significantly, and the bedside lamp came on. Gary sighed. "Whoever's there, are you related to our electrician, by any chance? Is there a Barnes here? Calling any relations of Vincent Barnes...? He likes switching the lights out on us, too. In fact, he likes the dark so damned much he should have been called Vincent Price!"

Poppy growled again, louder this time. She was trying to sleep, after all.

Gary rolled his eyes and rolled over, back into bed. He was too tired to mess with the lamp and left it on. He fell deeply and immediately back to sleep.

After what felt like about twenty seconds, the travel alarm clock went off, right next to his head. Before he could even take a breath to calm his racing heart, Poppy leapt on his chest, yapping for her breakfast.

Bright sunlight streamed in through the gaps in the curtains. He fell back onto his pillow with a groan. "I want to retire."

Gary descended the spiral stair and crossed the courtyard to the castle's small café, a characterful hall, complete with minstrels' gallery and a massive elk skull mounted above the grandest of two large inglenook fireplaces. Red-eyed, he greeted his men, blearily. Every one of them seemed bright as a button – the rotten swines.

A kindly old man was serving them breakfast and telling them stories about the castle. Setting aside his magazines, Willy Mammoth questioned him, eagerly. Eventually, their kindly chef approached Gary.

"What'll it be, young man?"

In his current state, Gary took a moment to work out whether he was being mocked. The cheery little man's smile was disarming enough, so he returned it and agreed to try a little of whatever was on offer. The grey-haired old timer introduced himself as Albert, the ticket vendor, gardener, cook and indispensable man-about-the-castle, before disappearing into the kitchen, humming merrily to himself.

"The old boy's just had a new grandson," Floating George explained.

"Some nice Elizabethan joinery in this place," Liam McGeegonnaroghonnaghy noted.

"The carved masonry's nothing to be sniffed at, either," Jimmy added. "Look at that stunning frieze above the fireplace. Beautiful work."

"Good morning, boss. Sleep well?" Jerry chirped as he sat down next to Gary.

Exhausted, Gary bowed his head and groaned.

When a plate of bacon, eggs, toast and baked beans appeared before him, he perked up a little, thanking Albert for looking after them. They passed a pleasant half-hour with a hearty breakfast and several mugs of builders' tea – meaning it was so strong, the spoon stood unassisted at the centre of the cup. Gary listened to his men witter on about needing to go shopping later for a few necessities – ingredients for sandwiches, toiletries, that type of thing – until they returned to the stories about Rookstone, especially the ghost stories, bombarding their friendly cook with questions.

Gary paid more attention when the old man began to explain how the north tower in which they were staying was said to be the most haunted, with footings and structural elements possibly dating back to before Rookstone was even a castle. Albert proved well versed with the castle records, relating how Rookstone was initially raised in the 12th century as a monastery. Later converted to a manor house, it became the Grey family home in AD1246, when Sir Henry's distant ancestors bought the estate. Fifty years later, it was razed again – this time to the ground, in a Scottish raid that saw the building burned and almost completely destroyed. Albert theorised that the core of the north tower might be a remnant of the first stone tower house that rose out of its ashes. "Although a competing story has it that the south – or King Edward I – tower is the oldest," he continued. "It's named for when the king stayed there, near the end of the thirteenth century – 1298, I think – on his way to meet the forces of William Wallace at Falkirk."

Wearing his 'restorer of ancient properties' hat, Gary had indeed noted a small but decorative stone window near the top of Edward's tower, on his first walkaround a few months earlier. Tom, the groundsman, had explained that the window was installed specifically for the royal visit. From the outside, it must have looked an oddity at the time – a nod to form within the decidedly functional and masculine square-lined fortress.

Wearing his 'man of the nineties' hat, it put Gary in mind of a shopping trolley filled with beer, with a small bottle of advocaat nestled in the corner, for the ladies.

"In the fourteenth century," Albert broke into his befuddled musings, "or AD1344, to have it right, Edward's grandson, King Edward III, granted Rookstone's owners a licence to crenellate. From there, the castle grew into the massive, four-towered, quadrangular structure it remains to this day."

So, we might be staying in the oldest part, Gary thought as he chewed distractedly on his toast. *Great. The bit burnt down and rebuilt in the middle of a war zone. I'm sure there'll be no negative energy associated with that!*

Poppy yapped, polishing the flagstones with her wiry little tail. Without even realising, he handed her a piece of bacon – it was all in the training.

After his experience in the night, he should have been more concerned. Yet, somehow – apart from the lack of sleep – he was fine with it. A couple of times, he made to chip into the conversation, to share his experience with the others, but each time stopped himself. He looked to Jimmy, wondering if his brother had experienced anything. No. Something told him that whatever had happened had been just for him. He was the eldest, after all.

He stopped chewing. Where had that thought come from? What did it have to do with anything? He replaced the remainder of his toast on his plate. Poppy yapped. He picked it back up and fed it to her, all without conscious thought. There was definitely something strange about Rookstone Castle, and Gary Stone could feel it. It was not like anywhere they had worked before. He was used to creepy – it went with the job – but this felt different. It felt deeper.

"You coming?"

Gary blinked. "What?"

"Come on." His brother gestured. "Lead from the front, and all that flannel you usually push on me. The lads are ready to go."

"Oh, right." Gary scraped his chair as he stood, digging in his pockets for some cash to leave for Albert. "I was miles away."

Jimmy looked at him strangely. "You OK?"

"Yeah, yeah. Just didn't get much slee—" He stopped mid-sentence.

"What?" Jimmy asked, looking round.

Gary was staring up at the Elizabethan minstrels' gallery above them.

Jimmy followed his gaze. "I'll ask again. What?"

Gary's mouth opened, but words temporarily eluded him.

"You sure you're alright, Gaz?"

"Yeah. *Oof!*"

Jimmy frowned. "Wassup?"

Gary pulled the Saxon cross from inside his T-shirt. "Ow! Feel how cold that is."

Jimmy held it between his fingers, shaking his head. "Feels alright to me."

Gary looked up sharply to the minstrels' gallery, once more.

Again, Jimmy turned to see. "What *are* you looking at?"

"I don't know. Just thought I saw someone."

"Who?"

"Not sure. Probably one of the staff going about their business, I expect."

Jimmy craned to look up at the gallery. Eventually, he gave up. "*Right,*" he drawled. "You're getting strange in your old age."

"There's only five years between us!"

"Yeah, but they're clearly a *big* five. I feel like I'm previewing my own decline."

Gary shoved him. "Get out of it!"

Hammer was not a happy camper. In fact, he was no kind of camper at all. The great outdoors held absolutely no appeal for the East End villain. He was cold, hungry and not a little shaken by his experiences of the previous evening. After a fright like that, a man needed people and normality around him, not a dark, windswept hillside, filled with alien sounds – and nothing between him and the unknown but a sheet of canvas.

Worzel nudged him, offering a small, plastic plate with something he could not even recognise on it. It was barely cooked.

Hammer looked around him to glare at the pathetic little camping stove sitting on the sheep-nibbled grass.

"You 'avin' a laugh? What's this, *Carry on Campin'*, or somefin'? Who you tryin' to be, Terry bleedin' Scott?" He snatched the plate and frisbeed it down the hill. "Get in the van! Let's see if we can find a caff in this godforsaken place. Come on, get up!" He kicked the other tents as he strode past to start the van.

He revved the stolen Mark II Transit's diesel engine aggressively, until Scott and Serj joined him, bleary-eyed.

"We need to let things settle. Let 'em get the tom installed and fall into a routine. Once we've grabbed something to eat, we're going home. I ain't staying up here with the bladdy sheep."

Worzel nodded behind him. "What about our tents and camping gear?"

Hammer leaned across the transmission hump and the passenger seat, into Worzel's personal space. "Do you know what you can do with your tents?"

Worzel rolled his eyes. "I actually *paid* for them, Ham."

Hammer let go a bark of unexpected laughter and Scott joined in.

Worzel soured. "I'm just saying."

Hammer was still laughing. "When we get the stones, feel free to submit your expenses."

Even Serj smiled at that.

"Now we're sure those cowboys are in the mix, I've had a better idea. One that'll get 'em involved for keeps."

"Was that a joke, Ham?"

"What ya mean?"

"That's the name on the side of their vans, innit."

Hammer glared at him, all humour evaporating. "*Shat* it! Let's get out of here. I need to get a few fings from down in the smoke. We'll tuck 'em up a treat."

Worzel's angry flush turned to a self-effacing grin. "Some of the tape the Bill[6] use?"

Hammer winked. "That and a few decent nights' kip away from... wherever the hell this place is. It's like being on the moon. When we get back home, I'm gonna lose this van. Serj, I want you to find me another. Doesn't pay to hang on too long to a hot motor. Even in a backwater like this, we might just cross paths with whatever passes for the law up here."

In a cloud of blue smoke, Hammer headed for the A1 and civilisation.

---

6. 'The Bill' or 'Old Bill' is a London slang term for the police. Thought to come from a 1914 play about a pipe-smoking Tommy (or Tommy Atkins – slang for a common soldier in the British army), Old Bill was a popular character and wore a heavy, walrus moustache, also favoured by the police of the period – hence they acquired the nickname. Between the Bill and the beaks (judges), Hammer wanted to get in and out, before the law could stick its nose in.

Liam-the-Leaver cut four pieces of shuttering plywood and some stakes from a length of scant to board up the sides of the sump hole. Together, they would prevent it from filling up when the concrete was poured. "Hobnob, fetch me the bar I left in the courtyard yesterday, can you? Floating George had it, just outside the door. I need to push back on the boards before I drive in the stakes."

"Stop calling me that!" Aleks fumed and stormed out.

"Sorry, Hobnob," Liam called after him. "After you've brought me the bar, you can get the kettle on!"

"Up yours!"

"Get on with it!"

Aleks returned a moment later, still complaining about bullying in the workplace.

Jimmy rolled his eyes. "Been reading the *Socialist Worker* again, have we?"

"What?"

"Never mind that," Liam interrupted. "Where's the crowbar I sent you for?"

Aleks shrugged. "Wasn't there."

"What do you mean? I left it there, just yesterday," the joiner replied, frustratedly, as he stood in the hole, unable to move, his shin propped against the board he was holding back.

"I know. I saw it," Aleks retorted, petulantly. "I'm telling you, it's not there now. And another thing, the big screwdriver's gone as well. Jeeves left it on top of the flagstones, but it's not there either. Someone must have been down here."

"For a crowbar and a knackered old screwdriver we use as a wrecking chisel?" Liam asked incredulously. "Come on, Hobnob, will you not look properly, now?"

"*I'll* have a look," Gary interceded.

"No rush. I'll just wait here, then!" Liam called out from his hole.

"Yeah, yeah. Keep your shirt on." Gary was gone for some time before returning with a blue crowbar as requested.

"That's not the one," Liam stated, irritably. "Mine's black."

"I know, this is mine. Got it from the van. Don't know where yours has gone." Usually, at times like these, Gary would berate his men for carelessness where their tools were concerned, but he held back, once again remembering Sir Henry's warning about the likelihood of things being moved around.

"So where the hell's that gone?" Liam protested, angrily. "I'd hardly used it!"

"Like most of your tools, then?" Aleks sniped.

Liam glared at him. "Get any sharper, you'll cut yourself. Here, let me lend you a panel saw so you can do it properly!"

"Alright, alright," Gary cut them off. "I'm sure it'll turn up somewhere."

They completed the shuttering and got a chain going, moving barrowloads of hardcore all the way from the outer courtyard. Two hours of solid shovelling and shifting, and they had the sub-base aggregate laid, levelling the uneven bedrock of the cellar floor. After the filthy sludge and broken surface, the grey chippings made the place feel clean and almost pleasant. Even the cellar's lamentable lighting gained a lift from the brighter floor surface.

Straightforward graft out of the way, it was now time for a much less pleasant task. The whacker plate was petrol powered – awful in an enclosed space. Gary had seen men emerge from basements, red-eyed and blue-lipped, choking – literally poisoned after consolidating a floor like this one and taking the rest of the day to recover. Consequently, he had built his own adaptor that allowed a pipe to be fitted onto the exhaust. The fumes were still appalling, but until an electrical version entered the market, it was all they had.

Blackout set up a large fan in the doorway, to draw any fumes that escaped their jury-rigged pipe from the cellar, and Gary took first shift. He got halfway across the floor when even the reduced fumes became too much. He switched off the machine and left the cellar.

The others were taking their break in the courtyard when Gary emerged, coughing. Jimmy stood, stoically. "My turn?"

"Sorry. Did as much as I could. Give it a minute for the fan to clear it."

After Gary's visitor in the night, word had indeed filtered down for those spirits not in-the-know, that the For Keeps crew were not there to demolish the place – despite the evidence of their first day on site. As Jimmy took his turn with the toxic, petrol-powered whacker plate, the castle's permanent residents gathered around him. With just a toe in the living world, they watched from a higher plane of existence. Despite several centuries of observing the living, they nevertheless wondered why a man would choose to choke himself just to pound the floor.

Making themselves known to the non-dead was taboo among the undead – at least, it was to those who still held themselves to certain standards. Yet, the onlookers marvelled at his behaviour and drew closer, in spite of themselves, wondering what the strange moderner might do next.

The dim light began to flicker alarmingly as the spirits unwittingly drew on its power. Nine-tenths of the way towards his goal, Jimmy switched off the machine hurriedly and ran from the chamber, leaving just a few square metres still to be compacted.

Gary turned as his brother emerged into the daylight at a run. "Got a bit much, did it? How far did you get?"

Jimmy was wild-eyed and breathless.

"You OK? Want to sit down?" Gary pulled up one of their folding chairs and offered him a drink from his Coke bottle. "What's the matter?"

"There was s-someone down there," Jimmy spluttered, breathlessly.

Concern crossed Gary's face. "We'd better get them out. The air will be poison."

Jimmy grabbed his sleeve. "Too late, Gaz."

Now Gary was really concerned. "What do you mean?"

"I think it was too late for them a very long time ago – if you know what I mean."

The older brother opened his mouth to speak, but decided to think instead, puzzling over Jimmy's meaning. "Oh," he muttered, softly. "Seen something, have you?"

"No. But I *felt* it." Jimmy shuddered. "Man, it was strong. I know we get some weird stuff sometimes. We've both been freaked out by things before, but... Look, I'm not going down there again – not on my own. Really not sure about this place, Gaz. Was like I was chased out of the room."

Gary tilted his head, pensively. That was not his impression at all. The term 'older brother' tripped across his mind again and he wondered if it might be important. He patted Jimmy on the shoulder. "I'll finish it, bro'."

Once the consolidation was complete and the air cleared, the team wheelbarrowed a ton of sand down to the cellar, spreading it evenly to 'blind' any rough edges still proud of the hardcore, before laying the damp proof membrane on top. They tamped the sand, patting it with the flats of their shovels to roughly consolidate it into the top of the coarse aggregate laid beneath – everyone had had enough of the petrol-powered machine. On that occasion, the DPM was not to prevent the transference of damp, but rather to prevent the underside of the slab leaching into the sub-base and becoming biscuity and weak. They would install cavity drain membranes to seal the interior environment of the room at a later stage, after drainage channels were cut into the slab while it was still 'green' and not fully cured.

Gary taped a few joints in the membrane, specifically where it joined the shuttering around the sump hole, tasking the others with carrying sheets of steel reinforcing mesh down into the cellar from the outer courtyard. At 3.6 metres long, they were ungainly things to move through the narrow passage and had to be bent around the corners before they could be laid on small, plastic feet to keep them off the floor, so that the concrete, when it came, would cocoon them. Overlapped, and tied together with wire, the reinforcement would prevent the slab from cracking and breaking in the unlikely, but not impossible, event of extreme water pressure striking up from under the ground.

Everything in place, they were all set for the ready-mix concrete to be delivered the following morning.

Wishing to make the most of the few hours remaining that afternoon, Gary walked the men through the other jobs they would be undertaking for Sir Henry Grey. However, the actual walking part of his show-and-tell was soon curtailed when they bumped into Secure Nation personnel, who explained that parts of the castle were now off-limits. At least a dozen of them were setting up their own operation at one end of the great hall.

Gary tried reasoning with one of the guards. "We're meant to be repairing some of the mullions in the south range. You know, the stone uprights in the windows?"

"Not today," was the abrupt response from a man almost as large as Willy Mammoth.

Unimpressed by the fellow's manners, Gary mentally assigned the clean-shaven giant the name of 'Nellie'. "Some of the stone has perished, see?" he pressed. "We only need to take a few measurements, so we can begin cutting the stone to size, ready for working."

"Not today."

Gary opened his mouth to argue, when Jimmy cut him off. "It's alright, Gaz. I'll measure up the best I can from outside – we've got stepladders."

Nellie turned to look down at the second brother. "Not today," he repeated, equally deadpan.

"We can't get to the ground floor windows from outside, either?" Gary clarified, growing exasperation in his voice.

Nellie returned his stare to the troublemaker in chief. "Not today."

Anger flashed across Gary's face. Jimmy saw it and took his brother's arm. "Come on, Gaz. We'll find something else to do, away from this lot."

Gaze still locked with the giant stopping him from getting to work, Gary eventually sighed defeat. "Thanks for the chat!" With that, he stormed away with Jimmy skipping to catch up.

They returned to their own men in the courtyard. Aleks was throwing a tennis ball for Poppy, while the others swapped some tools to and from the vans, ready for the next phase.

Liam approached them. "Hey, Gaz, these guys have been taking down our reg plates."

"Who has? The security people?"

The Irish joiner nodded. "Are we under suspicion for something? I asked the lead fella about it – that one there. No, *that* one – beardy. When he heard my accent, he wanted to know how long I'd been here and everything about me. What's going on?"

"I'm not sure," Gary confessed. "Think I'd better have a word with the customer. Maybe it would be best just to make ourselves scarce until these people leave."

They walked through the castle gates to where their vans were parked. Even before they passed outside, they could hear two separate arguments already in full swing.

"What now?" Gary chuntered under his breath.

"I'm a plumber, bonnie lad," Floating George announced, loudly and pointedly. "Not a bank robber!"

"Yeah, but what if we could be warriors?" Andy Wilson contested.

Gary turned his head to see Andy step up into the side door of one of their vans, still arguing with Willy, who passed him a heavy breaker – one-handed. *What on earth are* they *on about?* Gary wondered.

"Look," the bearded security guard stated, matching George's tone, "all *we* see is a bunch of guys with vans full of tools that could easily be used for breaking and entering. It's our duty to check out *any* threats to the items under our care – OK?"

"We might be wizards," Andy's voice cut across the altercation.

Gary stared at him again, distracted and more than a little baffled.

"Hadaway," Floating George rejoindered, disgustedly. "You're having a giraffe, man." When he spotted Gary and Jimmy, he called them over. "Gaz, tell this gadgie I need this tool to cut a slot for the inch-and-a-quarter pipe from the pump, will ye?" He turned back to the security chief, now joined by a woman in her thirties wearing a similar uniform.

Obviously sent to defuse the situation, she smiled apologetically. "I'm sorry, sir, but we're contracted to keep the installation clear of anyone who isn't employed either by our company or Rookstone Estate directly."

"*Howay,* man." George turned away, exasperated. He nodded towards Gary. "Well, this is who I work for, pet. Ye'll notice he's not the Pink Panther, is he?"

"Well, not necessarily," Willy stated, still debating Andy.

"Hello," Gary greeted the security man and woman, uncertainly. "Can I help you?"

"But that's the whole point!" Andy fired up. "What kind of fantasy have you walked into?"

Gary could only guess.

"Good afternoon, sir," the woman greeted in return. "I was just explaining to your operative that we can't allow certain items into the building at this time."

"But we don't know anything about weapons," Willy stated, witheringly. "Well, maybe Floating George knows a bit, but..."

Gary glanced nervously towards Andy and Willy, wishing they would shut up. "Erm... items, miss?"

"That cutting saw, sir." She pointed at the object in question, still in Floating George's hands. "We're under strict orders from the insurance company—"

"She means the grinder," George helped her out, unhelpfully.

"No, no, no," Andy pressed his point from the van. "We'd be well-skilled and tooled up for battle."

Ears pricked up. Gary, and more worryingly, security, turned to focus on the debate taking place between the two men, one inside and one outside the rearmost of the three For Keeps vehicles.

"You can't just step through a magic door and set off on some 'dashing bold adventure'," Willy continued, quoting a Faith No More song he liked. "Then, just as magically, become somebody else, you numpty. We'd still be us."

"You're missing the point," Andy shot back. "Just read the words. It's all there, in black and white. Just by being there, we'd be able to take on, well... anybody, I suppose, in a fight."

"But what if we got there, all armed to the teeth and ready for battle, and found that we hadn't got a clue how to steal gems, or fight castle guards, stuff like that? What if we found that we were just, oh, I don't know, quite good at plasterin', or summat?"

"Quite good? I'm a master plasterer, son. Don't you forget it."

"*Son?* I'm a year older than you!"

"Yeah, but it's about experience, mate."

"I've got six years' experience on the trowels!"

Andy barked a derisive laugh. "One year six times, more like. Besides, I could be deadly just with my trowel, me. Have you felt that edge? Go on. Try it. I've worn it down, razor sharp – hard work did that, sunbeam. Hard work!"

The Secure Nation personnel were now studying Gary like he might actually be the Pink Panther.

"Will you two shut up!" he shouted. "What the hell are you talking about?"

Andy stepped out from the van to stand in Willy's shadow. "It's a game we're playing," he muttered, sheepishly. "I bought this adventure book, see. You know, while we're away, like, and, er..."

Gary glared at him. Blowing out his cheeks with exasperation, he turned back to the lady guard, and the more diplomatic of the pair. "There are no weapons, or dungeony dragons, nor anything else weird on our vans, OK? Apart from those two idiots, maybe."

The woman smirked. "We understand, sir. We're just doing our jobs."

"Yes, miss, but unfortunately, you're stopping us from doing ours—"

"Hello, chaps," Sir Henry cut into the conversation, approaching from the castle gates. "Everything going swimmingly, I hope?"

Jeremy Horatio Jarvis giggled nervously.

The girl at the supermarket checkout chewed gum and blew a bubble. Staring, she clearly wondered where he had escaped from and what was wrong with him.

"I say, I seem to have left my wallet back at the jolly old castle," he explained.

She blew another bubble and reached under her station to press the alarm button.

A guard in his fifties appeared immediately, wearing a completely different security uniform and a Judge Jeffreys expression. "Problem, Jess?" he asked, stiffly.

"Sez he's got no money, Alf."

"Alright. With me, bonnie lad."

"Wh-what seems to be the problem, officer?" Jerry stuttered, nervously.

"Divvent[7] fret. You're not arrested. Not yet. Let's just have a nice little chat in my office to see where we all stand, eh? Then we'll know if it's a matter for the pollis."

"Erm... do you mean the police, erm, officer?"

"'S what I said. The pollis. Now, I'm sure you won't mind turning out your pockets, sir."

"Oh... Well, if you think it's necessary?"

"Trust me, I think it's necessary. Clearly, *you* think we've got nothing better to do than restack the shelves and check the stock, every time some tearaway wants to mess us aboot at the checkout? Back at the castle? Howay, man. That posh accent's not fooling anybody. Where you from, Wooler?"

"W-Worcestershire, sir. Where are you taking me?"

---

7. Divvent in Geordie dialect sounds like 'didn't' but actually means 'do not'.

"Southerner, eh? What's yer name?"

"Erm, my friends call me Jerry."

"That's nice. This way, bonnie lad."

Though Gary managed to extricate the fish out of water, just as Jerry was innocently handing over all his details to store security – along with his entire life story – the mood in the van was subdued. At the wheel, Gary shook his head. What a day. He had paid the young man's bill for the supplies he would need in the coming days and explained that they really were staying in a castle, thus reclaiming him for the team, but he marvelled at Jerry's innocence. He seemed far younger than his years. Gary blamed his father. It would be so easy for him to be led astray. *I'll have to keep a closer eye on him. At least, while we're away.*

Fully attuned to her master's emotions, Poppy jumped over the driver's seat into the back of the van, hopping into Jerry's lap to provide the underdog with some comfort – though she was not above sniffing at the contents of his carrier bag.

"Will I have a criminal record?" Jerry asked, morosely.

"They weren't the police," Andy sneered. "That bloke obviously just thought you were a suspicious character. A weirdo. Was he wrong?"

"But I've never been in trouble before. Not with anyone." Jerry sounded close to tears.

Gary felt sorry for him. "Leave him alone, Andy. He's never been north of Kidderminster before. It's been a shock."

Andy laughed.

Jerry forced a smile, though he wondered how his father would respond, if he ever got wind of him being held by store security.

"Come on, Jeeves." Andy slapped him on the back. "I'll buy you a beer."

Jerry cheered at that. "Thanks, Andy. What's that you have there?"

"Just a copy of *FHM*." The plasterer waved his lad-mag around, proudly.

"Yes, but what's that inside it?" Jerry pressed.

"Nothing."

Blackout Barnes snatched for it and a copy of *Dragon Magazine* fell out. Andy blushed.

"*Dragon?*" Blackout cried. "Eh, look, lads, what's this?"

"Nothing!"

"Is that that rubbish you were talking about earlier?"

"It's just a game, OK? Willy, tell him."

"Leave me out of it," Willy snapped, sulkily. "*I* haven't read it properly, remember? Besides, I probably lack the *experience* to help, don't I?"

Andy glared at the betrayal. Returning his attention to Blackout, he lashed out to sublimate his embarrassment. "Anyway, you'd know all about dragons, being from Bala, Blackout. Bet you used to blame 'em for all the sheep going missing, up in the hills! *Baa-a-a-a!*"

"Yeah, yeah," the electrician drawled. "Get some new material, boy."

"Look," Andy continued, the cat now well and truly out of the bag, "there's a picture of your mum on the cover!"

Blackout reached out to snatch the magazine. "Give that here!"

"Let go!"

Poppy leapt off Jerry's lap and ran in circles, yapping.

While they squabbled, Andy's *FHM* fell to the van's load bed. Jerry picked it up at the centrefold and gaped. "I *say!*"

"Jeeves, give that back!" Andy snapped, fighting now on two fronts.

"Oi!" Gary exploded. "Do I need to pull this thing over?"

Jimmy rocked with laughter in the passenger seat. "You better find a place where we can get this lot fed, before civil war breaks out."

"Wouldn't that be chisel war?" Liam called from the rear.

They all groaned, while Andy snatched back his magazines.

Gary eventually pulled into the car park of a little country pub. Complete with thatched roof, it might have featured on a postcard. Despite the welcoming scene, Gary's reasoning was more prosaic. He decided to give the establishment they patronised the previous evening a miss – at least, until the dust had settled – concluding it might be best to spread the discontent around. There was still the weekend to contend with yet. He sighed. Something was kicking off in the back of the van again.

"Oh, *man!*" Aleks whined. "I forgot to pick up my custard creams. I paid for them an' all!"

Andy laughed. "You've had enough biscuits, Hobnob! All that sugar's no good for you, you know. Your stupid moon face is already covered in craters."

"Up yours!"

"For crying out loud!" Gary bellowed. "You lot are giving my sphincter a migraine! We don't want to get barred from this place before we've even walked in! And I, for one, am starving," he admitted, as hangry as the rest of them now. "So zip it, will you?"

His men muttering and chuntering behind him, Gary crossed the car park. The pub's low, arch-topped door opened with the creak of age as he stepped in.

Apart from the barman, the interior of the beautiful old building seemed deserted. *Finally, a piece of luck!* he thought, tetchily, as he strode up to the bar, hoping his rictus smile passed for disarming. "Evening, barman. Can you squeeze in nine hungry workers for dinner, please?"

Woof!

"And might you have any scraps?" he added, weakly.

Wiping a glass and hanging it above the bar, the landlord returned his smile. "Of course we can. Come in, lads. Up from the smoke, are we?" He leaned over to glance down at Poppy. "Hello, boy."

Woof!

"Her name's Poppy," Gary explained, awkwardly.

"Sorry, girl. I meant no offence," the barman tried again, merrily. "I'll get the lass to show you to a table. Drinks, anybody?"

"*Yeah!*" the gang hollered.

"Why aye!" Floating George chimed in, late.

A head popped around a column at the far end of the bar. In the low light, Gary had not noticed the pub's sole other patron, but he saw him now. Pint glass in hand, and wearing a policeman's uniform with all its buttons done up and highly polished, he viewed For Keeps' personnel with, if not outright suspicion, then at least scepticism.

Gary cried inwardly, when out from the kitchens appeared a brunette in her early twenties. She treated them all to a dazzling smile. Pretty, buxom, she was quintessentially exactly everything he did not need at that moment. Somewhere, the gods were laughing.

"Oh, hello, Dad," she greeted the policeman.

"Oh, Christ," Gary whimpered.

"I'm sorry?" asked the barman.

"Oh, crisps! Anyone want any crisps, while we wait? I'm starving." Gary spoke far too loudly.

As the tradies spread out along the bar, the better to ogle the newcomer, Jimmy squeezed in next to Gary, wearing a broad grin; they were not brothers for nothing.

Jerry, left out at the end, found himself next to the girl's father. "Hello, Constable," he greeted cheerfully, bending and straightening his knees, theatrically. "Evening all."

The middle-aged policeman soured still further. "Sergeant," he corrected the young man, grumpily, showing his stripes.

"Sorry, Sergeant. What a smashing little place this is. My name's Jeremy – Jeremy Horatio Jarvis. How do you do?" He held out a hand.

The policeman glared at it. "Sergeant Gripper's the name, lad. I suggest you remember it. I shall certainly try to remember yours."

"Actually, it's interesting that you should be here, Sergeant," Jerry continued, oblivious and undaunted. "You see, I was accidentally arrested earlier."

Gary chewed on his knuckles and closed his eyes tight shut.

Chapter 3

Dead of the Night

*T**hump.*

Gary groaned, rubbing his eyes blearily. He reached onto the bedside table for his digital watch. Lighting up the screen, he read 02:17. "You have *got* to be kidding. Couldn't you be this punctual at seven a.m.? I wouldn't need to wind my travel clock!"

Thump.

He pulled the sheets up over his head.

Thump.

"Oh, for crying out loud, alright!" He sat up, swinging his legs over the side of his bed. "I thought we'd been through this last night. We're not trashing the place, OK?"

The next thump came from the interconnecting hallway between his suite's bedroom, at the rear of the tower, and the lounge-kitchenette at the front. He stepped into the hall, switching on the light. It flickered, buzzed ominously and went out. "Great!" The temperature dropped suddenly by at least five degrees. "Drop it any further and we're going to have rain."

Thump. This time it came from the lounge. "Alright, alright. I'm following. Who *is* this, the ghost of Lassie?"

Thump. "I'm coming, I'm coming. Would be easier with the lights on, you know!" He tripped over his work boots in the hallway and swore. "You're a funny man!"

Thump!

He stopped. "You were a woman?"

Thump.

"I'm very sorry, I'm sure." He waved his arms about in front of him, in the darkness, gingerly sliding his feet forward across the carpet. "Don't suppose it's worth me trying the lights in *here?*"

Thump.

"Thought not."

Poppy yapped in her sleep from the bedroom.

"Oh, sorry if I'm disturbing you!" he called tersely. "Lot of good you are – again!"

A disgruntled growl from the next room was followed by the unmistakable sounds of Poppy circling in her bed, pawing at her pillow before finally crashing down again.

Gary sighed. "Trapped in a haunted castle with two females and neither will talk to me."

Thump!

"That doesn't count. Look, what do you want, for heaven's sake?"

He expected another directionless and equally unhelpful thump, but instead there was a tap outside the window, making him jump – they were four storeys up. Suddenly, he felt a sense of dread completely unrelated to his already heightened and completely freaked out state.

Slowly, cautiously, he edged towards the window, half expecting to see a floating vampire trying to inveigle her way in – he had seen both *Salem's Lot* and *The Lost Boys,* and knew how it worked.

Perhaps unsurprisingly, no one was floating outside the window, but it was cold. So cold.

"Ow!" The cross about his neck was icy to the touch again. He pulled the leather necklace over his head and placed it on the kitchenette's worktop. "That thing really conducts the cold." Wearing only his pyjama bottoms, he shivered and rubbed his chest where the cross had hung, before wrapping his arms around himself.

Another tap on the window.

Hesitating, curiosity eventually got the better of him and he approached. Looking out into the darkness, he breathed out a plume of warm air that steamed up the small windowpane, immediately before his face. He jumped again, his hair standing on end, for written on the glass was 'HRÓK', and beneath it 'STÁN', in block capitals. It was no writing of his – he had no clue what it even meant. So, he took a step back, rational mind working overtime to suggest that it might have been written at any point, and by anyone – perhaps a previous guest. After all, the grease left by fingerprints might endure for weeks, or months, until someone cleaned the inner face of the window. The rest of his mind, the part that dealt with the here and now, and more usually associated with the business of keeping the body that carried it around alive, argued that fear might be a fair and reasonable response at that point.

He shivered, not literally frozen to the spot, but unable to move anyway – and it seemed to be getting even colder. "Are you still with me?"

Thump.

"D'you know what, I'm actually comforted by that. Did you write this?"

Thump.

"Erm... why?"

Thump!

"Alright, alright! Give me a minute to work it out, then. Erm... Rock Stan?" he guessed, mispronouncing the words. "Isn't that a song by The Police?"

Silence.

"OK. It was a shot in the dark. Erm... *Red* Stan?"

Silence.

"Stan the man?"

A coaster lifted from the coffee table in the darkness and struck him on the back of the head. "Ouch! What was that for?"

Thump.

"OK, OK. Bloody hell!"

Another coaster bounced edgewise off his backside. "*Ow!* What are you, my grandmother?"

A soft *thud,* just on the edge of hearing.

Gary's flesh crawled. He shook violently with fear and cold as inspiration struck. "Rook... *Stone?*" he hazarded. A modern pronunciation of Rhók Stán, this time *not* a complete shot in the dark, when he considered where they were staying and working. "Is that what it means?"

Thump.

The temperature rose slightly, and Gary perked up, pleased with himself. "Not an ancestor of Una Stubbs[1], are you?"

Silence.

Fear subsiding, his confidence returned as he refocused on his earlier remark. "When I said grandmother, was I close?"

Thump.

"So... are you associated with me, or this place?"

Thump. Thump.

That gave him pause. "Rook and Stone, not Rookstone?"

Silence.

He sighed. This was hard. "Are you saying that I, that is, the Stones – my family – have a connection with this place?"

Thump.

---

1. Una Stubbs appeared with Lionel Blair in a British TV panel show called *Give Us a Clue.* Based on charades, it ran from 1979-1992. Of course, participating with an invisible ghost meant Gary had to guess *without* mimes or gestures – though, in fairness, that was hardly the strangest thing about the game he neither asked, nor wished, to play.

"Wow! Really?"

Thump.

"But..." He considered. "I thought this place belonged to the Greys?"

Thump.

"*OK*," he drawled slowly, cogitating. "So *we* are related to the Greys, somehow?"

Another coaster bounced off his head. "Will you stop that! I'm doing my best, for God's sake!"

Coaster strike.

"Ow, ow, OW! How many of those damned things are there in here? Ouch! Stop. Sorry, I'm sorry. Were you religious, by any chance?"

Thuuump... The last was drawn out and somehow sarcastic.

"Right, I suppose you would have been, I mean, back then. Stupid thing to ask."

Thump. Thump!

"No need to be rude!" A thought struck him, making a nice change from the coasters. "Were you Christian?"

Thump.

"Well, that narrows it to most of the last fifteen hundred years. Nice one, Gaz. OK, I'll try the direct approach. When *did* you live?"

Silence.

"Hmm. Right. I found out this morning – or rather, *yesterday* morning – that the Greys took over this place, that is, the first building on this site, in the thirteenth century. Are you from then?"

Silence.

"From before then?"

Thump.

"OK. Good. Wow, that's incredible." It was still bitter cold, but Gary was so fascinated now that he hardly noticed. "So, twelfth century, then?"

Silence.

"Eleventh? Tenth? Incredible. *Ninth?*"

Thump!

"I suppose there's no way to thump *bingo,* is there? Weren't a fat lady, were you?"

He caught movement in the moonlight – another coaster hovered. "Wait. Don't. It's just that I... I can't believe it, is all." There was a slight change in the texture of the air. One of the previous missiles lifted again to hit the wall behind him with force. "Don't throw anything else at me! I'm not saying you're lying – it's just a turn of phrase. I mean, it's pretty amazing, isn't it? Talking with someone from eleven hundred years ago." He frowned. "Actually... how can you understand me?" Pondering a moment, his expression cleared. "Because you've been around long enough to follow many people's lives... bound to pick up the lingo, I suppose. I can only imagine what you made of rock and roll." Another thought struck him. "So I'm *not* related to the Greys?"

Thump.

"But I am connected with this place?"

Thump.

"Are you and I connected?"

Thump.

"So my family came from here, what, before there *was* a castle? They were from this land?"

Thump.

"Astonishing. What was it, this place? A farmstead?"

Thump.

"Incredible. Just incredible. So..." He swallowed nervously. "Are you, like, my great-great-great-however-many-times-over grandmother, or something?"

"At last – finally!"

The voice was the merest susurration in the frigid air, but it blew straight into Gary's ear, making him jump three feet from the carpet, almost leaving his PJs behind whilst at the same time very nearly filling them. Clearly a connection had been made, whereas they were merely sharing the same space before. Like the mystical relationship between the computer he used for his accounts and the printer he got to work one time in ten, the spectre was now, briefly, online. By recognising their relationship, the stars had aligned for that moment. There was so much he wanted to ask her, for he felt sure she would be able to answer all the eternal verities that plagued mankind. Was there a God? Was his favourite colour blue, or green? How do bumblebees fly? How *do* you take it all with you?

Ordering his scattered thoughts, Gary opened his mouth to speak.

The lights came back on in the hallway and the temperature returned to normal, almost instantly. Filled with disappointment and relief in equal measure, he let go a breath he had not even realised he was holding as he switched the lounge lights on, too – along with every other light in the suite – before making a pot of black coffee. *What the* hell *was all that about? Why did she break off as soon as we had a connection?* "Hello? Are you still here? What do you need me to know?"

Silence.

He knew he was alone again – apart from Poppy yipping in her sleep in the next room, doubtless giving some poor feline hell in her dreams.

Gary often suspected he might be in some way sensitive to 'spiritual stuff', as he called it, though he possessed little understanding of such things, and barely a passing interest. Regardless, he had experienced much that was difficult to explain throughout his career – not uncommon for builders working in old properties. He had read somewhere that the very act of building, or demolishing and rebuilding, shakes things up, psychically as well as physically. His personal experiences were not solely limited to ancient properties, either, though never anything so strong as this before. He raised the steaming mug to his lips, double-handed to steady himself, for he was still shaking, wondering whether he might be losing his mind.

Deciding to put it to the test, he walked over to the window and blew across his cup. There was no sign of HRÓK STÁN or any other writings in the steam. The windows looked recently cleaned, in fact. If he had been hoping to convince himself that he was not losing his mind, he had failed. Should he talk about what had happened with anyone? His brother, Jimmy?

Perhaps.

Otherwise, it might be best to keep such things to himself. He had no interest in committing career suicide, just because an ancient relative decided to drop by to say hello. He blew on the piping hot coffee again, taking another sip. One thing was for sure, there would be no more sleep for him that night.

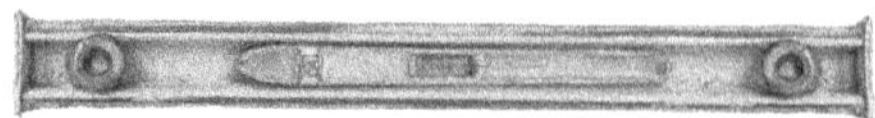

Sir Henry was used to visitors in the night. Weirdly, his wife never saw anything directly. She was cognizant of things being moved around from time to time, but whoever came, never came to, or for, her – perhaps because she had no blood ties to the Greys. In a way, Henry was glad. Though he, personally, had grown used to it over the years, it still unsettled him sometimes.

He lay awake, as he had so many times, considering the photograph taken on that faraway sunny afternoon in 1934, and all that it might mean. The grandfather he loved, smiling proudly with his new car, at his friend with the camera – a friend who went through the Great War with him but sadly was not to survive the second. When Henry was old enough, Grandpapa Harry explained how Roger had been killed at Gold Beach in Normandy, 1944 – tragically sacrificed along with so many others to uphold freedoms all too often taken for granted by their descendants, until they come under threat again.

Henry dwelled in the gloom. Saddened by the memory, unable to sleep and unwilling to disturb Eleanor by his side, he slipped silently out of bed, making for the kitchen to put the kettle on – a cup of local Ringtons[2] tea could solve practically anything.

"Ah..."

He always knew when one of his ancestors was near, but which one? Sir Henry would never call himself psychic, but when one's family home was *the* family home, for three-quarters of a millennium, one did not need to be. He knew they were there, they certainly knew he was there, and like all families, sometimes they got along nicely, other times, not so much. Henry had the distinct feeling that this occasion would prove the latter, and more than just a social call.

There was no point asking who was with him. Even if they answered, he had no sensitivity to perceive it.

He walked to the westward-facing window of his lounge. From the top floor of the tower his family used as their main residence, he enjoyed the view over the castle's ornamental gardens.

The sky had cleared since he went to bed, the moon high, bathing ordered pathways and manicured flowerbeds in monochrome. The large fountain at the garden's heart was a cascade of silver, casting long shadows in the haunting light,

---

2. No apostrophe required, only milk.

like a *moondial.* How Henry loved such nights – usually. They made him feel like some divine being was pouring the last bit of magic left in the world across all the land, and just for him.

He blew across his cup to cool his drink.

"Hmm. That's new."

The steam highlighted some finger-writing on the window glass. It read, simply, 'IT'S TIME'.

"Ominous. Wonderfully succinct, however. Don't suppose you chaps could expand a little?"

The writing faded as the steam evaporated.

"Didn't think so." He blew again before taking a sip, and nearly dropped his cup. The message had indeed changed, and not for the better.

Chapter 4

Boredinary World

Running wheelbarrows of concrete from a ready-mix lorry to an awkward room or cellar, through twisting, turning subterranean passages, was always a panic. Gary knew that well. Especially when the supplier charged waiting time after the first twenty minutes – he was already paying a higher tariff because the two cubic metres he required was only a part load for the lorry. In such situations, he normally ran around with a barrow like his life depended on it, leading by example. Unfortunately, having hardly slept for two nights on the trot, it was all he could do to remain upright. Consequently, he found himself in a vaulted cellar, shovel in hand, moving the heavy concrete around as though in a dream, while his team, using all four of their barrows, brought him a steady supply. Everyone knew they were on the clock.

Visibility in the cellar was worse than ever, the dark mix barely reflecting what little light there was to begin with. The chemical reaction within the material also shed latent heat, blending with local conditions to fill the room with steam so that it more resembled a swamp than a basement. Already exhausted, Gary felt like he was in a pressure cooker. Once poured and spread, Andy and Willy tamped the concrete with a length of three-by-two timber to consolidate it and bring the air out while levelling its surface, checking periodically with a spirit level.

Once satisfied, they cleaned down their tools and wellingtons and left the concrete to cure. Depending on ambient conditions, it would be at least twenty-four, maybe forty-eight hours before they could continue, but that was fine. Gary had scheduled the project to begin on a Wednesday so that the concrete would be poured Friday, giving it the weekend to harden enough for them to begin the next stage the following Monday.

A second delivery lorry arrived, dropping off many of the materials necessary to convert the cellar into a dry, warm space, suitable for its new life as a strongroom for Sir Henry's most valuable treasures. The gang soon had all the membranes, drainage channels, timbers, fixings, insulation, plaster and boards, along with everything they would need to construct the second phase of the project, stowed away in the tunnel just outside the vaulted cellar.

Depending on where in the country they happened to be, Gary and his team often went home for the weekend, but the journey from Rookstone was too far to justify the travel time. Despite that, Emma planned to join him, catching the train up from Worcester, having already booked them a room in a small hotel by the seaside, no more than fifteen miles from the site – close enough, should the lads have any troubles, and far enough away, should the lads have any troubles. He was looking forward to it and would be happy just to get some proper rest, after the last couple of nights.

Thankfully, Secure Nation were also scheduled to complete their work and get out of everyone's way that day. Gary would not be sorry to see them go.

With precious little they could be getting on with, he gave his gang the afternoon off. They were in a beautiful part of the world with much to offer and to see and to do – which naturally meant they would head for the nearest built-up area and sit in a pub until they were thrown out. Doubtless they would find one with a television they could yell at.

Part of him wished his wife had chosen another time to visit, for a nebulous sense of foreboding was growing within him. Impossible to tie down, it was just a feeling that he should stay with his team that weekend.

Shrugging his concerns aside with a wry smile, he told himself they were good lads really. A little rowdy sometimes, but they meant no harm. After all, they were young British men, once the backbone of an empire, and like all young men, as capable of acts of stupidity as nobility – possibly even at the same time, as the mood took them – yet he would never look for malice in any of his gang. He understood them, and loved them all, in his way.

Hammer knew his gang were hardened criminals, capable of any and all forms of deceitful malice, so he would never look for sympathy from them, let alone understanding. He would never reveal what he saw within the blackened heart of the woodlands around Rookstone Castle two nights earlier, either. Having grown up with Worzel, that put him ahead of the pack, but when it came down to it, they were a means to an end, and he cared about as much for them as they did for him, so he would find little support there.

A few days in London offered a dose of nineties urban normalcy, helping him get over the shock of his forest vision and allowing his mind to more easily attribute the apparition to a quirk of the moonlight through the trees, or indigestion from Worzel's disgusting campfire cooking. Yet, despite his rationalising, something of the experience still gnawed at him – probably because he knew he was lying to himself.

Their return home also yielded an unexpected bonus, for waiting on the mat when Hammer opened his front door was a package he had almost given up on receiving, after his contact went mysteriously silent. That was a welcome win, as when he opened the large envelope, it contained detailed layouts of Rookstone Castle's new security system, including appropriate entrance and exit points.

When their contact began ignoring his communications, forcing him to hire a photographer to gather information, with limited success, things had taken a bad turn for Hammer. He knew that proceeding without the schematics would place him in far greater danger, leaving him completely reliant on Worzel's innate skill with locks and alarms, but even that would have been the lesser of two evils when compared with the danger of cancelling the project. That would have led to a loss of reputation – and as he had taken the front money, an almost certainly fatal loss of reputation.

Whatever happened, he was committed to the project. His backers were very serious men who would see him successful, imprisoned, or dead, but with the plans in his hands, he was once again in a strong position.

Back behind the wheel, this time of their latest stolen panel van, Hammer nevertheless continued to fret about the coming weekend. Telling himself that the job was just another blag[1], he could not deny his nervousness went beyond the usual butterflies. There was something about Rookstone Castle...

Belting up the M1 motorway, he stuck to a diligent seventy miles per hour to avoid attracting any flashing blue lights. The journey up from London was long, but their trip back to the smoke had not been made merely as a balm for Hammer's unsettled psyche. It also allowed him to purchase a few little necessities for their upcoming caper – stolen gear ironically robbed from the Met's Criminal Investigation Department by a bloke he knew from the pub.

Not all his dealings were nefarious, however. Knowing a hotel stay would leave a trail of witnesses to their presence in the north, he had taken a leaf out of Worzel's book and, without telling the others, visited Millets to buy an airbed to mitigate the misery of camping out in the hills again – his back had given him hell last time.

---

1. In British criminal parlance, 'blag' is a deceptively innocuous term for armed or violent robbery.

At least the van Serj 'procured' for their trip was better than the last one. Obviously unmarked, it was also newer and more comfortable, with a more powerful engine – a suitable getaway vehicle, should the need arise.

He took a deep breath, releasing it slowly. *I don't like this job,* he admitted in the privacy of his own thoughts. Despite being in a stronger position with the plans in his possession, he just could not shake it. Unfortunately, his partners in the enterprise would care little for his gut feelings and might just remove him from pole position if he aired them, possibly even from the world, considering all he knew of them and what they planned – and he could never escape the limitless reach of those funding their operation.

Forcing aside his mounting anxieties, Hammer focused on the positives. At least their operation was scheduled for a Saturday night. With any luck, there would be hardly anyone around and no one would even realise what had happened until Monday morning, giving them a full day to get out of the country.

He backed off his speed and indicated, returning to the slow lane. They were well past the Midlands and would easily arrive before dark. Northern place names now dominated the road signs. In such a sparsely populated region it would be relatively easy to find a place out of the way to make a new camp. A good night's sleep was what he needed to settle his nerves – hopefully his new airbed would provide. Tomorrow, they would eat sensibly, rest when it suited them and generally take their ease.

It's just another blag. Get a grip! Hammer repeated over and over, but it changed nothing, because he did not believe it.

Gary awoke later than usual, but still annoyingly early. Despite sleeping like the dead in their hotel room, he could not break the programming of years in the building trade and rising before most. However, on this occasion, there was compensation.

Emma smiled down at him with a steaming mug of tea. "Here you go, sleepy head."

"What time is it?"

"Nearly eight. I'm surprised. If it were a Monday, you'd be out the door hours ago, by now." She sat on the side of the bed. "Happy Saturday." She winked. "There's a full English breakfast waiting downstairs in the restaurant, when you're ready to stir."

Gary smiled back, ruffling his hair as he took the mug from her. "What, no biccies?"

"Ta da!" She produced a hotel four-pack of biscuits from behind her back in one hand, while unconsciously flattening his hair back down with the other. "*You* haven't been getting enough sleep," she accused. "Anyway, how would you like to spend the day?"

He accepted the four bourbons that in later decades would be replaced by two, or one, and then finally by none. Opening the pack, he announced that he would prefer to spend his day, "Getting really, really bored, please."

She grinned. "I promise nothing." Kissing him on the forehead, she continued to tease, "I thought we might nip up the coast to see Bamburgh Castle. How would that be?"

Gary coughed, choking on a piece of biscuit as though she had fed him *bourbonic* plague. "A busman's holiday, you mean? People usually pay *me* to go into castles, not the other way around."

She smiled again, immediately demolishing his resolve. He slumped resignedly. "OK, darling, if that's what you'd like."

Eyes twinkling, Gary's capricious goddess chose to be merciful. "How about a gentle stroll along the beach, then – maybe a paddle? It's a beautiful day. I'm sure Poppy would enjoy a run and a swim. We could follow up with a ridiculously extravagant candlelit dinner for two this evening?"

He sighed, contentedly. "Hmm. Perfect."

"Excellent. That's decided, then." She kissed him again and left him to dress. "I'll go and get us a table. See you downstairs and don't forget your wallet."

"No beans? Seriously? You said *full* English." Gary stared balefully at the plate of salt before him. It needed sugar. "No beans..."

Emma sniggered unsympathetically as she tucked into her Frosties. "There's a grilled tomato, dear."

Gary's expression spoke louder than words about what the cook could do with his grilled tomato. "One sausage," he continued his litany of complaints. "No beans and one sausage?"

"There's a hash brown, sweetheart."

"What the hell's that?"

"Some kind of tasteless potato thing. I usually leave them."

"No beans, one sausage and some kind of tasteless potato thing you usually leave. You're really selling it to me!" He replaced his knife and fork on the table. "Can we find a greasy spoon café? *Please?* I'm starving."

"Shh. Not until you eat something. You'll cause offence."

"You eat some of it, then."

Emma wrinkled her nose. "No. It doesn't look very nice."

"Oh, thank you. Thank you very much!"

She laughed, lightly, leaning in close. "Just eat *something,* and we'll try somewhere else, OK?"

Gary picked up the rather small, dried-up sausage and chewed moodily, dunking it in his fried egg. At least there had been no calls to the mobile phone he hated but was now forced to carry everywhere with him. No police sirens, either. Things were looking up. He might get a weekend yet.

"Hello...?" Sir Henry called.

Footsteps rang down the north tower's stairwell, growing louder. Presently, Vincent 'Blackout' Barnes appeared. "Ah, *bore da*. Gaz— I mean, Gary's not here at the moment, isn'it. Hang on, I'll fetch Jimmy."

As Blackout disappeared back inside, Sir Henry heard a thump and the sounds of someone stumbling. "What's happened to the bloody lights?"

Blackout grinned as he met Jimmy on the way down. "I was just cleaning the contacts in the switch at the bottom of the tower. Thought it would help. It was on the fritz, like. Didn't want anyone tripping down the stairs."

"What a great idea!" Jimmy snarled moodily, rubbing his elbow where he had fallen against the wall.

"By the way, the customer's here, looking for Gaz."

Realising they had company, Jimmy stepped out sheepishly, into the sunlight. "Sir Henry, sorry about that. Good morning. I'm Gary's brother, Jimmy Stone. What can we do for you?"

Sir Henry shook the proffered hand with an easy smile. "Hello, Jimmy, how do you do? I'm going to be away for a few days. Just wanted to touch base with you chaps before I left. Secure Nation have completed their work, so I'm taking some time with the family before we reopen to the public – you know how it is. Richard, my secretary, and Tom, my groundsman, will be around should you need anything, and I have this key for you. I'll have to ask your men not to use the main gates now, as they'll be sealed for security purposes. This is for the staff entrance in the outer courtyard, do you know it?"

Jimmy nodded that he did. "We'll be here a few weeks yet. I think we have everything we need, but will you be back before we're finished?"

"Oh, certainly. This will be little more than a long weekend, I'm sure. We'll be staying with my wife's family down in Yorkshire. Richard knows how to reach me. Actually, that reminds me, here are Richard's and Tom's mobile phone numbers. We don't use them much, but I've asked them to leave them switched on while you chaps are here, just in case you need anything."

Jimmy accepted the scrap of paper. "Thanks. Well, have a nice time with your family, and a safe journey. We'll see you in a few days."

Sir Henry drove away in a gold Range Rover, with his wife, two children and their dog – a scruffy border terrier named Turnip. Turning left out of the gates to the castle grounds, he travelled two hundred metres, splashed through a shallow ford and pulled up in front of a twinned pair of stone cottages. Removing a bag of clothes, and another of supplies, from the car's boot, he swung a pair of binoculars around his neck and slammed the tailgate closed. Stopping to kiss Eleanor and his children, he tousled Turnip's ears and disappeared inside the left-hand cottage.

Eleanor moved behind the wheel, selected 'Drive' and pulled away with a muscular V8 rumble.

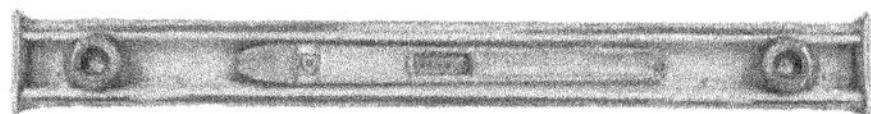

At the end of a beautiful day, a red sun hung low in the west, the whole landscape settling comfortably into the golden hour. Gary's restful day of sunshine and fresh air with his beloved was closing. Ensconced within a quaint, centuries-old restaurant, he awaited dessert, while the other female in his life lay curled up under their table. Fast asleep after her long run on the beach, Poppy was too tired to even beg.

A dozen miles west, Jimmy and the other For Keeps lads were propping up the bar in the *Stag's Head,* Rookstone's nearest public house that lay approximately two miles from the castle.

Sir Henry had also spent a pleasant afternoon, eventually nodding off in front of the cricket on television.

At Rookstone Castle, Sir Henry's secretary waited for the groundsman to wash up and change out of his work boots before leaving for home. "Good day, Tom?"

"Aye, not bad. Glad to get back into those flowerbeds in front of the south range again. There's a lot to do before we open in a couple of weeks."

"Yes, Henry asked me to thank you for working your Saturday."

"Got to be done. Is that new-fangled security system up and running?"

"It is. Set it myself." Richard smiled, ruefully. "Hope I got the codes right. If you pass any flashing blue lights on your way home, I might just need an alibi."

Tom chuckled. "Aye. Well, enjoy your evening, and your Sunday. Are you sure you don't want us[2] to do a few hours in the morning?"

"No. It's very good of you, Tom, but you know what summers are like in this place. I think you should enjoy a day to yourself while you still can – and while Katie remembers who you are."

Tom laughed. "Wor lass[3] understands. She asked me to pass on that she's happy to help out in the café and shop again this year, if you need her to."

"I'm sure we shall. We gratefully accept her offer. Goodnight, Tom. Enjoy the rest of your weekend."

Richard waited until he heard Tom's Toyota Hilux roar away up the lane before closing the door on its Yale lock. He left it unbarred, so that the builders could get back in later that evening, and returned to his suite on the ground floor of the West Tower.

---

2. In England's North-East dialect, the object pronoun 'us' – pronounced locally, *uz* – often replaces 'me'.

3. Again, in the North-East dialect, 'wor' in this context means 'our'.

He usually returned home at the weekends but had offered to stay over while Sir Henry was away.

Rookstone Castle was a beautiful place, brimming with character, but when night fell, her eeriness was tangible. Diurnal to nocturnal, the day people went to sleep, as the night people came out to prowl her dark corridors and silent halls. At the edges of perception, the ancient building came to life. No longer mere stone and timber and metal, she became the sum of all those things and more. Blended with so many lives – past and present – she gained energy. More than a building, more than a home, she *was* living history, and on that night, every stone carried expectation.

Richard crossed the inner courtyard. He could feel it. Rookstone was waiting, watchful. He shuddered. Before closing the main door at the base of the tower, he turned. Fully aware of all the ghost stories, he encouraged them – they were good for business – but no spectre nor spook ever intruded on his time within that ancient pile. Personally, he believed it all to be stuff and nonsense, but kept his opinions to himself, knowing that his boss was a believer. Nevertheless, spending the evening alone, locked within the walls of that sprawling medieval fortress, was enough to test any man's convictions. "There's nothing there." His voice rang loudly around the unnaturally silent inner courtyard. By verbalising his thoughts, he hoped the sound of a human voice, even his own, might offer some comfort. It did not. Rather, it left him with the disturbing impression that he had just given away his position.

He slammed the door, closing out the encroaching night. The spiral stairway leading up to the Grey family's suites above was gloomy and silent. The narrow windows at each floor, some of which were little more than glazed arrow slits, cast less and less light as the sun dipped ever lower. Richard shuddered. Despite working almost five years for Sir Henry, he had never spent the night in Rookstone alone and was beginning to regret making the offer.

He wiped perspiration from his forehead, which struck him as odd, because it seemed unusually cold at the base of the stairwell. Cooler air would naturally descend to the bottom of the tower, he reasoned, scratching the shadow of the day's stubble on his cheek. That said, an unpleasant feeling of isolation was growing within him, and even though their presence was an interruption to the castle's routine, he wished the builders would come back from the local pub. Taking a deep breath, Richard shook off his feelings. After all, it was all imagination. He reached for the door to his suite but hesitated, never turning the handle. Standing completely still, he could hear whispering from up the stairs.

"Hello?" His call did not exactly echo, but it certainly rang off the hard surfaces with a natural reverberation. Richard took the first few steps on the spiral to see around the corner, to glimpse the first floor. "Hello?" he called again.

A loud groan, right next to his ear, span him around in fright. Pressed against the wall, he looked up and down the stairs, nervously. Old buildings were full of strange creaks and noises, he rationalised. Calming his rapid breathing and thumping heart, he blew out his breath and cracked a nervous smile. "You're letting your imagination run away with you, Richard, that's all." He looked up the stairs again. "There's no one there," he cried, as if shouting it might make it so.

Another sound from above – a soft *clink,* like something made of metal coming gently to rest on the stone floor.

"Look, if there's someone messing about—"

A heavy block tumbled down the stairs, just missing him. In the low light it looked like rusty iron or steel. "Jeez!" he exclaimed, flattening himself even tighter against the wall. "Whoever's up there, you'd better stop messing around and come down. I'll call the police!"

It was a lie, and he knew it, but it was worth a try.

Again, whispering, but he could not make out the words – or word. It was hard to be sure, but as it continued, it began to sound more like a single word repeated over and over again.

"Listen, I'm not playing around. Show yourselves this instant, or it'll be the law!"

The daylight dropped several lumens all at once, leaving Richard peering into the near darkness. He switched the stairway's lights on. They fizzed and crackled, flashing on and off. A sudden *bang* threw him into darkness. True darkness now, the sun behind the hills no longer able to help him and his night vision blown. He swore, far more coarsely than he normally would. He was afraid.

Fumbling with the door handle to his suite, he turned it and reached through to switch on the lights inside, hoping they were on a separate circuit. A sickly, yellow glow spilled across the floor to pool at the base of the tower. It was as though the bulbs were at one-quarter power. Despite his circumstances and plans, the rational part of his mind made a note to speak with For Keeps' electrician the following morning, when he noticed what had fallen – or been thrown – down the stairs.

He bent to pick the item up. It was an axe head. Like so many castles, Rookstone was filled with such remnants and trinkets from bygone ages of war and violence. So that, in itself, was no great surprise. He was less than happy about it whizzing past him on a darkened staircase, of course, but what really gave him pause was that he recognised it – *that* axe head, in particular. "How on earth did you get here?"

It was an exhibit from one of the castle displays – part of a mock dungeon and torture chamber created to provide morbid entertainment for the tourists. It usually rested with its edge buried into a wooden executioner's block and was the head of a real headsman's axe.

The whispering began again. Paralysed with fear, now, Richard swallowed, straining to make out what was being said. Almost certainly there were multiple voices, the combined strength of whoever was trying to purvey the message making it just loud enough for mortal ears. *Treachery!*

Chapter 5

Hollow Man

"C ourse, I'm a *master* plasterer, me – best in Walsall," Andy Wilson assured the barmaid, sloshing his beer.

"Really?" she intoned, deadpan, wiping the bar. "Small place, is it?"

"No, it's a great town. You should visit – I could show you round the wossnames, the illoo-illoomi-illumination-emuns."

"Sounds wonderful."

"Ar. Gimme your, er… you know, your number… and we'll sort summat out, like, yeah?"

"I don't have a pen."

"It's alright. I'll memorise it."

She suppressed a sigh. "Good head for figures, have you?"

"Ar. I certainly won't forget yours. I'll be dreaming about it all night."

That actually drew a smile.

"Seriously, I'm brilliant at remember-umberers." He stopped, took a breath and tried again. "I'm brilliant at remembering numbers, me. Can take a dozen board measurements and cut every one of 'em perfect before I, you know, wossname, dab 'em up. Up to the wall, like."

She frowned. "Dab?"

"Ar. Drywall adhesive, you know?"

"Not really."

"*Goo* on, give us your number."

"Five-five-five, seven-six-three-eight."

Andy blinked. "That sounds familiar."

"Watch a lot of American TV, do you?"

"Oh, you've been to America, an' all? I went there a couple of years ago. Actually, I can tell you – *hic!* – tell you a story about that, as it 'appens—"

The blonde glanced at her watch and held up a finger. "Hold that thought." She walked away to pick up a school bell from behind the bar and gave it a single ring, catching the hammer to silence it as she called, "Time, ladies and gents, please. Have you lot not got homes to go to?"

Laughter and boos ensued.

The plasterer looked crestfallen. "Oh. Well, will you be here tomorrow night?"

She stared balefully at him. "It's my job. Drink up, please."

Jimmy threw an arm around the B-team Romeo, trying to suppress his own amusement. "It was a valiant effort, mate, and don't forget, it's not the winning or losing—"

"*It's the taking part that counts!*" the rest of the For Keeps gang joined in, suddenly grouped around him, slurring and out of time with one another.

"Get lost, yo lot!" Andy shot back, but his grievance was short lived, and he soon began to laugh with his mates. He could barely stand, without the bar to lean against. Besides, tomorrow was indeed another day.

After a night out with the lads, Jimmy and Jerry were the only members of the rowdy group still sober. Jimmy, because he was driving and nominally in charge, and Jerry, because he was learning.

They each took one of Andy's arms to help him out of the pub. "Hey! What're y'doing? I can walk."

Jimmy released him. Andy slumped. Jimmy caught him again.

"It's a bloody conspiracy!" Andy continued but managed to call over his shoulder, "I'll see you tomorrow night, Princess. I'm sure you'll have cheered up by then!"

The whole pub was laughing now.

Jimmy grinned at the barmaid, shaking his head apologetically, but she was already smiling. She had seen and endured far worse.

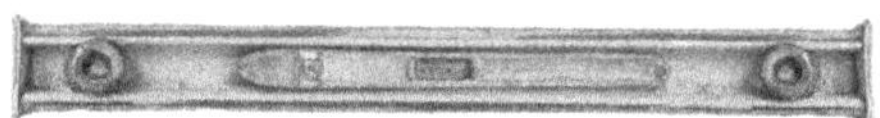

Jimmy cringed at the row from the back of the van as they drove down the lane towards Rookstone Castle. Its radio could barely compete as the lads serenaded Andy, after he struck out with the barmaid. Timing was everything – and what a track the DJ had chosen.

'*I'm a loser, baby, so why don't you kill me?*' seemed to be the only line they knew from Beck's hit single, but they sang it with gusto.

"Calm it now, lads. We're almost back." Jimmy believed the Grey family to have left, but it still felt somehow disrespectful to shout and bawl in such a tranquil and historic place. In the way that elderly drivers with flawless records never dwell on the numerous accidents that seem to happen in their vicinity, it was doubtful whether a gang of builders on their way back from the pub would take the time to dwell on words like 'uncouth'. Nevertheless, they all felt the urge to quieten down – even through the beer haze. A strange phenomenon, because the castle, like so many ancient properties, would have seen more than its share of wild parties over the years, without even mentioning the ruckus and criminality endured during times of conflict.

The van crunched up the gravel drive into the outer courtyard to park alongside their other vehicle, next to the skip – Gary had the third van with him.

Jimmy blew out his cheeks, missing his brother's calming influence and wishing that he, too, was in a nice, quiet hotel somewhere, rather than with a bunch of drunken lunatics in the middle of nowhere.

"*I'm a loser, baby...*" Floating George slurred, off key, managing to sing out of time even with himself. Somehow, in the darkness, that led to squabbling.

"Get off my foot!" Aleks cried out.

"Howay, Hobnob, man!"

"Don't push him onto me, numpty!" Willy Mammoth boomed.

Jimmy snorted. Yes, it was a good job the Grey family were not in residence. "Come on, you bunch of pillocks. Hangovers await."

In the end, the *Stag's Head*'s landlord had proven quite liberal with drinking-up time, so it was almost midnight when they let themselves in. Making their way through the labyrinthine hallways and corridors, they emerged into the central courtyard and back out into the moonlight.

Jimmy took a deep breath, filling his lungs with the sweet night air after the smoky stuffiness of the public house. The lads let themselves into the guest tower without so much as a glance around, already arguing about who should be first in the queue to use the toilets – some of them had invested in ridiculously over-spiced curries and were already receiving their dividends. As they stumbled up the stone steps, he heard someone drunkenly ask where James-the-Mason had got to.

He rather enjoyed his nickname and chuckled to himself. *Idiots,* he thought, benevolently.

Silence blanketed the courtyard once more. A beautiful night, and Jimmy was alone to enjoy it, when a conversation struck up with an old boy in the snug earlier that evening came back to haunt him. Apparently, the area was associated with a horned spirit – probably an ancient tale based on Herne the Hunter. According to the old man, it haunted the woods around Rookstone to this day. He even claimed to have seen it.

As a stonemason by trade, Jimmy was naturally interested in old structures and architecture. That, and his work for his brother's company, meant he spent a lot of time in places like Rookstone, though rarely at night.

The moon emerged from behind a cloud, instantly throwing all the ancient fortress' curves and angles into silver relief against black shadows. From the centre of the courtyard, the 360-degree vista was as stunningly beautiful as it was creepy.

A shudder ran up his spine. Imagination could run wild in such places – especially with a headful of local folklore – and standing there alone, he could easily believe it all.

The ghost rider slid gracefully across a mostly clear sky, fully releasing the moon to flood the courtyard in harsh monotone. Jimmy turned full circle, immersing himself in the moment – committing every inch of his surroundings to memory. He need not have tried, for that night would be burned into his mind for the rest of his life.

The increased light revealed that one of the castle gates was ajar. He frowned. Richard had made it quite clear that they would now remain locked for the duration of their stay. Jimmy took a step forward and caught his breath. The moon was throwing more than mere architecture into sharp focus. Wilfully forcing himself onward, he ran to the body it revealed slumped in the main entranceway.

Kneeling in something sticky, he checked to see who it was. Before he could ask if they were hurt, his jaw swung open, the thrill of terror stealing his voice as dread flooded his soul. He was kneeling in blood.

Two hours earlier...

Inga Hrók Stán played there as a girl, though the passage of centuries had seen vast, ancient forests reduced to a rump around the castle. During the day, it was a temple to life, but even in the black of night, and despite more than eleven hundred years wandering through them, she still loved Rookstone woods.

Gary Stone was her descendant – he was family – but warning him, the previous night, had left her exhausted. By the time he guessed who she was, completing the link between them so that they might communicate, her energy was spent. Hopefully, it would be easier next time, because she had much to tell him. Were she still alive, and blessed with living eyes, she would have rolled them,[1] for Gary was not even present on the night when it mattered most.

- She usually fared better with animals. However, it seemed Gary's dog was duff, too. Either that, or Poppy *had* sensed Inga and completely ignored her – maybe she was used to seeing ghosts? Who really knew why animals did what they did, but whatever the reason, it was time for desperate measures. It was time to search for... *him.* Having spent so much of herself trying to contact Gary, she was heavily

---

1. There were no microaggressions in Inga's day, and the macro ones were unambiguous, an axe to the head being impossible to misinterpret.

disadvantaged. After rolling her eyes, she would have sighed, too, were she also still blessed with living lungs, because as times went, now was a hell of a time to have no time to lose.

Her powers waxed nightly at 02:17 – a lunar cycle rather different from the one that regulated her body in life. Unfortunately, it was only 21:53. Hopefully, she would have enough energy to do what she must. At least she only needed to commune with a fellow spirit this time, which helped, because the dead were so much better at listening than the living.

Inga slowed, drifting through the woods as silently as air. Even the spiritual plane was controlled by laws of the physical world – and so it was, for anyone wishing to interact with that physical world. Though non-corporeal, she focused her energies within a volume of her environment exactly corresponding with her physical size in life.

Like all who passed, she was forced to learn how to respect floor levels. When she ran through those woods as a child in the 9th century, the overall ground level had been lower than in 1994. Indeed, it was easy to spot the less powerful dearly departed, not merely by their style of dress – often misleading among the poorer classes, rags being rags – but rather by *where* they haunted. More specifically, at what height. Less powerful spirits appeared rarely, and never really adjusted to how the world had changed. Inga saw it, even among some of the weaker residents of Rookstone. Often, they would appear upper torso only, sticking out of the floor, or floating three feet in the air – those were the ones who really terrified unwary tourists. However, dull-eyed, they rarely noticed the chaos erupting around them on those occasions when they were seen.

Alone now, Inga allowed herself the pleasure of feeling her *own* soil beneath her feet. To any outside observer, she would have appeared to float one minute, then disappear waist-deep into the ground the next, though in real terms, she did move through space. She had no mass that any meter might detect, but what she did have was *existence*. After she died, Inga realised that *that* mattered more than matter.

She alighted gently, once more on the forest floor of 1994. Even to apparitions, perhaps especially to apparitions, appearances were important – after all, they were all they had – and Inga would need to make a good impression, for the presence she sought was close now. She could feel him. He rarely strayed far from Rookstone. She often wondered whether he might have a connection with the ancient stones of her literal and spiritual home, deeper and more intrinsic even than her own. In life, her family even worshipped him.

Despite the controlling hand of Christianity across much of Northumbria in the 850s, faith became more fluid the further one travelled from a town or religious house. Many of the old beliefs, even the old gods, still loomed large in the lives of the peasants – and not only the peasants. Inga's family were landed, and by the standards of the day, well off.

At the moment of her death, as an old woman of fifty-one, she learned more than she ever had in life. Perhaps the nature of that death opened her, making her more receptive than most to its stark realities. Neither a beginning, nor an end – for she had learned there was no such thing as either – it was all true. All of it. The myths, the legends, the faith, the religion – it was all true and none of it was true. All there, and yet part of something else, something greater still. In the afterlife – or, at least, after *her* life – Inga now possessed very little. In fact, she no longer owned anything at all, but it was a good death, because the best things in death, as in life, were free, after one had paid with one's life – and so, aware of her surroundings in ways no living being could ever experience, she opened herself completely to the spirits of the night.

His presence flared like a beacon, the instant he felt her gaze seeking him. Inga slowed. Having located him, she must now wait for him to come to her. Only a fool would dare pursue him – and Inga was no fool. As with Gary's presence, she instantly knew who approached, and he was *very* close now. However, the coming encounter would be nothing like meeting her own far-removed kin and she felt exposed, especially in her weakened state. Even the dead were not immune to fear, and he could be capricious, that one – even dangerous – but she had no choice but to request and accept his help... assuming she could convince him to offer it. Perhaps her predicament might amuse him?

Even when rested, her power was far outstripped by that of the demigod who approached, yet he wielded less worldly power than her feckless forty-third-great-grandson. It was incredibly irritating. The living were such ungrateful sods. So whatever she did to adjust the odds, hopefully with her ally's assistance, could only ever be subtle, oblique even, if they wished to avoid calling down a terrible wrath upon themselves for interfering too far. Rules were rules, and passing through the veil only exchanged one set for another.

He was behind her.

Inga turned, looked up and up again. Not daring to meet his eye, she was not stupid enough to take her eyes from him, either. Like a wise martial artist, she bowed with eyes forward, focusing on his talisman, an unusually large heart stone hanging from a rough twine about his neck. It was an *os cordis,* the floating bone that reinforced a stag's heart. Inga could feel its power, had always wondered – though never dared ask – if it had once been his own.

In the near distance, they heard one of the infernal combustion machines moderners used in place of horses. Time had caught up with her, so she stated her case quickly.

The van was hidden in the trees, just off the lane.

"Got everything?"

Scott and Serj nodded.

"Yeah, Ham. Good to go," Worzel confirmed.

They closed the doors quietly, listening for any other traffic. Happy they were alone, Hammer signalled for them to move out.

Rookstone's walls ran for miles around the estate and grounds. Hammer led his men to the western entrance, sealed by a pair of massive wrought iron gates between two tall stone piers with decorative finials. Outside them was a further pair of ornate columns that served no purpose other than to reinforce the opulence of the castle beyond. Were they not enough, the drive was half a kilometre long before any visitor, living, dead, invited or otherwise, even saw the castle.

The walls to either side of the gates were surprisingly low – barely chest height to a tall man – so they were soon over and heading down the driveway, keeping right, hidden by deep shadows cast by the treeline.

On their return, this would be the danger point for them, being so far from their getaway vehicle. It was the payoff for keeping their approach and departure silent.

Rookstone loomed black against a deep blue, starry sky, in complete darkness but for a single light twinkling low in the west tower. A gentle breeze rustled the leafy boughs above their heads. Otherwise, all was silent as they left the tree-lined avenue to creep through shadows thrown by the high, crenellated walls enclosing Rookstone's ornamental gardens. They soon reached the point from where they launched their first assault on the castle, three nights earlier.

Hammer could see no movement, that single light the only evidence that anyone was within half a mile of their position.

"Worzel," he whispered, harshly. "Get the gates unlocked. Signal when you're in."

Worzel nodded and sidled along the edges of the building, staying low until he reached its main entrance. It was a job of moments to turn the ancient lock – a weakness that caused Secure Nation to butt heads with Heritage, but whether they were against building regulations, planning control or property owners themselves, the result was almost always the same: Heritage had their way. The lock stayed. Worzel smiled. "Lovely." He waved to his companions, and they entered the castle.

"Still got that screwdriver we filched from those cowboys, Scott?"

"Aye."

"Good. I want you to use it to butcher that old lock on the main gate. Make it look like some thick brickie mangled the mechanism to get in – got it?"

"Aye, but would they no' have a key?"

"I know, but it all muddies the waters. Catch us up." Hammer beckoned the others on, into the courtyard and turning right to approach the west tower.

Turning the handle gently, he let them in. Standing outside the door to the ground floor suite, he rapped on the door with a gloved hand.

Within moments, they heard a shuffling of feet. A light came on, evident only by the sickly glow that spread like melted butter across the flagstones from a crack under the door to illuminate their shoes. They heard the drawing of a bolt, and the door creaked open. Richard saw three dark, burly figures standing in the darkness, with a fourth arriving on the run. "I wasn't expecting you chaps for another hour at least." The lights fritzed again and went out. "Damn and blast! It's been like this all evening. I've no idea what's causing i—"

The sickening *clop* of metal meeting skull separated him from his words and he collapsed to the floor.

"What the hell was that?" Hammer demanded, furiously.

"Ah thought we were meant tae make sure of him?" Scott replied, now with the builders' stolen crowbar in hand.

"Idiot! We need to get the wand off him first. And you weren't meant to kill him!"

"It was only a wee tap."

Hammer cursed. "Leave that bar here. It's evidence. You haven't touched it, have you? Without gloves, I mean."

"Of course not. Ah'm no' an eejit. What should Ah do with this jessie?"

"Leave him. He's no good to us now! Come on, we need to find the wand – it's a black rod about a foot long. It contains a device that gives off an electronic signal. We won't get past security without it. Not without setting everything off. Get moving!"

The lights flickered and fizzed furiously.

"Here!" Worzel called from Richard's study, holding up a black rod of the proportions Hammer described. He grinned, swishing it about. "Izzy, wizzy, let's get busy."

Hammer scowled. "*Shut* it! Come on. Let's go."

They left Richard in the doorway to his apartment, stepping over him to run back across the inner courtyard.

Hammer took the stone steps leading up from the courtyard to the first floor of the south range, three at a time. At the top, he lifted the cover that protected a new security keypad. Using a small penlight to help him see, he typed the code his contact had provided. A small, red LED blinked out as a green one lit up. "So far, so good." He tried the heavy oak doors. "Locked. Worzel?"

"On it." Slipping to the front, he produced his lockpicks again, setting to work. "That's it." He opened one of the pair and stepped into a short corridor between two long, narrow rooms. One on the left, the other right, they sat above the stone colonnade below and were dimly lit by moonlight shining through windows that overlooked the centre courtyard. Hammer ignored the contents of the rooms as he passed Worzel, making for a second set of double doors ahead. Unlocked, he pushed them open to sweep into the great hall. Moonlight streamed much more brightly through the high windows built into the south range. Worzel joined him, whistling softly. "*Nice.*"

"Never mind the tour, give me the wand," Hammer demanded, roughly. "And no lights in here, remember? Not until I've disabled security. The new systems will detect any torch beams and we'll have the Old Bill here before we can turn around."

At the eastern end of the great hall stood a glass cabinet on a plinth, roped off to keep the public from getting too close, and within the cabinet was their prize. Hammer removed the glove from his right hand and pulled a sealed bag from a pouch in his combat vest. He unsealed it carefully and removed the single surgeon's glove from within.

While visiting London, he had secured fingerprint gathering equipment, and with the assistance of another dubious acquaintance, highlighted the prints present on the tools stolen from the For Keeps team. Using special tape to lift the best set, he had transferred them to the glove.

Gently, he fed his fingers in. His hand was sweaty, so he took great care not to tear the latex. "Right. Now we find out if this was worth all the trouble." Mounted on a column, two metres to the right of the display cabinet, was another security keypad. He typed a second, unique code, lip twitching to his approximation of a smile as the red LED also changed to green.

Making sure the wand was secure in his breast pocket, he stepped gingerly towards the famous Grey Emeralds.

Sir Henry nodded in an armchair, the television still playing to itself in the corner. He awoke with a jolt, instantly knowing something was wrong.

The ancestor, who had been screaming words to that effect into his ear for the past half an hour, sagged with exhaustion – or at least he would have, if he still had a body. Being dead and dealing with the living required the patience of a saint – though having met a few since his demise, the shade of Sir Edward Grey found most saints to be rather curt.

Sir Henry grabbed a torch and the field glasses from his bags. Reconsidering, he dropped the binoculars and picked up his Palmcorder with night vision, instead. He stepped out into a starry night, locking the cottage door behind him. After all, there might be thieves about.

He crossed the small pedestrian bridge over the ford and jogged down the lane back towards his home. Through the east gate, he ran up the short, twisting, tree-lined driveway and stopped, panting, next to the arched gateway that led into the outer courtyard.

Moon behind, the castle was a dark silhouette against the sky. He swung the Palmcorder from around his shoulder, removing it from its carrycase. Switching to night vision brought out the monolithic structure's details in eerie greens and blacks. He zoomed in on the main entrance. The small screen revealed that one of the double doors was ajar.

Henry's heart leapt. He was certain something was wrong now. He had locked the doors himself, leaving specific instructions with Richard to keep them so.

Wiping sweat from his brow, he waited for his breathing to calm, considering his next move.

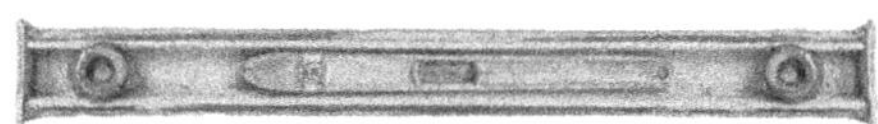

Still wearing the surgical glove, Hammer lifted the glass case that sat over the emeralds like a cloche. His reward nested comfortably, on a plush, ruby red velvet cushion. Even bathed in moonlight greys and blues, he considered them living things, hypnotic, possessing an inner light that held him spellbound. Manfully tearing himself away, he set the case aside, making sure he left stolen fingerprints on its glass.

His team gathered round, eyes lit with shared avarice.

"Are ye sure they're real?" Scott returned to business, throwing a dash of cold water on their elation.

Hammer took a deep breath, puffing it out quickly to calm his excitement. "They're the most beautiful things I've ever seen. How can they not be?"

Such emotive words were out of character and his team eyed him strangely. "Bet your life?"

Returning to himself, Hammer glared at Scott. "What're you saying?"

"That they'd *better* be real. Ah cannae tell in this light. No' even with an eye glass. Imagine turning up tae our investors with fakes?"

Hammer had no argument for that. He simply reached for the emeralds, lifting one of the three in his hand. It was smaller than a golf ball – maybe three-quarters of the size, but much heavier. He hefted it, feeling its quality, before handing it to Scott, who held it up to the moonlight.

Hammer held out his hand. "Remember that film last year, the one about the dinosaurs? Where that geezer asked the kid, 'Are they heavy? Then they're expensive. Put them down.' Remember that?" He snatched the stone back from Scott's hand. "Words to live by, sunbeam."

Worzel opened a small, black felt bag, offering it.

Gently, Hammer dropped each stone into its own bag, before placing all three into the larger bag with a soft *clink*. Worzel pulled the drawstring tight and tied it up, placing them carefully in his pack before swinging it back around his shoulders.

Hammer allowed himself another grin. "Right. Got everything?"

They nodded.

He turned to Scott. "When we get back to the gate, drop that screwdriver we nicked there, yeah?"

"Aye."

"Good. Let's go!"

They moved carefully back through the great hall, picking their way around the furniture in the moonlight. Once outside, they were down the stone steps and making for the main gates, when a figure appeared in the castle's entranceway to block their path.

"Hey, you! What the hell is going on here?"

The secretary had been dealt with and the voice sounded far too aristocratic to be a builder or groundsman. Hammer swore.

"What shall we do?" Worzel whispered, anxiously.

"We can't afford to stumble around this place in the dark, looking for another way out. Charge him!"

They ran.

Sir Henry stood his ground. Gripping his five-battery, metal-bodied torch like a baton, he waited for them at the gates.

Hammer swung for the man belligerently barring his way, but Sir Henry flashed the torch in his eyes, blinding him briefly, before it connected with his skull. Hammer cried out, but while Sir Henry focused on his attacker, Scott slipped around him, stabbing brutally at the baronet's side with the stolen screwdriver.

Sir Henry collapsed in agony, gripping a heavily worn wooden handle, already slick with his blood.

Hammer swore again. "Go, go, go! Get to the van!"

With the last of his strength, Sir Henry reached for the Palmcorder, but it slipped from his fingers as darkness claimed him.

Now...

Jimmy cried out in horror. "HEEEEELLLLLPPPP! Somebody, get help!"

Someone staggered into the entrance passageway, clinging to the wall.

"Get some help!" Jimmy demanded again, his wits scattered. He expected to see one of his inebriated workmates, but as the figure drew closer, he saw that if the man was drunk, then he was punch drunk. Dried blood covered the left side of Richard's face as he stumbled into Jimmy.

"*What?*" the stonemason yelped in disbelief. "W-what the hell's going on?"

"Help me," Richard slurred. "Wasn't meant to... I was... They weren't..."

Jimmy helped him down to a sitting position, propped against the stone wall of the entranceway. "What wasn't meant to what? Look, never mind. I'll be right back."

He ran, clattering across the cobbles and out onto the flagstones of the inner courtyard. "Call the police! Call an ambulance!" he screamed.

Richard saw Sir Henry, lying, bleeding onto the stones. "Oh, no. All... gone... wrong." Severe concussion caused his focus to drift. "Hollow man..." he breathed as he slid sideways, collapsing onto the cobbled coachway and into unconsciousness.

Chapter 6

From Out of Nowhere

Hammer's crew sprinted along the driveway for their van. Scrambling back over the wall, he pointed to the telegraph pole at the side of the road. "Serj, climb that and cut the phone lines. Worzel, get the motor."

Without a word, Serj pulled crampons and a leather strap from his pack. Clipping the crampons to his boots, he threw the leather belt around the pole and fastened the buckle with himself inside it. Kicking his boots into the timber, he shuffled the strap upwards until he reached the cables. Drawing a pair of wire-cutters from a pocket, he clipped the longer handles in place for extra leverage and snipped the phone lines.

The communications had to be killed on their way out. On their way in, the alarms were set and active. A dropped connection would have alerted the police to a possible robbery. Now the alarm was disabled, Hammer wanted to make it as difficult as possible for anyone to call out.

"Where's that bladdy van?"

Serj slipped back down the pole and packed away his equipment. Hammer patted him on the back for a job well done as he peered down the lane into the darkness. He deliberately ignored his third associate. Scott had just committed two acts of extreme violence, in rapid succession, on what was meant to be a softball job with benefit of insider information. Were it not for their need to vanish without further complication, Hammer would have been tempted to leave a third body behind. Hammer was well known for his temper, but the cold fury burning within him at that moment might consume them all, if he let it out. Sometimes things went bad, but the underground had ways of dealing with operatives who deliberately went off script, and he would make sure Scott would get his, for that night's work.

Still no van. "Stuff this. Come on."

The gateway formed the eastern branch of a crossroads. He ran to the lane opposite, which sloped downhill through the woods.

He met Worzel coming the other way.

"Where's the motor?" he demanded.

"Won't start, Ham."

"What do you mean, won't start? Serj picked us a peach. It was mint!"

"Yeah, well, it's sugar free! Kaput!"

Hammer swore. "We need to get out of here. It's a murder job, now."

A dark figure glided through the trees. Interfering with the course of human events directly was frowned upon, if not outright prohibited. Part man, part stag, the challenge appealed to the man in him, making it more fun. Especially as he knew the loopholes.

Affecting the everyday movements of animals was less strictly controlled. Though more sensitive to the spirit world, their simpler psyches took less or no harm at all from exposure. The Hornèd One released his hold over the mice that chewed every cable they could find under the bonnet of the white steel box. He had little understanding of technology but doubted it would be going anywhere for a while.

He was well known for skirting the edges of permitted intervention. Inga placed her trust in him to think of something and was not disappointed. Watching him drift through a nocturnal murk of rustling boughs and shifting shadows towards the main track, she would have shuddered, if she still possessed a corporeal body, for his presence was truly terrifying. Perhaps it was because he was old. So old. She could not even guess how old, but suspected he had walked those lands long before the sons of Adam arrived. Perhaps man and deer arrived together, before the Storegga Slide sacrificed Doggerland to the North Sea, creating the English Channel, 6200 years before the coming of Christ? When alive, she could never have guessed at the age of their world. Now, as *part* of the Earth's story, and even with the knowledge of death, the Hornèd One's past was still hidden from her – though, in truth, she was content to remain joyfully ignorant of any union between man and deer, absolutely refusing to consider who might have done what to whom.

Almost dragging on the ground, his robes hung, torn and frayed, blacker than the forest night around them, the heart stone hanging at his chest seeming to pulse blue light with every beat of his heart. Horns resembling the antlers of a stag were in perpetual motion, pausing only for a split second here or there before jerking to new, sometimes impossible angles – unpredictable as lightning. His face was barely a collection of shades, hinting at movement within the darkness, revealed only in glimpses and chances of the light, making it impossible to ever guess exactly where the head would appear next. The apparition presented as twelve feet tall, even taller as he floated above Inga, arms stretched wide, beckoning. Drooping, ragged sleeves hanging. Hands spread, long fingers grasping.

Whereas their monks and priests were concerned only with men, Inga's people worshipped him as protector of the land and *all* its creatures. Bearing witness to his work, Inga waited near the thieves' getaway vehicle as the horned spirit approached, radiating power. She bowed respectfully, grateful for his assistance.

As the criminal gang also approached, on the run, she sensed that her descendants might need any support she could bring that night. She was about to return to the castle when one of the criminals screamed. That surprised Inga. Few, if any, ever saw her. Had they? A cold smile tugged at her lips. What an interesting evening it was turning out to be. No. They had seen *him*.

Gary's day by the seaside with Emma and Poppy, followed by a superb meal in a local restaurant big on oak beams and roaring fires, had been blissful. Back at their hotel, his head hit the pillow with a sense of serenity he felt all too rarely. He was actually smiling, until his mobile phone rang. In the days before sophisticated, polyphonic ring tones, the irritating, repetitive beeps conveyed all the heart-attack dread of an alarm clock – without the benefit of it being time to rise.

He sat bolt upright in bed. "Don't let it be them, *please.*"

He looked at the tiny screen. It was them – more specifically, it was his brother. Hitting the green button that lit up accusingly in the darkness, he answered, "What have they done?"

"Gaz, you need to get over here, quick!"

Gary expected Jimmy to sound annoyed, possibly even harassed – a normal response to whatever fracas his lads had caused – but this time, he sounded anxious to the point of fear.

Gary threw his legs over the side of the bed, adrenaline shock driving all soporific contentment from him instantly. "Let's hear it."

"One of our vans has been nicked."

"Oh, *what?* Seriously? Up here?" Then his small businessman's instinct kicked in as he almost subconsciously began worrying about the dealings to come with his insurance company. "It *was* locked, wasn't it?"

"Yeah, but it gets worse, Gaz. Richard, Sir Henry's secretary, has had a right kicking. The ambulance and police are here."

"Oh, my God. Is he OK? What the hell's been going on over there?"

"Not sure yet. Oh, and I think our client has been murdered."

"WHAT?"

"Shh. You'll wake the whole hotel!" Emma whispered, urgently. Also sitting up now, she placed her arm around Gary's shoulder. "What's happened?"

He told her. She swore.

He shushed her in return.

"*That's not all, Gaz. There's someone here who'd like a word.*"

"Who?"

Jimmy told him. "*And he's trying to pin all this on us.*"

Gary jumped out of bed, throwing the duvet to the floor. "What? Oh, for f—" For the sake of decency, Emma jumped out of bed to slap a hand across his mouth.

The eeriness of Rookstone Castle was only enhanced by the spinning blue lights that threw harsh, unworldly shadows across her façade.

Gary braked hard, digging his radials into the gravel drive. Almost forgetting to apply the handbrake, he was one foot out of the door before he turned and yanked it harshly on its ratchet.

Emma and Poppy jumped out of the passenger door and followed more hesitantly. Poppy growled at the nearest ambulance.

Five emergency vehicles were spread out along the driveway: two ambulances, two police cars and a small, K-reg[1] police van, based on a Ford Escort Mark V. Gary recognised it as the same vehicle strategically hidden behind a large oak tree, on the car park of a pub they had visited a few nights earlier. No one had noticed it on the way in, which was clearly its owner's intention. He sighed. "That's all I need."

Emma joined him, anxiously. "What is it?"

"I think that's the local bobby we met a few nights back. A Sergeant – and I'm not making this up – Gripper."

Almost as though he had heard his name, Gripper turned to face them.

Poppy snarled.

"Put her on a lead, Em. Last thing we need is for Colonel Blimp to arrest the dog as well." He approached the local representative of Her Majesty's Constabulary, greeting him with trepidation. "Sergeant Gripper. What's happened?"

"Gary, isn't it?" Gripper replied, making it clear that he had memorised all their names at their first meeting, despite never having spoken with Gary before that moment. "That is, I assume it's Gary. I heard your *people* call you Gaz, the other night at our first meeting. Didn't catch your surname, sir?"

Gary resisted the urge to reply that he had not thrown it. Gripper's question was perfectly polite and reasonable, though the 'sir' was clearly an affected device,

---

1. Registered 1992.

implying no genuine respect for the consenting, law-abiding and law-funding taxpayer in his sights.

Gary sighed. "Stone. Gary Stone."

"Very good, sir." A notepad and pencil magically appeared in Gripper's hands. He smiled, licking the pencil's tip, before ostentatiously taking a note with the satisfied air of a man completing a set.

Gary was about to ask again what had happened, when someone or something blew ice-cold air right down his ear. "*I'm with you...*"

"Aaargh!" Gary jumped sideways. "Ow! Ow! Ow! Ow!" He span around in panic, pulling the Saxon cross from under his shirt. It was cold enough to give him a freezer burn.

Gripper frowned, curiously. "Been drinking, have we, sir? I noted that *you* were driving the vehicle, and not the lady. Is that your good wife, sir? I'd better take her name, too. Just in case we have any questions."

"Emma S-Stone." She shivered, the early May night air possessing none of the summer's warmth yet, but she was also afraid. "This is Poppy," she added, hoping to ingratiate any human qualities the man might possess.

He looked down at the little terrier with disdain.

Poppy wagged her tail, offering him the benefit of the doubt one last time, but her overtures of friendship were entirely wasted. She immediately sensed his thinly veiled contempt and hostility as though he were shouting abuse. The stink of it came off him in waves.

Doggy politics being simpler than ours, their mostly superior senses interpret all that humans think they are hiding. Unfiltered and perfect, they react accordingly. Poppy jumped at the uniform. Fortunately for Gary, she got no further than the end of her lead before being yanked back, barking and snarling aggressively. No one ever accused a dog of hinting.

"Sorry, Sergeant. She's nervous," Emma apologised, also nervous.

Gary was at sea, barely even noticing. Who had just breathed '*I'm with you*' down his ear?

"We're all nervous," Emma continued, trying to mask her own concerns about Gary's behaviour. "Can you tell us what's happened? I understand people have been hurt."

"*I can help you...*"

Gary cried out again, spinning around as if searching for someone or something no one else could see.

Gripper's eyes narrowed. "I think I'll get that breathalyser. If you wouldn't mind stepping this way, sir."

Gary had known better than to take more than a single glass of wine with his dinner, not while working away with a gang of builders far from home – anything might happen – so he was unafraid of the policeman's tests. However, the voices in his head were another matter.

"Hey, that crowbar's mine!" The voice that cut across them belonged to Floating George, For Keeps' plumber.

Gripper turned to Gary with a practised gotcha smirk. He did not need to add: *and* it's covered in the victim's blood.

Gary placed his head in his hands. He would never want to see wickedness or serious dishonesty in his lads, but just sometimes, a little guile might have been useful.

Two hours later, they were all grouped in Rookstone's café, helping the police with their enquiries. A forensic team arrived from Newcastle to monopolise his crew, collecting fingerprints from everyone – for the purposes of elimination only – which Gary thought about as likely as 'bank error in your favour', but had to comply.

Another hour dragged. No one so much as nodded in their seats as they waited to see what the police intended next. All drunkenness left them hours ago as the gravity of their situation sank in.

Gary struggled to believe what was happening, but there were two pieces of good news to lighten his mood. Firstly, Jimmy had overreacted when reporting Sir Henry's murder. The screwdriver – *his* screwdriver – penetrated the baronet's side but missed all major organs. Henry passed out from blood loss, now replenished from the ambulance's ubiquitous stock of O-negative. He remained in one emergency vehicle, while Richard stayed with a second pair of paramedics in the other. Both victims had been lucky.

Furthermore, his forty-third-great-grandmother, if that *was* who she was, seemed to be leaving him alone. Perhaps she realised that freaking him out in the presence of the law was not helping. Gary was sure that Gripper already suspected him of some form of substance abuse, and who knew how much else?

Speaking of the devil, the sergeant returned with two of the recently arrived crime scene investigators. He pointed out two of the builders, questioningly. *What now?* Gary thought, wearily.

Floating George and Jeremy Horatio Jarvis were both asked to stand.

Gary straightened in his seat, concerned. When both men were cuffed, hands behind their backs, he jumped up in alarm.

Dawn broke across the eastern seaboard, moving inland to Rookstone in moments. Sir Henry was now sitting up in the back of the ambulance with a bandaged torso and a mug of steaming, sweet tea in his hands. "Didn't catch sight of the blighters – not clearly. Pitch black, see?"

"And how many of them were there, Sir Henry?" Gripper asked, teasing the information gently from the injured man.

"Three or four. They rushed me in the dark, but certainly three, anyway."

"Three or four..." Gripper repeated slowly, pencil scratching at his notebook, "but could have been more. Actual number unknown. Yes, that fits with the evidence as I see it."

"That's not what I said," Henry qualified. "And what evidence have you found? Do you know who they were?"

Gripper smiled, blandly. "We have a couple of suspects in the bag, sir."

The young constable, present to provide a witness for Sir Henry's interview, looked less certain. Doubt flickered across his face as he briefly locked gazes with Rookstone's owner, though he dared not gainsay his older, more experienced superior.

Gripper continued. "And we have another man under observation, whom – except for the collaboration of his wife – we know was unaccounted for at the time of the crime. As we can't force a wife to testify against her husband, make of that what you may, Sir Henry."

"Who?"

"All in good time, sir. Now, about the emeralds that were stolen. How valuable were they?"

"About seven or eight million."

Gripper lifted his pencil from the pad, his face a mask of astonished excitement. Were he to bring this case to a successful conclusion, Mrs Gripper could begin gathering quotes for that new extension they had always wanted, for there would surely be a promotion in his near future. He had always liked the sound of 'Inspector Gripper'. "And the insurance, sir?"

"Are going to have a bally fit!" Henry snarled, testily. "We invested thousands and thousands on that new security system. How did they disable it, Sergeant?"

Inspector Gripper's dream bubble burst, as he realised that *Sergeant* Gripper would need to make a few more arrests first.

"Erm... it appears that they simply keyed in the codes, Sir Henry."

"*What?* Ouch!" Henry made to stand and sat back down hurriedly, nursing his side. Agony dragged the colour from his face and his voice cracked. "How can that be?"

"Perhaps you might tell me, sir?" Gripper replied, neutrally, though accusation ran like a river of poisoned honey through the man's every word.

"Just what is that supposed to mean?" Henry asked, irritably, pain adding to his annoyance. "I'm the victim here, don't you know."

"Indeed, sir. Please remain calm, sir. As you yourself stated, they're well insured – aren't they, Sir Henry?" Gripper's smarm could have greased a goose.

"Now, you look here..."

The sergeant held out a placating hand. "I'm merely asking if you have any theories, Sir Henry. After all, you know the alarm system better than I do. Better than anyone, I should imagine."

Henry seethed. The message on his window had warned him of troubles ahead, but he had not expected this. Why was communication from beyond the veil so peskily light on detail?

Sir Edward would have told his descendant why, had he been physically present in the back of the large, white metal box with the flashing, blue devil's plant pot on top. Unfortunately, Sir Edward was dead – had been for well over four hundred years, so the condition would probably not get better. Worse than that, there were rules – and the Tudor nobleman found them damnably frustrating. About as far away from the great Henry in the south as it was possible to be, whilst remaining in England, he enjoyed almost complete autonomy throughout the lands that fell under his writ in life. In death, it had come as a shock to learn that rules made by others now applied to him.

He would have sighed, if he had any breath, but the fact was that no spirit – he disliked the term ghost, for it implied a lack of will – should affect the lives of family or those they knew. Where deep ancestors were concerned, they were allowed a little more latitude, but direct intervention would still be prevented – with prejudice. Sir Edward certainly knew what that meant. He had lived under Henry VIII. In a way, it might be even worse – after all, *deceasement* had been good to him, and he did not want to throw his death away over someone else's problems.

He considered. The situation definitely required cunning. If only there was some way to send a message via a third party. Although, that raised the question, would Rookstone's current incumbent, having narrowly avoided death himself only a few hours ago, welcome another despatch, so to speak? He would have winced at that turn of phrase four and a half centuries ago, but now he saw things exactly as they were. Like the flattening of a crumpled piece of paper, all life's peaks and troughs were clearly legible to him, and what he saw made him fear for his far-removed son. Sir Edward would have told him why, had he been physically present in the back of the large, white metal box with the flashing, blue devil's plant pot on top.

Gary held back angry, helpless tears of his own, as Floating George and Jerry were bundled into a police car to be taken in for further questioning. They looked both lost and impossibly young.

"What on earth's going on?" he asked a young constable.

"We found their fingerprints on the iron bar used to beat Sir Henry's secretary down." He checked his notes. "Er... Mr Richard Clarence."

"Of course you did!" Gary exploded. "It's our tool – obviously used by someone else, in this instance. My lads weren't even here when the crime was taking place. They found the injured men after returning from the pub – almost certainly saving their lives by calling in the emergency services when they did! Thank God they had a mobile with them. My brother said the phone lines are down. Are we responsible for that, too? None of this adds up. Surely you see that?

Furthermore, one of those lads is a Gulf War veteran – a man who, regardless of the political mess, fought for this country. He deserves better than being treated like a common criminal!"

"Please remain calm, sir. Your men have been arrested but not charged. Not yet. I will check out their story and visit the local pub in the morning to check the timelines we've been given. Be assured of that, sir."

"It's a miracle that *all* our fingerprints weren't on that crowbar, that's all I'm saying," Gary added in a calmer voice, massaging his temples to head off a galloping stress headache.

"That might be so, sir. However, the fingerprints on the alarm keypad and the glass cabinet that contained the Grey Emeralds are, I'm sure you'll agree, more difficult to explain. Perhaps you would like to give it a go..." he checked his notebook again, "Mr Stone?"

Gary's jaw fell open. "That's impossible. Whose fingerprints?"

The young man glanced down at his notebook again. "Those of Mr Jeremy Horatio Jarvis. Quite a handle, that."

Gary ignored his attempt at levity. "But none of us have been anywhere near that display. Ask Sir Henry – he'll confirm it. His security people wouldn't even let us in the room to measure up the stonework we're contracted to replace."

"And yet, the evidence was there, sir. However, if there's a simple explanation, I'm sure it'll all come out in the wash."

"Look... What's your name, Constable?"

"PC Josh Charlton, sir. This is my collar number. Please feel free to ask for me at the station if you have any questions or remember anything else that might help us." He looked Gary earnestly in the eye. "I'll do what I can for you and your lads, sir."

Gary took a deep breath, reining in his anger. The young policeman was only doing his job, whilst trying to remain open-minded. "Thank you, Josh, but will it?"

"Sir?"

"Will it all come out in the wash? Seems to me, that arrogant sergeant of yours has already made up his mind – no doubt has his sights on a promotion, if he can wrap this up quickly – and then there's this sudden, impossible evidence. From out of nowhere! Can we really rely on this situation being handled fairly?"

"Just let us conduct our investigation and help us where you can, sir."

"Will my boys get a solicitor?"

"They'll be assigned a brief from legal aid, unless you wish to appoint your own representation, sir."

"At five in the morning on a Sunday?"

Constable Charlton shrugged. "Can't help you there, sir. I'm sorry."

Gary blew out his cheeks, running his fingers through his hair in frustration. "I'll try to organise something."

"Very good, sir." Charlton scribbled something on his notebook and tore out the page. "You can reach me on this number, sir."

"You're leaving? All of you?"

"Not quite yet, but we're only a small team, sir. And like you say, we need to get out and confirm everyone's whereabouts, including your own, sir, and those of your wife – everywhere you've been in the last twenty-four hours."

Sensing they should take advantage of the apparent fairness the young constable demonstrated, Gary called his brother over. Between them, they reiterated their stories and gave a blow-by-blow account of everyone's movements throughout the previous day.

Gripper approached them with the air of a man pleased with his night's work. Even after being up all night, his uniform was crisp, his silver buttons gleaming. "Gentlemen, I take it you two are in charge of these... *men?*" He looked around, taking in the scruffily clad tradies slumped in their seats, all of whom had been up for the past twenty-two hours, having spent a significant portion of them 'as the newt[2]'.

Gary was not in the mood to be taunted by the arrogant fool and bridled, squaring his shoulders.

Jimmy stepped in front of his older brother. "Yes," he bit out, tautly.

Again, the smarmy smile. "Good, then I shall only need to say this once. You will not leave the area until our broader investigations are complete and we give you clearance, got it?"

"But you've been through all our things and found nothing. How much clearance do you need?"

"We still have fingerprint evidence, so you stay."

"Here?" Gary was aghast. "In the castle? After all this?"

"Don't worry. Our forensic teams have completed their part of the investigation, so you won't harm the evidence. I hereby give you permission to remain. In fact, I insist."

"Don't worry? Harm the evidence! Are you for real?"

Gripper's expression was composed and patient, with just an unprovable hint of mockery. "As I understand it, sir, your guest quarters were unaffected. Yes, I think it would be best for everyone if you were in one place – don't want any of you to get lost, do we?" He winked.

"After you!" Gary growled.

Gripper smiled again, blandly this time, feigning misunderstanding. "Right. I'll be getting along, then. I suggest you and your lads get some shut-eye. You might need it. Oh, and by the way," he turned back, "we'll be keeping *our* eyes open, so don't stray too far."

"Are we allowed to purchase food to keep us alive?" Gary was tired and riled, but Gripper took no offence.

Smirking, he replied, "There's a little shop in the village. Just a couple of miles down the lane, sir. They sell sandwiches, pasties, crisps, that sort of thing. I'm sure that'll be gourmet for most of your boys, eh?" He chuckled. "Goodnight, gentlemen."

Gary grimaced. "Oi, not so fast!"

Gripper turned again, this time in surprise.

"How about doing your job?"

"*Gaz,*" Jimmy warned.

"Sod that!" Gary pushed past his brother. "What are you lot doing to find my stolen van and all the tools on board? They don't grow on trees, you know. Local authorities won't just give *me* a new one!"

Gripper waved his little notebook. "I have the details, sir. We'll be proceeding with our enquiries in due course."

Jimmy grabbed Gary's arm. "We need to look after our lads, Gaz."

Gary nodded, turning his back on the man to whom he had taken a serious disliking, then changed his mind. "You know, it should be obvious to anyone that we're all victims here, *Sergeant* Gripper. You might do well to remember that the police are the people, and the people are the police. You're *of* us, not above us. Paid to uphold the law and protect, not harass! Those young lads you've bundled into your squad car have done nothing wrong and will be terrified. This action of yours will destroy their trust."

Gripper reactivated his bland smile once more. "Very good, sir. Rest assured, we'll get to the bottom of it. We *always* get our man."

"We'd be grateful if you'd get our *van*, Constable," Jimmy shot back.

"That's Sergeant."

It was Jimmy's turn to smile blandly. "Please, let me lock the gates after you – on your way out."

Gripper shrugged. "As I said, forensics have been all over it. However, the lock itself seems to be broken, by one of your tools, if I'm any judge – the very one used in the attempted murder of Sir Henry Grey."

"Your people aren't going to secure the place?" Jimmy asked, frustrated himself now. "This isn't just an ancient monument. It's Sir Henry's home. The last thing he needs now is to be worrying about it while he's laid up in hospital."

"How fortunate for him, then, that you lot are here, eh? Eh?" Gripper grinned. "If you're just honest tradies here to do a job of work, like you told us, then I'm sure you'll find a way to shore it up or do something with it, won't you?"

Jimmy glared as he replied through clenched teeth, "Bet on it. Fixing things that are broken is what we do! Keep us posted about our van, if you would be so kind, *Sergeant*."

Gary caught Constable Charlton's eye. "I'll call you tomorrow."

Charlton waited for Gripper to turn away before giving the brothers a reassuring thumbs-up. "If I don't call you first. Goodnight, gentlemen."

Chapter 7

Cashes to Ashes

The Interview: part III, August 1994

S o, two of your lads were carted off by the police and you were all under suspicion. How did that make you feel? Were you angry?"

Gary's eyes lost focus as he recalled the memories. "I was damned well furious! We all were. And afraid. Two men almost lost their lives, and two innocent men were in cuffs – *my* men. We were reeling. What you must understand is, at that point, we hadn't got a clue what was going on. It was like we'd walked into a nightmare where everyone was out to get us, but we hadn't done anything."

He took a deep breath. Two months had gone by, but he was still losing sleep over it. "We were beyond exhaustion. The only thing that kept us going was knowing we really *hadn't* done anything wrong. I was focused on getting some legal support for my boys and trying to put everything back together so that, hopefully, we could just get back to work." His jaw clenched as he relived the feelings of helplessness.

Brandon let the moment breathe, building the tension, sensing his viewers would be on the edge of their seats, hanging on Gary's every word. Gently, he nudged his guest to continue. "And what happened next?"

Gary sighed, shaking his head. "We had no idea how much worse things were about to get."

The small hours. Sunday, May 8th, 1994

"Stop! Stop!" Scott bellowed from the back of the van. He looked around and found a flashlight.

Hammer pulled over in a layby several miles away from Rookstone Castle, up in the nearby hills. "*What?*" he snapped savagely, in no mood for any more aggravation from his associate.

"Hang on, wull ye! We're well away and Ah cannae see what we have, with the van bouncing up and doon like tha'." Scott raised a jeweller's magnifying glass to his right eye, frowning to keep it in place as Worzel handed him one of the gems. He shone the powerful torch through it, squinting intently.

"Well?" Hammer demanded. "How much are we looking at?"

"Two million big ones, each," Worzel suggested, grinning hugely.

Scott put the torch down, letting the eyeglass fall into his hand. "Two million dong, maybe."

"What are you talking about?" Hammer growled. Always on the verge of a sudden, forced vacation – and never knowing just how far he might need to abscond – it paid to keep constant tabs on the value of his suitcase's contents within the international currency market. After a moment's calculation, he announced, "That's only about sixty nicker!"

"Aye. Sixty-two on a good day." Scott also lived with an emergency travel bag.

Hammer pulled on the handbrake, roughly, and jumped over the seats into the back of the van. "What the 'ell are you talking about? Worzel, give me the other stones."

He pushed one of the remaining two into Scott's hands. "Check that one."

Scott replaced the eyeglass and focused. "Will ye no' hold the damned torch steady!"

"Give it here." Hammer snatched it from Worzel and shone it through the emerald. "Well?"

The Scotsman threw it, hard, at the back door of the van. "Glass! Bloody glass! We've been had!"

Hammer leaned in dangerously. "You what?"

"Give me the last stone." Scott held out his hand.

Hammer passed him the final gem. "Well? Is it any good?"

"Oh, aye. As a paperweight!" He threw that one angrily, too. The fake emerald boomed off the side of the panel van.

Worzel's mouth hung open. "What we gonna do, Ham?"

"Shat it! Lemme think."

"We go back." Scott filled in the silence.

Hammer glared at him, not sure he fully believed the Scotsman, though he doubted he would have treated the real emeralds like that, even as a ploy. "Not tonight."

"Now!" Scott shouted.

"I said not tonight! Got it? The Bill will be everywhere. We still need to torch the van an' all."

"I'm not going back there, Ham," Worzel complained. "Not in the dark!"

"I said shat it!"

"We all saw it," Worzel bellowed, refusing to back down. "That floating goat thing in the trees, so don't try and tell me you never!"

"Ye simple-minded Sassenach! It wasnae the goat of Mendes!"

"Where's Mendes, somewhere in Scotland?"

Scott rolled his eyes in disgust.

"Look, I don't care where it's from—" Worzel continued.

"It was more of a stag, anyway," Scott cut him off.

"Oh, so you saw it, then?" Worzel rounded on him.

"Shat it! Both o' you!" Hammer bellowed. "Serj, what do you fink?"

Still in the front passenger seat, Serj shrugged.

Hammer grabbed Worzel by his coat. "Did you hide the van well, in the woods?"

Worzel nodded.

"Did you hide it *well?*" Hammer demanded again, shouting this time.

"I did, Ham. I did."

Hammer let him go. "Good. If the Bill are still looking for this heap as a getaway vehicle, they'll be focused on that bunch of cowboys."

"But, Ham," Worzel asked, tentatively, expecting another explosion of temper, "surely they'll realise that all the builders are there..." He tailed off.

Hammer nodded, calming his tired mind to think. Worzel was right. "But at least one of 'em *weren't* there. They had three vans when they turned up. There were only two at the castle when we lifted this one. That'll throw the geniuses from the local Bill off for a little while, at least. They'll be used to investigating stolen bicycles and broken shed windows up here – they'll put two and two together and get five. Hopefully, it'll confuse 'em long enough for us to get away. Then we'll need a plan to put this right and finish the job. Serj?"

The eastern European glanced over, into the back.

"We're gonna need another van, old son."

Serj nodded stoically.

"And you'd better get us to somewhere we can lose this one," Hammer continued. "We'll burn it out."

Serj nodded again, sliding over into the driver's seat. He reached under the steering column and touched together the cables that Hammer yanked from the ignition system when they stole the vehicle. The engine fired and he revved it, engaging the clutch, but before he could select first gear, the engine hiccupped and died.

He touched the cables again but was rewarded only with the dry cough of the van's starter motor. He checked the instruments. Sometimes known as Silent

Serj, he hardly ever spoke, so it came as a double shock when he turned to his companions in the back and said, "No diesel."

Eight hours later...

Four angry villains sat in individual seats on the bus, all glaring out of the windows, aggressively ignoring one another. The single-decker roared up a steep incline along the edge of a popular local viewpoint known as Corby's Crag, but the broad and beautiful vista across the hills was entirely lost on Hammer. All he could see was his rapidly approaching violent end, after such a catastrophe. His life of crime had provided a tidy nest egg over the years – most of it, thankfully, locked up in a Swiss bank account – but he knew there was no running away from this one. Someone would find him. If he was lucky, someone with a badge. No. He had to fix it, before one of those someones fixed him.

He became aware of a constant wittering that cut across the doleful drone of the Dennis Dart as it struggled up and down the northern hills. Momentarily distracted from his woes, he turned to see what was going on.

Worzel had never been good with the public; his criminal record was strewn with failed interactions, yet the old lady in the florid bucket hat seemed determined to strike up a conversation with him.

"Of course, when you get to my age, you can't carry all your shopping home. That's why I bought this shopping trolley. Do you like the tartan? Reminds me of my dead husband. He was a Scot, you see. Sometimes, it feels quite threatening, travelling alone on the bus these days. But with four strapping young men to protect me, what could happen, eh?"

Worzel tried to smile – by necessity, they were now undercover as law-abiding fellow travellers on the hamster wheel of public transport – but what began as a smile turned into a rictus grin of impatience and disbelief.

"Now, when I moved north – I'm from the south, you see, as you can probably tell by the accent, my lovely. Anyway, when I moved north, as I was saying... actually, I've got a quite a funny story about that. I was talking about it with Gladys just the other day. Gladys is from my church – do you go to church? Anyway, I was saying to Gladys... Oh, is this your stop?"

Worzel was making his way to the front of the bus to sit behind the driver as though seeking his protection.

"Nice talking to you, dear," the old lady called after him. She began to hum loudly.

Hammer placed his head in his hands, fuming. Just hours earlier, he had been at the top of his game, beating security, getting away with the swag. Now, he was the proud owner of some worthless, if exceptionally well-made, *objets d'art,* and desperately trying to distance himself from what, as far as he knew, might yet turn out to be a double homicide. He honestly believed himself at an all-time low, when he felt something pressed into his ear from behind. It rustled.

"Would you like a mint, dear?"

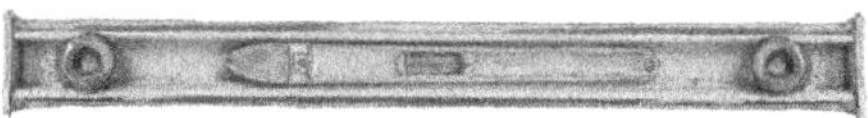

After barely a couple of hours sleep in four, Gary eventually gave up. He left Emma and Poppy to get what rest they could and went down to the castle's café, which had become a common area for them over the last few days.

He found Willy Mammoth staring into the ashes of a long-dead fire in one of the large stone fireplaces, a couple of magazines on his lap. "Couldn't sleep either?" he greeted.

Willy looked up. "Oh, alright, Gaz. I was just wondering how Floating George and Jeeves are doing."

Gary patted him on the shoulder. "I know, lad. Me too. I'll have to try to get them some competent legal representation this morning. God knows how."

"On a Sunday?"

"I know." Sensing the young plasterer's distress, Gary tried changing the subject. "Still reading two magazines at once, I see. How *do* you do that?"

"I like to swap between them. I take things in better in small chunks."

"What are you reading?"

Willy held up the May '94 editions of *Kerrang!* and *History Today*. He blew out his cheeks. "If I was home now, I'd be having a nice lie in and looking forward to band practice." He looked around the hall sullenly, at the many stag heads, goat skulls and weapons adorning its walls. "Enough history in this place, without us adding to the drama."

"True." Gary sighed and tried again to lighten the mood. He knew Willy usually loved historic places as much as he loved his music. "I thought you'd left the band?"

"No. I quit Queens of the Steel Age – too many egos, you know – but I joined this indie-crossover band about a month ago. We practise at Rich Bitch Studios in Brum[1], twelve o'clock, every Sunday."

"Right." Gary nodded, injecting enthusiasm into his voice to lift the young man's spirits. "I've heard of that place. Haven't they had some big names rehearse there, over the years?"

"Yeah, Rob Plant, Sabbath, UB40, The Wonder Stuff. It's got some history."

Gary smiled as Willy's favourite subject revived him from his torpor. Though his mind was inexorably drawn back to deeper concerns, he staved them off with a further question. "So what's this new lot called, then? Your new band?"

Perking up, Willy announced proudly, "We're called The Flux Capacitors!"

---

1. West Midlands dialect for Birmingham.

Gary let out a bark of laughter, instantly feeling guilty. Despite being close to fifty, even he had noted a recent swathe of new 'The' bands popping up everywhere to rival even the sixties. "Erm, cool name," he added, lamely. "Weren't you in that punk band, too? Are they still going?"

"Hospice? Yeah, well, sort of. We don't practise that often. We had those great T-shirts made, though, remember? The one with the shire horse taking a leak?"

"That's a bit close to the knuckle, isn't it?"

Willy snorted, softly. "It's punk. We're not gonna offend the oldies singing *I'm a Pink Toothbrush*, are we?"

"Do you have to offend, erm, the oldies?" Gary paused, realising that probably included him.

Willy shrugged, matter-of-fact. "It's punk! Anyway, we changed our name since those days."

Gary was almost afraid to ask. "To...?"

"Urine8." Willy etched the symbol in the air to illustrate how clever and fashionable it was. "We do a cover of that ancient Journey song, you know, the one everybody knows."

Gary brightened. "I really like that song."

Willy gave him a compassionate look that clearly said 'you poor old fossil'. "Yeah, but we sing *Don't Stop Relievin'*."

"Oh."

Willy grinned. "Yeah, usually goes down well with the crowd, that one."

"I must really be past it," Gary admitted, glumly.

Willy laughed. "Never mind, Grandad. The fire's gone out. Would you like me to bring you a blanket?"

"Sod off!"

The door creaked open, first a crack, widening gradually. No one appeared, but both men clearly heard shuffling. Willy leapt out of his seat, moving quickly to help whoever was struggling to get in.

"Morning, chaps. Blast these crutches!"

Gary blinked. "Sir Henry? I thought you'd be in hospital, after what you went through last night." He drew a seat over to where they were sitting and helped the injured man into it.

"Couldn't do it, old man. Checked myself out. Got to get this place secured, what with poor Richard being out of the frame, too. Doubt if Albert or Tom even know anything's wrong yet. Damned phones are down!"

Gary nodded. He remembered all too well how unhelpful the local police sergeant had been when it came to securing the property. "We'll take care of that, Sir Henry. Gratis. It's the least we can do to help you out."

The baronet smiled. "Please, just Henry, and that's awfully good of you fellows. Not sure how much use I'd be with the old hammer and nails just now."

"I'll ask Liam to fix up the gate when he gets up. I'm letting them get all the rest they can after last night, but we'll get it sorted for you. Be assured of that."

Henry winced at a jab of agony from his injured side but smiled again. "Thanks. Am I correct in saying that you've had your own share of problems over this?"

"Two of my men were arrested last night, by Sergeant *Gripper*," Gary replied, sourly. "For nothing, I might add. Just because they found their fingerprints on our own tools! Man's an idiot."

Henry winced again, placing a hand to his side. He remembered the screwdriver intimately.

Gary sagged. "I'm sorry this happened and that you were injured by our tools. We thought the castle was secure, or we'd have stored them in our vans each night – especially with your new, expensive alarm system."

"Don't remind me, old man. Not your fault." As he said it, Henry found that he believed it, too. He had known for years that the owner of the van in his grandfather's out of context photograph was somehow tied up with his own destiny. The evidence continued to stack up, especially over the last few months. Knowing that the Grey Emeralds would soon be returned to Rookstone, he had tried to employ For Keeps three months earlier. They were well known in heritage circles and easy enough to find. Gary's team had been fully engaged on other projects at the time, leading Henry to try a firm from Middlesbrough, but the owner was immediately involved in a car crash, finding himself unable to work – also for three months. Henry tried to employ a second company from Lancaster, but an unexpected bad debt left them suddenly insolvent and unable to fund the Rookstone project, their accountant advising them against invoicing Sir Henry for an upfront payment to get them started, as the project alone was not profitable enough to restore them to solvency. Bad luck, and more of it. Henry felt the hand of fate intervening, to make sure that For Keeps Ltd and the Grey Emeralds were brought together at Rookstone at the same time. It had seemed, and still seemed, that all he could do was hang on for the ride.

Despite obscure partial messages and hints from his long-dead ancestors, Henry had no idea whether Gary Stone was there to save his family heirlooms or steal them, or to help him or kill him, for that matter. Naturally, he had kept the fact that the emeralds on display were fake a close secret. Not even his secretary knew – at least, not as far as he was aware – but now he could clearly see that Gary had no idea about it, one way or the other. He only seemed to care about his men in those police cells, twelve miles down the road. Indeed, if he had stolen the copies, he would surely have been far away with them by now.

Henry decided to trust, and was about to reveal the rest of what he knew when a thought struck him. *Unless Gary has already identified the emeralds as fake, and is playing a clever double bluff, hanging around hoping an opportunity to snatch the real ones presents itself? There's also the matter of my attackers. I would find it hard to believe that any of Gary's team were involved, but all I can say for certain is that I was assailed by four burly men. I can't be sure...* However unlikely, Henry dared not take the risk. Not yet. Especially while he was so weakened by injury.

"I've got a number for a young constable," Gary broke into his thoughts. "His name is, er..." He searched his pockets for the piece of paper. "Constable Charlton."

Henry recognised the name. "Oh, young Josh. Smashing little chap. Local boy. Bagged a century against the Berwickers, don't you know. Cracking batsman. You'll be alright with him."

Gary smiled at Henry's extremely well-bred enthusiasm, and the fact that the basis for his holding Charlton in such high esteem revolved around cricket. He reminded him of young Jerry. "Yes, Charlton seemed fair and reasonable," he accepted. "Actually, Henry, that leads me on to my next point. Wouldn't happen to know where I could find a reliable lawyer up here, would you? One willing to represent a couple of tearaways at," he checked his watch, "ten past eight on a Sunday morning?"

Henry nodded. "You should use my man in Alnwick. I'll... oh, blast, the phones are out. I won't be able to get onto Telecom until tomorrow, earliest, and I've no idea what happened to my mobile phone – not after last night's fracas."

"We can help you there. We have a couple of mobiles between us. Would you mind if we called your lawyer now?"

The injured man's expression clouded.

"Henry?"

"Don't know the number, old chap."

"You don't have it written down somewhere?"

"I *do*," he replied thoughtfully. He grimaced, standing with the help of his crutches, his side complaining as he transferred his weight to them. "It's in my desk..." He blew out his cheeks. "On the fourth floor."

"We'll..." Gary tailed off as a loud snore rumbled through the empty cafeteria. Willy slumped in his seat, fast asleep. He continued in a whisper, "*I'll* help you with the stairs. If you think you can make it?"

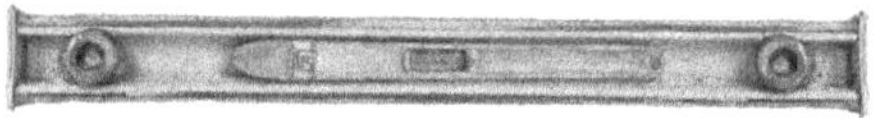

Gary waited on the railway platform for the 10:30 to New Street, Birmingham, holding Poppy's lead in one hand and Emma's hand in the other. "It'll be alright. I promise." He kissed her.

Emma wiped a stray tear. "I can't believe this is happening. I don't like leaving you like this, Gaz."

"I know, Em, but I need you back in the office. That's where you can do the most good. It's all going crazy up here and we're completely disconnected from all our contacts and documentation, and anything else we might need before this is over. I'll feel better knowing you're safe at home, too."

"But what about you?"

"The worst is over now, love. Trust me. Just got to meet with Sir Henry's lawyer down the cop shop at eleven. He sounds a decent chap. Was certainly good of him to help us out on a Sunday morning. We'll soon have that couple of misfits out, so we can start putting things right. You'll see." He smiled down at her with a confidence he hardly felt. "*We* know they had nothing to do with all this, don't we? I'm just hoping we can still finish the project, and more importantly, get paid!"

Poppy growled, winding up to a *woof!*

Her taller associates eventually turned to notice the train rounding a bend, just before the station. They stood back from the edge of the platform as it pulled in. The train was almost empty, so Gary hefted Emma's bag onto the seat next to her, kissed her again and stepped back out, onto the platform. Emma sat at a window seat and waved as the train left the station.

Gary watched it out of sight, releasing a great sigh. He had absolutely no idea if he really could put everything right, but if Emma was safely out of it, then at least he would feel a little less exposed. When Sergeant Gripper grudgingly granted permission for her to return home, Gary wanted her on a train out of there straight away, before the capricious copper changed his mind. It was true that she could best support him from their office in Worcestershire, but that was three hundred miles away, and despite himself, he felt some of his resolve slip away with her leaving. It is a sad irony that nothing gives a man greater courage and strength than a good woman at his side, but when danger threatens, it's the one place in the world he would never want her to be.

He looked down and smiled. "At least I've got you with me."

Poppy sat and yawned, scratching behind her ear.

He snorted softly. "When you're awake, maybe. Perhaps I should have got myself one of those big, ferocious-looking breeds?"

Dogs *can* be offended and have subtle ways of showing it, ranging from ear-dropping heartbreak to growly irritation and everything in between. Poppy treated her two-leg to bottom plonked down, mouth closed, staring into the middle distance, unimpressed – the canine equivalent of crossing one's arms and scowling.

Gary tousled her ears. "Come on, girl. I didn't mean it. I wouldn't swap you for anything. Now, let's get out of here, before those headbangers get into any more trouble."

Sir Henry made his way back down the tower, gingerly, carrying a few necessities. As Richard was to stay in hospital for at least another twenty-four hours under observation, Henry intended to camp out in his secretary's suite until he came back. Despite being built at a time where injury and illness were a far greater part of everyday life, medieval castles were not constructed with infirmity in mind. Of course, Henry hardly blamed his ancestors. With the constant burning, rape, pillage and slaughter of border warfare, they would have been in a rush to build the strongest, most defensible walls they could afford – it was easy to see why disabled access never made the specification, and yet, for Henry, the spiral stairs were purgatory itself that day.

The door to Richard's apartment was still ajar from the night before. Breathing heavily, Henry brooded, waiting for the pain to subside as he stared balefully at the bloodstain on the carpet, where his friend had been beaten to the ground with a crowbar.

"Damn those blighters," he cursed, shoving the door further open to make his way in. He could already hear sawing and hammering from outside. Presumably, good as his word, Gary had put his men to work fixing the gate.

Henry went into Richard's small study, looking for his book of contacts. He needed to inform Secure Nation of the break-in, not to mention the insurance company. He sighed again. The insurance could wait until the morning – there would be no one there on a Sunday – but Secure Nation had an emergency line. Having paid them so much money, seemingly for nothing, he felt no scruple about calling them at the weekend.

Going through Richard's drawers, he found the Filofax where his secretary stored Rookstone's business contacts. He opened the clasp, and a collection of photographic negatives fell out. He replaced them without thinking and was about to resume his search for the details he wanted, when he hesitated, the warning received from one of his ghostly ancestors a couple of evenings previously suddenly troubling him again. Although he did not know it, it was the same warning Richard had received, right before he was attacked. He would never usually have gone through Richard's belongings, but these were in with the Rookstone Estate files, so it was hardly an invasion of privacy. Perhaps he was getting paranoid, but Henry held them up to the window and peered.

Floating George looked drained and exhausted.

Jerry stared, wide-eyed and shellshocked.

After vouching for their good character, and making a generous donation to the 'Policemen's Benevolent Fund', Gary knew how they felt.

They sat in silence on the journey back to Rookstone. Even Poppy seemed subdued as she curled up in Gary's lap, peeking out from under her tail to keep an eye on his passengers.

Gary kept his eyes on the road; they could talk later, once the young men had been given chance to come back to themselves. Something caught his eye in the door mirror – flashing blue lights.

"Oh, for the love of... What now?"

He pulled over and a small Escort van pulled in behind.

Gary opened the van door and stepped out. "Wait here, lads. I'll be right back."

Gripper smiled. "Well, well, well, if it isn't my favourite builders."

"What is it, Sergeant? It's been a hell of a night – we've filled in all your damned paperwork *and* got it all signed off with the lawyers—"

"Excellent. Very diligent, sir. Pity you don't show that kind of diligence when it comes to maintaining your vehicles."

Gary frowned. "What are you talking about? These vans are nearly new and are kept in excellent order."

"I have to differ, sir. Your offside brake light isn't working."

Gary gritted his teeth. *Of all the times!* He took a breath to calm himself. "I'll pop to the nearest car factor and get it sorted, first thing in the morning."

"Good, good. That's very good, but I'm afraid I'll have to issue you with a producer, sir. If you could bring your licence and insurance details down to the station."

"I don't have that information with me, Sergeant. We're working three hundred miles from home – as you well know – but I can have my wife fax copies to your station this evening. She's travelling back to Worcestershire at the moment."

Gripper smiled blandly and began writing on the pad in his hand.

"What are you doing?"

"Filling out a fixed penalty notice. Don't worry, sir, you'll have fourteen days to pay it. Oh, and I've taken the liberty of including my station's fax number at the bottom, there. I'll expect the details this evening as promised, sir."

"Just excuse me for one moment, please." Gary left him and returned to his van to rummage through the glovebox. He came back with a Polaroid camera.

Gripper frowned, wondering what he might be up to.

Gary smiled. "This is a lovely part of the world. I'd just like a record of everyone we've met while working here."

Baffled, Gripper merely stared, while Gary took a photograph of the police sergeant before stepping back for a second, wider shot of Gripper next to his police van – parked very clearly on a public highway. As he strolled back towards his nemesis, the camera flashed again. "Oops. Went off by accident, that time." It had done no such thing. Having owned one himself, Gary knew that the Ford Escort Mark V was prone to wishbone issues that usually showed themselves by very quickly ruining the front tyres. He also knew that the driver of any vehicle in Britain was ultimately responsible if that vehicle was not roadworthy, even when that driver was a policeman and the van a registered police vehicle. Ever an observant man, when it came to spotting things that needed fixing, he checked his Polaroids, giving them a shake – three beautiful photographs of vehicle, driver, registration and a front tyre completely bald on one side down to the steel, developed within moments.

He smiled. "Thanks."

Gripper was looking at him strangely. "Enjoy the rest of your weekend, sir." He turned to walk back to his vehicle.

"Just a moment, please. What about my stolen van?"

Gripper halted. "Our enquiries are proceeding, sir."

"Really? You could have fooled me." Gary was livid. The attitude of the man. However, he buried his fury deep, saving it for a time when revenge might be served up cold. He screwed up the fixed penalty notice and shoved it roughly into his pocket, not trusting himself to say any more as he stormed off back to his own vehicle and slammed the door. "More money! I might as well just set *fire* to my bank account and have done with it! Put this camera back in the glovebox, will you?"

"Everything alright, Gaz?" Floating George asked, quietly. "Why's that gadgie got it in for us?"

Gary ran his fingers through his hair and sighed loudly, calming himself. "I don't know. But we'll get our own back on him."

"Yeah?"

"Believe it! Come on, let's get back to the others. I think we could all do with a drink."

H ey! I said, hey! What's going on?" The man took a step forward, shotgun held in the crook of his arm with its barrel broken. "You there! I say, you, fellow! Hey!"

Hammer froze.

Worzel bumped into him from behind.

"Watch it!" Kneeling, Hammer gently moved a few leaves aside to peer out from the trees across fields drenched in bronze russet by the setting sun. Concerned that they might have been spotted creeping through the woods, the beauty of the spring evening was entirely lost on him as he spied on the armed man in the flat cap. He was shouting at another man in a light brown jacket, who seemed to be looking in completely the opposite direction.

"Fenton!" brown jacket bellowed. "*Fenton!*"

Flat cap called after him. "I say, fellow! Get your hound under control! These aren't just cows, they're wild cattle – and they have young! Little blighter will get himself killed!"

Hammer grinned. Even Scott's lip curled into a sneer.

"Fenton!" brown jacket hollered again, ignoring flat cap and running after his errant Labrador.

Ignorance of the countryside can sometimes be dangerous. After stealing a car, Hammer had brought his team back to Rookstone just before sundown, the Grey Emeralds growing on his mind like an obsession. The fakes were things of rare beauty. He could only imagine what the real things must be like, how they might feel in his hand. Securing them would get him off the hook with his backers and net him a tidy sum, but it was more than that.

Having spent the day planning his next move, he was gambling that no one would expect them to return the following night. Not after the recent commotion and police involvement. He had no idea there were wild cattle near the castle grounds, or that cows often had young calves with them by May. Unlike domestic livestock – that can also be extremely dangerous – the wild cattle experienced no human contact at all and would kill anyone they considered a threat. Fortunately for the gang out of London, the cattle had been drawn to their attention by an exceptionally naughty dog. For his owner, who most certainly could *not* outrun the cows now eyeing him with murderous intent, things were about to become exceptionally hazardous.

"Get back here, man!" flat cap screamed at the top of his lungs.

"Fenton!"

"Get out of there!"

"Fenton!"

"They've seen you, man!"

"Fenton!"

Flat cap shook his head, snapped his barrel closed and fired a cartridge into the air.

That got brown jacket's attention. Finally realising his peril, he turned and ran for his life as a rumble travelled across the land behind him. He cleared the fence before a ton of angry mum stopped just short of smashing through it. She jumped and bucked around in frustration.

Hidden within the bushes, Hammer and Worzel were doubled up in stitches.

Brown jacket was back on his feet. "Fenton! *Fentooooon!* Oh, Christ[1]!"

"Alright," Hammer stated in a low voice. "Make yourselves comfortable. We'll wait here until the time's right."

Still chuckling, Worzel asked, "What time we goin' in, Ham?"

Hammer checked his watch. "We'll go about three a.m. That'll be about as dark as it gets. Now, get some shut-eye. Gonna be a long night – again."

---

1. Yes, the original, hilarious Fenton incident was a later internet sensation involving a naughty dog and some deer. Even out of sequence, funny memories are timeless and surely worth reliving.

Katie helped out around the castle during the peak tourist seasons. Married to groundsman Tom, she was naturally concerned about all that had happened at his place of work during the previous evening, just a few hours after he had returned home for the weekend.

Despite a visit from his own wife, Eleanor, during his morning in hospital, Sir Henry had forbidden his family's return until things were settled, so Katie and Old Albert conspired to bring Rookstone's forced residents some much needed cheer in the form of a giant Sunday dinner. Katie and Albert worked on it all afternoon, sending the scent of roasting meat drifting across the courtyard to make everyone's tummy growl. The side of beef, purchased from a local farmer, would have fed them three times over, which was fortunate, because Willy Mammoth was hungry.

By evening, the great hall was already prepared for their faux medieval banquet when the builders drifted in, in ones and twos. Swapping the smell of plaster and stone dust for aftershave and deodorant, they arrived fresh from the showers to a long table laid for twelve and adorned with blazing candelabras.

Within moments, the places were filled. Sir Henry sat at the head of the table with Gary to his right and Jimmy to his left, with Gary's team lining each side. Tom, Katie and Albert sat at the end of the lines, the easier to serve the men who – for some, at least – had been through the worst day of their lives. Only one place remained empty.

Gary looked down the table, taking a quick headcount. "Where's Andy?"

"Looking for his boots," Willy informed them. "Andy-the-spread[2] will be sorry he's missed this spread, if he doesn't shape himself."

The door at the east end of the great hall opened, revealing Andy Wilson.

Gary stood, to point out his place at the table. "You hear us talking about y— What the *hell* have *you* got on?"

Andy paused as he walked down the long hall. "What do you mean?"

Gary pointed, slack-jawed, at the plasterer's golden basketball boots. The others turned and a whoop of delight filled the huge chamber.

"What's wrong with 'em?" Andy asked, tetchily. "These are classics. LA Gear. Limited edition!"

Gary was laughing heartily now. "Really? Limited, you say? You'd think they'd be more popular! Can you turn 'em down a bit? I'm going blind!"

"Get lost! You're just jealous – all o' ya!"

"I think you mean envious," Willy pointed out. When parted from his guitars, he read.

Andy, not known for his witty repartee, glared at him. "Cobblers[3]!"

Laughter and catcalls filled the hall, further adding to the atmosphere of a medieval banquet.

---

2. Spread is builder slang for plasterer in some regions.

3. Possibly a corruption of cobbles, meaning small, round stones – also a British euphemism for *men parts*.

"What happened to your work boots?" Jimmy asked, grinning. "Couldn't you find them?"

"I found one. God knows where the other one's gone. I left 'em in the hallway when I went for a shower and one of yo' lot nicked it! It had better be back there in the morning – I'm warnin' ya!"

Gary and Sir Henry shared a glance. "I did caution you about things going missing," Henry whispered. "Happens all the time. They always turn up... eventually."

Gary nodded. "It seems even the dead have a sense of humour in this place." Sometimes the devil works mischief, even in the best of men. Already guessing the plasterer's well-worn response, he asked, innocently, "So, Andy, what do you think happened?"

The builders waited expectantly.

"It's a bloody conspiracy!"

A roar of laughter and bangs on the table rattled the cutlery.

As the merriment subsided, replaced by the rapture of tucking into the biggest roast most of them had ever seen, Gary spoke quietly with Sir Henry. "You know we had some of our tools go missing a few days ago."

"Yes, as it happens, one of them turned up sticking out of my side!" Seeing the misplaced guilt of the decent man cross Gary's face, he softened. "Sorry, old chap. Only joshing. Nothing too expensive, I hope?"

Gary shook his head. "It's not that. It's more *what* went missing."

Henry paused with his fork halfway to his mouth.

"We lost a crowbar and a large, wooden-handled screwdriver. Both tools that were used in last night's attack – I don't need to remind you of that."

Henry's side twinged at the memory.

"We turned the place upside down looking for them, but I swear, they weren't here."

Henry replaced his fork on the table. "So how did last night's thugs get their hands on them?"

Gary could only shrug in bafflement.

"Doesn't look good for your chaps, that, does it? Hard to see how anyone else could have gained access to them. I just assumed they picked up tools lying around on the job and put them to malefic purpose, but I'm not sure Sergeant Gripper will see it that way."

"Oh, that git!"

Henry grinned. "I'm not a fan, either. Chap tried to imply that I organised all this for the insurance!"

"And almost got yourself killed to... what? Make it look convincing?"

Henry snorted. "So he seems to think."

Gary shook his head. "I'll be dealing with young Charlton from here onwards, rest assured. Those scum pinched one of my vans – and all the tools we had on board."

Henry looked pensive for a moment. "Yes, I'd forgotten you were also a direct victim of these fellows."

"But back to your theory about them simply using what was at hand," Gary continued. "That's completely logical – and the only explanation I can think of – but we simply could not find them. I just thought it was young Aleks giving up and not looking properly, but, Henry, *I* looked everywhere. They weren't here. Unless I missed them by some fluke, and the robbers found them by another such fluke, then something strange happened. I know things go missing here, but..."

Henry gave Gary a penetrating stare. "Go on."

Gary looked around to see if they were being overheard. Content that his lads were involved in their own boisterous conversations, he leaned close. "Since I've been here, some strange things *have* been happening."

"You don't say?"

Gary rolled his eyes with a smile. "OK, apart from the obvious, I mean." He took a moment to collect his thoughts. "Do you ever see anything here? That is, things that, erm... shouldn't really be?"

"You mean ghosts?"

"Yes."

"No."

"Oh."

Henry smiled. "Don't worry, old man. I don't *see* them, but I certainly know they're here."

Gary brightened. "You do?"

"Indeed. One sent me a message just a couple of evenings ago, as it happens."

"You too?"

Henry blinked. Clearly, he had not expected that. "You've experienced the same? What did they tell you?"

Gary puffed out his cheeks. "That's a long story."

"Fine, then I'll go first, as mine was only a short message. One word, in fact – 'treachery'."

Gary's jaw dropped again, Henry's revelation being even more astounding than Andy's trainers. "What did you infer from that?"

It was Sir Henry's turn to shrug. "The very next night, I was stabbed by villains using one of your screwdrivers, while stealing *my* family heirlooms, so I'm not sure what to make of it."

"You still suspect we might be involved?"

Henry pulled a weary hand down his face to relieve the tension he still felt. "It all comes back to my grandfather's photograph."

"The one with my van in the background, somehow in 1934?"

"The same. You're obviously part of all this." He held up a placating hand before Gary could protest. "I'm not saying a nefarious part, but it seems to me that we are linked in some way – and this has been a long time coming. Longer than you know."

Henry sat back, taking a moment before continuing. "I have a private drawing room, just through there and up the stairs." He pointed towards the door behind him, at the west end of the great hall. "Perhaps it's time to compare notes? Bring the glasses, would you? Can't carry anything with these wretched crutches."

When Gary rose, Willy grabbed his arm. "Weren't planning on leaving that beef, were you?" he asked, hopefully.

Inga Hróc Stán opened her spiritual mouth and closed it again. "Look, Edward, shall we swap to modern speak? We'll be here all night, else, and things are afoot."

"It *would* save time," the shade of Sir Edward Grey agreed. "Your *Saxon* sounds more like German to me, anyway," he added dismissively.

Inga frowned. "Don't forget, we *made* England, Sir Knight – and I'm as noble as you are! *I* remember the Great Alfred."

"Knew him, did you?" He sniffed.

Inga glared.

Sir Edward bowed. "Of course, dear lady. I meant no offence."

Ruffled feathers partially smoothed, Inga continued, "Those brigands are hiding out in the woods over yonder. I heard them planning another attack on our descendants this very night."

"No one says 'yonder' any more."

Hands on hips, Inga's glare intensified.

"*Our* descendants, you say?" Sir Edward moved on, swiftly. "Yes, I've heard the others talking about this builder chappie. One of yours, is he?"

Inga nodded.

"So you want to intervene." It was not a question.

She nodded again. "I'm not sure he's very bright, but he seems a nice boy. I can't just leave him to his fate."

Sir Edward chuckled. "Not sure my lad's any better. When that obnoxious little man from 'the heritage' came calling, telling Henry what he could and couldn't do in his own castle – *my* castle – the boy practically grovelled for permission! I'd have had the fellow stripped, whipped and sent running across the fields, his backside bared and bloody!"

Inga sighed, a hard habit to break when considering the state of the world, even when one has – corporeally, at least – left that world. "Yes, they've regressed a long way since our day, but we are where we are. Now, what are we going to do about the current situation? They have a castle but not the wit to defend it. The fools are in there now, eating most of their food supplies in one meal! That would have kept our entire household fed for a week!"

Sir Edward wilfully reduced his girth, tightening his spiritual belt. "Yeees," he drawled, hoping the act had gone unnoticed. He failed.

"Of course, *we* worked hard, in our day," she added, pointedly. "Even the lord didn't have the luxury of lording it."

"You think I had it easy? *I* lived under the Great Henry. Forsooth, one learned how to dodge and weave, I can tell you! I fought the French, too, don't you know!"

"Really? They're still there. Anyway, no one says forsooth any more," she returned his jibe.

Edward reddened, no mean feat for a blue-lit ethereal apparition.

Refusing to be intimidated, Inga crossed her arms as though she were still alive, while treating Edward to a wry smile. "But of course, *we* only had the Danes to contend with."

Edward looked uncomfortable. "Well, it's not a competition, dear lady. Perhaps we should focus on the job in hand, eh? If we get involved, we'll be for it. We'll be risking our very deaths."

"I know, but young Henry almost joined us last night. We can't stand idly by."

"*Oh...*" Edward sighed, gently, seeing where her thoughts were leading. "So you're thinking about asking *his* help again."

"He's good at walking the line, Edward."

"But he's still constrained by the rules, Inga, and remember this – if *he* calls down the wrath, it won't only be him who burns for it."

"Hmm... burns for it," Inga repeated, as she drifted thoughtfully through a tree trunk.

"Lady?"

She turned back to him with a new light in her eyes. "Perhaps you're right. We shouldn't involve him. After all, he's not like us. He chose the body of a man, sort of, and the head of an animal—"

"Sort of..."

"Quite. But my point is, he – what's the phrase? – nailed his colours to the mast, with those choices. We'll need a little more humanity to deal with this."

"Compassion?" Edward asked, doubtfully.

"No. The other thing."

"Oh, that. Really? Are you sure?"

"Play to your strengths. Look, if we pull this off, I don't think *he* will want to be anywhere near, but we'll attract everyone else, from miles around – place will be like a hornets' nest!"

"Right. It's time. Get up!" Hammer went round kicking the others awake.

Worzel lit up his digital watch. "It's only just after two, Ham."

"Since when could you tell the time? Get up! I've got a plan to take care of the van. The second one we nicked. The one that's still covered in the woodland the opposite side of the castle. We can't risk just leaving it behind, but we can't risk drawing attention to it, neither."

"So what's the plan?" asked Scott.

Hammer grinned. "Worzel knows."

"I do?"

"You'll get there. You're pretty good with time, it seems."

Worzel groaned. "It's the middle of the night, Ham. Just tell us!"

"Just get your stuff together. We're going – now."

The thieves left the copse where they had slept the evening away to step out under another clear, starry sky. Climbing over a fence, they cut across fields of suspiciously short grass towards the castle. The moon cast a pale light across a landscape of midnight blues and sharp-edged shadows.

Worzel tripped and swore.

Hammer turned. "Keep it down!" he hissed. "It's all quiet out here."

"Too quiet," Scott seconded.

Hammer rolled his eyes. "Worz, what are you playing at?"

"Bootlaces have come undone. With you in a sec."

Hammer stormed off, shaking his head. He approached the fence at the far end of the field when he heard what sounded like a sneeze. Looking back over his shoulder, he could barely see Worzel, dressed all in black, which was good. *Less* good was what approached Worzel. A mucky, yellowy white in the day, the giant bull positively glowed under moon and starlight. "Worz," he rasped as loudly as he dared. "*Worz!*"

Nothing for it, Hammer covered the remaining distance to the fence in a heartbeat, clearing it in a single leap – followed closely by Scott and Serj.

Worzel tied off his boot and stood. "What?" he hissed back. At his rear, the drumming of heavy hooves suddenly increased in intensity to what could only be described as a gallop. As ever, timing was important, and as the thuds fell ever more closely together, it was obvious that acceleration was also taking place. "Oh, *sh—*"

"Shall we help him?" Scott asked, in an interested-but-not-serious kind of way.

Hammer was incredulous. "You first!"

Worzel was flat out, but unless Lady Luck intervened soon, he would shortly be flat *and* out – although 'Worzel was' would probably still be accurate.

The bull gained.

Worzel ran.

The bull lowered his head.

Worzel whimpered for his mother – though, he had no idea where she might be.

The bull snorted.

Worzel cried out, throwing himself forward, desperately hoping his legs would catch up.

The bull sprang.

Both chaser and chased were head down, but there was no photo finish, only a pine fence. Worzel's terrified "Aaaargh!" instantly turned to an "Oooooohhh!" as he flew straight over it, slam-dunked unceremoniously into the next field. Winded, he was nevertheless fortunate to roll across soft grass, otherwise his next stop might have been a pine box.

Hammer and the others ran over to him. "You OK, Worz?"

"No," he whimpered in a small voice.

"What's wrong?" asked Scott.

"*What's wrong?* That... that *rhinoceros* just tore me a new one! *Ow!* Don't touch me!"

Scott was already suppressing laughter. "Sorry, Ah meant, what's *up?*"

They fell about.

"You fink this is funny, do ya?" Worzel rounded on them, angrily. "I'm bleeding to deff, here!"

Hammer tried to keep his face straight. "Did it, er... you know, go in?" He burst out laughing again, immediately shushing himself and everyone. "Come on, help him up, lads. We can't stay here. Didn't that second van we nicked have a first aid kit in the back?"

Chapter 9

999 Emergency!

If Sir Edward still had a belly, he would have been laughing all the way down to it. Inga covered her mouth delicately with a hand, for dignity, but also found the sight of Worzel limping down the lane towards their ex-getaway vehicle hilarious.

When the villains arrived at their hidden, mouse-disabled van, they stepped inside and removed some effects there had simply been no time to retrieve the last time. After being forced to steal one of the For Keeps vans to make their escape, Hammer was concerned that their previous vehicle might be discovered. No matter how careful they always were, there would almost certainly be some genetic material left behind, perhaps even an unguarded fingerprint here and there. It needed to be burned out, which presented him with another problem – they could not leave yet, not without the emeralds. He had taken his backers' money and must come through with the goods. A fire would bring the law, and he could not have that. Not yet. Not that night.

Wincing and whinging, Worzel used a bandage wrap from the van's first aid box to patch the bull-inflicted hole to his gluteus maximus – fortunately, just left of the one he had been born with. In terms of pain and discomfort, his was a horn of plenty. He would not be doing any sitting for a while.

"Pity he couldn't wait until one of the nights next week," Sir Edward commented, wryly.

Inga frowned. "Next week?"

"Indeed. He could have had a new moon!" Edward barked with laughter.

Inga smiled wanly. "If I follow their speech correctly, they're doing our work for us."

"So I understand. Yet, we must be careful. If we're caught breaking the rules..."

Inga knew he was right. She followed one of the criminals underneath the vehicle, to see what he was up to.

"Serj?" Hammer hissed.

Serj poked his head out from under the centre of the van, near the fuel tank. "Are we all set?"

Serj raised two fingers, Churchill style.

"Two minutes, great. That's two minutes, Worz. You finished with your eye patch?"

Scott sniggered. "We'll call him Nelson after this."

"No, he only had the one!" Hammer exclaimed, in a rare burst of good humour.

"You *could*," Worzel chuntered from the rear of the van, "if you want a brick thrown at your head!"

"Alright," Hammer calmed them. "And slide the door shut all *quiet* like, when you come out."

The criminal gang closed all the doors, setting off once more for Rookstone Castle.

Edward watched them go. "Did you see what they did?"

"Yes. The one underneath fitted this contraption with an engine that cuts time into slices. Do you know, I remember when they started chopping the day into two-dozen pieces – no idea how they came up with that number. Anyway, it's almost the end of the twoth hour—"

"Second."

"What?"

"It's what they call it now. The second hour. Some say two of the clock, I believe," Edward explained, knowledgably. "Of course, we'd pretty much got time all worked out by my day," he added proudly.

"To us, it was light, or it was dark. Only kings and bishops cared about counting the hours, with their fancy marked candles. For the rest of us, time was short, and it was best not to dwell over what we didn't have. Still, if I understood those malefactors correctly, the numbers shown underneath this steel wagon are counting down from five... what could it mean, hours?"

Sir Edward nodded. "Dawn, then. If we're about to go into the third hour. They've set the device for dawn. I heard them tell of something combustible in the belly of that monstrosity, too. Probably some source of Greek fire, I should expect. Its stench is pervasive, oily, and..." he stooped to look under the van, "it's leaking from where that rogue nicked one of those, what are they, *pipes?* There, underneath. You see it? What do you propose we do?"

"We need to raise the alarm now. Dawn will be too late, for I do fear for our boys in the castle."

"Can't do it. Interference, remember?"

"We can't intervene for *good,* but anyone can intervene for evil. Whenever that happens, it's just fate and 'to be regretted'. You see, the rules aren't so different from when we were alive."

"And you think detonating this, this *thing* would come under the latter?"

Inga smiled. "I remember, ooh, centuries ago now, one of those men visiting Rookstone – you know, the ones with those ridiculous wigs and the big brains? He said everything in the universe tends towards chaos, a sort of lowest commonality. Entropy, he called it – you know, my memory's much better since I died."

"What was his name?"

"Can't remember."

Edward blinked, but did not press the point. Instead, he frowned in concentration, trying to recollect. "Yes, I remember him now. What *was* his name? Sounded like Sir Nigel Luton, or something like that. Interminably boring fellow. I must confess, I tuned out and went down to the guards' room to listen to their tales of ale and wenching, instead. Had a much more entertaining evening, I can tell you."

Inga scowled. "Hmm. *Anyway,* how I see it, is that we're helping the natural order, the tendency for things to be *reduced.*"

"You mean go up in smoke."

"That's a narrow interpretation."

Sir Edward's eyebrows rose. "And *that's* a fine line. I'm starting to wish we'd asked *him* for help now. He's a less dangerous associate than thou art."

"I thought we'd agreed not to speak like that. And don't be silly. Besides, I can't possibly be held to account."

"Forsooth, why?"

Inga smiled, mischievously. "I'm only a *woman.* What could I possibly know about these devices?"

Sir Henry slept well after an extremely interesting conversation with his builder – a healing sleep he desperately needed. After a solid four hours, he awoke reasonably refreshed. He was still in agony, but no longer tired.

He switched on the bedside lamp and looked at his clock. 02:17. "Hmm. What a coincidence." After what he had heard, he wondered if Gary was also awake and whether it was by choice. "Something's telling me it's time to act." Gingerly, he swung his legs over the side of the bed and reached for one of his crutches to help him stand. He dressed as quickly as he was able, left Richard's apartment and began the long climb up the winding spiral stair to his own suite on the top floor. "Didn't think this through, did I?" he stated ruefully, barely halfway up and wincing from the pain in his side.

Eventually, he reached the top of the stairs and entered his family's private accommodation. Hobbling painfully to his study, he reached for a sconce on the wall. The torch it held was for decoration only, but he pulled it, and a secret door popped open within the wall panelling – no castle should be without one.

Henry pushed the door fully open and looked inside. It was too dark to see properly. Unfortunately, he was no electrician, and employing a tradesman to fit a light would have given the game away, rendering his most secret hiding place useless, for even the most trustworthy people can speak out of turn or make mistakes. He sighed, realising what he had to do next.

After propping one of his crutches against a wall, he slowly – desperately slowly – bent to reach the bottom drawer of his desk. Leaning on the other crutch as though his life depended on it, he reached into the drawer. With ragged, chopped breaths, he removed a leadlight. Placing it on his desk, he straightened, taking a moment to gulp several calming breaths, until the urge to cry out subsided. He was not done yet. No building regulations set the minimum heights for power points in that medieval pile, and so, screwing up his courage, he bent again, to plug in the cable.

Swearing over and over in silence, he straightened again and switched on the lamp. "Idiot!" He cursed himself for looking at the bulb to check it was on.

Blinking away the spots before his eyes, he leaned on his single crutch and limped into the secret room. Mounted into the side wall was a safe, installed by one of his forefathers in the late nineteenth century – a secret handed down from father to son along with a key. No one alive knew of it, not even his wife, just Henry Grey III and a few dozen ghosts. He looked around, fancying they might be watching him at that moment. "I know you chaps won't talk. Haven't for years, eh?"

A stiff breeze blew through the apartment.

"Sorry. Gallows humour."

Leaning his remaining crutch against the wall, he worked one of the earliest combination locks of its type. Hearing the *click,* he took his keys from a pocket, inserted one of them into the secondary lock and gave it a twist. Turning the handle, he pulled. The door swung open, easily.

Inside were several confidential documents and deeds, a little money, and two sets of the famous Grey Emeralds. "Better make sure I take the right ones."

In fact, there was no way he could have confused them. The second set of copies were in an expensive-looking, modern box with a Swiss jeweller's logo on the side. He checked the real ones were as he'd left them – after the weekend Henry had endured, one could not be *too* paranoid. Smiling to himself, he rewrapped them contentedly and relocked his safe.

Closing everything up and replacing the leadlight in his desk drawer took far longer than it should have and left him feeling weak. He considered stopping for a fortifying cup of tea but decided against it. "No. Let's get this done."

Henry was working on a hunch. After the discovery of those negatives in Richard's Filofax, he was on full alert and suspected his troubles were far from over as he slowly made his way back down the stone steps.

A few minutes earlier...

Gary woke up with a start, followed immediately by a sigh. He switched on the bedside lamp, pleasantly surprised that it actually worked. He checked his travel clock. 02:17.

"OK. Let's get this over with. What do you want to tell me tonight? Or do you just want to throw things at me again?" He was still tired and had woken up tetchy. "I've heard of angry ghosts. Does chucking things at people provide you with some form of therapy? Perhaps for tomorrow night I'll bring some coasters from the lounge to bed with me. At least that way I won't have to get up!"

Silence.

Gary waited for a thump. When nothing came, he continued his berating. "Pity you didn't actually tell me anything useful the other night. You know, something like, 'Hey, Gaz, your workplace is about to be broken into by dangerous criminals who are about to try and murder your employers, putting you squarely in the frame for the whole thing!' Too much to ask?"

After running off at the mouth, Gary realised his ill-tempered, middle-of-the-night witticisms were going entirely to waste. He was, in fact, alone.

Grrrr!

Almost alone. Poppy was clearly terrorising someone in her sleep.

Gary leaned over the side of his bed to check on her, shaking his head. "Could sleep for England, you could."

Grrrr!

"Right." Now thoroughly annoyed that his internal clock had woken him up for nothing, he decided to go and make a cup of tea. Coffee would doom any hope of getting back to sleep again, but he needed refreshment. Slipping out of bed, he first went to the toilet. While emptying his bladder, a thought struck him. After several frigid experiences, he had decided to leave his Saxon necklace on the bedside table while he slept. After washing his hands, he went back to his bedroom and touched it gingerly. Retaining all his fingerprints, he dared pick it up to rub it between his forefinger and thumb. The cross was slightly cooler than his skin, roughly room temperature.

He looped the lace over his head, wearing the necklace like an early warning system, for it was dawning on him that whenever he received 'visitors', the small silver cross became freezing cold to the touch – although, weirdly, only for him. Jimmy was unaffected when Gary showed it to his brother in the café. In an odd way, he felt disappointed when his ghostly caller failed to show – especially now he was awake anyway. He had so many questions. Concern crossed his mind. *Could* ghosts also get themselves into trouble, or danger, or be harmed in some way? He walked into the lounge-diner area of his suite and strode right up to the window. He breathed heavily on the glass, just to be sure.

Nothing.

He shook his head again. "Most people keep a memo pad!"

Yawning, he filled the kettle as Poppy padded into the room to leap up onto the sofa.

"Oi! Off! We're not at home."

She skewered him with a glare, demanding that he explain himself further.

"Come on, off!"

She hopped down, growling indignantly.

"There seems to be some confusion about who's in charge here," he grumbled, taking Poppy's blanket from the armchair opposite to spread it over half of their two-seater sofa, for her to sit by him. Having turned down Poppy's bed, the man nominally in charge turned to find her already curled up on the armchair. "You little— Get off!"

Poppy raised her head, her scowl stating as clearly as Queen's English, *Make up your damned mind!*

"Come on, hup! Up on your blanket."

Indolently, she slid from the armchair to hop lightly onto the sofa as instructed, pointedly turning her back on Gary before drifting immediately back to sleep.

"You know, the thing I love most about owning a dog is the company."

Gary sipped his tea in wordless solitude, fully expecting a disturbing visit at any moment. He must have been psychic.

Now...

"The lock's knackered!" Worzel stated, irritably.

"Well, do *something* with it!" Hammer hissed, harshly. "You're meant to be our locks *man.*"

Having so recently been 'bullied' by a master, Worzel was in no mood to take any more. "Don't blame me. He knackered it!"

"As per orders," Scott shot back.

"*Orders,*" Worzel mocked. "He'll be goose-stepping next."

"Ye're tha expert on farm animals!"

Worzel balled his fist around his lockpicks. "You want some? Do ya?"

"Enough!" Hammer shushed them angrily. "What the hell do you think we're doing here? Now sort yourselves out!"

The villains turned away from each other grumpily. "So what do you wanna do, Ham?" Worzel asked, eventually. "They must have barred the gates to secure 'em."

Hammer thought for a moment. "We use the tradesman's entrance, of course." He grinned at his own cleverness, and grudgingly Worzel grinned, too.

They followed the line of the building to where it intersected with the wall of the outer courtyard. Keeping low, they ran along the base of the wall as it turned sharply east. Sticking to it, they came to the gateway that led into the outer courtyard. At one end were the remaining pair of For Keeps vans and an eight-cubic-yard skip.

Hammer led them to the door, while Worzel limped painfully by the rear[1].

"Now listen," Hammer began, "we'll need to memorise our way through here, 'cause we might not be able to use the main gates to get out, neither. Understand?"

They nodded.

"Right. Worz, it's just a Yale lock – if you'd be so kind, sunbeam?"

Worzel moved forward, removing his lockpicks from a pocket. "Give me some light."

Hammer switched on a small pencil torch with a three-volt, lensed spotlight bulb.

Worzel applied the picks and was able to turn the lock in seconds.

Hammer pushed past him. "Follow me – and keep it down. There's a small army of brickies asleep somewhere in this place. We don't wanna get into nothin' we don't need to. Got it?"

They made their way through short, interconnecting corridors and hallways that eventually led to the castle's café and tea rooms.

"This place is really freaky, Ham," Worzel noted, staring balefully up at the giant elk skull above the fireplace, while trying not to dwell on the various skulls of other dead animals that decorated walls dripping with antique weaponry. "Who *owns* this place?"

"Who cares? Get your mind back on the tom. That's what we're here for, remember?"

"Hey, Ham." Worzel began a stuttering laugh. "Bet you didn't expect to be in your own Hammer film, eh? Eh?"

"Shat it! Come on."

Serj admired the weaponry on the walls, noting their locations – just in case.

"De ye reckon these skulls are any relative tae that thing we saw out in tha woods last night?" Scott asked, in an unusually subdued tone.

Hammer turned on him. "Look here, that was nuffin'. *Nuffin'!* Got it? There's no such things as ghosts—"

The bang made them all jump.

"What the hell was that?" Worzel cried.

"Shat it, you muppet!" Hammer hissed, furiously. He bent to pick up the object that had fallen – a long pole with a spearhead combined with a hook and a wicked-looking spike on either side. Hammer stared at the halberd in wide-eyed horror. "Who knocked this off the wall?"

---

1. Yes, that was a bad joke.

Moonlight streamed through high windows and Hammer could just make out their faces, seeing nothing but confusion and more than a little fear in them. He placed the centuries-old weapon on a table covered with a cheery red and white checked tablecloth and looked around cautiously. At the end of the tea rooms, high up at first floor level, was a minstrels' gallery. He fancied he saw a shadow move, but when he squinted, scrutinising the area, it was gone. "Let's get out of here."

He led them out through a door underneath the minstrels' gallery and along another corridor to an external door. Opening it a crack, he checked the coast was still clear after the clang of a weapon hitting the café's flagstones. Fortunately, Rookstone's walls were thick. Satisfied, he followed them round to the west tower. Standing outside the door where Scott had bludgeoned Sir Henry's secretary with a stolen crowbar, he waited for his men to catch up.

After their attacks on both Richard and Sir Henry, Hammer expected to find the apartments empty. He was surprised to see a yellowish light spreading under the door.

"Crap!"

"What shall we do, Ham?" Worzel asked. He sounded jittery, and though he would never admit it, Hammer could fully understand why.

"We go in," Scott prompted.

Hammer turned. "I'm calling the shots here."

"Ye'd better call them fast, then, laddie, 'cause ye know what'll happen if we come back empty-handed on this one."

The muscles bunched in Hammer's jaw. He knew Scott was right, but did not want to admit that, either. He made a snap decision. "Pick the lock, Worz."

Worzel did as asked, but the door remained unopenable. "Bolted, Ham."

"They werenae strong bolts," Scott assured him. "Ah clocked them last time we were here."

At last, information he could use. Hammer nodded. "Stand back." Granted some room, he jumped at the door, giving it an almighty kick. As Scott predicted, the bolts gave, their keeps flying off the doorframe and clinking across the floor inside the apartment.

No sooner had Henry closed Richard's safe, with the second batch of emeralds securely inside and their cardboard box roaring on the fire in the hearth, when a crash at the door made him straighten in shock. Leaning heavily on his crutches, he cried out, unable to help it as white-hot pain shot down his side. Alone and trapped, he gripped them, standing ready to defend himself. "Who the hell are you?"

Scott grinned, nastily. "How's the side, yer worship?"

"You!" Henry accused, catching his meaning instantly. "Get out of my home this instant, you hear? I'm not alone, you know!"

"We know," Hammer assured him, "and we don't care. This should save us a long and difficult search. You know what we're after. I suggest you hand them over. Now."

"I don't know what you're talking about."

"Do you honestly think that line has *ever* worked? Come on, be sensible. Hand over the emeralds. My friend here hates leaving a job unfinished." He gestured towards Scott with a nod. "Give us what we want, or he'll make sure of you this time."

Rookstone Castle was full of historical memorabilia, and not just from the castle or the medieval period. Scattered about Richard's study were many items collected from his and Henry's travels around the world, all awaiting a good clean before being put on display. On that day, there was a buccina mounted on top of the oak mantel above the fireplace. Desperate, and having no clue whether it would even work – let alone how to make it sound – Henry grabbed the curved, C-shaped Roman horn and blew it for all he was worth, ignoring the agony that tore once more through his side.

Made for signalling manoeuvres within the legions, often in the heat of battle, the horn reverberated at a teeth-chattering mid-range. Perfectly pitched for the human ear and surprisingly loud, it shattered the stillness of the night.

Poppy jumped off the sofa and ran around Gary's suite, barking like the gates of hell had just opened in the next room.

Nodding in the seat next to her, Gary spilt the cold tea in his lap and swore. He was about to remonstrate with Poppy for going crazy for no reason, when his wits caught up with his galloping heart and he realised something was wrong. Rookstone was a creepy castle, but even here, a war horn sounding at three in the morning was unusual. Had he dreamt it? The horn sounded again, the second time ending with a strangled *parp*. Never mind. Gary knew he was not dreaming that time. "Better wake the troops!"

Dressing quickly, he stepped into his steel-toecaps and raced out of the apartment, down the spiral stair. He banged on Jimmy's door while tying his laces. "Jimmy! There's something going on!"

After much hammering, Jimmy appeared at the door, peering blearily out into the stairwell. "Gaz?" He wiped sleep from his eyes. "What's up?"

"Didn't you hear that horn blaring?"

"No."

Poppy ran up and down the stairs, yapping for the men to follow. "Get dressed. Get everybody, and bring something you can use to defend yourselves. Come on! This is not a drill!"

"You want a drill?"

"Wake up, Jim! It's hitting the fan."

"What's going on, like?" A sleepy voice called from the next floor down.

"Blackout?" Gary called. "Get everybody up and arm yourselves!"

"I've only got my snips and a thousand-volt screwdriver in my pockets, Gaz."

"Never mind. Grab something. Seriously, *move!*"

"Alright, alright. Hobnob, wake up! Gaz is tampin' and ragin', isn't it."

"Don't call me that!"

"Get a move on!" Gary bellowed as he ran down the spiral stairs, banging on everyone's doors in the teeth of extreme apathy, moaning and some choice invective. He ran out into the courtyard, immediately spotting the light spilling from the open doorway of the west tower. Checking his mobile for signal, he dialled 999.

Poppy stood before him, hackles raised and growling like a hammer drill.

"Sir Henry?" He stepped out further into the centre of the courtyard, while he waited for the line to connect. "*Henry?*"

If there was any reply, Gary never heard it. An enormous *BOOM* rolled out across the landscape. He felt it through his boots as the flagstone vibrated in sympathy. The western sky lit up, visible even above the high castle walls. "What the...?"

"*Please state which emergency service you require.*"

"Hello? Hello? Yes, we need the police, please, to Rookstone Castle, Northumberland. I think someone's broken in. And you'd better send the fire brigade, too. All hell's breaking loose here. *Help!*"

"*Can I just take your name, sir?*"

"Gary, Gary Stone. Please hurry!"

"*Very good, sir. Is that Gary with one 'r' or two?*"

"What? One! Does it matter?"

"*Thank you, sir. The police ha—*"

The line died. Gary checked his signal and swore. So far from the city of Newcastle, and all the large conurbations along the east coast, coverage was patchy at best. There was a way up onto the roof and the battlements to get a better reception, but it was locked.

Willy Mammoth ran from the tower with a finishing trowel in his hand. "What's goin' on, Gaz?"

"God knows. Where are the others?"

"Getting their boots on. 'S why I wear Riggers."

"A trowel? Was that the best you could find?"

"I was in bed, man – lucky I found this. Andy sleeps with it by his bed. He calls it Jacob. He'll have a fit when he sees I've nicked it. It's well sharp, though."

"Alright, alright. Thanks for backing me up. I think Sir Henry's in trouble."

"What was that massive bang?"

"No idea. Come on, lads!"

The For Keeps crew spilled out into the courtyard in various stages of undress. Floating George brought up the rear, hopping about trying to get his second boot on.

"What's all the commotion, boss?" Jerry asked, wide-eyed with excitement.

Gary expected him to be terrified, especially after his recent experiences, but he was beginning to realise there might be two sides to the young man's character. This time, he was behaving like the crisis was the most exciting event of his life – perhaps it was, so far.

"OK, lads. Let's see what's going on." Gary stuffed the useless phone into a pocket and picked up a shovel leaning against the wall, hefting it. Shovels worked

everywhere, and this would not be the first time he had used one to defend himself
– he often worked in Birmingham.

A man screamed.

"Henry?" Gary looked to his men, and as one, they ran forward.

A few minutes earlier...

"Any luck?" asked Sir Edward's shade.

"It would go a lot quicker if you helped me," Inga replied, tersely.

"Ah... well, you see, I'd love to, but best clothes on, don't you know?"

Inga appeared from under the van, coalescing in front of him. "You're not
wearing any clothes – you're dead. They're not real!"

"Steady on, old girl. Chap still has to keep up appearances. Can't let standards
slip just because we've gone on, can we? Besides, I can't help it if my wife buried
me in my best rig, can I?"

Inga was lost for words trying to follow that logic. She changed the subject.
"There seems to be a little round thing that makes the numbers move. I've pressed
it for all I'm worth, but it's exhausting."

"How far have you got?"

"Three hours. I think. It would really help if you could—"

"Well, you seem to have things under control," Edward blustered. "Would be
a waste of time bringing me up to speed—"

"I *say,* chaps, isn't this exciting, what?"

Sir Edward and Inga shared a glance and, as one, rolled their eyes.

"Well, if it isn't the Honourable Geoffrey Grey. Where have you been all this
time?" Edward greeted, wearily. "What's exciting?"

"Back at the castle. It's all kicking off, what? And please, call me Geoff. Let's
not stand on ceremony, what? It *is* the 1920s."

Edward was about to correct him but found that he lacked the will.

"I say, hello, Inga, old girl. What are the two of you up to?"

Inga smiled tautly. "*I* am trying to blow up this infernal machine. Couldn't
help, could you?"

"I *say,* what fun. You clever old thing. I'd love to help, but I'm an absolute
duffer with anything like that. It's my brother Henry you need. Clever as a tack,
what?"

"You mean sharp as a... oh, never mind," Edward muttered. "We haven't seen
Henry Grey, that is, the *first* Henry Grey, for a while, have you?"

Geoffrey, known to the other ghosts as Enthusiastic Geoffrey, frowned. "No,
as it happens. Wonder where he's hiding himself, what?"

"Probably staying out the way because his grandson is in so much trouble,"
Edward guessed. "Doesn't want to call down the wrath, should he be tempted to
cross the line and interfere. They'll be watching him more closely than any of us."

"Hmm," Inga agreed. "Drawing their attention up there, so we can act. Yes, that sounds like something he'd do."

"I *say*. Young Henry's in trouble? Really?"

"Where've you *been?*" Inga asked, the annoyance – to anyone else, at least – clear in her voice.

"Oh, I've been hanging around at the *Stag's Head*, what?"

Inga allowed her form to dissolve in a way that somehow purveyed disapproval and went back to work. She had not been able to check in on Gary that night, gambling that continuing with her plan would help him the most. She certainly had no time to waste exchanging banalities with a fool. Focusing all her energy on the control mechanism, she watched the numbers scroll, painfully slowly, down to zero.

Click.

In all honesty, she had been expecting more. However, the spark generated by the device's small battery ignited the diesel dripping from the nicked pipe, conducting the flame all the way back to the fuel tank. When the whole vehicle detonated above her, flinging glass and burning plastic in all directions to start smaller fires in the trees, she vanished from Edward's sight.

The initial ball of white-hot accelerant rose high into the sky, drawing a funnel of yellow flames in its wake to convey sparks well above the canopy to carry on the breeze. The sonic boom shook the earth as it rolled away across the wide valley.

But for the crackle of burning material, a silence fell as Edward stared in shock and awe. "Lady?" he enquired, anxiously.

Inga stepped out from the inferno like the Devil's daughter.

Geoffrey stepped back on impulse. "I *say*, are you alright, old girl?"

Inga raised a delicate eyebrow. "Warm work."

Sir Edward's jaw swung open.

She allowed herself a half-smile. "I think that will attract attention, don't you?"

After the recent robbery at Rookstone Castle, Sergeant Gripper called in a surveillance team from Northumbria Police to watch the building, and the builders within it. Sir Henry had no choice but to inform him that the stolen gems were actually worthless fakes, because he suspected the perpetrators might try again when they worked that out.

Rural Northumberland almost entirely lacked late-night doughnut dispensaries, so the two officers on duty relied heavily on flasks and boxes of sandwiches provided by their loving wives.

While pouring themselves a revitalising hot drink, their radio erupted to life. The nearby explosion that followed caused most of the piping hot tea to end up down their trousers.

Now...
Sir Henry was shoved against the wall. Black spots swam before his eyes, threatening to steal his consciousness as Scott grabbed his side and *squeezed.*
"Where're tha real emeralds – Ah can keep this up all neet, ye ken?"

Hammer placed a firm hand on the arm of his overzealous partner in crime, pulling him back. "Steady. Turns out it's *not* a murder job. We got lucky – so let's not push it if we don't have to. OK?"

Gary and his team burst into Richard's apartment, bearing an assortment of unlikely weaponry.

Hammer pulled a knife and backed away. "Well, look what we have here," he snarled. "A bunch of have-a-go heroes. You and that bunch o' clowns had better stay out of this, sunbeam."

"Henry? What's going on?" Gary demanded, ignoring the gangster, though his voice shook with nerves.

Unable to speak, Henry doubled up and collapsed, his side bleeding.

"You *toerag!*" Gary growled at Scott, raising his shovel and moving forward.

Scott grinned and surprised everyone, Hammer most of all, by sliding a Browning Hi-Power 9mm L9 pistol from his jacket.

Silence fell as everyone froze.

Outside in the world, the night came to life with the distant two-tone sirens of approaching emergency vehicles.

Completely exhausted, Inga smiled with satisfaction and faded away.

Chapter 10

Under Siege
(Regnum Trullae)

There he is – Jacob! Give him back here. No wonder I couldn't find him. Honestly, it's a bloody conspiracy!"

Scott stared, as Andy wrestled 'Jacob' out of Willy's hands.

Taking advantage of the split-second distraction, Gary raised his shovel, but Scott saw it and fired.

"*Ouch!*" Gary shouted, putting a hand to his ringing ear. His shovel had a small, circular hole through its blade. Furious, he glared at the gunman. "I've had this shovel twenty years!"

"Next one's through yer hid! Now, back off!" Scott kicked Sir Henry in the leg. "Get up!"

When the injured man did not move, he glared at Hammer. "Get him up! He knows where they are."

"What're you after?" Gary demanded, unable to help himself. "You took the Grey Emeralds last night. What more could you possibly want?"

"They weren't real," Worzel snapped.

"Shat it!" Hammer barked, furiously.

"It don't matter, Ham. Anyway, they might know somefin'."

"No names, idiot!"

"Sorry, Ham."

"*Christ!*" Hammer twisted his lip disgustedly before turning his fury on Gary, wondering if he might indeed know something.

Gary glowered back. "Look, I'm no criminal mastermind, but have you looked, oh, I don't know, in the *safe?*" he spat, contemptuously, pointing with his shovel at the floor-mounted strongbox in the corner.

"It's a combination, Ham."

"Shat it!" Hammer repeated. He nodded towards Sir Henry, curled up on the floor. "Get him up and in that chair. Bring him round, *gently!*"

Sir Edward knew the stag-headed demigod, the creature they referred to simply as the Hornèd One, never stepped inside the man-made ring of stone that was Rookstone Castle. At least, not during the last five centuries of Edward's lived and unlived experience. The nearby forest fire alone was enough to keep him at distance. Inga had been right about that, forcing Edward to search further afield. An experienced hunter in his day, he had to try something, and so called on that knowledge to track down his quarry. Though the only arrows in his quiver were words, he nonetheless aimed straight for the heart. "Will you help, sir, *please?* The lives of our families depend upon it – including the one who cares for and protects these lands – yet you know we can't take direct action."

The giant spirit loomed over the shade of the Tudor magnate. He said nothing, yet his demonstrative shrug eloquently purveyed that he, too, was forbidden under the same rules.

Edward slumped, understanding perfectly. "But..." he tried again, desperate to form a persuasive argument, "aren't the rules that bind us more, sort of, *guidelines* for you?"

The erratic movements of the giant stag head stabilised for just a moment, as Herne the Hunter stared down at his petitioner, pupils contracting to points as silver-white as moonlit snow. He leaned closer to look Edward in the eye.

Terrified, Edward stood his ground. This was no time to back down; the loss of Henry Grey III might threaten the very future of Rookstone itself. Braced with legs apart and fists on hips, he dared to stare right back.

The face of a stag was never designed to smile, yet somehow, Herne's lightning bolt stare softened, and he straightened. Again, he shrugged.

Edward could sense that, though he had earned a few points for courage, none of this mess was the Hornèd One's business – he had already helped them enough.

There really was nothing else for it. He knelt before the forest god. "*Pretty* please?" It was at times like this that he really missed Inga. Even before that night, she was always the firebrand, and yet more eloquent with it. Unfortunately, his only other ally was a drunken fop, whom Edward was not entirely sure even realised he was dead. There would be no help coming from that direction.

"I *say!* Those antlers are top hole!"

Edward hung his head.

Enthusiastic Geoff offered Herne a drink from his hip flask.

The stag nose wrinkled, recoiling from the whiff of gin.

Unaware that he might have caused offence, Geoff built on that foundation and continued. "Six, seven, eight – sixteen tines! A monarch[1], no less. I think Grandpapa shot and mounted a couple of twelve-tine royals in the great hall, back in jolly old Rookstone[2]. Brought them back from Prussia, or somewhere, long before the Great War, of course – but those heads are nothing when compared with your remarkable rack, what?"

Sir Edward closed his eyes and raised his hands to hide his face. Unfortunately, both eyelids and hands were as transparent as his dismay. He opened his eyes and opened his mouth to apologise, but it was too late. Geoffrey and he were alone. "Imbecile! Now what are we to do?"

"We could drift on back to the *Stag's Head* for an early snifter?"

"Will you stop talking about decapitated deer!" Realising he was shouting, Sir Edward lowered his voice, nervously. "Couldn't you see we needed his help? After all that talk of trophies, we won't see him again for an age!"

"Sorry, old man. Not sure I see the connection?"

"Oh... *disappear,* will you!"

"OK." Hammer leaned close, right in Sir Henry's face. "Now you're back with us - for now."

Worzel chuckled.

Hammer turned on his associate. "Shat it! And check these lot for mobiles. Do it!"

"Sorry, Ham. Right, Ham."

"Names!"

"Sorry, Ha— erm... sorry." Worzel frisked the builders, confiscating Gary's phone.

Hammer returned to his prisoner. "Right, Sir Herbert—"

"Henry."

"What?"

"The name's Henry."

"Shat your face. Now you listen 'ere, Lord Fauntleroy—"

---

1. Tines are the points on a stag's antlers. A deer with sixteen tines or more is a monarch, fourteen is an imperial stag, and twelve is a royal.

2. As a keen hunter in life, Sir Edward was well aware of that, too. He was also painfully aware that his companion was a royal idiot.

"Henry," Henry repeated, softly. "And I'm not a lord, I'm a knight – a baronet, technically."

"Is that a fact? I'll inform the press." Hammer grabbed Henry roughly by the collar. "Now, you listen 'ere, I've 'ad enough lip from you. You're gonna tell me the combination for that safe, right now – got it?"

Henry sat in silence.

Gary held his breath, shaking his head, willing Henry to speak. The emeralds were not worth his life.

Hammer waited.

Henry looked ahead stoically.

Hammer lost his temper, shaking him again. "Well? Out with it!"

Still not a sound escaped Henry's lips.

"Oh," Hammer breathed, softly. "Looks like we've got another 'ero 'ere, boys."

Henry's eyes swivelled to lock gazes with Hammer.

Hammer waited. Still Henry remained close, so he leaned in again. "Do you really fink I won't 'urt you? Or one o' them?" He gestured behind him with a thumb to where Gary and the others stood crowding the door to the small office.

"Erm," Henry rasped, clearing his throat.

"Well?"

"It's just that…"

Hammer leaned in closer still, smiling menacingly. "Go on, my son. Get it off your chest."

"It's just that you said 'shat your face'. I rather assumed that meant stop talking."

Gary snorted, unable to help himself.

"Fink it's funny, do ya?" Hammer rounded on him. Catching Scott's eye, he added, "If Sir Baronet don't talk, right now," he pointed at Gary, "you can shoot that clever Herbert."

"Ah thought ye didnae want tae kill anybody."

Hammer looked at him as though he were simple. "He's got kneecaps, sunbeam."

Scott grinned and aimed.

"Wait!" Henry cried out.

Gary sagged with relief.

"*His* name's not Herbert, either."

Gary surreptitiously lowered the blade of his shovel to cover his knees, for what it was worth.

Hammer's patience was all spent – in fairness, he had lost most of it by the age of seven, so he was well overdrawn by that point. "Combination!" he bellowed.

Sir Henry's reply was almost silent. "OK."

"What?"

"I said OK. I'll tell you. Never said I wouldn't – you just assumed, rather."

Hammer clenched his fists and seethed. Collecting himself, he nodded for Serj to work on the safe. "Right. Very clearly, one number at a time – and yes, you can talk. Begin."

"One, then six, right."

Serj spun the combination lock carefully, counting the digits.

"Thirty-seven left – no, wait. Thirty-two, er... Oh, hell! It's very difficult to think with you breathing down my neck like that."

"Maybe you need something to jog your memory." Hammer's arm shot out and he grabbed Jerry, pulling him off balance and holding a knife to the young man's throat.

"I say, steady on, old chap," Jerry exclaimed.

Hammer laughed, nastily. "Well, what have we got 'ere? Another *lord*, boys."

The villains laughed.

"Or is this one Jeeves, the butler, eh?"

"No, I am bally not!" Jerry shouted, angrily. "I do wish people would stop calling me that. It's not funny!"

The gangsters disagreed. Even Serj was chuckling.

"Now, *'Enry* the Knight, where were we? Ah, yes. Why don't you give me the correct combination – now, *please*. Before we 'ave to 'urt anybody."

The Interview: part IV, August 1994

"How did you feel, facing down the villains who'd attacked Sir Henry Grey and his secretary, Richard Clarence, so violently?"

Gary fiddled with his collar. "Anxious. Angry. That sort of thing, you know?"

"Brave?"

Was Brandon throwing him a lifeline or just trying to make the interview more spicy? Everyone loves a hero, after all. Gary decided on honesty. "Not really."

"But you had your men to back you up, didn't you?"

Hmm... so much for building me up, Gary thought. "They were a gang from the violent underworld of organised crime – we're just a bunch of lads, tradies, but I think we could have given a good account of ourselves, if we'd had to. Especially as Sir Henry was in such a bad way. I wanted to get him out of there."

"Noble, noble," Brandon replied, thoughtfully. "But you did outnumber the criminals two-to-one, didn't you?"

"Yes, we did." Gary stared the interviewer in the eye. "And none of *us* are weak men," he added pointedly. "However, when they pulled the gun, any advantage we might have had went out the window. From then on, I just wanted to get my lads out of there alive—"

"That's when things took a much worse turn for you, didn't they, Gary?" Brandon interrupted. "For you, personally, I mean."

The small hours. Monday, May 9th, 1994

Multiple sirens rang and rebounded from the walls of the ancient stronghold. For the second time in as many days, Rookstone Castle provided the back canvas for a flashing lightshow.

Gary opened the door at the top of the north-east tower with Sir Henry's key. Scott shoved him roughly from behind, pushing him out onto the lead-covered roof. The grey sheeting glowed eerily in the moonlight, making it easy to see where they walked. Scott pushed Jerry out next, and they walked to the northern battlement to look down. Below was a carpet of white vehicles, also washed in rippling blue and orange electric light. After the recent violent robbery, the police were obviously not taking any chances. Gary glanced east to see more on the way. To the west, maybe half a mile or so from the castle, the night was lit by the fiery reds of a large conflagration. Whatever exploded earlier had clearly set the woods alight. Further emergency vehicles converged on the problem from the south. He stared, finding it hard to believe everything that was happening all around him.

The gun barrel, poked hard into the small of his back, restored his faith that it was all real.

"Well? Talk tae 'em, then, or the laddie here gets it!" Adding force to his words, Scott grabbed Jerry roughly by the arm and held the pistol to his head. "And dinnae forget yer lines. *Lives* depend on it."

Gary swallowed and turned back to the battlements. Leaning over, he cupped his hands to shout. "Hey! Up here!" He waved his arms.

A powerful searchlight came to life on top of a police Land Rover and swivelled until it found him. He blinked against its brightness, spots swimming before his eyes.

"Is that you, Mr Stone?"

Gary recognised the voice.

"Sergeant Gripper." Gary's was not a question, nor was it a greeting, more an indictment on the state of his fortunes. Taking a deep breath, he tried again. "Sergeant Gripper, yes, it's me. I..." He faltered.

Scott twisted Jerry's arm, making him cry out.

Gary nodded, despairingly.

"What's going on up there?" Gripper demanded, using a megaphone someone just handed him.

"We have..."

"Get on wi' it!" Scott snarled. He fired a single shot into the night, making everyone jump. Jerry went rigid with terror. "That ought tae get their attention!"

When Gary looked back over the battlements, he could see the police were crouching behind their vehicles and did not doubt that armed officers would soon be on the way. He cleared his throat. "We have a hostage," he called down, with all the strength he could put into his voice.

"Who?" asked Gripper.

"Sir Henry Grey. And as you can see, we're armed." Gary looked to Scott, who nodded that he should continue. "We have a list of demands."

"What was that? You'll have to shout up, if we're to help you."

"I said we have a list of demands!"

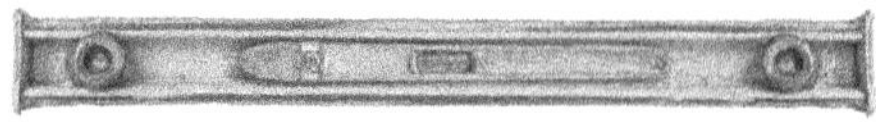

Sir Edward watched balefully as the fire consumed trees, bushes and last season's dead brush beneath them. Inga caused this crisis specifically to attract attention, and it had certainly worked. Three monstrous horseless carriages arrived, all at once, and all coated in vivid orange paint, followed by a smaller one in a white livery. Every vehicle lit the area around it in blinding white and blue light. Sir Edward would have shuddered, if he still had muscles and a nervous system. It was unnatural – and he was alone now. Inga would be spent after her efforts. He would not see her again that night.

The firemen worked efficiently and effectively. A practised and highly trained team, they ran hoses to spread tons of high-pressure water across the fire.

"I say, these chaps are rather good, what?"

Edward closed his eyes with a spiritual sigh. No, he was not entirely alone. Enthusiastic Geoff had returned.

"I thought you were going to the castle, to see what was going on?"

Before Geoff could answer, a loud *crack* rang out across the wide valley.

Edward span, anxiously, looking back towards Rookstone. "What was that?"

"Sounded like a gunshot," Geoff postulated, a curious mix of excitement and trepidation on his face. "Do you think we should go back? These chaps seem to have everything under control here, what?"

"Yes." Edward nodded, thoughtfully. "That might be a good idea. What in Hades is going on over there?"

"Oh, didn't I tell you? Jolly old Rookstone's under siege."

Chapter 11

When Will I be Famous?

I *can* answer that, as it happens," Sir Henry allowed. "That safe is used primarily by my secretary, Richard. He has all the details, including the correct combination, at his fingertips. What a pity it is that you put him in hospital!"

"We should get out of here, Ham." Worzel sounded nervous.

"*Names,* idiot!"

"That explosion must have been our van going up early. They'll have the area sealed off tight any minute. I don't want my face smudged across every newspaper in the north."

"Relax. They don't know who we are. Nor will they, if Scott can get that lump-headed brickie to snag the Old Bill's attention. They'll be focused on *him*."

Jimmy exchanged glances with the other lads. With the gunman up on the roof, they might have been handed an opportunity.

Hammer caught it. "Leave it out! You really think that Scottish lunatic won't shoot anyone who plays up? And he'll start with that simple kid – the posh one – and Plod will think it's you lot."

"They'll soon find out the truth!" Jimmy spat, defiantly. Although, having met the local police sergeant in charge, his reservoir of faith was barely deep enough to get his shoes wet.

Hammer smiled, without humour. "Perhaps, but when they call in armed coppers to deal with this, *they* will think *you're* the problem, savvy? Who d'you think's gonna get it first, eh?"

"Look, chaps," Sir Henry placated. "Let's all just stay calm. I..."

Hammer glared at him. "You what?"

"I think I might be able to open the safe – if I try it myself, I mean. I can't remember all the numbers to the combination, but if I worked the lock personally, then maybe, you know, muscle memory, perhaps...?"

Hammer nodded for him to try.

Henry leaned heavily on his crutches to reach down, awkwardly kneeling to turn the dial. Making a show of experimenting with several combinations, he finally used the correct one, and they all heard the mechanism *click* as the tumblers fell into place. Pain stabbed at him and black spots danced before his eyes as he stood, straightening carefully. "There. You can do the rest." He lowered himself gingerly back into the captain's chair behind Richard's desk with a groan.

Serj looked to Hammer for direction before kneeling to twist the handle and pull open the door. Among all the papers in Richard's safe was a black felt bag. He reached for it, removing it from the safe with an unmistakable *clink* of gemstones knocking together. He grinned.

Henry watched the last of the fake gems' box shrivel in the fireplace, all evidence vanishing up the chimney. He allowed himself the merest of smiles.

Hammer took the three emeralds out of their bag. "So these are the real ones," he murmured to himself. He could not tell any difference between them and the last set. He needed Scott to check their authenticity. Even as he thought it, he bitterly regretted having to rely on the most psychotic and least dependable member of his totally disreputable bunch for clarification.

The gunshot caused everyone to tense up. Hammer slipped the emeralds into his pocket for safekeeping as the builders inched ever closer to a fight or flight stance. He could sense that, at any minute, they might do something everyone would regret. He spoke directly to Jimmy as the eldest and obviously most senior. "I told you, don't get no ideas. Even I don't know what he'll do if you kick off, so don't push your luck!"

Jimmy gave him a sideways look. "You really didn't know he was carrying a gun?"

Hammer ignored the question, but the anger that crossed his face confessed the truth of it.

"So," Jimmy pressed, "you're a hostage here as well."

Worzel glanced nervously at Hammer, who glared at him. "*I* am in charge here. Don't no one forget it! And you," he jabbed a finger at Jimmy, "shat it!"

Everyone perceived a dynamic shift in their shared situation, though no one seemed to know how to exploit the change. For now, Jimmy simply logged it.

It was 08:15 on Monday morning. Tom had called by Albert's home earlier, to collect him for work as he often did, and they had arrived together to find Rookstone under siege. A police sergeant had just explained how builders recently employed by Sir Henry were now holding him hostage.

"I doubt that," Albert stated, flatly, finding it impossible to reconcile the young, high-spirited working men he had served with hearty breakfasts the previous week with armed desperados holding his boss at gunpoint.

The young constable standing in Gripper's shadow also seemed to have doubts. "What can you tell us about them, sir?"

Albert squinted. "It's young Josh, isn't it? Judy Charlton's lad?"

"Yes, sir."

"Sarge?" A WPC caught Gripper's attention, and he went to answer the squad car's radio.

PC Charlton watched him go.

"Don't think much o' that 'un, lad," Albert pronounced, unequivocally.

Charlton would never have dreamt of gainsaying the old man – Albert's generation had fought a world war for the right to speak their mind – so he hid his discomfort with a question. "You were about to tell me about the builders, sir."

"Not much to tell. They came up here from down south somewhere – last week. Seemed a nice bunch o' lads. Didn't see no guns with 'em. Their gaffer looked white as a sheet, last time I saw him, though. Like he'd seen a ghost." He chuckled. "He probably had – he's staying in the most haunted suite in Rookstone!"

Charlton looked up at the tower. Even in the morning sunshine, the place had a forbidding air, its windows black and lightless. He scanned along the battlements to the place where Gary Stone called down to them, some hours earlier. The builder had sounded nervous and scared then, too – perhaps unsurprising in the middle of a stressful hostage situation – but having met the suspects, something just did not add up. If the For Keeps team had perpetrated the robbery two nights earlier, then why all this now? Had they discovered the gems were counterfeit? That made sense, but why attract so much attention? There was also the matter of the burning van in the woods. Forensics believed the fire to have been caused deliberately by some sort of device – doubtless to remove any fingerprints or DNA from the getaway vehicle. However, if Gary's men were responsible for that then why had they, firstly, *not* gotten away, and secondly, drawn all eyes to them so spectacularly? They had completely blown any chances they might have had to ride this through – and talking of riding, he suspected his superior was riding for a fall. He considered trying to point that out as politely as possible, but saw that he was already too late, for Gripper was talking with a press team, piling out of a local news station camera van.

"Let him dig his own grave, son."

Charlton turned back to see Albert smiling up at him.

"He's got this all wrong."

Charlton wore a pained expression, but it was more than his job was worth to agree with the old man. "Do you know another way into the castle, sir? A quiet way?"

Albert thought for a moment. "Well, I have the key. Would that help?"

"To which door?"

"The one in the outer courtyard, but if it's barred from within..." He tailed off, considering.

"The doors can be barred?"

The old man chuckled. "Rookstone's a castle, lad. Don't let those fancy windows the Elizabethans knocked through her walls fool ye. She's a war machine!"

The WPC who called Gripper away now tugged on Charlton's sleeve. "Josh, sorry to interrupt, but as you're the local boys, and the sarge is busy, I'm just letting you know there's an Inspector Harrow on his way from Newcastle, to take command, OK?"

"Thanks." He smiled. "I'll tell the sarge, when he's free."

Albert felt a chill run down his spine. Hairs rose on his arms and neck, despite the mildness of the morning air. He turned to see... something. It was hard to describe, yet he knew it, had seen it before, especially when there was trouble afoot. "I take it you don't want to make a big song and dance about breaking in, young Josh?"

Charlton looked over Albert's shoulder, trying to make out what the old man was staring at. "If our armed response team break in, it might cause the gunman to react, or overreact, sir."

"'S what I thought. So, what you could really do with," Albert was speaking slowly and loudly now, exaggerating his point as though to someone hard of hearing, "is someone drawing the bars from across the sallyport door, yes?"

Charlton looked around Albert again, wondering what on earth the old man saw that he did not, and why he was suddenly behaving so strangely. "Erm, that would be nice, sir, but I don't see how..." He tailed off. There was movement. Just something out of the corner of his eye. When he looked directly at it, it vanished.

Albert winked. "We should give it a little while and then try my key. I suspect the door will be—"

"May I have it, sir?" Charlton interrupted, distractedly.

Albert handed the young constable his key. Staying close to the outer courtyard wall, Charlton made his way to the door where the builders let themselves in the previous evening. He inserted the key into the Yale lock and turned it, and the handle beneath it. The lock opened, but the door moved barely a fraction. It was indeed barred from within. *No way of opening that without making noise – and lots of it.* He sighed. *Worth a try.*

Albert was shaking his head when he returned. "You'll have to give them longer than that. Try again later, lad."

Confusion clouding his expression, Charlton pocketed the key.

Sir Edward listened carefully to the conversation between the old retainer and the young... what was he, some sort of soldier? He watched the uniformed man try the door and knew what he must do. After all, there *was* no one else.

"I say, can't get in. What a fix, what?"

Edward slumped and then turned quickly to Enthusiastic Geoff, suddenly at his shoulder again. "Wait, *you* can help me!"

"Oh, I say, what fun. What are we doing, what?"

"You can stop saying what, for a start! Where did that come from? Never mind. Come with me, young man."

He drifted through the castle walls to arrive on the other side of the locked door. "How old are you, anyway? That is, how old were you, erm, originally?"

"Nineteen, what?" If anything, Geoff became even more effervescent. "Until July, of course. Then it's the big two-oh for me, what?"

Sir Edward gave him a searching look, his expression softening. "You do realise... how can I put this? You do realise that's not going to happen, don't you? Not ever."

Geoff blinked, innocently.

Edward felt like he was punishing a very young puppy, who genuinely had not realised there might be consequences for stealing the Sunday roast. He opened his mouth to speak but instead patted the younger man on an ethereal shoulder. "Perhaps we'll have a chat about it later. Right! Help me draw this locking bar. Come on, heave!"

To an outside observer, the bar remained stoically unheaved.

"Again. *Heeeave!*"

Nothing moved.

Sir Edward had no breath to puff, but he could feel his death force ebbing away. He had very little energy remaining before he, too, would need to slip off to limbo for a while, as Inga had, to recharge. The trouble was, he knew his son – many times removed – needed his help now. "Stop pushing!" he snapped. Geoff, too, was fading and would have kept going until he popped out of existence had Edward not stopped him. The Tudor nobleman shook his head. The lad was dim enough already. "We need to find another way to get that door open. Any ideas?"

Geoff looked blank.

Edward patted his shoulder again. "No. I suppose not."

"Could we find a way to blow it up?" he tried, earnestly giving it his best shot.

"No. The men outside could do that. They don't want to alarm that damned Scot upstairs. The one with the dagg."

"Got a doggy, has he?"

"No. A dagg. A wheellock. You know, a pistol?"

"Oh, the chappie with the gun, *riiight.*"

Edward frowned.

"What is it, what?"

Lost in thought, Sir Edward murmured, "The doggy?"

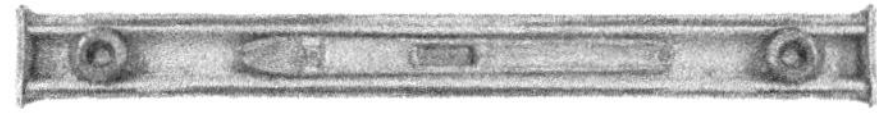

Rookstone café and tea rooms
"I just want to let her out into the courtyard to do her business. It's not like we can go anywhere. Come on."

Scott leered disdainfully at Gary. "Do Ah look like tha sort o' man who cares about a comfort break for yer wee hound? She can crap all o'er yer bed for all Ah care."

Gary glared at him. "What a guy. You must have so many friends."

Scott's lip curled in amusement.

At the top of the spiral stair within the north tower, Sir Edward was confronted by another solid oak door. It was unlocked, but even lifting a latch can be problematic to those without physical hands.

"Ooh, ooh, ooh, I can do these!"

Edward blinked in astonishment as Geoff leapt about excitedly. "You can?"

"Yes, yes. I can open it for you!"

"Really? How did you learn to do that?"

"Remember when we had the Durham University girl's lacrosse team stay, a few summers ago? It was well worth the effort, I don't mind telling you, what?"

"You learned to open latched doors so you could spy on some young wenches, prancing about in their linen smocks? They wore little enough while they were out and about!"

"Ah. Saw them, then, did you?" Geoff grinned, pointing accusingly. "Don't think they wear linen smocks these days, old chap, what?"

Sir Edward made a show of clearing what used to be his throat. "Well, I... erm. I mean, we all keep our eye on those who come and go, don't we?"

The younger man smiled and gestured towards the latch. "Shall I?"

"Erm, of course." Edward frowned. "Wait a minute. *Why* did you learn to lift the latch?"

"I rather thought I'd just explained that, what?"

"No. I mean, why bother? You could have simply walked through the door."

Geoff looked affronted. "Walked through the door? Steady on, old man. That wouldn't have been cricket, would it, what? Dear me, no. Not the sort of thing at all."

Sir Edward blinked again, completely at sea. "Perhaps you should just open the door."

"Erm?"

The Tudor magnate pulled himself up to his full height, standing with hands on hips. "Well? Out with it, boy. What now?"

"Why don't *you*, erm, you know, just go *through* the door, as it were?"

"I don't want to get in there, you damned fool. I wish to get someone else *out*."

"Oh, I *see*."

Geoff focused all his enthusiasm to lift the latch, and between them, the long departed managed to budge the door ajar.

Poppy stood in the hallway. Hackles raised, she looked up at them and growled.

"Careful what you wish for, old man," Geoff muttered with misgiving.

"Hmm. Indeed. For one thing, I'm wishing that Gary fellow had a bigger dog."

"I'm afraid I can't release any names, sir," Gripper explained, patiently, "what with this being an active case – a *very* active case. So active, in fact, that we don't even have the suspects in custody yet." He gave an ingratiating smile.

The reporter ignored it. He wore a brown, tailored camelhair overcoat with a navy-blue suit and held a large microphone with the channel name on its shaft. "Tammy, over here."

He whispered into the ear of his assistant, who walked away to make a phone call.

"Will we be live, sir?" Gripper asked nervously, hopefully.

"Yes, yes. I expect so. They'll want to get in ahead of the big boys, at the nationals, you know. Not much happens up here, must be quite a boon for you. In fact, I'm surprised you weren't reposted – or whatever the boys in blue call it – to Newcastle, years ago, or pensioned off, maybe?"

Gripper soured but managed to ratchet a smile back up his face. This was his big chance, after all.

The girl named Tammy returned after her quick call to Companies House[1] with a note scribbled on a small scrap of paper. The reporter read it quickly and slipped it into his coat pocket. This might be his big chance, too, if he could generate enough interest to get noticed at a national level – placing himself to the fore, naturally. Might be his ticket out of the rain to get his backside into the anchorman's chair.

His cameraman switched on the overhead light to combat harsh shadows thrown by the bright sunshine. "You ready, Brandon?"

"Just a second." The reporter looked to Tammy. "Is my tie straight, Tam?"

Tammy moved in to order the offending apparel, also flattening a lapel. She nodded, happy with her work.

"OK, Stan, let's roll it." Brandon hitched a smile onto his face, while Stan the cameraman gave his equipment a final check.

"OK. Five, four..." Stan switched to hand signals. *Three, two, one. Thumbs up.*

"Good morning, Tim, in the studio, and to all our viewers watching at home. I'm here outside Rookstone Castle in Northumberland with," he checked his notes, "Constable Gripper. Now, Constable, we understand a robbery with

---

1. Where all companies in the UK are registered – a large house by now, also full of ghosts.

violence took place in the castle behind us over the weekend and is now under attack for a second time in as many days, with armed men still within, holding the owner hostage."

It was not exactly a question, but the microphone was nevertheless thrust into Gripper's face for comment.

"Sergeant."

"Excuse me?"

"It's *Sergeant* Gripper."

"Don't worry, we can cut that in later."

"I thought you said we were live."

"Don't worry about the details, Constable. Now, these violent gunmen, I understand the ringleader is one Gary Stone from Claines in Worcestershire?" He thrust the microphone further up Gripper's nose.

"How did you...?" Caught off guard, Gripper struggled to quickly get a grip on himself. "We can neither confirm, nor deny, nor discuss the identity of the *alleged* offenders, due to this being an active case."

"Of course, of course, Constable. So you're saying that the builders' vans, parked round the back with For Keeps Limited written on the side, *may* be linked with the crime taking place within these walls? Can you get those in shot, Stan? Great." He gestured expansively to their fortress backdrop. "Can you confirm *that?*"

A tic worked at Gripper's cheek. "As I said, sir, we can neither confirm, nor deny—"

"Sure, sure," the reporter cut across him, re-hogging the microphone. "So, what can you tell us about the Grey Emeralds that were stolen?"

Unconsciously, Gripper pulled at his collar, which suddenly felt tight. "Unfortunately, we can't discuss details of that either, sir, due to that matter also being an active, and possibly related, case—"

The microphone was once again taken away before he had finished speaking.

"*Possibly* related? Word has it that the priceless emeralds were stolen on Saturday, and after talking to people here, we've since been told the gang responsible returned last night to take Sir Henry Grey hostage in his own castle. Are you now saying that you suspect there might be two gangs, working in tandem or with separate agendas? Your comments on that..."

"We can't, I mean, we don't—" Floundering, he cast a censorious eye towards his own people. "Who have you been talking to?"

"Sure, sure," Brandon deflected. "You can't tell us about the robbery, either, but do you expect to get the precious stones back soon – or ever, Constable?"

"Ha ha, as I said, sir, we cannot—"

"Sure, sure. Was anyone killed in the attack?"

"It's Sergeant, sir." Gripper looked directly at the camera, upping his smarm, his chest swelling proudly. "Sergeant Gripper of Northumbria Police, and no. Thankfully, no one was killed."

"Right. At least, not yet." Obviously completely losing interest, the reporter turned away.

Seeing the initiative slipping from his grasp, Gripper pulled the microphone back towards himself. "However, there *were* two men seriously injured during the assault on Rookstone Castle late Saturday night."

The 'assault on Rookstone Castle' line seemed to reinvigorate the reporter. "And who were the injured men, Constable?"

Gripper gritted his teeth. "Once again, I can't—"

"Thank you. That was Constable Gripper from Newcastle—"

"*Sergeant* Gripper from Northumbria Police."

"Right, of course. Thank you, Constable. As you heard, local police are so far baffled about the motives of the men inside Rookstone Castle and don't seem clear on the identities of those involved, either, but rest assured *we* will stay abreast of the situation here and keep you up to date with the latest developments as they unfold until we get to the bottom of all this for you." The reporter flashed a dazzling smile, and slowing his delivery, completed the broadcast. "And you've been watching Brandon Porkpie on *Whopper TV* – telly it, like it is!" His smile froze for a few seconds. "OK, Stan, you can cut it there. Loving that American vibe – I think people will enjoy it. We may as well hang around here for a while, in case anything interesting happens. Keep an eye on the battlements up there, too. If anyone gets thrown off, I want to catch it, got it?"

"OK, Brandon."

Effectively switched off, Sergeant Gripper waited a few moments before eventually sidling away.

Sir Edward looked down at Poppy and shook his head, sadly. "When the Hornèd One calls upon animals, I can't help but notice that he gets better results than this."

"Who, old Ernie?"

Edward waved his hands, urgently. "Careful, Geoffrey, he might hear. And don't call him that, he hates it. His name's Herne. There's no 'e' at the end."

"I rather beg to differ, old man."

"There's no 'ie', then – pedant!"

"Besides, he won't hear us. The old boy never comes inside, does he, what?"

Edward nodded, knowingly. "Yes. We think he's afraid of stepping within a ring of stone. Either that or he's not allowed in for some reason. Waste of time asking him about it."

"Never was one for geometry, but I believe Rookstone is square, what?"

Edward rolled his eyes. "Figuratively. Figuratively, it's a ring of stone."

Geoff considered. "Never was much for figures, either. Not unless they're holding a lacrosse stick, what? Eh? Eh?"

Edward buried his face in his hands as the public schoolboy sniggered and ribbed him with an elbow. Once again, he could see through his hands, but it was a hard habit to break – especially when one spent time with Enthusiastic Geoff. "Shall we figu—" He stopped himself. "Shall we *work out* how to get this very small dog to reach and move this very heavy bar?"

"Oh, I *say* – a puzzle! What an absolutely spiffing idea!"

Edward slumped. He looked down at Poppy. "Have *you* any suggestions?"

Willy Mammoth switched on the small transistor radio behind the counter of the castle's tea shop, thinking to brighten the mood and relax his troubled companions with a little normality.

"Switch it off!" Scott snapped.

"Just a little music, to pass the time," Willy argued.

Still in the news cycle, the radio played Nirvana.

"Ah said, switch it off!" When Willy did not move immediately, Scott shot at the radio, blowing it to pieces. As the gunshot rang around the old stones, the cavernous room fell once more into complete silence but for the buzzing in everyone's ears.

"Hope they don't blame *us* for that," Willy muttered.

Scott pointed the gun at the giant man, menacingly. "Let's hope ye're around long enough tae pay fer it!"

"I like that song," Willy chuntered, massaging his ears.

"Are ye tired o' life, son?"

They all fell silent.

Down the corridor and just inside the door leading to the outer courtyard, another teen spirit was trying to get a little dog to jump for one of the two handles that protruded from the drawbar. They were simple, barrel-shaped, thick wooden dowels. Although Poppy's jaws could easily close around them, she would be hanging a metre off the ground by her teeth if she did so. So far, Geoff had failed to make a compelling argument for her to make such a move.

He stood back, seeking inspiration. "Strange how animals see and hear everything we do, isn't it?"

Sir Edward stared down at Poppy, who in turn looked up for further instructions. "I've watched this little one grapple with some very large sticks while she's been here. She's got the stuff in her. If only we could find a way to compensate for her lack of stature."

Poppy whined.

"I think you've offended her, what?"

"Don't be ridiculous. She's a damned dog. She's not aristocracy!"

Poppy turned her back on him and trotted down the corridor.

The ghosts looked at each other. "Come back!" they called in unison.

"*Why don't you come back, please hurry...*" Jimmy drummed his fingers on the table in time, while singing softly to himself.

"That's an oldie," Willy stated, moodily.

"What, Paul Young? It was only eighty-three," Jimmy retorted, irritably. His stomach growled.

"I was thirteen."

Jimmy puffed out his cheeks. "I'm working with foetuses."

"You're livin' in the past, more like."

"Alright, alright, that's enough!" Before Jimmy exploded, Gary stood, slowly, to head off a row before anyone got theirs blown off. He raised his hands placatingly before the Scotsman with the gun. "Look, we're all a bit strung out and none of us have eaten, right? Perhaps we should at least do that, before anyone does anything they might regret." He gave Willy and his brother a meaningful look to calm down. There might later be the need for a distraction, but that time had not yet arrived. He hoped they understood.

Scott nodded to Hammer. "OK. Let boss man see what's in tha kitchen, but keep an eye on him. After we've had something tae sloch, we have our next appointment with the new friends outside." He grinned lopsidedly at Gary. "Ye'll soon be famous – get yer picture in the papers, laddie."

Gary glared, but said nothing as he led Hammer into the adjoining kitchen to ransack the fridge. They were disappointed. "They must have been bringing stuff in for us daily," Gary surmised. "The castle doesn't open for the season fully until next month, as far as I know, anyway."

Hammer looked in the various cupboards and pantries before turning, angrily. "You lot must 'ave something."

Gary shrugged. "We bought a few provisions last week, from the supermarket. They're up in our suites. We could rustle up some sandwiches or something, before those lot freak out."

Hammer was immediately suspicious. "I'll come with you – and don't forget, I've still got this..." He brandished the fixed-bladed knife he drew several hours earlier, when Gary's team had burst into Richard's suite to surprise the criminals.

Gary shrugged, noncommittally, secretly thinking, *Snap, me old mate.* For while Hammer was rifling through the cupboards, he had slipped a mid-sized kitchen knife into his own fleece pocket.

Hammer explained the situation to Scott and he and Gary left the café to track down some provisions.

The Interview: part V, August 1994

"Took a turn for the worse for me, personally," Gary repeated, ruefully. "Yes, you might say that. I was about to come to your attention and fall under the media bus, wasn't I?"

"Actually, I meant that the police now believed you were the gang's ringleader," Brandon corrected him.

Gary smiled, blandly. "Of course. Well, I was, really. Just of a different gang."

A titter went around the studio and the interviewer chuckled, politely. "You must have been desperate to communicate your situation to the people outside at that point."

"Yes, but who would have listened, I wonder?"

"The police? The reporters gathered in front of the castle?" Brandon answered the rhetorical question, dimly.

"Actually, it turned out that the only useful help we received from the living world – at least, up to that point – came from a very good friend of mine."

08:30 Monday, May 9th, 1994
Begrudgingly, Poppy returned to the sallyport door. She really had nothing else to do and the see-through, two-legged ones in the funny clothes were at least interesting.

Enthusiastic Geoff redoubled his efforts to encourage her to jump for the handles on the drawbar.

Poppy sat, tilting her head to one side as she tried to work out what the man with wide-legged trousers tucked into his long socks, that gave off no scent, might be up to.

Sir Edward rolled his eyes. "There must be a better way to make a dying. She's not getting it, Geoff. We need to—"

Poppy stood and peered down the corridor. Wagging her tail, she let go a loud *Yip!*

Gary stopped. "That sounded like..."

"Never mind," Hammer growled. "We've got a job to do, remember?"

"Hang on. That sounded like my dog." In no immediate danger from the knifeman, Gary opened the door that led to a series of passageways, eventually leading to the tradesman's entrance they had been using over the last few days. He moved quickly to find the source of the sound, Hammer following on his heels, growing angrier by the second.

"Look. There she is. How did you get out?" He leaned down. "Hello, girl."

Poppy jumped into Gary's arms and licked his face, feverishly excited. It felt like years since she had seen her favourite two-leg.

Gary chuckled, despite their predicament.

"See! She can jump," Geoffrey stated, triumphantly. "I was on the right lines all along, what?"

Sir Edward ignored him, focusing on the two men.

Gary sneaked a quick look around, taking in the door where Poppy seemed to have been looking for a way out. He allowed her to jump out of his arms. "Oops. Come back here, girl. We've got to go and feed the troops. I may as well give you some din dins, too, eh? Bit early maybe, but... well."

He stooped to collect her once more in his arms. In one smooth movement, he turned back towards Hammer, surreptitiously shoving the handle on the drawbar with his back as he stood, sliding it several inches to the right. Gary suffered a bruise to his back, but he felt the bar move. Not daring to look behind him, in case he gave the game away, he had judged the action to perfection.

The spirits of Enthusiastic Geoff and Sir Edward Grey watched them go with open dismay. "Our only chance," Sir Edward sputtered, furiously, "of helping a rescue team gain entrance to the castle, and it's scuppered by one of the damned fools we're trying to save! Honestly," he bellowed down the corridor, "how do you put up with yourself, sir?"

Eventually, he calmed enough to return to the door, hoping another plan might present itself, when he saw what Gary had done. "Ha! Ha! Look!"

He nudged Geoff, pointing to where the drawbar hung a bare millimetre into its keep – just enough purchase to stop it from falling, but not enough to prevent a semi-muscular push from outside from opening the door.

The ghosts grinned at each other, and with a complete reversal, cried out.

"Stout fella!"

"I say, top hole! What?"

Years of running a business with her husband had taught Emma that when things are on a downward curve, sometimes, no matter what you do, things just keep getting worse until the unlucky streak breaks – and only a fool would think their current trajectory was on the up. That was the ebb and flow of life, written in block capitals. All they could do was keep fighting – and just as importantly, keep *looking* for an opportunity to change that trajectory. Constant vigilance and readiness were essential, because when opportunity knocked, no one wanted to be caught looking the other way.

That understood, she knew better than to lounge around in her dressing gown feeling sorry for herself. Moping only made matters worse, so she began getting ready for work from the moment she got out of bed. She had hardly slept a wink anyway, after a restless night mithered by all that needed doing the following morning. Things like finding all the documentation Gary might need, should they have to mount a legal defence for their team members, while making sure all the usual day-to-day tasks of running a company were not neglected. She was taut as a bow string, but there would be no relief that day. If she failed to stay on top of their admin or pay bills on time, they would have no company to come back to, once the current crisis passed.

She fully understood all that and yet, waiting for the kettle to boil, she fretted. Caffeine offered no answers, only resolve, but she would take it, as she gripped one hand with the other to stop it from shaking. There was a message in that, and Emma closed her eyes, in spirit, throwing her arms around the man she loved, though he was hundreds of miles away. She hoped he would feel it.

Small business has always been like no man's land, where one stands, puny weapon in hand, taking fire from all sides, while trying to work out which way to run. Fortunately, it differed in that it was usually only one's wallet that ended up shot full of holes, although Emma knew how dangerous construction could be. She worried constantly about that, too, always noting the daily cuts and contusions Gary tried to hide from her, when he noticed them at all – so conditioned was he to minor injury – but their current situation was different. Two people had been brutally attacked, lucky to be alive, and although Gary was absent at the time, he might just as easily have been one of the victims.

Now he was effectively stranded at the other end of the country, with the police breathing down his neck over something about which he knew nothing. Intellectually, Emma knew the truth would have to come out eventually, and the best help she could offer her husband was from the office attached to their home, but that troubled her, too. She may have lacked the physical strength of her man, but she matched him for courage and wanted to be at his side so badly that it hurt, yet she also understood why he wanted her out of the firing line. For all she was his strength, she might become his weakness, too, if there was any further trouble. She did not want him worrying about her safety when he should be guarding his own.

She wiped a tear of frustration from her cheek. How many times had she watched Gary's van leave before dawn on filthy, windswept mornings? How many times had she sent him off with only a kiss and box of sandwiches for comfort, to drive endless miles to a dangerous, dirty job – often to deal with a customer she patently did not trust – praying he got there safely? She had no choice and nor did he – they had to work. There was no safety net for them. No sick pay, no paid leave, no meaningful or honest insurance against injury – just the conspiracy they paid into, like a votive offering to a capricious god. It was the gamble they took every day, hoping for a better life to come. Errors were common, malicious intent doubly so, and Emma knew how so many businesses ended in failure and bitterness, with their owners far worse off than if they had not bothered at all.

Worry and lack of sleep turned her thoughts increasingly negative. Her feelings were valid, but she could spot the cycle, mentally calling herself out before she was overwhelmed. Nevertheless, the challenge they faced was real, and being separated from her soulmate only made matters worse. Darkness seemed to swirl around her as she imagined how her mother had felt when her father went to war. Awful for those who had to go, but never a picnic for those who had to stay. As far as she knew, their own situation was not so extreme, not really... as far as she knew.

She chided herself. *Get a grip on yourself, girl. It's the 1990s, Cool Britannia is out of recession, and we can achieve anything, if we just keep at it.*

She sipped her coffee in the kitchen, letting the caffeine work its magic, sharpening her thoughts and perceptions, and then it came – an idea. It was a good one, too. An epiphany. The first in what seemed like a long time.

Downing her drink, she grabbed her car keys and set off across Worcestershire.

She pulled up outside the family seat of the Jarvis family – eventually; the driveway was well over a mile long. However, the journey was well worth any visitor's while, for the house at its end was a stunning masterpiece of Georgian confidence – and that was just its current form. There had been a grand house on that site for almost nine hundred years, and every one of them was etched into the magnificence and time-honoured presence of the building before her. Each column and carving a self-possessed display, stating unequivocally that these were people who knew where they came from.

The façade was daunting, as it was meant to be, causing all lesser mortals to quake in a sense of unworthiness. Emma might have been daunted herself, but for two things. One, For Keeps Ltd dealt with the owners of such properties daily for their bread and butter, and two, she was in no mood to be messed about by *anyone*.

She rang the bell and was rewarded with a deep, sonorous *bong* from within. Emma shook her head wryly. It was like walking onto a movie set, a Hollywood perception of Britain – wonderful, quaint even, but so overplayed.

Eventually, one of a pair of massive doors, easily twelve feet high, opened with a drawn-out *creak* – although that could just as easily have been the faithful retainer who now stood in their mighty shadow. He looked like he had been answering those doors since the day after the builders installed them.

"May I help you... *miss?*"

"Actually, it's *Mrs.* Mrs Stone. Is Sir Kenneth in residence, please?"

"Do you have an appointment, madam?" His question was polite enough, though he clearly had doubts.

"No."

Had he been wearing a monocle, the abruptness of her response would have caused it to fall. "Then might I enquire as to the nature of your visit, madam?"

"Of course. His son, Jeremy, works for my husband and seems to have gotten himself into a spot of bother." It was an understatement, but she knew better than to use emotive language with the old-school man of service who guarded the gates against her.

The elderly retainer's expression changed from polite enquiry to disapproval. "You had better come in, madam. I'll show you through to the drawing room. Please take a seat. Would you mind waiting, while I inform Sir Kenneth that you're here?"

Ten minutes dragged by. Emma drummed her fingers on the arm of an exquisitely upholstered Queen Anne armchair, one of a pair placed before a magnificent marble fireplace. The room was stuffed with antiques, its walls dripping with beautiful artwork. Unfortunately, she was in no mind to enjoy any of it – and knowing she had work to be getting on with at home only increased her impatience.

When the finely carved oak door opened, she stood, quashing her annoyance and mustering her best smile – she needed this man's help.

Sir Kenneth Hornesby Jarvis was a man in his fifties with a square, rigid, military bearing. Despite the earliness of the hour, he was immaculately dressed in a grey suit and red tie, looking like she had just called him out of a cabinet meeting – although possibly with Neville Chamberlain.

Much about young Jerry became clear.

Emma offered her hand as he approached.

He shook it quickly, but with gentle deference to her sex. "Mrs Stone, I understand?"

"Thank you for seeing me without an appointment, Sir Kenneth."

"Please." He gestured for her to retake her seat as he took the one opposite. "I understand young Jeremy might be in some sort of trouble."

Emma explained the situation at Rookstone Castle, three hundred miles north.

Sir Kenneth listened attentively but gave nothing away.

Driving back down what suddenly seemed an incredibly ostentatious driveway, Emma fumed. Going in, she had known better than to expect a gush of emotion from the blue-blooded aristocrat, but Sir Kenneth barely even acknowledged her story before ringing for the butler to show her out. She *inferred* there was nothing he could do – or was willing to do. He hardly said a word.

After that, her way home was a blur. She scarcely even noticed which roads she took. Butterflies swarmed around her gut like bats in a cave. Was that it? No help at all? She knew Sir Kenneth Hornesby Jarvis was connected at the very highest levels, both within the government and the military. She could hardly believe he would refuse to lift a finger to get his own son out of this ridiculous situation.

"OK!" she announced to the world from her driver's seat. "If that's the way it is, we'll just have to do it alone, then!"

Waiting at traffic lights, her hand trembled on the gearstick. Raising it slightly, she realised it was not merely vibration from the engine. She was shaking with nerves. Fearing her hopes might be dashed, she railed at the unfairness of their situation. All Gary wanted was to do his job and get paid, so he and his team could get on in life. Why was it always so difficult?

She shook her head. *That sort of thinking gets you nowhere. We're just going to have to fight a little harder, is all. Regroup and plan another sortie, as Gary likes to say. God knows we're used to it, so calm down and breathe!* She felt a little better after giving herself a stiff talking to. Taking her own advice, she inhaled deeply and, letting it out slowly, switched on the car's radio to brighten her mood. Catching the end of Supersonic by Oasis, she tapped along to the beat on her steering wheel, her spirits lifting, just slightly, right up until the news began. Within minutes, the BBC had completely undone her hard-won, fragile optimism with endless droning on about the passing recession. They seemed desperate to keep it alive and in the misery cycle by squashing any good news as it arrived and stamping all over whatever green shoots were to be found. Just when she thought she could take no more of it, the state propogandist interrupted herself to bring some breaking news from all the way up in Northumberland – a place called Rookstone Castle. Emma turned up the volume, listening with growing dread.

She had been hanging around with builders too long, for when the loathsome presenter finally returned the airwaves to music, she punched the off switch, in no mood to listen to some pretty, sunny Australian girl sing about being so lucky. Emma sucked her knuckles and was in such a foul mood by the time she pulled onto her own driveway, that the police car parked there barely even registered as a surprise.

Emma opened the door and stepped out, slamming it closed much harder than necessary as she demanded, "What's happened – this time?"

The young constable took a step back. "M-Mrs Stone?" he enquired.

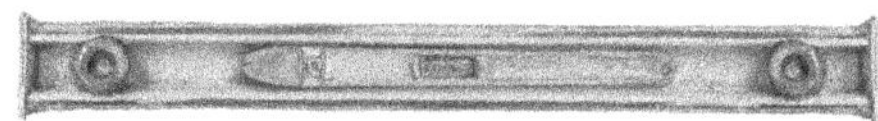

09:00 Monday, May 9th, 1994
"Hello down there!" Gary hollered from the battlements.

Sergeant Gripper checked his watch. "Well, at least they're punctual." He watched the man on top of the tower turn away, out of view, as though also checking something.

He reappeared, cupping his hands to shout, "How are our demands going?"

Gripper's megaphone gave a squeal of feedback as he lifted it to his mouth. Grimacing with annoyance, he reported, "A negotiator is on his way from Newcastle – due any minute. I'm sure he'll be able to..." He tailed off as Gary disappeared once more.

Up on the rooftop, Scott held Floating George hostage this time, with his gun at the young plumber's back. Usually full of life and mischief, George had not been himself since the police released him on bail. Having served his country, his country turning on him was a bitter pill to swallow, and he now stood morose and motionless.

"Tell him tae organise tha flight we ordered, or ye'll toss someone o'er the side."

"*What?*"

"Tell him! Or we'll start with this one." Scott grabbed George around the neck, pulling him off balance, holding the gun to his head. "Now."

Gary opened his mouth and gawped in horror.

"*Now!*"

Nodding, he turned and leaned over the parapet. "Hurry up, or I'll, I'll, erm..."

"Speak up, man!" Gripper's amplified voice bounced and rebounded off the high, crenellated walls.

"Aye, speak up – or he goes down!" Scott encouraged.

"He said, I mean, *I* said get our transport here and our private flight ready to take off right now, or I'll, I'll..."

"Tell him!"

Gary swallowed and gabbled, "Or I'll throw someone off the tower. One of the hostages, probably!"

Down below, a flock of cameramen fluttered excitedly into position.

High above, Scott scowled at Gary as though he were simple. "*Probably?*" he spat, furiously.

"I know, I know. I'm sorry. I'm new to this."

"Eejit!"

A four-door saloon car roared up the drive, skidding to a halt behind the other parked vehicles. A man flung the front passenger door open and strode purposefully towards Gripper to introduce himself gruffly. "Detective Inspector Mellow. I'll take over from here, Sergeant."

"Be my guest, sir," Gripper replied tautly, handing his superior officer the megaphone. His chances for promotion were slipping away. Frowning, he recalled the earlier message from Constable Charlton. "I was told it was Harrow, sir."

Mellow aggressively sucked the last life out of his cigarette like he hated it, before flicking it away. "He's on holiday, down south somewhere, so you've got me."

"Of course. Much experience with this type of thing, sir?"

Mellow shook his head, his expression promising violence.

Gripper took a step back, despite himself. If pressed, he would guess the man had no other expressions.

"My *experience,* Sergeant, is in getting little snots like these lot down to the cells for a right kicking! But today, somebody decided to send me here to *talk* this scum down."

Panic flashed through Gripper. Not only could he see his promotion, and subsequent extension, receding, but headlines began to write themselves large across his imagination. "Erm, they have someone at gunpoint up there, sir. Probably best not to..."

Mellow turned angrily towards Gripper, silencing him instantly. "Best not to what?"

"I mean, perhaps we should try to keep them calm – put them at ease, sir. That sort of thing. Don't you think?"

The detective inspector growled noncommittal annoyance. "Can you get one of these layabouts to fetch me a bacon sandwich or something? If such a thing exists out here. I got the call early and I haven't eaten."

Gripper did not doubt it. If this was Mellow, he could only imagine what Harrow must be like. Removing his police sergeant's hat, he wiped his brow anxiously as he called over the nearest constable to run his errand.

Mellow stood with his hands on hips, the megaphone still in his right, glaring up at the north tower. Roughly fifty, while still obviously strong, he looked older.

Gripper guessed he would have joined the force in the late sixties, early seventies. Was that what city policing did to a man? It certainly threw into sharp relief his reasons for remaining a country copper.

The megaphone squealed again as the inspector raised it. "This is Detective Inspector Mellow. I understand you have some demands up there. How about some good faith?"

Gary appeared once more, as though he had been pushed between the crenellations. "Erm… what did you have in mind?"

"Dickhead!" Scott seethed. "Dinnae give them an inch, ye hear?"

Unaware of the running commentary above, Mellow called again. "I *mean*, I'll arrange your transport if you release the hostage."

Gary did not possess a criminal bone in his body, but even he rolled his eyes at that. He looked to his advisor for confirmation.

Scott sneered.

Gary leaned back over the parapet. "I don't think we can agree to that, Mr Marrow."

"DI Mellow!"

"Sorry."

"*Sorry?*" Scott was spitting nails, desperate to take over from the rank amateur but afraid to blow his anonymity.

Far below, Mellow frowned. "Gripper, come here."

Gripper appeared obsequiously at the inspector's elbow.

"There's something strange going on here."

"Yes, sir. I don't believe it's usual for builders to take hostages when negotiating their fee."

Mellow snorted, despite himself. "Do I understand correctly that they failed to steal the Grey Emeralds a couple of nights ago and came back?"

"They never left, sir. Could be a ploy, maybe?"

"A ploy? For what? Not exactly proving their innocence, are they? I want a chopper. Now. Get on to Newcastle and organise it, will you? We need eyes up there and it will lend the impression that we're taking their demands seriously." He spoke once more through the megaphone. "We're organising your flight, but just in case you get a bit twitchy, like, know this – if anything happens to Sir Henry Grey, the marksmen surrounding this castle have orders to turn you into purée, got it?"

"Oh, my God! Who *is* that man?" Emma exclaimed, as the video flickered bottom to top in freeze-frame. A female officer brought her a cup of tea, while a detective sergeant glowered at her across the table in Worcester Police Station.

Emma glared back. Via the power of television, the story was even more damning than it had been on the radio, especially now the nationals were broadcasting live updates. Everyone would have seen it. She placed her head in her hands, shaking it in disbelief. "Gaz's mum's going to have a fit."

"You can make this a lot easier for yourself, Mrs Stone, if you just tell us all you know about your husband's plan to steal the Grey Emeralds."

A bark of laughter escaped her lips. Was he joking? "I think I'll call my lawyer now – not that I don't trust you, or anything!"

The DS nodded to the WPC, who slipped out and returned with a cordless telephone.

The sergeant stood. About to leave, he smiled, sardonically. "This has just gone international. I'm sure we'll have another update in a few minutes. So, don't go anywhere, will you?"

After agreeing to give the inspector in charge some time to organise a helicopter, Scott grew impatient and sidled up to the battlements, sneaking a glance down below at the forces ranged against him. His grip on Floating George loosened as his attention shifted. George caught Gary's eye and nodded, almost imperceptibly.

Gary lunged for the gunman's right arm, grasping the weapon as George twisted away. A builder for most of his adult life, Gary was a strong man with a grip like a vice from years of tool use. Scott was overmatched but possessed with a meanness Gary entirely lacked. Immediately realising his mistake, his arm rose as he also tried to twist away.

The pistol discharged.

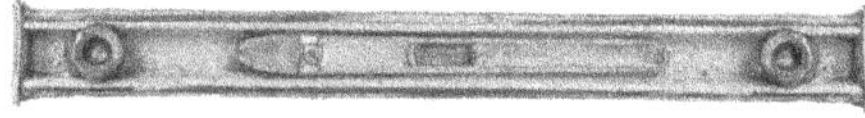

The same smug commentator in the camelhair overcoat appeared back on the portable television screen in Worcester Police Station. Emma forced herself to watch, despite the growing knot in her stomach. She had to know all that was happening if she was to stand any chance of being able to help.

That knot turned into a boulder as the camera blurred away from the newscaster on impulse, to catch the action up on the tower. Everyone watching the live news feed heard the presenter, Brandon Porkpie, exclaim, "Oh, my God! Did everyone see that?"

Emma screamed, knocking her chair over as she reached uselessly for the small TV and her husband.

Fortunately, when the pistol fired, George had the sense to duck as he span away, allowing the bullet to *zing* harmlessly off one of the stone parapets to cut a fresh scar into its weathered face.

Before he could return to help his rashly courageous boss, Scott gave the builder a brutal undercut to the belly with his free left hand that bent the larger man over, winded. The stolen knife fell from his pocket, but neither man noticed in the mêlée. Without stopping to consider further, Scott shoved the builder between two of the stone crenellations, and with the lightest lift of Gary's leg, helped him the rest of the way over the edge.

Gary Stone fell like one.

part two

Chapter 13

What a Fall

L ife flashing before the eyes of the dying is an old cliché, so what remained of Gary's rational mind registered no surprise when something similar happened to him. Other than being thrown over the side of a four-storey building, the surprise, when it came, was that the life flashing before his eyes turned out to be several lives. Even more disturbingly, none of them appeared to be his – he would have remembered.

Sunlight streamed in through a stone window set into the west wall. Looking closely, he fancied he recognised its decorative mullions. Rich tapestries hung from the remaining walls and fresh, scented rushes carpeted the random width, oak floorboards beneath. Gary felt sure he recognised the room, too, had visited it before, though there were significant differences. The chamber he visited previously was like an historically dubious *version* of the one he now saw and boasted a Tudor period minstrels' gallery around three of its sides, high above. He instinctively knew he was looking into an earlier time, before the structure was built. Another difference his builder's eye could hardly fail to notice was that the window was obviously recently installed and flawless, for it bore none of the perishing of ages For Keeps were contracted to restore in the late spring of 1994.

His first impulse was to call his brother, so that Jimmy could see its original state before getting to work. Realising how impossible and ridiculous that was, on so many levels, he forced himself to concentrate. There was bound to be a test – assuming he was not already dead.

A richly carved bed was pushed tight against the south wall. When Gary was first shown around Rookstone, months earlier, it had been a four-poster – not common in England until the 15th century. The fact that this bed was not a four-poster was hardly conclusive, but did add to his suspicions about what he was seeing, though it was far from the only clue about when he found himself. Two men sat before and to the side of the bed, their table in the light of the window. Pawing over primitive maps and charts, one could have been sixty-ish, the other, somewhat younger.

Gary stepped closer. Neither appeared to notice him as the older man jabbed a finger at Falkirk, just south of Stirling, on the map. Gary squinted. The quality was low, Britain drawn much fatter than the satellite view moderners like him took for granted. Indeed, to Gary, it looked more like a treasure map from a Rupert Bear annual than the Ordnance Survey map he used to find Rookstone Castle when he drove north. The men spoke fluent French – or so he believed. After three holidays in France, two with his wife, Gary barely got past the *'un demi-litre de bière, s'il vous plaît'* phase, with associated hand gestures towards his beer font of preference.

Another shock. One of several experienced over the last few seconds. This latest was that he understood what they were saying, despite their antiquated and decidedly foreign tongue. What was going on? *Was* he dead? He had not felt it, but having never been dead before, how would he know?

"No, you're not."

Gary jumped out of what he was no longer sure was his skin. "You!"

Inga Rhók Stán gave him an understanding smile. She was perfectly clear to him now, large as death. Presenting in her mid-twenties, her blond hair long, with a pretty plait to each side of her face, she was quite the looker.

Gary turned away with a shudder, remembering she was his many-centuries-removed grandmother.

She gave him a moment to compose himself. "Don't worry. You haven't passed on. Not yet."

"Don't *worry?*"

"You've been granted a great gift."

Understandably shaken, Gary bridled still further. "It feels like it! Should I be flattered before I'm flattened?"

"No need to be sarcastic."

"I disagree. Might be the last chance I get."

"Calm yourself. You're here for a reason."

Gary slumped. Could he not even die without someone piling on his workload?

"Do you still have your necklace?"

He looked at her sharply. "You know about that?"

Inga nodded.

"And how frigid cold it gets when you're near?" Though, as he spoke, Gary realised it was not freezing him at that moment.

She nodded again. "If you're wondering why you're not feeling anything now, it's because you're only here," she smiled knowingly, "in spirit. Like I said – a great gift." She reached out to place a hand lightly on his chest, where the cross hung beneath his clothing. Her hand shook, as though she were straining against an invisible force, like the repulsion of two identically polarised magnets. She pulled back.

Gary frowned, trying to comprehend what was happening. Without thinking, he reached down the neck of his shirt and pulled out the ancient cross. "You can't touch it?"

She shrugged, gazing longingly at the small cross.

He waved it left to right, to see if she would follow.

Inga blinked and skewered him with a glare. "What are you doing?"

"Nothing. Just hoping you're not going to start calling me Frodo."

She wore a pained expression. "What?"

Relieved that the pretty girl before him, the one holding all the answers to his immediate future, had missed the Gollum comparison, he cleared his throat and tried again. "But you and it are linked, right?"

"In a way."

"Can you just give me a straight answer, please? It's like talking with the damned Sphynx!"

Inga's irritation faded and she smiled enigmatically, entirely failing to deflect the accusation. "You're not ready."

"Trust me, I'm ready, and bloody annoyed!"

"Then understand that *I'm* not ready." She gestured back to the men still engaged in an intense conversation over their maps. "You must pay attention to this."

Exasperated, but with no obvious alternative, Gary turned back to them, listening closely. The older of the pair's shoulder-length, leonine hair was whitish grey, shot through with remnants of black. His left eyelid drooped slightly, marring an otherwise still-handsome face – though, at that moment, it was a face full of fury as he gesticulated indignantly, speaking of the Scots in most unflattering terms. Recently pitched off a building by a Scotsman himself, Gary empathised.

"That's Edward."

"Edward? Should I know him?"

Inga nodded. "I believe our people began numbering them some centuries ago, but you might know him as Edward Plantagenet – the first one."

Gary's jaw swung open. He stared stupidly, first at Inga, and then at Edward I of England – Hammer of the Scots. He knew Edward had visited Rookstone on his way north to fight his Scottish campaign, but to *see* him... His astonishment was released by way of a coarse, thankfully short, two-word expression – one that described something he had no intention of doing to himself, but it had been a trying day.

Inga huffed.

"What?"

"I see *some* of my Saxon tongue endures, even in this Godless age. Small mercies."

"Uh?"

"Never mind. Listen..."

Gary listened. The younger man, if anything, seemed more furious even than the King. Though respectful to his liege lord, anger rolled off him in waves as he described the burning alive of women and children.

"They were his kin," Inga explained, sadly. "They died when Rookstone was attacked by the Scots. Those were dark days."

Engrossed and unable to help himself, Gary asked, "What year is this?"

"The year of our Lord 1298. Some horrific crimes were perpetrated here, drawn out over many years, with so many victims – and villains – on both sides." She shook her head. "Terrible, terrible times. And I remember the women and children suffered most of all."

"Hmm..."

Inga looked him squarely in the eye. "You disagree?" Annoyance flashed blue in her stare. "I *witnessed* some of that savagery."

"No, it's not that. I read in the paper recently that an Australian actor, erm... a *mummer*, you might say, is about to make a film— that is, a *play* about those times. You know, the chap from Lethal W..." He remembered who he was speaking with. "Look, that's not important. Apparently, they start filming next month for release next year. My point is, I wonder if any of this will be in it?" He shook his head. "Doubt it'll be big on history."

"You watch plays about such horrors?"

"We do."

"Do you not crave escape? Entertainment? Humour?"

"Of course. It's just that most of our escape and entertainment is about war, death and murder. We're a funny old species."

"That's *funny?*"

"Yes. Films and books help us remember war, so that we can learn from our mistakes."

"You still have wars." Inga had been around a long time, so it was not a question.

Gary frowned. "Hmm. We always seem to forget everything we learned, just when it matters most. That said, we've had no big ones for a while. Not here, at least. We still have the modern equivalent, though."

Inga frowned, too. "Modern *equivalent?*"

"Yeah. We call it football."

Inga blinked. "I hear your words, though I struggle to understand."

Gary blew out his cheeks. "Sometimes, so do I." He looked at her intently. "Inga?"

"Yes?"

"Why am I not dead yet? I was falling from the castle roof – surely I must have hit the ground by now."

"There *is* no time here, not for you. Like I told you, a great gift."

"OK. So why am I here? Why *here*, exactly?"

"To learn."

"But..." his brows knitted with confusion, "if I do learn something really important, I'll only retain the memory for about half a second before my head is six feet wide and an inch deep."

"We'll ford that river when we come to it."

"Either way, it sounds like I'm going to get my feet wet," Gary muttered, miserably.

Inga smirked. "How you get out of this is up to you. I would rather you remained with the living."

"I'd prefer that, as well – funnily enough."

"You have unfinished work here," she explained, her smile softening. "More than that, you are my son, through many daughters, and sons. Now, take heed. Here comes the first clue. Listen closely, if you can bear it."

"Bear it?"

Inga shuddered. "When I hear the Norman tongue, I..."

Gary stared, waiting for her to continue.

She shrugged. "It was a long time ago. When the Normans came they killed everyone they could find and scorched the earth so that all they missed could no longer feed themselves. It was long after my time, but I'm still Saxon. I still felt the agony of my people."

"The Harrying of the North," Gary muttered, comprehending. "We'd call that a genocide if it were to happen now. We learned about it in school. You saw it happen?"

She nodded. "Northumbria, especially southern Northumbria[1] was devastated. But enough of this. You must pay attention." She turned him to face the two men at the table.

King Edward passed his companion a small leather pouch. Whatever was inside it clinked softly. Unsure what he might find, the younger man opened the bag tentatively and looked inside. His eyes lit, not with green-eyed envy, but with green-eyed jealousy, for the contents were now his, granted by the King himself. Gary craned over the man's shoulder, also to look inside. What he saw were three exquisite stones. Emeralds.

"Use this gift to build back your walls more strongly than before – stronger than ever – for I need Rookstone sturdy, if it's to keep my northern borderland safe from Wallace's dogs."

Inga squeezed Gary's arm for him to pay special attention.

"You have no idea how it pains me to let them go," the King explained. "You may use them as collateral. Borrow against them to raise the funds you'll need to refortify." He closed the younger man's fingers around the small pouch, gripping them in a massive hand, for Edward was a giant for his time. Six feet and two inches, he stood head and shoulders above most men of that age. "Offer them as surety, but *never* let them go. I give them to you on trust, you understand?"

---

1. The modern, English county of Northumberland represents only the north-eastern tip of the much older, much larger Saxon kingdom of Northumbria.

Gary turned to Inga for explanation, but she merely led him from the room. They no sooner walked through the solid oak door, literally *through* the door, when the floor fell away.

Chapter 14

Losing My Derision

G ary found himself in what appeared to be a chapel. "Whoa!" He staggered, disoriented. Whether he was there only in spirit or not, corporeal habits were baked in – as were building site habits. "What the f—"

"Fond of that word, aren't you?" Inga accused.

"Flippin' 'eck," he finished, weakly. "Give me a break. I'm absolutely terrified! What the *hell* is going on?"

She slapped him around the head.

"Ow! What was that for? Hey, how come I felt that?"

"Because you were *meant* to! Do not curse."

Gary rubbed the back of his head, grouchily. "You mean 'hell'?"

She nodded, tautly.

"So you're OK with f—"

She glared at him, cutting him off.

"*Far* worse words – I was going to say – but not that one."

She looked around, cautiously. "We never know who's listening."

Still rubbing his head where she struck him, Gary felt like a plaything and wanted to know what was going on. "OK, so why have you brought me here, oh, ghost of crapmas past?" he snapped tetchily. "Is this where we meet up with Jacob Marley, or something?"

"What are you blathering about, now?"

"Nothing."

"Stop being so moody. It's undignified."

"Oh, sorry, *Nan!*"

Inga glowered and pointed. "Actually, she's a nun."

Kneeling before an altar in silent prayer, there was indeed a nun before them. "You're here to see her. And you will certainly need her help. So I warn you, mind your language!"

Gary glared at his guide in return, but did not answer back. The slap really hurt. Eventually, he asked, "How can she...?" He tailed off as armed men ran into the chamber and dragged the prostrate woman to her feet roughly, only to knock her down again.

"What's going on?" Gary asked, frantically. "What are they doing to her?"

"It's called martyrdom," Inga replied, quietly. "The meaning was a lot more specific back in her day. Less – what's the word – *metaphorical.* Yours is a pampered generation. This is the year 1540. The dissolution of the monasteries is in full flow. Hard times for any practising the old faith – the Church of Rome. It was bad enough when the pagan Danes came to rape and kill and burn, plundering our churches. We never expected the English would turn on their own that way. This is what happens when ideology runs out of control, when one belief replaces another. Remember it well."

"I can't take this." Gary tried to turn away from the screams and the vile spectacle, but Inga forced him to watch.

"You must see. This evil will leave its mark on you both, creating a link between you. Witnessing her suffering is crucial and your only hope. I can do very little to help you, but she... she is *different.*"

Gary sniffed and wiped his eyes, disgusted and horrified by the treatment of the young woman, so recently at prayer. Now it seemed she had no prayer at all. "Can't we do something?" He reached for a floor-standing, silver candle holder, almost as tall as Gary himself, fully intending to smash whatever the monsters before him used for brains right out of their grinning heads. He had never felt such fury, but his hand passed straight through it, without so much as a flicker of the candle.

"Not like that." Inga pulled him back as he staggered. "Reach out to her."

Gary took three steps forward, but his anger flared again, and he followed up with a running kick at the beast now pressing himself on his victim. He fell over.

Inga rolled her eyes. "Not like *that,* either!" After witnessing eleven centuries of history, she was no longer easily shocked. "You still have the force of life. Open your spirit. *Lend* her your strength. She will need it."

Gary took a deep breath to fortify himself – he had no idea why. Taking a final step, he reached out to the dying woman, both spiritually and with his hand, just as the base creature, now finished with her, drove a dagger through his victim's heart. The 20th century builder, lost in time, screamed along with her, a wordless cry of anguish.

With her dying breath, Sister Beatrice looked up into Gary's face, seeing him for the first time. Through her agony, she reached out to touch the cross at his throat, managing a final, beatific smile.

Hers was the lightest touch, but it knocked Gary across the chapel like a battering ram to the chest. Fortunately, he had no breath to lose as he managed to cry out coherently at last. "No!"

In his fury, he was back on his feet instantly. Beyond rational thought now, he ran to the altar, reaching for its small crucifix to launch it at the ringleader who had just committed the vilest of acts a man can carry out against a woman. Despite lacking physical presence, Gary's white-hot anger caused it to wobble and topple to the floor with a crash.

The murderer stopped laughing. Suddenly uncertain, he turned back to the altar, concern flashing across his face. Without thinking, he crossed himself, unconsciously – a baked-in habit inculcated by the old religion, so recently disavowed. Fortunately, his two comrades failed to notice his lapse into papism and began laughing once more. He joined in, though his merriment seemed forced as they began looting the chapel and the murdered nun.

Gary stood with his head in his hands, completely traumatised, unable to do anything to stop them.

When Inga placed a hand on his back, he jumped. "*No one* should have to witness such things. I am sorry," she asserted, softly. "You did well."

"I barely managed to knock the cross off the table."

"Not what I meant, but that, too, was impressive. When your time comes, your spirit will remain strong." She inflected pride into her words. Gary was, after all, and in a manner of speaking, her son.

He spread his fingers, revealing a gap through which he could stare at her.

"Don't worry. That time is not yet," she assured him. "You've achieved our main goal."

"I have?"

"Yes, and you now have vital clues to defeat your enemies and recognise your friends, but there is more you must see and do. Come."

"Is it over?"

Inga and Gary turned towards a voice behind them to find Sir Edward Grey standing by the door, quite deliberately facing away from the horrific spectacle of the soldiers stripping and stealing.

"Who are you?" Gary demanded. He was rattled, and way past any social niceties.

Inga introduced them. "Sir Edward has been helping you, too, haven't you, Edward?"

Gary was still in shock, and now another ghost was speaking to him, as though he were just another passerby in the street. "S-so, are you related to Edward the First?"

Sir Edward frowned at the builder as though he were a halfwit. "Are *you* related to everyone named Gary?"

"Oh. Probably not."

"Sir Edward was master of Rookstone during the time of the dissolution," Inga explained.

His wits beginning to catch up, Gary asked, "Right, so you're a ghost, too? Can you all travel through time like this?"

"Not exactly, and please refrain from using the G-word."

"But you are ghosts, aren't you?"

"Dead noun me again, sir, and I'll have you horsewhipped!"

"We prefer spirits," Inga intervened. "Ghosts are just memories, caught in an action they're doomed to repeat forever."

"Ah, like recordings," Gary caught on. "I read something about that once. Something about the magnetics of stone – the stone tape theory, I think it was called."

The spirits stared, clearly wondering what on earth he was jabbering about.

"No," Inga corrected him. "I mean, they're no longer aware."

"We hope," Sir Edward added, darkly.

She shrugged.

"I'm sorry," Gary tried again. "You'll have to forgive me. I'm still only halfway through a fall to my death, so this is all quite new."

"It's alright, dear." Inga patted him on the hand. "Edward doesn't like coming back to this place, at this time. It unsettles him. You can see why. That's why I've led you thus far. In answer to your question, we move through time just the way you do, but with one exception – we can also see the world as it was when we lived."

"We think that might be why some of us become trapped," Edward joined in the explanation.

"The *ghosts?*" Gary suggested, nervously.

Edward nodded.

Inga continued, "I'm only able to travel with you because the strongest among us are joining forces to help cover my tracks."

"Strongest among you?" Gary was suddenly afraid again. "And who are they?"

"You just met one of them."

"Sir Edward?" Gary hazarded.

Sir Edward shook his head, sadly. "Boy's an imbecile. A complete doddypol."

Inga smirked. "No, silly. Sister Beatrice. She has more power than any of us. All of us!"

Gary was at sea. "Because of the way she..." He tailed off, swallowing like he lost the knack, unable to bring himself to speak of the things he had just witnessed.

The spirits looked at each other. Sir Edward shook his head again. "Not exactly. Her power is due more to what she *was.*"

"And what was that?"

"Pious."

Gary's brows knitted in confusion. "Weren't you all, you know, back in the day, I mean?"

Sir Edward straightened, hands on hips; belly protruding over his highly decorative belt, he glowered haughtily. He was far too well-dressed to be considered a pound-shop Henry VIII, but nor was he wearing full kingly rig

– perhaps a Savile Row Henry VIII described him best as he glared at Gary. "Presumptive little chap, isn't he? God's wounds, art thou always so quick to judgement, fellow?"

Gary's mouth fell open. Mystified, he just wished he knew the rules.

"Beatrice," Inga began, "was, erm..."

"*Too* pious," Edward affirmed. "Let's call a spade a shovel – they couldn't stand her!" He paused, pointing upwards, adding in hushed tones, "Up there. Booted her out, didn't they, and that matters. We're restricted, see? Non-interference, they call it. Especially not with anyone we knew or are related to – even if they are our descendants down many centuries. *She,* on the other hand—"

"Sister Beatrice?" Gary guessed, running to catch up.

"Indeed. *She* can act more or less freely."

Gary's brows furrowed again. "Why?"

"She was a pure soul, as close to perfect as anyone who ever lived in this world," Inga explained.

"So they can't kick her downstairs," Edward clarified. He grinned. "But they don't want her *upstairs,* either."

"I'm confused," Gary admitted. "If she was so perfect and pious, isn't 'up there' exactly where she belongs?"

Sir Edward laughed, sharing a secret look with Inga, who smiled. "Let's just say she had one flaw. Wait 'til you meet her again, lad. You'll see!"

Inga seemed to fade. "I must leave you with Sir Edward. He'll take you the rest of the way."

"Are you alright?" Gary asked, suddenly concerned.

"You got me up many hours before I was fully regenerated – with your antics!"

"Me?"

"I pushed myself past endurance to make that, that metal box on wheels burn like hellfire."

"That was you? The fire in the forest over the way?"

"Yes. I did it to draw the attention of the ones in uniform."

Gary soured, turning away. "The ones waiting to arrest my corpse the moment it hits the ground. Thanks a heap." Slow on the uptake, he turned back. "Hey, I thought you didn't like the H-word?"

Inga shook her head at his ingratitude. "Never mind that. We knew those villains were coming back to the castle. We also knew they were dangerous, most specifically to Sir Henry. We didn't expect you to dive from the battlements."

"I wasn't exactly given a choice, you know!"

"Yes, I saw the clumsy way you handled the situation. You wouldn't have survived the week in my day."

"Nor mine," Sir Edward vouchsafed.

Gary's anger flared again. "That's right, gang up on the nearly dead guy!"

"Anyhow," Inga continued, wearily, "I'm exhausted. I had hoped to call on you later, in the night, but you forced my hand."

"Yes, I can't tell you how I've started to look forward to our little chats at quarter past two in the morning. Some of us have work the next day, you know."

"Ungrateful barbermonger!" Edward exploded.

"He's a man, isn't he?" Inga jibed.

"How dare you, madam!"

"Whoa, whoa, whoa." Gary waved them down. "I thought you were here to save me. This is only my entire life on the line, you know. So we're all tired, I get it. If you don't help me, I'm going to get the chance to sleep it off forever! So please tell me what I must do to avoid my impending splat."

"I'll take you on," Edward agreed, grumpily.

Inga thanked Sir Edward before gripping Gary by the arm. "I'll return as soon as I'm able. Keep your wits. Learn all you can. You will survive this." She smiled and faded.

Edward gave a short wave, his temper forgotten. "See you anon, dear lady. Now, come with me, lad. Let's leave this awful place."

"They've been a long time up on the roof," Jimmy fretted.

Hammer checked his watch. He was forced to agree.

"You think the police will give you a safe way out of here and then out of the country?" Jimmy pressed.

Hammer glared at him. It was his way. "They'd better, sunbeam, or you lot are gonna have a really bad day. Starting with Lord Muck, over there."

Sir Henry shifted uncomfortably in his seat, though due to injury rather than fear.

"Don't like nobs," Hammer continued. "I've waited a long time for these." He took the Grey Emeralds from his pocket, when confusion crossed his face. Why had he just said that? He had only planned the caper a few weeks ago, yet he was already extraordinarily jealous of the stones. It occurred to him that, when it came time to handing them over to the sponsors of his criminal enterprise, he was not entirely sure whether he would be able to do it. Unused to such nebulous emotions, and as brutal as his name, he always knew exactly what he wanted. Getting it usually involved hitting something – or someone – but now he was deeply troubled. Something was niggling at him – something over and above the total disaster their venture had become.

"So what do you still need *us* for?" Andy Wilson demanded, breaking into his thoughts. The plasterer still cradled Jacob, his beloved finishing trowel.

Hammer smiled nastily. "In case we need a spare. You might just have volunteered, sonny Jim."

"It's a bloody conspiracy," Andy chuntered under his breath.

Before anyone else spoke, they all heard the *crack* from the roof. Heavily muffled through countless tons of sandstone, it was still loud enough to cut through their conversation and was undoubtedly a gunshot.

Hammer and Jimmy stared at each other, each wondering what was happening and whether the advantage may have just shifted dramatically.

Jimmy leaned forward. "You never planned for this, did you?"

"What are you on about?" Hammer snarled.

"That madman with the gun. You didn't know he was armed. Come on, you didn't, did you?"

Hammer glared, admitting nothing.

Jimmy tried again. "You still have time to get out of this with a relatively light sentence. Hopefully, no one has been killed yet." A pang of concern for his brother shot through him. "But that Scotsman will be going away for a long time – you know that. However, *you* still have a choice."

Hammer leapt to his feet, arm shooting out to point at Jimmy. "You, shat it! And you," he swung round to point at Worzel, "go and see what the 'ell's going on up there. Move it!" He made eye contact with Serj, who nodded, selecting a halberd from the terrifying array of antique weaponry adorning the ancient stone walls. Testing its weight in his grip, he glowered at the builders, daring them to misbehave, though it was concern for their colleagues up on the roof that really kept them under control

"Damn, damn, damn!" Sir Edward cursed.

"Problem?" Gary asked, nervously.

"Perhaps." Concern bled into the nobleman's voice. "As we explained, we can't normally travel back and forth outside the current time or our own."

"Rules?"

"That and we don't know how – or have the power. We're being helped by... by a colleague. Inga asked for his help, and he showed her how this might be done, but I..." Sir Edward pondered. "Oh, Inga was always better at remembering things! Let me see. I went through the process she showed me. Hmm... Must have missed a step."

Gary walked to the north-facing mullioned windows of the beautiful long gallery where they had just reappeared. "You sure it hasn't worked? We certainly moved. Made me feel travel-sick again." He turned to Sir Edward. "It's chucking down outside, though."

Edward joined him at the window. "Yes, that's a problem."

"It is?"

"It was meant to be sunny. Oh, God's wounds, it's all gone wrong!"

"Why does it matter what the weather's doing?"

"It's not the damned weather that matters. This is still 1540. All I've done is move us from the front of the castle to the rear!"

Gary frowned. "Isn't that the other way around?"

"Not in 1540."

"Oh, I see. So, what does that mean for us?"

"It means that unless I can remember what our *colleague* told us, we're stuck here. And when I say we, I mean *you*."

"You'll return to 1994 without me?" Gary could feel panic rising again.

"Not intentionally, my boy. I won't have a choice. I can move around within my own time for a while – it's sort of like a memory. A memory imprinted on reality. I'm not very good at explaining this type of thing. Never was much of a theologian. Trouble is, when I get pulled back..."

"I'll be stuck here!" Gary was having a full-blown anxiety attack now. "Why?"

"You're... How to describe it... You're in a strange place right now."

"I bloody know that – worked it out all on my own!"

Sir Edward had not taken a breath in centuries. Nevertheless, he appeared to sigh, patiently. "I mean you're in a bad position."

"You *think?*"

The spirit frowned. "Of course I think. What sort of damned fool question is that?"

"That's not what I... Look, just forget it. Let's see if we can walk you back through the memory. Where were you when your 'colleague' showed you the technique?"

"He showed Inga. We were in Limbo."

"OK. I'm guessing, not too many visual prompts there, then?"

"It's like," Edward puffed out his cheeks, another residual behaviour, while thinking how he might describe the concept, "like a *nothing* soup."

"Don't suppose there were any croutons floating by to hang a memory on?" Gary was grasping and he knew it. "A bit of potato?"

"What on earth are you blathering about?"

"Nothing, sorry. You didn't have potatoes in your day, did you? That was Sir Walter Raleigh, wasn't it? Bit later. Erm... turnip?"

"Will you be quiet! No, wait! What did you just say?"

"Erm... turnip?"

The Tudor nobleman slapped a palm to his brow. "Of course!"

"Really?" Gary queried, sceptically.

"Look." Sir Edward beckoned him close. "See this?" He showed Gary the gold medallion hanging about his neck on a gold chain. "We all have one of these."

"A gold pendant? Wow, will I get one when I hit the ground?"

"What? No, no, no. You take everything so literally!"

"I've never been dead before."

Sir Edward's face flushed with annoyance and then softened. "Yes. Not your fault. We have a plan to prevent that, young man."

"I'm forty-seven."

"Truly?" He looked Gary up and down. "By the time I was your age, I was, I was... Well, I was dead, as it happens," Edward muttered, weakly. "You really have led a pampered life. Never mind. Also, not your fault. Look at this. It doesn't matter what it is. Mine is an item of jewellery, Inga has a... well, I'll let her tell you. Lady's prerogative, you understand? We all have a totem of some sort. A talisman that focuses our power – what remains of it. This is mine. It's usually something we treasured in life. For some of us, it might even be what got us killed. No one ever said the powers that be had no sense of humour."

Sir Edward closed his eyes, concentrating hard.

"And how does turnip come into this?" Gary spoke before he could stop himself.

His spirit guide opened one eye. "What?"

"I said how does a turnip help?"

Sir Edward's pained expression said, 'what the hell are you talking about?' without need of words, so Gary explained again. "I just said 'turnip' and you made me repeat it."

A light came on in Sir Edward's eyes. "Oh, is that what you said? Turnip? What good is a damned turnip?"

"Well, that's what I thought—"

"I thought you said *turn it!* That's what Hern— I mean, that's what *he* said. It was one of the steps to make the process work. I forgot to do it." Sir Edward gave Gary an appraising look. A smile slowly tugged at his lips. "Seems you have luck on your side, my boy." He laughed. "Turnip! Haha, oh, my old bones – wherever they are. Good for you!" He closed his eyes once more, concentrating with all his might, when the door to the chamber opened and who should walk in but Sir Edward. He looked furious, striding straight through his future shade.

"I *hate* it when they do that!" Sir Edward's spirit complained. "Especially when *I* do that!"

His living self moved to warm his hands over the roaring fire at the eastern end of the long gallery.

"He's just returned home to find out what happened to Sister Beatrice," Sir Edward's spirit explained. "I remember this day – though I try hard enough not to," he added, darkly.

Gary felt it necessary to whisper. "How do you know he's just come home?"

Sir Edward's shade gave him a look.

"Ah... because he's you, and you're him, or whatever." Then a more important question crossed Gary's mind. "So, you were against what happened – when you were alive, I mean?"

"I was."

Gary felt a sense of relief about that. "Held with the old religion, did you, with Catholicism?"

"Young man—"

"I'm forty-seven. I did say," Gary muttered.

"Very well, *old* man—"

"Hey, steady on."

Sir Edward glowered. "*Man!* Back in civilised times, we never discussed money, politics, nor religion. It was seen as uncouth. Furthermore, any or all of them could get you killed!" The nobleman's noble spirit sagged. "But if you must know, I supported the King. Perhaps I should say the Crown – whoever wore it. He was anointed by God, you see?" His look was one of guilt mixed with a plea for understanding. "Those were dark days. We had not long finished rebuilding after the siege."

Gary was spellbound. "*You* held Rookstone during a siege?"

Sir Edward nodded. "Percy came north, during the Pilgrimage of Grace, back in '37."

"1537?"

Edward nodded again. "They came to demand I join the rebellion against the King, during the religious strivings. Never was much of a theologian," he repeated softly. "After all that blew over, after the executions, I tried to shelter a few who cleaved to their faith."

Gary began to understand. "Sister Beatrice."

"Yes," Edward sighed. "I never forgave myself for not being there when she needed me. I dealt with the noisome serpents who... who..."

"I saw what happened," Gary muttered. "Will never forget. You got them, then?"

Sir Edward glanced at him sharply. "Believe it! Of course, after I... *moved on*, I realised that Beatrice was at peace with what happened. They were such brutal times, young-old Gary. Your people must remember. You really must, you know. I tell you, when times change, they change quickly. Never forget."

Gary watched the living Sir Edward at the fireside, pensively. To Sir Edward's spirit, he whispered, "Please take me home."

Edward looked uncomfortable.

Gary slumped. "What's wrong – specifically?"

"I can't do it."

"Why?"

The spirit tugged on his beard frustratedly. "We're in the right place but almost four hundred years too soon."

"I thought you'd remembered how to fix that?"

Sir Edward was suddenly awkward. "I have. I think. It's not that. I mean, it's... That is, not with..."

"Not with? Not with what? You can't leave me here! I have a dog waiting for me back in the future. Who's going to look after her? Oh, my God, I still haven't paid off the mortgage!"

"What about your wife?"

"Yes, *yes*. Her, too. I was getting round to that," Gary added, tetchily. "Emma will kill me if I die here!"

Sir Edward shook his head, trying to make sense of Gary's priorities, having already decided his logic was not worth examining. "You don't understand. It's not with what, it's with *whom*. I can't do it. Not with *him* watching." He nodded to his living self, the former Edward, who stood stock still, staring into the roaring flames, too angry to sit or to see anyone.

Gary looked between them. "Rules again?"

"No, it's not that. It's just, well, you know?"

Gary's temper snapped. "Oh, give me a break. I'm not asking you to take a pee with him looking! He can't see you anyway!"

Sir Edward looked even more uncomfortable. "But you're asking me to perform, erm... How should I put this? A chap can't just practise pagan death magic right in front of himself."

"Will you just bloody well get me out of here?"

"Of course, you're right. You're right, of course. Ahem." He cleared his throat for effect and concentrated one last time.

Eventually, he opened one eye again. "Is he, that is, am *I* still here?"

Gary placed his head in his hands. "God give me strength!"

"Sorry, sorry. It's just that, if he sees me, I'll have to live with it."

"You're dead."

"Short on manners, aren't you, boy— man, or whatever you are! I mean, *he* will have to live with it. Just feels wrong, because I remember how he felt about witchcraft."

"Is that what this is?"

"No, but he would see it thus, and to just do it in front of him – that is, for him to see himself practising it right in front of him. I mean, really..."

"For crying out loud, if you're that worried about him seeing you, how did you ever take a bath? Bad example. Sir Edward, will you *please* try?"

"I'll have you know I bathed monthly – whether I needed to or not!"

"Yes, yes, sorry. Please, Sir Edward, *concentrate.*"

"Right. Suppose I should get into the spirit of things, eh? Eh?" He nudged Gary with his elbow.

"*Stalling,*" Gary noted in a singsong voice.

"Right. Right you are." The Tudor nobleman's face screwed up in concentration as he took his talisman to 'turn it'. Once the pendant was upside down, Gary felt the gut-wrenching sickness again as they reappeared – exactly where they were.

"Oh, man!" Gary exclaimed. "I'm going to get left behind, aren't I?"

"I say, chaps, good show!"

Gary turned to see a young man he had not met before. Dressed in the style of the early 20th century upper classes, he assumed he must be another spirit. *Getting closer,* he thought, before trying to retch. Without a stomach that was impossible, which somehow only made the nausea worse.

Sir Edward bent double, like he was genuinely winded. Straightening, he walked to the window and looked out into glorious sunshine. "Ha! Knew I had it in me!"

Chapter 15

Cars (and Vans)

I did it! I got us here!" Sir Edward exclaimed, proudly, though he shimmered, becoming faint.

"Are you, er... I hesitate to use the word 'well'?" Gary asked the dead man, cautiously.

"Exhausted," Sir Edward replied, and sounded it. "Need to rest, to replenish."

"But you can't leave me like this. I don't know what to do," Gary pleaded.

"Almost home, lad." Sir Edward's usually booming voice was much weakened. "This young fellow is the Honourable Geoffrey Grey – grand-uncle to your Sir Henry Grey. Poor chap never lived long enough to really grow up." He paused, meaningfully. "As you'll no doubt see, soon enough."

"But, Sir Edward, you can't leave me."

The spirit smiled sadly. "No choice, my boy. Sorry. And it gets worse."

Gary pinched the bridge of his nose from habit. "How," he breathed, softly, "is that possible? I'm caught somewhere in time and in the middle of a near-death experience."

"It's even worse than that, I'm afraid. You're about to be caught in the middle of a near-Geoff experience, too."

"I say, chaps, I'm right here, you know, what?"

"Sorry," Sir Edward repeated. "I have to go."

"No!" Gary raged. "My head's about to connect with the driveway out there. You do realise that if I headbutt the world, I'll come off worse, right? And you're leaving me with the *B*-team?"

"Talking of bees, I rather think I hear a buzzing, don't you chaps, what?"

Gary turned to the window, instinctively. He *could* hear a buzzing, now the Honourable Geoffrey mentioned it. "What's tha—" His question went unanswered, because when he turned back, Sir Edward was gone.

"Don't worry, old man. I'm here to save you!" the shade of the young man enthused. "Just call me Geoff."

The pistol *crack* echoed around the towers and courtyards of Rookstone Castle. "Gaz!" Floating George screamed as Gary was tipped over the parapet. He took a step forward, hopelessly. To do what exactly, he had no idea, but many cameras below now zoomed in on his horrified face, allowing millions of viewers to draw exactly the wrong conclusion. He barely noticed the gun aimed at his midriff as Scott regained his balance and composure. What he did notice was that he had kicked something to the wall that now rested under his boot.

"You want tae go next, laddie?"

George ignored the jibe and continued to stare over the battlements. His heart leapt from his mouth to his stomach as he watched his boss and friend fall.

"*Nooo,*" he cried softly, sagging to his haunches. With his back to the gunman, he risked removing Gary's small kitchen knife from under his boot, transferring it to a pocket inside his own work fleece. Saying nothing, he stood and turned slowly, blocking the gap between the crenellations where Gary had fallen. Carefully draining all emotion from his face, he locked gazes with the jewel thief and probable murderer.

"Ye can take his place," Scott growled.

On the storey below them, they could hear Poppy barking and snarling for all she was worth. Perhaps she knew, or sensed, that her master was in the direst of straits?

Despite being a former soldier, Floating George had no experience whatsoever with gun-toting criminals, or hostage situations – like Poppy, he felt like running around screaming himself – yet something told him to play for time. He could not help Gary, but there might be something he could do for his friends, or even to help the police. "How's that going to work for you?" he asked, tentatively. "If you throw any more of us over, even that genius, Sergeant Gripper, might suspect there's something amiss, bonnie lad."

They stared at each other in silence, each wondering what their next move should be when Worzel burst onto the roof. "What's happening?"

Scott instantly turned the gun on him, relaxing once he recognised his fellow lag. "Their boss man tried tae take ma weapon, so Ah showed him tha easy way doon!"

"He tried to grab the shooter?" Worzel repeated, slowly.

Floating George stole another glance over the battlements and closed his eyes tight shut against the trauma of what he saw.

Scott's lip curled into a sneer, and he took a step forward.

"What do you want me to say to them to explain this?" George deflected him. "Before those marksmen start shooting at us. That new bloke in charge down there seems about stable as, as... well, you!"

Scott thought quickly and placed his order.

Floating George sighed, leaning back over the battlements, deliberately looking away from where Gary had fallen. He cupped his hands. "Sir Henry just made a mistake. He's lucky to be alive. If that helicopter doesn't arrive in the next thirty minutes, his luck will run out."

"And the rest," Scott snarled.

George took another shuddering breath and called, "And divvent bother trying to get into the castle. The hostage will be..."

"Tell him!" Scott struck George in the kidneys with the pistol's barrel.

George grunted, stumbling against the battlements. "That'll look great on camera. Why don't you give me the gun, so I can wave it around to prove I'm in charge?"

"Dinnae push yer luck, Geordie. Tell him."

"If you try breaking into the castle, Sir Henry will be dead before you're even inside," George repeated accurately, if half-heartedly. Turning back to Scott, he asked, "Are you planning on waiting here, where they can pot shot us, or are we going back down?"

"He's right, Scott," Worzel agreed.

Scott glared distrustfully at the Geordie plumber and took another step forward to look over the castle wall.

George panicked, desperately trying to contrive a way to stall further, when he was saved by Worzel.

"Hammer said we should get back down ASAP. Doesn't trust that bunch of brickies not to go radio rental[1] ."

Scott stopped in his tracks. Deciding it would be best to remain hidden, he waved Worzel back through the roof door, and George after him. Closing it behind them, he marched them back down to the castle tea rooms. Hammer had a point. He was only one man with one gun. He could not be in all places at once, and that gave him an idea.

---

1. Cockney rhyming slang for 'mental'. How Radio Rentals' ownership received this boost to brand recognition is unclear.

"What *is* that buzzing?" Gary looked left and right from the mullioned windows at the centre of Rookstone's northern façade. Outside, the sky was brilliant blue. Crisp, noonday sunshine obliterated the shadows. He looked down at the driveway and the breath would have caught in his throat, had he been breathing.

Where myriad police vehicles had filled the driveway, just a split second ago in his personal timeline, there now stood a single car – a beautiful, highly polished, burgundy Bentley. Leaning against it was a man he recognised, who bore a marked resemblance to his current customer, Sir Henry Grey. However, that was not why he recognised the man. He had seen him in an old photograph from 1934, pasted into Sir Henry's family album.

Another man faced away from Gary, holding what he assumed was a camera. He could not catch their words, but the overall tone was of jovial banter between friends. A woman walked into view, approaching from the main castle entrance beneath him. She wore beautifully tailored clothing, also obviously from the 1930s, and would have been striking in any period.

"I say." Enthusiastic Geoff tugged on Gary's sleeve. "I was told not to linger, what? Something about not missing our window of opportunity – that sort of thing."

Gary tore himself away from the scene below with difficulty. It felt like walking onto the set of an old black and white movie, where everything was magicked into full colour and everyone still lived. The experience was thrilling, yet incredibly creepy.

The buzzing grew louder. "Where do we go from here?"

"This way, old chap." Geoffrey took Gary by the arm, and instantly, he was outside and retching ineffectually again.

They were in the lane that led away from the castle. Using nothing but willpower, Gary forced the stomach he was no longer connected to, to settle. "You can travel outside the castle?"

"Oh, *rather,* old man." The Honourable Geoffrey flashed a toothy smile. "Spend most of my time down in the *Stag's Head,* what?" He pulled a hip flask from his pocket. "Fancy a nip of gin, old chap?"

Gary was about to refuse when he realised that he really needed a drink after his recent experiences. He took the flask and, rather than a sense of relaxation, the alcohol brought him an extraordinary clarity – assuming it was alcohol. Whatever it was, his surroundings came into acute focus. He might actually have been there, he might not – he had no idea any more – but the one thing he was sure of was that he could no longer tell the difference.

The sun warmed his skin. He touched a hand to his face, feeling stubble. What had been in that drink? Nothing more than gin, his taste buds informed him, but how had they caught up? As far as he understood things, his real body was suspended, mid-fall, just over the edge of Rookstone's north tower.

All that flashed through his mind as the buzzing grew louder. He tilted his head to listen carefully. No. Not merely louder; it lowered in pitch, too. Or was it slowing down? He could not tell. There was something familiar about that groan, for it was no longer a buzz.

"This is our ride out of here, old chap."

Gary followed Geoffrey's gaze and his jaw dropped. Of *course* he recognised that sound. It was the sound of his own van, barrelling down the lane straight at him.

Geoff grabbed him by the arm again and he was immediately at the wheel. Driving towards himself, or rather towards where he had so recently been. He saw both himself and Geoff fade away like shadows in the sun.

"Woo hoo!" the spirit of the young man cried, exuberantly. "She goes like a witch!"

Each time one of the spirits shifted Gary through time and space, he felt profoundly nauseous, but the previous occasions were as nothing compared with the nausea he felt now. Whether it was because the van was moving when they 'landed', taking him from zero to fifty miles per hour in no seconds flat, or whether it was a cumulative effect of being literally spirited away through the continuum, he could not be sure. All he knew for certain was that he was sick of being toyed with and had lost all sense of humour. Angrily, he rode the horn while reaching out of the window to make a hand gesture towards Roger, the completely undeserving cameraman, as he went by.

Braking hard, he turned in through the gates to the castle grounds and drove up the rough, winding track to the D-shaped driveway in front of the castle. For the second time, he slammed the brakes on, his tyres cutting deep elevens into the gravel.

He turned to Geoff. "Now what?"

His guide was fiddling with his hip flask. "Er, just a tick, old man. I think it was something like this—"

'Without warning' is often overused as a narrative device. However, when Gary moved instantly from sitting in a parked vehicle to falling headfirst from the battlements of a castle, and no one told him it was about to happen, other phrases, though available, do not really cut it. Naturally, Gary screamed for his life – what little remained of it.

The view of the ground accelerating towards him came back to him exactly as he remembered it, just before Inga whipped him away to the year 1298. This time, he fully expected his *own* life to flash before his eyes. However, he was disappointed again. For once, in a good way.

The sash window to his own apartment flew open as a stiff breeze tugged at the full-length curtains from within, flinging them outside to hang, Rapunzel-style, down the castle wall. Instinctively, Gary grabbed for them – he would have grabbed for a spitting cobra at that point – and waited for the inevitable sounds of terminal tearing. About that, he was *not* disappointed. Several of the hooped curtain rings were stripped, bringing the rail down after them. Gary desperately pulled hand-over-hand as the fixings holding the curtain rail in place gave up. Feverishly, he tugged and leapt, just managing to get a hand to the windowsill. Releasing the curtains to fall, he slapped his other hand onto the base of the window frame and hung on, whimpering for his life. Unable to trust himself not to look down, he snapped his eyes tight shut as he tried to recall how to breathe. Fortunately, his hindbrain had little to do with his wants or fears and was way ahead of him. His lungs inflated with the life-giving oxygen his muscles would need to pull himself inside. His terrified consciousness had little to add in that regard, either. His feet kicked, all on their own, desperate for purchase so that he could scramble up the wall to eventually pull himself in through the window. Breathless, nauseous and scared out of his wits, his dexterity was slower to catch up and he banged his head on the sash. Losing his balance, he tipped backwards, arms flailing, and was just past the point of no return when a tug on his Saxon cross pulled him back, just to the right side of balance, so that he could grab the window frame once more.

Ducking this time, with exaggerated care, he pulled himself inside to collapse on the carpet, panting.

Poppy immediately leapt onto his chest, yapping and licking his face in a febrile panic of her own.

Gary's chest heaved as he tried to bring his body, and his nerves, back under control.

Once his breathing regained some measure of normality, Poppy hopped back up onto the sofa to wag her tail.

Gary's head thumped down on the carpet, exhaustion claiming him.

Living in the moment, and noting that his behaviour was no longer interesting, Poppy span around three times before dropping back into the depression made earlier in her new favourite cushion.

Still lying on his back, Gary lifted his head again, understandably put out. "Was that it? Bored now?"

Yap!

"Oh, *sorry.*"

Without Poppy pinning him to the carpet, he raised himself to his elbows. His Saxon cross was still suspended, taut on the end of its leather lace. His eyes crossed to look down at it, when he noticed something more – a hand. Barely visible on such a bright day, it was yet somehow luminous. Unable to help himself, he allowed his gaze to follow the hand up an arm to a shoulder, and eventually to a face, one he categorically *knew* belonged to someone who was dead.

He wailed – in a most unmanly fashion – although, before his breath was fully expended, that wail turned to a string of astonishingly coarse invective.

The floating apparition scowled down at him. Releasing the necklace to fall against his chest, she crossed her arms, shaking her head disapprovingly. Clearly visible, the nun's veil did little to disguise Sister Beatrice's thinly veiled annoyance, nor her holier-than-thou expression on a face that, after the last time he saw it, was the stuff of nightmares for Gary – or would be, assuming he ever slept again.

Also unsympathetic to his emotional outburst, Poppy growled with annoyance. Kicking her feet, she knocked another cushion onto the floor as she moved seamlessly from the 'I'm so glad to see you' to the 'how dare you leave me like that' phase of their reunion.

My Friend of Misery

The Interview: part VI, August 1994

In spite of himself, Brandon was on the edge of his seat as Gary explained his bizarre near-death experience. "So these ghosts—"

"Spirits," Gary corrected him.

"I'm sorry, these spirits took you on a journey through *time?*"

Gary blew out his cheeks. "I'm not sure I'll ever really understand what happened, but they saved my life. *That* you caught on camera, though all you saw was me falling and scrambling through a window that miraculously flew open at exactly the right moment."

The interviewer sat back, slightly embarrassed that he had become so rapt. "But of course, we can never really know *what* you saw…" It was a weak half-question, and Brandon knew it. However, he was also aware that he must tread the fine line between credibility, for those who thought the whole story nonsense, and keeping the people who wanted to believe onside.

Gary shrugged. "There was no one in the room but my little dog. That's provable from the witness statements of everyone in the castle at that time. All our movements are easy to corroborate. You're surely not suggesting a terrier could unlatch and throw open a heavy sash window, are you?"

"Well, I... erm."

Enjoying the smarmy interviewer's floundering for a moment, Gary decided to throw him a bone. "I understand your scepticism, but I swear to you, that were it not for the dead, *I* would not be alive – and let me tell you, my day was far from over..."

09:15 Monday, May 9th, 1994

Jimmy leapt at Scott. Fortunately, Willy Mammoth and Floating George grabbed him and pulled him back before the gunman felt compelled to fire. Jimmy screamed and raged at the man so casually announcing the death of his brother.

"Calm down," George insisted. He winked, so that only Jimmy saw. "Getting shot won't help Gaz." He winked again and nodded, gently.

Unsure what he was being told, Jimmy finally decided to err on the side of self-preservation and stopped struggling. His chest heaved, his every instinct telling him to tear the murderer limb from limb, but George was right; he had to wait.

"You!" Scott pointed to Jerry. "What's yer name again?"

"Jeremy. Jeremy Horatio Jarvis."

"Right. Come with me."

Hammer stood. "What are you doing?"

"Splitting tha herd. Ah'm locking this one up for safekeeping. So, if any of yous try any more tricks, he willnae be coming back. Got it?"

Jimmy's glare was pure hatred, but he nodded acquiescence for Jerry's sake.

The young man looked back in alarm.

"It'll be OK, lad," Jimmy assured him, though he had no idea if that were true.

Albert sneaked into the outer courtyard, slipping under the police crime scene tape that now sealed off the area. Keeping to the wall, he made his way past the builders' skip and remaining van to the sallyport-cum-tradesman's entrance. Despite giving a key to Constable Charlton, he still retained a second copy for himself. Inserting it slowly and quietly, he gently turned it in the lock. The door was still barred from within. With all the strength of a young man, the policeman had been unable to budge it earlier.

Albert raised his eyes to the heavens and uttered a silent prayer. With a quick shove, he managed to nudge the door open, just a few millimetres. The *clonk* of a baulk of timber falling to the quarry tiled floor inside brought a smile to his face.

He knew one of Rookstone's many past residents had indeed been listening to his conversation with the constable. Over his many years working at Rookstone, Albert had developed a feeling for them. The ghosts never showed themselves to him, though he sensed that was more about wishing to avoid frightening him than anything else – perhaps they even considered it crass – but he knew they were there, and they knew he was there. It was a relationship that worked well. The door slid open the rest of the way with ease.

Scott pushed Jerry outside into the courtyard, shoving him once more towards the north tower. When he climbed to the roof earlier, he noted a sign – obviously for the benefit of tourists – to the dungeon. It was conspicuously nowhere near the faux torture chamber, also set up for the tourists. Reasoning that a dungeon would make a perfect holding cell for one of the builders, he climbed a half twist up the spiral stair, exiting left into a high-ceilinged room with a stone fireplace at its southern end. Set into the wall, opposite the entrance, was a small doorway. He shoved Jerry for a third time, banging the young man's head on the low lintel. Jerry did not complain. As far as Scott could tell, he was too scared.

A narrow passageway turned left into darkness. Scott searched for a light switch. He threw the switch to illuminate a small antechamber with a vaulted stone roof. The low-wattage bulb buzzed and flickered as the two men squeezed themselves in. At the end of the chamber was an ironbound oak door. Scott's lip turned up into an approximation of a smile. "Open it!"

Jerry did as instructed. The room beyond was tiny, a stone box barely long enough for a man to lie down on the cold, uneven floor, and set into that floor was a hatch, sealed with a wrought iron grill.

Lit for gloomy effect, the oubliette cut from the living rock beneath them also had a flickering bulb, a 20th century device just bright enough to illuminate what an awful place would have awaited any whom Rookstone's lord wished to forget. No one had died in that stone tomb for hundreds of years, though the atmosphere, even high above in the holding cell, had lost none of its potency. It was a place of suffering and death, of starvation and torment, of terror and darkness; it was a monument to man's capacity for evil literally carved into stone.

Scott could see a heavy lock preventing the grill in the floor from being opened. Mildly disappointed, he noted, airily, "Looks like yer lucky day. Ye get to stay in the penthouse above." He laughed, a sickly, vile sound that bounced around the stone vault.

Jerry was shaking. "Y-you're going to lock me in here on m-my own?"

"*Now* ye're gettin' it." Scott grinned again, stepping backwards out through the low, narrow door. He slammed it shut, barring it from the outside.

Jerry leapt for the door, beating on it. "Don't switch the light off, *please!*"

Scott chuckled. "Do ye know, Ah hadnae considered that. Thanks for tha idea." He switched off the light and walked away, leaving the prisoner screaming and beating on a completely immovable iron-strapped door.

Realising he was wasting his time and only hurting himself, Jerry eventually turned and leaned against it, sliding down to the floor to sit on his haunches with his knees tight to his chin. He could hear the thumps of the Scotsman's footfalls across the wooden floor of the fireplace room as he walked away, chuckling to himself. After a dozen steps, the footfalls ended but the sickly laughter remained.

Jerry wondered what his jailor was up to when he realised that Scott had left, and still the horrible laughter remained. Partway between a choking cough and a snarl, it had no place in the light. If it could be considered mirth, then it was twisted and demonic, and belonged only in dark, damp chambers of terror. Jerry covered his head and screamed.

Gary almost bumped into Scott and Jerry as he came down the stairs. Beating a hasty retreat as silently as possible, he waited two floors up, listening hard. In the silence of the stone tower, he could hear nothing from outside the castle, but did hear the scrape of a heavy door from within – followed by cries of fear and alarm.

Every instinct urged Gary to run down the spiral stairs to help young Jerry, but sense told him that if he did, the Scotsman would have no compunction about shooting him. After all, he had already tried to murder him once. Gary shook his head. His surprise resurrection might buy him a split second, no more. He could not risk himself on such a foolhardy attempt – his men needed him, and so did his wife. He could hardly imagine what she must be going through. With all the press outside, his tumble from the tower was probably viewed on half the television sets around Britain – and about to hit the other half on *News at One*. He might even be a celebrity across the globe by now.

It is often said that there is no such thing as bad press, but being thrown to one's death from the tower of a medieval castle would certainly have rendered any potential profit from the exposure – like himself – short-lived. He had been outrageously lucky – a multiple Pools[1] winner with just one dive, and he loved to play the Pools. Although 'it could be you' was yet to become a catchphrase in Britain, it certainly applied, for added to his survival of almost certain death, he had also left a winning Pools coupon behind on his kitchen table in Worcestershire. One that, given their recent trials, Emma had completely forgotten to pass on to the Pools man who collected them – sure evidence that,

---

1. A mixed metaphor, for as well as the wet kind, the Pools was also a popular weekly game allowing participants to place bets on football results. It declined after the introduction to Britain of the National Lottery in November 1994.

while it's rare to get what we want, we tend to get what we need. Of course, had he known, Gary would still have been furious, because, having got what he needed, he would have already taken it for granted and forgotten how lucky he was to be alive to get angry about not getting what he wanted.

Blissfully unaware of that conundrum, he listened for sounds of the Scotsman leaving. He did not have to wait long. Making his way back down the spiral stair, he slipped past Rookstone's strongroom and tiny dungeon. Jerry's shouting and banging continued after the gunman left, so Gary assumed he was alive and well, at least for the moment.

Cautiously, he looked out into the courtyard.

All was still.

He hesitated. Chewing his lip in nervous fury, he raged about all that had happened and was still happening to him and his team. Torn between a strong desire to release the obviously traumatised young man, and a wish to stay off the gunman's radar, he mulled over his options.

Though it might cause his people, and especially his brother, great pain, there were advantages to letting everyone believe he was gone – he was unaware that Floating George had seen him disappear inside the window one storey down. Taking a deep breath, he forced himself to calm down and to think clearly. Anger was good – it meant he was alive – but if he let his anger rule him, that might change.

After a few deep breaths, he decided that he would stand a better chance of moving around the castle undetected if he were alone – assuming he *was* alone. The shade of Sister Beatrice made it quite clear that she would be keeping her eye on him. In his younger days, he had known another Beatrice, who enjoyed reminding him that her name meant 'bringer of joy'. Highly debatable in both cases, as far as Gary was concerned, but as he still enjoyed life, he was happy to go with it for now. Apparently, she almost never left Rookstone's chapel. Having met her, he could see why the other spirits avoided the place. Leaving her sanctuary certainly seemed to have made her cross, even though it was to save his life. Poor gratitude after he offered her whatever strength *he* possessed at the moment of her violent passing. It seemed her love of God left little room for anyone else – was that what passed for the purest of souls? Still, she had not let him down when it really mattered. Fluttering those curtains out of the window, just as he fell to his own violent passing, saved his life. He shuddered at the recent memory. *Why always castles, abbeys and haunted mansions? Can't someone, just once, hire us to renovate an old Butlins, or a pier in a bustling seaside town, instead?* The mouthwatering smells of fish and chips, and even candyfloss, trumped damp and decay, any time, but then he reconsidered. *Hmm, but they also have clowns, don't they? And worse... karaoke.* He shuddered again. He was a fan of neither. There was also Poppy to consider, still sleeping in his suite high above when he left, snuggled up on her warm cushion. Between capering clowns and fast-food stalls, she would be unbearable.

He kneaded his brow. His mind was drifting. Exhausted and stressed beyond breaking point, he had barely slept in days – days that were, coincidentally, the worst of his entire life. *Come on, Gaz, focus!* He still had to work through the clues his trip through time had provided. After dressing him down, Sister Beatrice gave him another clue as to how he might potentially turn their situation around. He was no gangster, nor did he have any expertise in understanding the criminal mind. He was a builder, and that gave him power, for Gary was of the class who created the environments in which those others chased one another around. Often dangerous, *his* job was to bring safety and shelter to his fellow man. When working away, he always packed a book for bedtime and his current situation brought to mind Conan Doyle's *The Speckled Band,* where Holmes remarks that there are few more dangerous than a doctor who turns their mind to evil. Wearily but determined, he smiled. *What about a builder who has just about had e-bloody-nough, Sherlock?*

He made the decision to come back later for Jerry and moved quickly out into the courtyard. Taking strength from the brief kiss of bright sunshine on his face, he stooped to pass quickly under the windows of the tearoom where his men were currently held, to disappear back into the shadows beneath the arches spanning the courtyard's southern elevation. Passing behind the central stone staircase that led up to the great hall, he approached a couple of old carts parked against the wall, out of the weather.

One of them was missing a wheel. Gary noticed it on his first walk about the castle, in the way that he usually noticed things that needed fixing – it was in his DNA. The absent wheel revealed the axle, attached to the vehicle's body via a single-leaf, steel cart spring. It was held in place by a spindle at each end, fixed with a nut. One was missing, the other was beyond finger-tightness. He cursed under his breath, casting about for inspiration. He found it. Within the bed of the second cart were some mild steel straps. Quietly, carefully, he took two of them.

Placing one strap each side of the remaining nut, he married them to opposing flat sides of the small, hexagonal fixing. Pressing them as hard as he could together, he twisted anticlockwise.

Nothing.

Taking a deep breath, he applied every joule of energy his tired muscles could muster and twisted again. This time, the rusty nut gave. It was no easy task to remove it, for the entire thread was also rusted, but Gary was determined and eventually the nut fell to the floor.

With no time to enjoy his triumph, he took the steel leaf-spring and disappeared into the mock torture chamber set up years ago by Sir Henry to delight and horrify the tourists. Although *it* was not real, most of the horrific objects within it were. Following the train of his earlier thoughts, the spectacle on display showed just what evils might be imagined by an inventive man competent with tools. He passed an iron maiden[2], a headsman's block[3], a rack – no torture

---

2. A hinged, man-shaped box with long spikes fixed to the inner face of its door that, were they able to get away, would make anyone 'Run to the Hills'.

3. The axe head that was usually buried in the block still rested on the floor outside Richard's apartment, after being thrown down the stairs by unseen hands.

chamber should be without one – and a chair with iron spikes in place of a cushion, with manacles on the arms designed to hold a person in place and kill them by inches, as they weakened and eventually sat to bleed out. The entire chamber was filled with devices of evil genius, and just as Gary was about to leave, he noticed a particularly gruesome barrel with hundreds of rusty, wrought iron nails protruding from its inner face. He imagined being bundled into that barrel, for it was very specifically man-sized, and rolled down a hill for the entertainment of the castle torturer. He shook his head, easily envisaging the man currently holding his team at gunpoint as a throwback to such a creature. He passed it by and slipped silently down to the cellar where they had so recently – and yet, so long ago, it seemed – laid a new concrete floor.

Jerry's eyes snapped open – pointless, for the room was blacker than an executioner's mask – but though he could see nothing, he could *hear*. Within his tiny chamber, there was nowhere to hide or even to evade as he heard the scraping grow steadily closer. Each scrape was followed by a heavy step, like someone was dragging a useless leg behind them. Jerry also heard harsh, rasping breaths. He jumped to his feet, but what could he do?

"Wh-who's there?" he asked, voice faltering as he reached out, waving his arms before him. Senses stretching to their limits to compensate for his lack of sight, he nevertheless felt nothing. "Who's there, I say?" he called again, forcing strength into his words.

The scraping-dragging drew up right before him. Still, he could feel nothing with his flailing arms. But for his own, all susurration of movement ceased. Jerry stood stock still, his heart beating so hard that all he could hear was blood rushing in his ears, until the choking cackle struck up again.

Jerry jumped back against the locked door. It was a distance of mere inches, and he barely even registered the pain when his head struck the stone lintel above. His focus and stress levels were so heightened that he felt nothing but terror, could no longer even cry out. It was as though an invisible hand tightened around his throat, closing his airway. Scrabbling at his collar, he could feel no invisible hands, just a terror that was restricting his breath. He forced himself to calm, to breathe.

"I said who's there?" he demanded again. Anger helped, and he straightened, tensed to fight.

His blood continued to rush, loud as a waterfall, so loudly now, that he almost missed the low hiss that answered his question.

"*Drag... foot.*"

Almost driven insane with fear, Jerry tried to repeat what he had heard as his rational mind, barricading itself into a safe space within his head, demanded clarification. No words came, just an animal cry of terror from down in his gut.

Choking laughter.

Trapped within his stone sensory-deprivation capsule, Jerry swallowed hard, steeling himself to shout. "Who's there, damn you?"

"John Sage, Lieutenant to the Great Edward."

The words were so soft, so ethereal, that he barely caught them – would not have, had he been in an ordinary setting. His heightened state shunted Sage's words straight into the speech centres of his brain, where his terror worked an effects bank to really squeeze the most out of his imagination's budget. With mocking laughter, the shade added, *"And Rookstone's torturer – at your service."*

Jerry grabbed at his own hair, bringing his elbows in close to cover his face. "HELP!"

Gary moved as silently as possible past the entrance to the tea rooms, tiptoeing as delicately as his steel-capped boots would allow. He closed the door to the cellars behind him, wincing as the door ground against the gravel and dust left behind by many booted feet the previous week. He could not help marvelling at how quickly this situation had crept up on them. Just a few days ago, everything was in hand, Rookstone, just another project. Now they were being held at gunpoint inside a medieval castle, surrounded by police marksmen on the outside, all of whom believed Gary's team to be the villains. Added to that, three people had been very nearly murdered. As one of them, Gary was keen to bring their siege to an end as quickly as possible and by any means.

Barely having the time to appreciate, let alone get annoyed by the events ensnaring them, he stood alone in the dark, suddenly livid.

With the door closed, he risked turning on the lights. It was no longer pitch black in the cellar, but that was about all that could be said for the quality of the illumination. He would just have to do the best he could. With a sigh, he got to work.

A grin tugged at his lips as he collected the tools and materials he would need. He felt like a one-man A-Team, a MacGyver of sorts. Taking a short piece of four-by-two, about the length of a baseball bat[4], he took a narrow chisel from his toolbox and began to work the timber.

It was imperative that he labour as silently as possible – a tall order when using tools to construct anything. At any minute, the crazy man with the gun might burst in on him, so he tried to distract his mind while his hands carried out well-practised tasks.

Which member of the A-Team would I be? The certified insane man, who was probably the most intelligent among them? Probably not. I've no record of instability

---

4. Two-by-four in US reckoning, and not to be confused with two-by-two, which references a barge-like boat. Disclaimer: there may have been bats on board.

or criminality at all. Gary considered his recent conversations with people who were not there, before his thoughts strayed to the ring of armed police, currently laying siege to the castle outside. *Until now. OK, let's not go there, so what about the conman?* Really *not me. So, no again. The big guy who liked to turn people upside down and chuck them around? I like to think I'm fairly strong, but that's not my style at all. OK, what the about the lieutenant-colonel nominally in charge – the one that was* actually *crazy. Hmm, let me see… Nominally in charge. I choose, every day, to work with a bunch of drunken lunatics hundreds of miles from home and my wife, and when anything goes wrong, it's all on me.*

The most tired of all adages dragged its feet exhaustedly across his mind – 'you don't have to be mad to work here, but it helps'. He nodded to himself in the gloom. *Yep, just call me Hannibal and cue the music!*

The immensely sharp chisel made short work of the softwood without need of a hammer, and he soon had a six-inch-long slot cut into the top as he sighted down its length. The piece was *reasonably* straight – at least, over a short run. It paid to select the timber personally from builders' merchants. Unfortunately, Gary knew that was not always possible and consequently, whenever it was delivered direct, he got what he got – anywhere between perfect and something washed up on a beach – but at least he had wood[5] . Now he needed steel.

Returning to his toolbox, he retrieved the old-fashioned hand drill kept specifically for those occasions where a site was without power – quite often due to the unthinking antics of their electrician, Blackout Barnes. He selected a high-speed steel drill bit – not that he would be achieving any great speed with a hand drill. He simply needed its hardness to make two screw holes through the old cart spring.

'The music' must have been the extended prog-rock mix because, sadly – and without benefit of montage – Gary was forced to bear down onto the steel and keep turning the handwheel until the boring labour of boring was complete. Drilling two holes took roughly the amount of time it would have taken the real A-Team to build a Sherman tank from a cheese grater, a rubber glove and a bag of fertiliser, but eventually, he had them. Finding a box of woodscrews from the recently delivered building materials, he fixed the cart spring to the end of the length of four-by-two.

Now he was going from memory, and hoped he was right. Set into the doorframe at the entrance to the cellar, there was an old, wrought iron keep for a latch long removed. He noted it when their work began. Pleased to find he had remembered correctly, he closed a pair of plumber's grips around the hooked end of the keep and tugged. After much twisting, pulling and persuasion, it popped out of the ancient wooden frame.

Gary nodded, satisfied and doubly pleased that the stem inserted into the door frame was longer than expected.

Back to his toolbox.

---

5. *That* was neither a pun, nor appropriate to his predicament, and anyone drawing inference from it is entirely responsible for their own thoughts.

He picked up the drill for a second time and made a hole through the wrought iron keep at the centre of its length. The wrought iron was much softer than the steel spring, so he was soon able to place it within the slot cut into the timber. He marked halfway along its length and, retrieving his chisel, sloped the end of the slot downwards, towards the cart spring at the end of his new device. Considering for a moment, he reached for a steel rule and a Stanley knife, to cut a V-shaped slot along the centre-top of the timber, also down to the spring end.

Driving a screw through the side of the timber, he pinned the keep in place, allowing it to rock forwards around its fulcrum point, into the slot where it deepened.

Pleased with his work, Gary returned to his toolbox once more, this time taking out his builder's stringline. The string was very strong, but also inherently stretchy – not ideal, but it was what he had. Still in full A-Team mode, he would make it work.

He began by doubling and re-doubling the stringline until he held eight threads in his hands. After cutting them to the required length with his knife, he twisted them to create a single, extremely strong twine. Passing them through the loop at one end of the cart spring, where it was originally connected to the cart, he began twisting the cord again. Now sixteen-fold, he tied it strongly at the opposite end of the spring.

Gary now held in his hands a steel bow connected to a wooden stock. Time for ammunition. He cast around for inspiration. "Perfect."

Leaning against the wall, in the corner of the cellar, were several lengths of dowel cut longitudinally into quadrants. Gary bought them to use as a simple trim around the planned internal doors within Sir Henry's new strong room. *Who knows if that'll ever happen now,* he brooded. Grabbing all nine pieces, he set to work cutting them into eighteen-inch lengths. He filed the ends to remove any sharp edges but did not sharpen them. Tempting though that was, he was not a killer.

Once he had his 'bolts', he cut a heavy groove into one end of each.

Time to try out his new friend.

Squeezing down the latch keep with the palm of his hand as he held the stock, he prevented it from rocking freely in its slot and used his left hand to pull back the twine, hitching it onto the hook. He was impressed by how much effort that took, even with the inherent stretchiness of the stringline. Nocking one of his quarter-dowel bolts onto the latch hook, he slotted its ninety-degree corner into the V-cut he had made in the top of the stock.

He turned to face the stone wall of the cellar. "Right, punk, make my day." With that, he released his right-hand grip. The taut stringline instantly pulled the hook on the latch keep down into its slot, releasing the full power of the cart spring. The quarter-dowel shot out, hitting the wall with enough force to reduce itself to splinters.

Gary whistled softly, respectfully, as he considered the weapon in his hands, for that it surely was.

Gripper's eyes narrowed. He strode quickly to where the old man emerged from the outer courtyard. Albert saw him coming, affecting pantomime nonchalance. Unsurprisingly, it failed to deflect the police sergeant bearing down on him.

"Care to tell me what you were doing behind our cordoned-off area, sir?" Gripper queried in his characteristically passive-aggressive manner.

Albert looked around, hoping to catch the eye of Constable Charlton, but could not see him. Cursing inwardly, he tried the 'confused old man' approach.

That cut about as much ice with Gripper as the nonchalance.

Albert accepted defeat. "Oh, alright. I've found a way into the castle. One that I'm pretty sure the men inside won't realise we have."

"And just when were you going to inform us of this? In fact, why didn't you tell us when you were questioned earlier?"

"The door was barred then. Young Josh Charlton tried it."

Gripper stared intently down at Albert. "I know about PC Charlton's attempt to open the back door. It was locked. You're telling me it's now open?"

Albert shrugged. "In a way."

"And I'm supposed to believe you had nothing to do with this?"

"Not me. I just talked about it with Josh and..."

Gripper leaned in closely. "And?"

"Someone must have been listening," Albert admitted, weakly.

"I *see*."

Albert doubted whether he did, but kept his real suspicions to himself. "Look, Constable—"

Gripper soured still further. "*Sergeant.*"

"Aye. Well, as I was saying, that door wasn't open before, but it is now. Maybe someone inside drew the bar away?"

The policeman considered that. "Perhaps, but it changes nothing. If we go in, the chances are, those ruffians might shoot Sir Henry and that would ruin everything."

Albert looked up at him, squinting into the noonday sun. "That's very compassionate of you."

Gripper was unsure how to take that, but suspected he might have given something away. "Just doing my job, sir."

"Aye. So when are you going to?"

"Going to what?"

"Do your job. That door's open, but it might not stay open."

"We must show caution."

"Aye, I thought you'd say that, an' all."

"Did you see the way that Gary Stone fell, and managed to save himself? We're clearly dealing with a highly trained, quick-witted and dangerous scoundrel. Probably a criminal genius."

"Erm..." The flare of inspiration Sister Beatrice lit in Gary had gone out. Added to that, the force of his homemade crossbow frightened him. "Erm..." he repeated, not knowing what to do next. In his moment of doubt, he found that he was also missing Inga's equally disapproving presence. Failing that, he would have welcomed Sir Edward, or even Enthusiastic Geoffrey's company at that point.

It occurred to him that maybe they *were* there, but his back-in-body experience was preventing him from sensing them. Dealing with the spirits was becoming frustrating. He must rely on himself and his own wits. "Erm..."

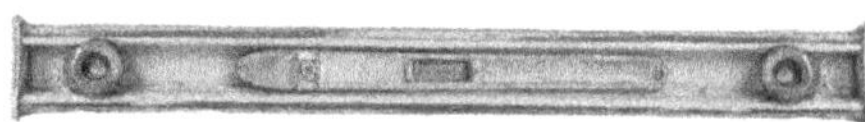

The spirits were governed by a very specific set of rules. Although some, like Inga, dallied optimistically with the notion that they might be guidelines, that was unwise, for those who made the rules came down hard on any unwilling to abide by them. Therefore, only two spirits within Rookstone remained relatively free to interfere with the living, and to understand why, we must return – on Earth, at least – to AD1540.

When Sister Beatrice achieved her life's dream and died, she naturally took the express elevator to Heaven, reserved only for the purest of heart. Upon her arrival, Saint Peter simply waved her through with a smile and a cheery 'have a nice day'. Any irony was unintentional. Heaven being timeless, all dates naturally defaulted to *Aeternum Domini,* rendering all chronological references metaphysically metaphorical. Of more importance to Beatrice, however, was that he barely glanced at the meagre pamphlet listing her sins before stamping it 'APPROVED'.

Beatrice knelt dutifully to kiss his hand, when she caught sight of a man heading the long line of people all waiting to step off the *escalator* to Heaven. Hardly visible behind his porter's trolley, overloaded as it was with boxes of files, the man was followed onto *nubes firma* by several angelic beings – all complaining about having to push the rest of his paperwork, for it appeared that *his* sins were more than one man alone could bear.

Saint Peter rolled his eyes and sighed, thinking of his backlog. On his beautifully carved, white marble desk sat a vintage candlestick telephone in pearly white. Holding the earpiece to his ear, he rattled the cradle and lifted the microphone to his mouth. "Hello? Hello, it's Pete at Gate One."

He heard whoever picked up at the other end call out, in a harsh whisper, "*It's the gaffer! Quick, do something – look busy!*"

Saint Peter rolled his eyes again. "I can't tell you how much your selfless service and attentiveness means to me. Look, we're experiencing delays again, I'm afraid, chaps. I think we might have another politician trying to get in, so we'd better open the *stairway* to Heaven as well, to relieve the bottleneck... Er, excuse me a second, would you?" He leaned in close to one of his angelic aides, who whispered into his other ear. "Really? An accountant? A bean counter, carrying all that lot? Who did he work for, Al Capone?" More whispering. "*Oh,* a senior government *official?* Good grief, this could take forever, and we don't have... well, actually, we do have forever, but that's beside the point. Heaven is meant to be a reward, not more of the same. Oh, alright, thank you."

He pulled the body of the telephone away from his chest with a sigh, lifting it back to his mouth. "Hello again. Sorry about that. Did you hear? I know, I know. I don't know why they keep sending them up here. I keep telling them, but... What? No. We'll have to check it, and check it all. If *they* think they're worthy, then *we* have to check. Dem's de rules... Hmm? Are you kidding? Send him away? With all the crooked lawyers they have downstairs? He'll be back up here on appeal before we've even filed his paperwork. Sorry, you'll have to excuse me again..."

The aide returned to Saint Peter's side. "We've had to stop the escalator, sir. We're already getting complaints from the bottom."

Saint Peter shrugged. "Well, they're dead, aren't they? They're not going anywhere. They'll just have to wait, like the rest of us."

He lifted the telephone once more. "Sorry. Back again— What? No, no, no. Will you just open the stairway, please? These lot will be needing the *ladder* to Heaven if you people don't shape yourselves up down there, and then where shall we be? Handing out ropes? Telling them to climb a tall tree? What? Of course I mean the stairway to Heaven, what else? Yes, I'm sure. Just do it, will you? I *am* in charge, you know. The big guy did make me Pope – the first one, I might add! Say again? I don't care if you were saving it for Led Zeppelin, most of them are still down there, and we need it now – and while we're on that subject, it's 'glisters', by the way, not 'glitters'. So when their time comes, they can just jolly well ride the elevator like everyone else!"

He slammed the earpiece back on its hook, replacing the telephone on his desk. "It's about time someone cleared that up! As for hogging resources like that... honestly, the amount those chaps have smoked, they'll probably float up here on their own." Remembering Beatrice, he raised her to stand, blessed her and shoved her inside before trolley man ran her over.

Stumbling into Heaven, she could not help noting that seeing was not the same as believing. Although Heaven was beautiful – breathtaking, in fact – it was also impossibly old, and with great age comes a certain sense of ease and comfort. Indeed, some say that is great age's greatest perk.

It fell short of Beatrice's expectations. Soon, everyone else in Heaven noticed that every frayed, comfy armchair, every peel of time-honoured paint, every bum note in the choir of angels was being *logged.*

Soon after that, a top-level meeting was called. The problem they had was, as a genuinely pure soul, the Wrath could not simply cast her down – at least, not all the way down. That would have been against the rules they enforced on everyone else, and unfortunately for the powers of creation, pretending to exist by their own laws while secretly doing whatever they wanted, or could get away with, was out of the question. They were not allowed to run corrupt government. There was no point them making protestations of innocence, either. *They* could not blame it on *them,* because *they* would know – *they* were *them* and consequently would know that *they* had broken their own rules and were trying to blame it on *them,* and, like a self-fulfilling prophecy, *they* would be forced to punish *them,* too.

Pointing out the failings among those not living up to the advertising was Beatrice's only crime, but it was a big one – the crime of noticing. A crime that no regime would tolerate. That, coupled with the need to report it. All of it.

Their problem was 'the rules'. She drove them to distraction, but whichever way they looked at it, she was genuinely pure of heart. Angelic Resources were at a loss. Fortunately, after receiving a particularly savage three-hundred-million-page review on his shortcomings, the head of maintenance piped up with the suggestion to give Sister Beatrice a second chance to fix things... down in the world.

Clutching at his suggestion with both wings, the head of AR grabbed the nettle, the bull by the horns and the sharp end all at once, by delegating someone else to send Beatrice back. Her secretary sighed and began the long walk.

Every action has an equal and opposite reaction – as does every*thing*. The concept of Heaven and Hell is overly simplistic, and so we return to Earth and AD1994 and to the other soul, free to wander Rookstone Castle, interfering where he liked.

John Sage, possibly one of the evillest torturers in British history, was not so much kicked out of Hell, they just did not care whether he was in or out. *They* never had much use for the rules, which explains why evil always has such free rein. It was not like Sage was in any danger of being dragged *upstairs,* so he retained autonomy. Only the other spirits kept him in check. It took a group effort, too, restrained as they were by the rules.

Jerry would have doubtless found Rookstone's localised theocracy fascinating, had he been in possession of his faculties. Terror drove him deep within himself, the dragging and the voices in the dark enough to break any living soul trapped alone in such a place. Thoughts completely scattered, his heart beat and his lungs breathed, keeping him alive – lucky for him, while John Sage was up to his old tricks.

In life, Sage the monster delighted in choking the life from his victims – those who survived his other 'games'. His disgusting rapture as life left the body of his victims was recorded in Rookstone's histories.

Fortunately for Jerry, Sage's black spirit was less potent than the man in life, and his youthful body was able to keep itself alive, despite his conscious mind's almost total surrender to terror.

The darkness gave way to the flicker of firelight from a brazier. Jerry could feel no heat from it, but he saw everything. A vaulted chamber filled with unspeakable things; monstrous creations designed by twisted minds to cause harm in hideous ways, there was nothing so honourable or straightforward as a weapon.

He was no longer in the small dungeon chamber, nor was he in the fake torture chamber. He was transported somewhere else, somewhere fouler than either, yet somehow, he knew he was still within Rookstone, in a buried place no one ever saw. The stone flagged floor sloped, adding to his confusion and disorientation.

The scene before him seemed to blur and skip. He tried to retch but could not. Blinking to clear his vision, he became aware of a subterranean space gradually filling up with the lost and the damned – two very specific camps – and then he saw *him*. John Sage, Rookstone's torturer. He blinked again, hoping to remove the sight before his eyes – even a return to the terrible darkness would have been preferable. However, this was no vision, no rerun nor memory, for Sage looked directly at him, grinning a broken-toothed sneer.

Jerry's privileged background had afforded him the very best education at the very best boarding schools, where he had benefited from the very highest calibre of bullying from the absolute cream of the world's richest progeny. He had seen the face, and often the faces, of evil every day, and again every night in his dorm. It was his own Hell, the place of torment that haunted his dreams and probably always would. He now had something to replace it, for never could he have imagined anything like what he saw at that moment – though he had little doubt some of his school chums might well have graduated along those lines. Despite the beatings, despite the burnings, despite the shaming, Jerry never turned, never became like them. His tormentors believed him weak, as did his father. He was about to find out if they were right.

The hellish vision was all around the young man, though his other senses registered nothing.

Sage stepped towards the brazier, dragging a useless leg behind him. Jerry wondered whether the limb had been ruined in war. Perhaps an injury that destroyed the promising young lieutenant's military career, twisting his mind as well as his leg and sending him down the darkest path imaginable. He was clearly insane.

The torturer wrapped the end of an iron poker with a filthy rag and lifted it from the flames. He spat on its glowing end. It hissed. He turned to Jerry, ignoring the screaming souls around him, some of them children, and grinned again.

"We all have a totem, boy. Usually something we loved." Sage's rasping laugh soon cracked into a hacking cough. "This is mine. We did so much work together."

He approached Jerry, dragging his leg, still chuckling and hacking. "Let me introduce you."

When Gary drank from Enthusiastic George's hip flask, the past become a tangible place of tactile experience, a place of touch and taste and feeling.

When Sage touched the red-hot poker to Jerry's arm the flesh burned, and he screamed. White hot as the pain itself, everything around him was thrown into the sharpest focus. The stench of John Sage, of years of baked-in sweat; the cooked-meat smell of his own flesh; the sharp stink of urine and faeces from the dead and the dying; the iron smell of blood, so much blood. Even the damp cold of the stone floor striking up into his bones. He was there, actually within the demon's lair with England's vilest torturer and there was no escape.

Lost in the darkness of his own soul, Jerry shouted not for, but at, his father. So many nights' sleep had he lost to their endless arguments replayed over and over. His arm was numb after the burning, but in all other respects his experience was still acute, every sense overloading his mind with information he could not use, driving him further into his terror. Yet still his father's face was before him, berating him for his weakness when he closed his eyes against the savagery and evil all around him.

His head lolled to the side and was slapped savagely awake by Sage, but it was not Sage – at least, it was not Sage's face, but that of Sir Kenneth Hornesby Jarvis, his father.

On the periphery of his senses, Jerry could feel something wet seeping through his clothes. The reek of blood and effluent was overpowering, and he tried to retch again, still unable to do so. The blood, and worse, ran down the sloping floor to the drain near where he sat. He was soaked in it.

His father continued to yell furiously in his face, taking the torturer's place. Jerry tried to look away, but was slapped again. Weirdly, despite the iron discipline with which Jerry had been raised, his father had never hit him.

He stared, unable to speak or even think. "Don't let me down!" Sage bellowed, or was it his father? Jerry could no longer tell. "Man up! What the hell is wrong with you?" *That* sounded like his father.

With everything he was going through, how could his father betray him so completely? They had never understood each other, never gotten along, but this was too far. Could his father not comfort him, just this once? He was dying.

With a shock, Jerry realised he *was* dying, and yet still his father bawled into his face, spittle flying in his fury. "Get... on... your... feet, damn you!"

His spirit broken, Jerry was close to giving up when a surge of anger ran through his veins like molten lava. "I'll never be like you!" he bellowed back. Forcing himself to his feet, he felt angrier than at any time in his life.

His father backed away... smiling. The cruel, vindictive swine was actually smiling, and then Sir Kenneth was gone, replaced once more by Sage, who was not smiling. He looked afraid.

Jerry realised his anger was keeping him alive, forcing his heart to beat strongly, so he released it with a roar of defiance. Grudgingly, he began to understand his father's point; there *were* times when you had to fight, and rather than turn away from the task his father set him, he should own it. That only through that crucible would he emerge his own man.

He sought the position with For Keeps Ltd to escape his father, despite it being Sir Kenneth's idea, and now he felt like he was floating above himself, looking down at a terrified boy.

His father wanted him to be a man. What he meant by that was something about which they would never agree, or had Jerry merely misunderstood? Perhaps there was nothing hard and fast about it?

A recent memory flashed through his mind, one of him spinning around on a cement mixer, howling for help, while stupidly hanging on to his shovel. When he finally fell, it had hurt like hell and he was ribbed mercilessly by new workmates for his stupidity, but there was no malice in their treatment of him – no sympathy, either. When he got back up, taking their insults with good grace, he had felt his spirit increase in size, rather than diminish, because he *had* got back up, despite the obvious pain he was feeling. Young men's rituals often begin with an act of stupidity; it was how the fool coped with the aftermath that counted. Whether it was a moment of shame or a proud anecdote to be shared and reflected upon for the rest of his life was up to him. He had taken the first step towards earning their respect at that moment, while they, in turn, made their opening offer for acceptance. Jerry knew he was better for it. For the first time in his life, he felt he had friends – people who might just help him if he needed them. His was such a lonely childhood that it had taken him a while to realise that they only insulted him because they liked him. Only men who dislike each other remain courteous and *en garde.* Perhaps his father berated him so because he understood that the only way Jerry would ever be accepted was by falling flat on his face and getting back up again – preferably while bringing wild hilarity to his peers. It was the glue of men, a necessary irony that so many of their fondest memories cost them dearly at the time.

Jerry had no intention of following in his father's footsteps, but then, maybe he did not need to. Nor did he have to believe all that his father believed to learn from the man. He had grown up on military stories. They all sounded so horrid to him as a child. Only now was he beginning to gain a glimmer of understanding. On impulse, he decided to complete this one task for his father – perhaps that was all Sir Kenneth Hornesby Jarvis ever really wanted?

Jerry stood in the darkness. He stood straight, staring ahead at nothingness, the horrifying screams fading around him, as did that chamber of suffering and death. He was in the darkness once more, but not alone. He could still hear the wretched Sage, dragging his leg and cursing, using all his might to frighten him, wanting his death. His dank, sickly presence prickled Jerry's skin. Despite his fears and the foulness of his situation, the young man took a deep breath, filling his lungs and balling his fists. He had made the decision to stand alone in that place and there would be no argument. "Go!" he commanded.

Sage was gone. Instantly.

Exhaling deeply, he relaxed against the door – only to find himself on the uneven stone floor of the antechamber outside, blinking up into the face of his new boss.

Gary held onto the now-open door with one hand, reaching out with the other to pull Jerry back to his feet. "*Jeeves?* What you doing down there?"

Jerry snorted. Yes, he had been accepted. A friend *had* come to help him. He would not say that his father was always right, but there were benefits to being a man over running and hiding, even when it cost him. He would carry out his father's wishes this time, completing the task Sir Kenneth had set for him. He would do his duty and then go his own way.

"What happened to your arm? You OK?"

Jerry glanced at the burn left by John Sage's red-hot poker, his own totem to a rite of passage. Reaching up, he accepted the older man's hand. "Thank you, Gary. It's nothing, and yes, I'm OK now."

Gary assessed the young man with concern, giving him a once over. "Good, because I need your help."

Jerry straightened, looking him squarely in the eye. "Then, you shall have it."

Chapter 17

Always the Son

12:00 Monday, May 9th, 1994

Aleksander Kaminski was young, still in his teens, and he was afraid. The older men were also subdued and anxious, most believing Gary to be lost over the side of the tower. Just before that crisis shattered what remained of their morale, Gary and Hammer retrieved all the food they purchased from their rooms. Thoughts of sandwiches distracted them for a while, but soon led to another argument.

Nominally in charge of the builders in his brother's absence, Jimmy called Hammer out on his division of resources. "Look, if you want to use hostages to get out of here, then those hostages need to be alive."

Blocking the kitchen door, Hammer glared at him. "Even I know it takes weeks to starve, so what's your point?"

"My *point* is, you haven't seen those lot when they're hungry. They haven't eaten since yesterday, don't forget. Shock is keeping them quiet for the moment, but if you steal most of the food for yourselves, it'll only be a matter of time before one of those nutters loses it, and if your crazy Scotsman starts shooting people, *you* will never see the sun again – none of you!"

Hammer considered. "Half a sarnie each, to keep them going, the rest in the fridge – got it?"

Jimmy nodded and reached for a kitchen knife.

"Oh, no you don't, sunbeam. *I'll* do that."

"Alright, you be mother then – whatever – and wash your damned hands first!"

Willy Mammoth swallowed his half-sandwich in two bites. "Is that it?" he asked, with his mouth full. "I'm starving!"

"Me too," Aleks seconded.

"Course you are," Worzel agreed, his own mouth full. "You're a growing lad."

"And if ye want tae grow any further, keep yer mouth shut!" Scott snapped.

"I only said I was hungry," Aleks grumbled.

"Right, you're it. Come on."

The teenager's heart leapt. "What do you mean?"

"I mean it's time to talk to the pollis." He dragged the young man to his feet. Holding the gun to Aleks' back, he nodded to Floating George. "*You.* Ye're up, tae. Let's go."

The plumber sagged, swallowing his half-sandwich with difficulty past the nervous lump in his throat.

With perfect timing, a helicopter flew over the castle, hovering directly above the centre courtyard. Scott smiled with satisfaction. "Tha head pig's learning."

Jimmy chanced a look out of the window, wondering if that were true. He still had no idea what had happened to his brother. All his hopes were pinned on Floating George's strange demeanour when they returned from the roof. The plumber got along well with Gary; he would have expected him to behave like a man stricken with grief, but he had not. Jimmy wished he knew what Floating George's meaningful look actually meant.

Scott shoved Aleks and Floating George out of the room. Before following them, he turned to remind the builders that he still had Jerry locked away in the dungeon. "So if ye play up, ye'll never see him again."

As the door slammed behind them, Jimmy gave Hammer his own meaningful look. "How long are you going to let this go on?"

"What's that?" Jerry asked, wide-eyed.

"Oh, just something I knocked together," Gary replied nonchalantly.

"Is it a crossbow?"

Gary scratched his head, thoughtfully. "Sort of. I didn't have time to shape the stock or give it a sophisticated trigger mechanism, but it works. Maybe a little too well."

Jerry was impressed. "But how did you...? Never mind. Gary, I need something from my room."

Gary misunderstood. "If you're hungry, you're too late. I already collected our supplies and took them down to the café's kitchen."

"No, it's not that. Come with me and I'll explain."

Again, Gary almost walked into Scott and his hostages and was forced to push Jerry back into the room that led to the dungeons, placing a finger on his own lips.

Jerry nodded understanding, as Scott, Floating George and Aleks stomped up the spiral stairs, presumably on their way back to the roof for another powwow with the police. Gary was tempted to use his homemade weapon there and then. Stealing a glance around the doorframe as the three men continued up the steps, he saw Scott bringing up the rear with his gun pointed at Aleks' back. He closed his eyes, cursing inwardly. He had always ironically told Jimmy, and their sister, Kim, that they would be the death of him. Now he suspected that dubious honour might fall to his nephew, Kim's son. *Damn, damn, damn!* There was no way he could risk firing when Aleks himself was held at gunpoint by possibly the twitchiest man he had ever met. He shook his head, angrily. *Imagine explaining that when I get home!*

Nothing for it, he simply waited for their footsteps to disappear before making his way to the shared rooms where Jerry was staying.

He closed the door as carefully and silently as possible behind them. "OK, let's hear it."

Jerry explained that he had taken the job to get away from his father – Gary already knew or suspected that part – but Jerry continued to explain that his mother had died when he was young, causing a rift between father and son that never truly healed.

"I'm sorry to hear that," Gary acknowledged, earnestly, "but what does it have to do with what we're doing now?"

"My coming to work for you was really Father's idea. You see, my family is... that is, my father is... erm."

"I'm sorry to rush you, lad, but we don't have much time before they come back."

"I know. I'm sorry, and I hope you won't think any less of me."

Gary frowned. Jerry told him the rest.

Two and a half hours earlier...

After several cups of tea and many digestives, Emma was just beginning to calm down. She had collapsed across the interview table when Gary fell from the castle roof. When she came round, the female police officer comforted her, reporting that her husband was alive and well, as far as they could tell.

Desperate to understand what was happening, Emma forced herself to watch a recording of the entire incident, including all that occurred after she fainted. Gary's escape from certain death was like something from an Indiana Jones movie. She watched, incredulous, her heart, broken by terror and grief, now bursting with pride.

Though she still believed Gary to be a villain, even the WPC watching with her wore a rueful smile of respect.

"You've got this completely wrong, you know," Emma announced, harshly; her nerves were shot. "He's neither a criminal mastermind, nor some kind of cat burglar. He's just an everyday hero, one of the millions who keep our world turning, so we can literally keep a roof over our heads. He's *my* hero," she added quietly. Batting tears from her eyes, she added, "You just wait 'til I get my hands on him. I'm gonna kill him!"

The WPC smiled again, but before she could respond, the detective sergeant who originally interrogated Emma came back into the room. "You're free to go," he announced without preamble.

Emma looked up in surprise. "I am?"

"Apparently. Better make the most of it before I file my complaint!"

"What? What's happening?"

He glowered, working the muscles in his jaw. "Come on. With me."

She looked to the WPC, who merely shrugged. Clearly, information about this turn of events was above her paygrade. Emma stood and followed the obnoxious DS from the room.

"Here are your things. Check them carefully and sign for them with the desk sergeant," he gritted his teeth, "*please.*"

Collecting her things, she was all but pushed out of the police station's front doors and out onto the street.

"This way, madam, please."

Emma swallowed, wondering what on earth was happening now. The man speaking looked like a chauffeur. He walked to a black, long-wheelbase Range Rover LSE with blacked-out windows, parked at the kerb. Opening one of the rear doors, he gestured for Emma to get in.

Emma was understandably rattled by her experiences, but not *that* rattled. "I don't think so, whoever you are. On your bike!"

"It's OK, Mrs Stone. You're quite safe, I assure you," drawled an aristocratic voice from the rear seat. "Maybe I could offer you a drink. I have an excellent Scotch decanted. Shame to let it go to waste, and you look like you could do with one."

Emma squinted in the sunshine, trying to make out who was within the darkened interior. "Sir Kenneth Hornesby Jarvis?"

Now...

Hammer poured himself a cup of coffee behind the café's counter. Jimmy gripped his arm. "We need to talk – now."

Hammer tried to pull away but could not break the mason's grip. Concern crossed his face as Jimmy took the kettle out of his other hand, not letting him go.

Serj raised the halberd, threateningly, aiming its spear point towards Jimmy without a word as he looked to Hammer for instructions.

Jimmy nodded to Serj, not taking his eyes from Hammer's. "Keep your dog on his leash, or this won't end well for you. This kettle's hot!"

The builders rose from their seats – plasterers Andy Wilson and Willy Mammoth, electrician Vincent 'Blackout' Barnes – strong men all, and dangerously hangry, they eyed the three men with menace. Worzel pulled a knife from his jacket.

Willy Mammoth was the last to stand, muscles in his arms bulging like those of a Norse god, blond head shaking in warning as Serj gripped the halberd tight and looked around nervously.

Jimmy brought everyone's attention back to Hammer and himself. "You need to listen."

Gary shook his head in disbelief. "How many of those things do you have?"

"Six. I'm sorry I couldn't tell you chaps anything about this. Aside from the fact that I really wanted the job and to get away, it would have been a breach of the Official Secrets Act and technically treason. You see, my father works with some very serious people."

Gary blew out his cheeks in astonishment. He did not doubt it. Picking up one of the small devices Jerry laid out on his bed, he turned it over in his hand. "I assume this little pull-out aerial means they transmit and receive?"

"Yes. There will be a van somewhere close, waiting for the signal to communicate with them. I had intended to disappoint those chaps because..."

"Go on," Gary prompted.

"Well, I just thought it was one of Father's paranoid national security stories." He shrugged. "When you're wrong, you're wrong, eh?"

Gary nodded. "So let me get this straight, the people your father works for want to get their hands on whoever these gangsters work for?"

"Yes. I should have spread these things around the castle days ago, but I didn't believe any of it until it was too late. These listening devices will gather evidence, hopefully evidence linking those thugs to whoever's paying them. When the government types hear what's really going on in Rookstone, it should completely exonerate our chaps."

"But..." Gary was struggling to understand. "If your father put you up to this, then surely he knows we're just a bunch of builders here to carry out work for Sir Henry Grey."

"Understand this," Jerry explained seriously. "Father never told me anything about his work – when we spoke at all. He pushed me into this, with almost no information. Everything on a strictly need-to-know basis. He basically just told me to do my damned duty! I doubt he suspects you have anything to do with all this. He just wants it to play out so that his people can get *their* people."

"With you in the middle," Gary noted, flatly. "Sounds a real charmer, your old man."

Jerry sagged slightly. "You understand why I wanted to get away?"

Gary took a deep breath. "OK, so where do you suggest we place these things?"

Floating George opened the door at the top of the north tower and stepped out onto the roof and battlements. The glorious sunshine, the only blessing on their trip north, had now deserted them, too. A few spots of rain pricked his skin, but the black clouds above Rookstone carried the promise of worse. He peeked between the crenellations, out over the police and other vehicles gathered below. Turning to ask for instructions, he found himself alone.

Waiting in the doorway, Aleks stood with one arm up his back and a gun to his ribs, Scott hiding in the darkened stairwell.

"You not coming out?" George asked, not unreasonably. "Divvent tell me a Scot's afraid of the rain?"

"Oh aye, and with that helicopter up there, stuffed full o' cameras and who knows what other surprises?"

Floating George curled his lip. "Just a shyness thing, then, is it?"

"D'ye have any idea how easily a sniper hovering overhead might blow that jessie's grin right off yer face? Ye can carry on tha negotiations – Ah'll direct from here." He pulled back the hammer on his pistol, giving it a hair trigger. "One misstep and the bairn gets it, understand?"

George swallowed, but before he could answer, something happened high in the air a hundred feet above them. The helicopter seemed to misfire, its pilot suddenly struggling for control.

"What tha hell's gan on?" Scott cried, trying to steal a look from the doorway without being seen.

A squeal of feedback sounded from the base of the tower. "This is Detective Inspector Mellow, speaking to the men holding Sir Henry Grey."

Floating George tore his eyes from the crisis happening above to stare at Scott. He raised his arms to ask, *what do I do?*

"Answer him, ye muppet! See what he wants," Scott spat, viciously, though he kept looking up with concern.

George leaned over the battlements and shouted down. "We're listening."

"The helicopter we sent for to transport your men has developed problems."

You think? George thought, constantly checking the aircraft's position above. He had no wish to be decapitated by a flying hedge cutter. He cupped his hands. "We worked that out for ourselves!"

Still appearing to struggle high above, the helicopter's motor cut out altogether. George's eyes widened. "Oh, crap!"

"Wha's happenin'?" Scott demanded.

Floating George's arm shot out instinctively, towards the chopper. "It's going down!"

Scott risked pushing Aleks outside so that he could look up. He was just in time to see the pilot execute a controlled fall. Fortunately, the large lawns to the rear of Rookstone provided a place for him put down. Without power, the rotors sliced the air like the buzz of a giant wasp. All three men on the roof gaped as the stricken machine fell from view behind Rookstone's south range.

"You got a plan B?" George asked, quietly.

"Tell him we want another one!"

George sagged. "Aye, I'm sure he'll have a spare in his back pocket."

"Dae it!"

The plumber leaned over the battlements to call down. "We need you to organise another helicopter ride out of here!"

DI Mellow brought the megaphone to his lips. "It's broken down – had to crash land. We cannae get another here before tomorrow – they divvent grow on trees, bonnie lad. But look on the bright side, as long as you deliver Sir Henry safe and sound, there'll be plenty of time now, to arrange your plane."

Scott swore his frustration. He did not believe a word the policeman in charge said and could sense everything unravelling.

Noting his distraction, Aleks jabbed him in the ribs with his free elbow, spinning quickly to reach for the weapon.

"No!" George shouted.

Scott squeezed the trigger, releasing his fourth bullet at point blank range.

Jerry ran as quickly as he could across the courtyard, disappearing inside the west tower where Richard, Sir Henry's secretary, usually resided during the week.

Closing the outer door gently behind him, he turned to enter the apartment. However, the internal door would not open. He sighed. It must have closed on the latch. With the tower deserted and the door to the courtyard closed, he decided it was worth taking a chance and looked around for something he might use to force the door.

An executioner's axe head nudged against his boot. He bent down to take it, expressing his thanks automatically, when he realised what had just happened.

The hairs on the back of his neck felt like they were marching to the top of his head and back down again. He gulped. "Hello?" There had been no time to reflect on his recent, awful supernatural experience, but he certainly had not forgotten it.

"*I said, you're welcome, fellow,*" Sir Edward repeated. "*Couldn't lift it to hand it to you, I'm afraid. Did what I could.*"

Jerry glanced up the stairs, oblivious. Clearly, whatever was happening was something else to consider *later.* Holding the axe head like a hammerstone in his right hand, he struck the door immediately to the side of its Yale lock. Inside the tower where they resided, Richard and Sir Henry had no great need for security. The lock was little more than a symbol that the rooms were engaged and gave instantly. As the door shunted ajar, Jerry's hand was suddenly icy cold, which was odd – the fact that the blow made no sound, doubly so. He suspected someone was helping him. "Thanks awfully," he acknowledged. The situation would have seemed disturbingly bizarre to him just a few days earlier; he was doing his best to keep up. Besides, not being able to see his benefactor was no reason for discourtesy, and Jerry was nothing if not polite.

He let himself into the apartment.

Out in the courtyard, Gary removed the seal from the sticky pad attached to one of Jerry's listening devices and, keeping low, gently stuck it to one of the café's windowpanes. He pulled the small aerial out to activate it, when another gunshot rang around the courtyard from the top of the tower.

"Oh, God, no!" he hissed, dreading the worst, when he heard the scuff of a door opening into the courtyard. He recognised the sound as coming from the entranceway to both the cellar where For Keeps had been working and the tea rooms where most of his men were being held. They must have heard the gunshot, too.

Hands shaking, he pulled back the string on his jury-rigged crossbow and took a quarter-dowel bolt from one of the side pockets in his combat-style tradesman's trousers, placing it into the groove along the top of the stock.

Worzel shot out from the doorway with a knife in hand, skidding to a halt when he saw Gary. The two men eyed each other for a split second. Worzel reacted first. Flipping the knife so that the tip of its blade was between his thumb and forefinger, he raised it to throw.

He was fast, but nocked and ready, the eighteen-inch dowel quadrant was faster. It struck the would-be knife thrower right in the centre of his forehead, flipping him backwards off his feet to crack the back of his head against the flagstones. The knife fell limply to the floor and Gary ran to snatch it up, slipping it into a screwdriver loop on the pouch attached to his trousers. He looked about him, anxiously, but Worzel was alone.

Reasoning their leader, the one the unconscious man referred to as Ham, would not want to be left alone with a bunch of hairy-backsided builders, he now knew where everyone was. Seizing the moment, he put an arm through his bow, swinging it over one shoulder. With his hands free, he dragged the unconscious

Worzel back towards the north tower, up the first quarter-turn and back into the room leading to the tiny dungeon and even tinier oubliette.

Roughly, he pulled the injured man by his feet, bouncing his head up and down steps and across rough stone flags until he lay crumpled in the dungeon where Scott locked Jerry away earlier. Gary closed the door and barred it, switching off the lights with satisfaction on his way out[1].

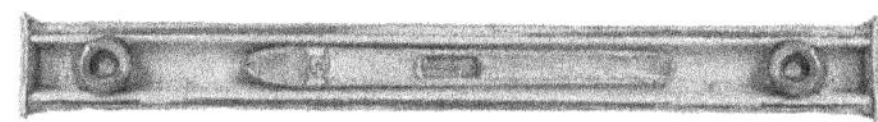

"You people are crazy!" Emma shouted, breathless and livid as she was terrified.

"I'm sorry, my dear, but it was a necessary deception."

"Don't 'my dear' me, Sir Kenneth Hornesby Jarvis. You almost got us killed!"

"Please, calm yourself, my d— Mrs Stone. Timothy's done that heaps of times, haven't you, Tim?"

The chopper pilot turned in his seat, giving Emma a toothy grin and thumbs-up.

Emma shook her head. "Bloody lunatics!" she hissed, exasperated and still shaking from their helicopter crash into the gardens at the rear of Rookstone Castle. "Anyone care to tell me what the hell that was all about?"

"Just a ruse cooked up with our friendly, local boys in blue. That little manoeuvre just bought us several hours, while we 'rustle up' another transport to take those villains and their hostage out of here. Which will be more than long enough."

"By villains, I hope you don't mean my husband and his men?"

Sir Kenneth smiled. "I suspect not." He straightened, puffing out his chest proudly. "It seems my son has finally carried out the task I set him. My people will be assessing the situation directly, and if your husband is innocent—"

"He is!"

"Then all will be well. Trust in the process. Now, please, Mrs Stone. We must get away from the helicopter and find cover, before we're identified."

Not waiting for the rotors to come to a full stop, Sir Kenneth opened the rear door and stepped out, bowing his head. Emma stepped out after him and he placed a gentle hand to the back of her head to keep her low, too, until they were beyond the rotors' reach.

At the south-east corner of the great lawn, they arrived on the run at a set of wrought iron gates. Sir Kenneth quickly ushered Emma through to a narrow dirt track, where a black Ford Transit panel van waited. The side door slid open expectantly. Inside, Emma saw a sports bag. "Hey, that's mine!"

---

1. The least he could do for Sir Henry. After all, it would be some years before energy saver bulbs became popular in Britain.

"Quite," Sir Kenneth assured her. "Didn't think we'd bundle you up here without so much as packing a bag, did you? That would be uncivilised."

"You've been in my *house?*"

He smiled blandly. "We're government, Mrs Stone. We're in everyone's house in one way or another."

The *crack* of a pistol shot rang around the grounds, forestalling Emma's next outburst. They both looked back through the gates, Sir Kenneth tensing with concern, Emma grabbing his arm without thinking. He did his best to keep his smile confident. "This way, Mrs Stone."

They climbed into the back of the van.

Aleks cried out as his legs collapsed under him. Floating George went cold, shock freezing him to the spot.

"Stupid little..." Scott let the teenager fall.

A patch of dark red was spreading across the side of the young man's green work fleece. Waking from his stupor, Floating George moved in to apply pressure to his side like he had seen people do in the movies. "We need an ambulance."

"Tough!"

"He'll die, you dickhead! Look at all the blood. Oh, my God. Hang on, bonnie lad. Hang on." He glared up at Scott. "I'm going to call over for help."

"If ye do, ye'll be taking a swan dive like yer ex-gaffer, ye ken?"

George's hatred almost got the better of him, but he realised that the gunman really would shoot him. He could not help young Aleks if he was dead. Quickly whipping off Aleks' fleece, he tied it as tightly as he dared around the young man's torso. Lying him down, he removed his own fleece and placed it under his head for a pillow. Aleks' lips were already blue and he was losing consciousness. "Stay awake, Hobnob, y'hear me?"

"Don't... call... me... aah." The last was a sigh as he passed out.

"Aleks!" George shouted.

"Who are *you?*"

"My name is Inga."

"I'm Aleks." The young man grinned. "You're a fox!"

Inga raised an eyebrow. "I'm your great-great, forty-four times, grandmother."

He pulled a face. "*Ew.* Sorry."

Inga snorted, gently. "I can see you're a Stone."

"I'm a Kaminski – that means stone cutter."

"Close enough."

"My uncles are called Stone. We call one of them James-the-Mason." He grinned.

Inga had no idea why that might be funny. "I know. He's my forty-*third*-great-grandson – they both are."

"Wow. How do you keep track? Am I dead?"

She answered the easiest question first. "No. Not yet."

"Will I die?"

"Certainly."

"Oh."

"But not necessarily yet."

"Oh?" He brightened, looking down at himself. "Trying to take the gun was stupid, wasn't it?"

"Yes, but it was also brave. If nothing else, I approve of your courage, though your execution left much to be desired."

"My execution?"

"Sorry. Poor choice of words. You're lucky to have good friends. That boy might just have saved your life by slowing the bleeding."

Aleks looked at her askance. "Boy? Floating George is an old man. He's like, thirty, or something. He looks older than you."

"He's really not."

Tearing his gaze away from himself, he stared intently at the spirit woman. "I'm scared. I've been scared for the last few days. Didn't want to tell the lads."

"Yes, I observed you becoming more subdued. When you arrived, you habitually shouted *'aciiiid'* at random intervals and for no reason. What was the meaning of that?"

"It's about clubbing, innit?"

Inga frowned, not sure she understood. "You glorify being beaten about the head?"

"No. Look." He pointed to a small, yellow smiley face badge on his spiritual T-shirt. It had Xs for eyes.

Baffled, Inga tried again. "Is that meant to be the sun? I remember the children in Rookstone singing *the sun has got his hat on*. Never really understood that one, either. Is your brooch's meaning related to that in some way?"

It was Aleks' turn to frown in bewilderment. "No, it's about taking, you know, *cid*... I mean, my mates... not that many of them did, like, but..."

"Who's Sid?"

Aleks looked down. "I'm not really sure."

It hardly mattered to Inga; she merely wished to keep him distracted. His body would keep doing what bodies do so long as his mind believed there was a chance. "Why do your friends call you Hobnob?"

"They don't!"

Her eyebrows rose with amusement. "As you wish."

Annoyance flashed across the teenager's face, but that was good. A little anger was essential if he was to fight for his life. It would also give *her* friends a little more time to fetch help.

"I heartily disapprove of what your progeny is doing in *my* castle!"

Inga winced, winding up her smile as she turned. "Hello, Sister Beatrice. It's very good of you to leave your chapel."

"Again!"

"You know, you've been in constant prayer for centuries..." Inga immediately realised she had taken the wrong tack. "That is, we're all very grateful to you, for taking time out," she finished, lamely.

The nun scowled, but knelt at Aleks' side to place a hand on his wound.

Inga watched with approval. "You would surely have been canonised if you'd been more famous, you know. Very unfair that, I thought."

"*That* is flattery!"

Inga pulled a face.

"I saw that! I've said it before, I'll say it again – the spirits in this castle would all benefit from joining me in prayer."

"But we were there just recently."

"*That* was Christmas!"

Inga squirmed. "Oh, you know how it is – commitments."

Beatrice glared. "You're dead. What could possibly be so important?"

"Maybe next Sunday?" Inga offered, weakly, with her fingers crossed behind her back.

"I saw *that,* too! That's a pagan symbol – the devil's work!"

Inga frowned, her lips moving while she tried to make sense of that.

Aleks took a deep breath and some of the colour returned to his cheeks. Beatrice stood. "I've done what I can. I'm going back to work! You have *no* idea how much they need praying for up there! I'll see *you* on Sunday. Don't be late!"

"As we're all dead, isn't that like being damned if you do, damned if you don't?"

Her attempts at gallows humour were wasted because Sister Beatrice was gone.

After hiding a bugging device, Jerry also heard the gunshot and ran out from Richard's apartment at the base of the west tower. There was no sign of Gary, so he ran back towards the north tower where they were all staying. Whatever had happened, the pistol crack almost certainly meant his friends were in trouble, and he wanted to help.

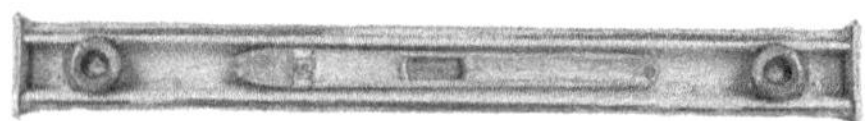

"If you let him die, there'll be no way out of this for you," Floating George snarled at Scott.

"It wasnae ma fault. The little eejit grabbed for ma gun. What did he expect tae happen?"

George stood to look him in the eye. "You were holding us at gunpoint, what did *you* expect to happen? He's only a kid! But let's say that's true – it was an accident. Letting him die now won't be. That'll be a choice, and it'll mean life for you!"

Hammer glared at Jimmy. He hated that the builder was right. Scott was indeed going to earn them all a life sentence, and if things really went south, that might only last the next few minutes. He glanced at Serj, who shrugged. Neither man was a stranger to a little prison time, but a murder charge would be a different matter. Hammer's experience of the legal system informed him that they might indeed be found jointly culpable.

"I'd like to know something," Sir Henry asked, standing with aid of his crutches. "You chaps broke in here, but once inside, you knew exactly how to disable my brand new, state-of-the-art security system. The police found no damage to the alarm. Only some rather unlikely fingerprints left by one of the builders. How *did* you get the codes?"

Hammer snorted sardonically. "Wouldn't you like to know?"

"Yes, I would, actually. And frankly, the more you come clean, the less time you're likely to spend at Her Majesty's pleasure. You had help, didn't you? An insider."

Hammer's lip twisted into a sneer. "You should be more careful about who you employ, sunbeam."

Jimmy was confused. "Does he mean the security firm you employed, Sir Henry? 'Cause I have to say, I didn't trust that Nellie."

Now Sir Henry was confused. "Nellie?"

"I mean..." Jimmy tailed off, remembering guiltily that he had named the giant security guard after noting he was the size of a clean-shaven Willy Mammoth. "Nothing," he muttered and then fired up again. "Hey, if he's trying to insinuate it was us you shouldn't have employed—"

"No," Sir Henry cut Jimmy off, keeping his gaze locked with Hammer's. "I rather fancy he was referring to someone else, weren't you?"

Hammer's nasty streak went as wide and deep as the Thames, and was equally filthy. He enjoyed the idea of stitching up their inside man, for no other reason than he despised Hooray Henrys. However, he possessed an equally deep undercurrent of cunning and knew, firstly, that betrayal ran both ways. Were their inside man to be outed, their whole organisation would be in jeopardy. Secondly, forced or not, should that inside man become a grass, it would be down to Hammer to cut him, or they would all be eliminated. Another job he really did not need. Better to keep their identity to himself.

He sat at a table and removed the felt bag containing the emeralds from his pocket. Unable to help themselves, the builders craned to see as he poured the three stones onto the checked tablecloth. Hammer was unsure why he poured them out for all to see. He only knew that he needed to check on them, to make sure they were safe.

Sir Henry frowned. Even though he hardly knew the villain, he could tell by the reaction of the other man, holding the halberd, that his behaviour was strange and out of character. Wondering whether there might be some initiative to be gained, Sir Henry pressed on. "I found the photographs."

"Hmm?" Hammer was clearly distracted as he turned, holding the gems up to the light of the window.

"The photographs," Henry persevered, "of the blueprints to my new security system. At least, I found their negatives. They recorded every passcode and location, and were in Richard's Filofax, where he keeps all the estate's contact information. Was he the hollow man?"

"If you know who got us in, why are you asking?" Hammer replied, absently. He held all three emeralds up to the window, frowning with confusion. He could not quite put his finger on the problem, but he knew there was one – or would *be* one. "Are *these* gems real?"

Everyone tensed.

Hammer had no idea why he even asked, yet for some reason he was suddenly suspicious. He skewered Sir Henry with a glare. "Well?"

"Of course they are. You know they are – you already stole the fakes. That's why you came back, isn't it?"

Hammer studied him closely. He needed Scott to check them as soon as things calmed down. "I remember it well," he answered, eventually. "Should have known better than to trust a toff!"

"That means exactly *nothing* from the likes of you!" Sir Henry bridled.

"Your mate was the contact, alright. He was also the liaison with our backers – the money. You're all the same, you lot, ain't ya? Looking down your noses at us – us, who do the work and take the chances. While you just front the money and take the biggest cut." He approached Sir Henry, a dangerous look in his eye. "These had better be the real stones, or when my mate comes back down here, I'll just tell him to shoot ya! You know he's been dying to, and you'll be dying, too. Ha!" He laughed at his own joke. "Now, I've got a bad feeling about these stones, so given your weakened state, sunbeam, I suggest you tell me the truth this time, and don't try to body swerve the issue, or it'll be lights out, understand? I'll ask you again, just one time and one time only. Do you want to confess anything, Sir High-and-Mighty?"

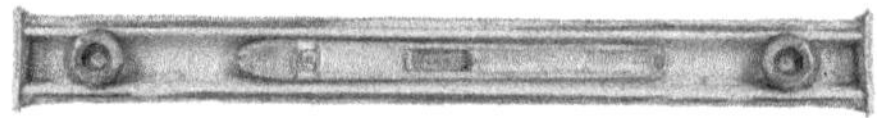

In the back of the black van, Sir Kenneth sat at a communications console, holding a headset to one ear. The MI5 operative who ran the desk turned to him. "Looks like they bought it, sir. Hook-in-mouth. Jeremy did well."

"What's happening?" Emma asked, anxiously.

Sir Kenneth smiled proudly. "We just took a giant step forward – and it's all thanks to my son."

Chapter 13

Barklife

Jerry ran up the spiral stair for all he was worth, throwing himself off the walls. He banged against the door to the top suite, knocking it open before he ran on to the door that led out onto the roof.

Scot span around, aiming his pistol.

"Jerry, stay there!" Floating George shouted. A sudden cloudburst soaked all three men already on the roof, in seconds. "Look," George tried again, holding his hands out to keep everyone calm, "can we at least get Aleks inside? His temperature's dropping as it is. Getting drenched might kill him."

Rain dripped from Scott's chin while his mind raced. He peered into the darkness of the stairwell and his eyes widened as he recognised Jerry. "How tha hell did *ye* get oot?"

"I... erm," Jerry stuttered as he looked down the gun barrel.

"Does it matter?" Floating George cut in. "Jerry can help me carry the lad, here. We'll have our hands full – no threat to anybody, OK?"

Scott could not have cared less about the young man bleeding on the roof, but the other two men, one in front and one behind him, could only be covered one at a time. If they rushed him, one of them might possibly take him down. Recent evidence suggested they might be stupid enough to try.

He waved George around to the door with his weapon. "Aye, tak' him in. He can go in tha top suite."

The open door to Gary's suite had not gone unnoticed. Poppy sniffed up and down the stairs. The reek of blood and fear from above was overpowering. She turned right, and hopped lightly down the stairs, her dexterous little legs carrying her swiftly to the bottom of the tower.

Stopping once more to sniff, she became confused. Her master's scent seemed to have crisscrossed the lower staircase several times, and very recently. There was no doubt that he, too, was fearful and confused – which was most inconsiderate. On the occasions when she looked to Gary for guidance, it was just like him to let her down by being useless when she needed him most.

She licked her lips and whiskers, yawning nervously, as she sat down. Looking out into the courtyard and then back up the stairs, there was nothing for it; she would have to go and save him.

At that moment, a fundamental change swept through the ancient stones of Rookstone – a heavy atmosphere that settled over the entire castle, and one that Poppy's nose recognised all too well. Blood.

The blood scented at the top of the stairs belonged to Aleks. She knew the scents of all Gary's men as well as her own. Even their blood, for cuts and grazes on building sites were as common as the bad language that usually followed – or preceded, depending on what sort of a day it had been. This new scent was not from Aleks, nor any of them, and it was overwhelming.

Poppy whimpered, now shivering with fear – and her idiot two-leg was nowhere to be found.

A thump from up the stairs made her jump. Up on her feet, she span to face the threat, growling and wagging her tail – it paid to wager both ways.

A *whoomph* of air descended the stairs after a door was closed. Undiscernible to humans, she instantly scented Gary and *woofed*. Suddenly extremely nervous of the tower stairwell, she thought it best to wait for him to come to her.

While she waited, the stench grew worse, now closing in from behind her, too. Even the free air of the open courtyard did nothing to disperse its malignance. She turned and growled again, not sure which way to run. Every instinct told her to find and leap into the arms of her master, because he usually understood bad things and how to make them go away, but somehow, *she* understood that whatever was coming was more than even her tame giant could cope with – it might even get him hurt.

That was unacceptable. She had become used to having him around. Besides, he was her biccie dealer and therefore important; she had to save him[1]. Her fear spiked again as the reek of death overwhelmed her senses. She ran.

"How did you know all this was happening?" Emma demanded, suspiciously.

Sir Kenneth replaced his headset on the control panel. "I apologise for our first meeting. I rather think I left you with a poor impression. Let me assure you that I do, in fact, care about my son – idiot though he might sometimes be."

She gave him a sideways look. "Convince me."

He chuckled softly. "You're a forceful woman, Mrs Stone. Your husband's a lucky man."

"And we both know it. You were saying?"

He smiled. "We knew, or suspected, that this attempt would be made to steal the Grey Emeralds. It's not the first crime of its kind across Europe over the last five years. However, the principal architects of these crimes never try more than once within a sovereign territory. After four such robberies, Interpol began making connections and informed MI6, who informed MI5, and so, here we are."

"You're MI5?"

"Not directly, but this is an MI5 Security Services operation. I... have an *open* portfolio."

"That's comforting. Now get to the part where your son and my husband became enmeshed in your schemes."

"Indeed. The directing minds behind these jewel robberies always outsource to a... shall we say, a local firm."

"You make it sound like business as usual."

"You have no idea, madam."

"I think I'm glad about that."

Sir Kenneth acknowledged her point with a nod. "When this particular crime was carried out, it threw us, as the Americans say, a curveball. You see, my son's fingerprints found their way onto the police computers. Unfortunately, as he was so slow to undertake his part in all this, that was the first we heard of it.

"When you came to my home, I was in the middle of a call from the Ministry. They were updating me as to the situation. I did not keep you waiting to slight you. When we spoke..." He sighed. "Let's just say, I already had quite a lot on my mind, and was fairly certain I already knew what you were about to tell me. I apologise if I seemed curt. You see, my son's failure to act had not only jeopardised

---

1. Dogs tend to live in the moment, dispensing with one thought at a time. Having no concept of either/or, Poppy's devotion for her master would certainly have been on the checklist somewhere.

our operation, but may also have placed him in some considerable danger. We already had people ready to swoop in, as it were, to catch the gang red-handed, while your husband's merry men were all at the pub."

"How did you know they'd be in the pub?"

"Firstly, each of the previous crimes were carried out by four-man teams. Despite being hardened criminals, we doubted they would make such an attempt while the castle was filled with security personnel and a large group of builders. It seemed most likely they would wait for Secure Nation to complete their work and for your people to leave for their evening's refreshment and entertainment. I must confess to a little snobbery there. I simply assumed that might involve a public house – particularly as it was a Saturday."

Emma opened her mouth to pull him up on that point, but, in good conscience, changed her mind – it was a fair cop. "How were Jerry's fingerprints left at the crime scene? We spoke to him, and the other lad, Floating Geor— that is, George Robson, before the police arrested them. They had us penned in the castle tea rooms all night. Although I've only known Jerry a short time, I found it hard to believe he was involved with a gang of dangerous villains. I was absolutely certain George had no part in the attack on Sir Henry. He served his country, you know."

"We know all about Mr Robson's record, and I think you're right," Sir Kenneth agreed, simply, "but we had to let the police carry out their investigations. The crooks had gotten away. If MI5 stepped in, they would have covered their tracks and we would have lost them."

Emma frowned. "But... they had their prize, didn't they? What did they come back for?"

"Fakes."

"Excuse me?"

"The emeralds they stole were nothing more than beautifully crafted copies."

"You might have led with that!"

Sir Kenneth's expression gave nothing away, making her immediately suspicious.

"You *knew* they'd come back," Emma stated, coldly. "And you left our team, your son, my family, right in the middle of it!"

"Madam—"

"Don't give me that. Those lads were frightened and in shock, and you left them in harm's way with no idea what might happen next! You total, complete and utter s—"

"Sir Kenneth!" the comms operative interrupted excitedly. "There's something happening."

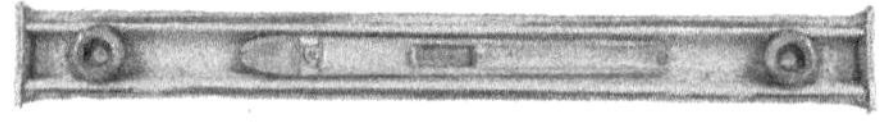

Poppy found her way back to the sallyport the builders used to come and go. The locking bar was on the floor and the door was ajar. Open by no more than an inch, it swayed gently back and forth as the wind carrying the new weather front grew stronger.

She reached her paw into the gap and tugged, skipping back. The door opened enough to squeeze her head through, and she was gone.

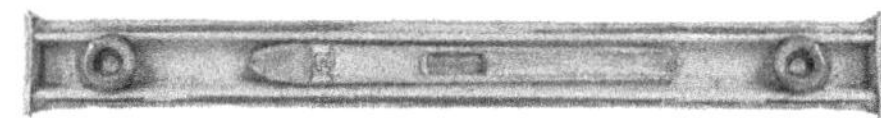

The spirit of Sir Edward kept his gaze lowered. "I hate to bother you, old fellow, but we have a real crisis here. One of the chaps in there is in danger of losing his life. You know we don't have the power to intervene, so we thought you might, you know, be able to bend the rules again."

The Hornèd One shrugged. At least, that was how it appeared to Sir Edward. Even to a man who existed the other side of death, the movements of the antlered head were disturbing.

The Tudor magnate and once lord of Rookstone wracked his brains for an argument that might sway their monstrous colleague before he drifted away again.

Cunning arguments were not really his forte, but Inga had flat refused to leave her distant relative's side, in case he crossed and needed immediate help, before Deceased Support were sent down from *upstairs*. He was about to suggest some form of *quid pro quo,* perhaps some kind of woodland surveillance sharing strategy, when he was interrupted by a skittering sound through the brush on the forest floor.

Poppy saw and recognised Sir Edward and *woofed* a greeting. She was fully used to seeing ghosts – dogs always did – especially when they frequented the sort of locations where *her* humans worked. She sat to look up into the face of the forest god and growled an enquiry. Her wiry tail scattered dead leaves from the previous season across the forest floor as it wagged to show that she came in peace.

Herne stared down, his gaze boring through her bright little eyes to a feisty mind so full of life.

Poppy growled a warning – there were limits.

The face of the ancient god was not capable of a smile; nevertheless, he was amused by her rebuttal and backed off politely – no one respected the non-human animals more than he. Patiently, he allowed Poppy to show him what was in her mind. The Hornèd One was always amused by animals who lived with humans. They carried so much unnecessary baggage. For example, Poppy had two names, the first, designated at birth from her first moment of consciousness. It was not a name in the way that people had names; it was more an identity code born from complex smells and chemical constructs. Compared with that, the name Gary and Emma gave her was like equating five years' life experience with a badge saying 'I am five'.

However, there was a flipside to living with, or at least alongside, the human condition. Such creatures learned so much that their would-be masters never thought to hide.

Again, Poppy pushed back. She was part of the animal kingdom, but she was also Gary's best friend.

Herne backed away again, and then he saw it. Always in motion, his head that saw in all directions at once froze in place, glaring down at the little messenger.

Sir Edward bravely stepped to the side.

The ancient forest god opened his arms wide, threw his head back and barked. A deep rumble shook the ground in every direction.

Poppy whimpered – and so did Sir Edward.

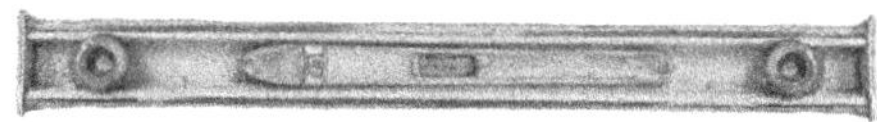

A small town now gathered outside Rookstone's walls. Tents and awnings filled many of the spaces between TV-channel vans and emergency vehicles as people hunkered down for the long game, waiting to see – and record – how events would play out.

First on the scene, Brandon Porkpie, along with his cameraman, Stan, and aide, Tammy, had secured a prime spot for themselves. Safe enough from the action, they were still within earshot of much that passed within the ad hoc camp springing up around the castle.

Brandon prepared to give another piece to camera, updating his viewers about the latest gunshot, when a tremor rocked the ground beneath them.

Vehicles shook and people stumbled; only the massive walls of Rookstone remained resolutely unmoved. The heavy clouds above them darkened further as lightning struck a weathervane in the form of a bat, atop the north tower.

Stan wiped rain from his lens, unconsciously adjusting the umbrella Tammy held for him, as he looked up at the medieval war machine. Stripped of its sunny, blue-sky background, Rookstone dropped all pretence of being just another quaint English country house. Black storm clouds now framed the ancient pile, creating an impression of malice.

Lightning struck again, this time incinerating a high branch near the top of a tall oak in the grounds. There were many large trees close enough to fall into the camp, and that made the people gathered within look out nervously.

Stan was anxious, but as an experienced cameraman and occasional director, he was also excited. This would look great on film. Mirroring the swirling clouds in the heavy skies, ideas formed and surfaced and reformed in the maelstrom of his thoughts. *What if I were to make a documentary series about the most haunted buildings in Britain? And why stop there? I could put together a crew easily enough, then gather a few experts on the supernatural – parapsychologists, mediums, ghost hunters and the like. Hmm... I'll have a chat with the missus, see what she thinks.*

Thunder rolled across the landscape, shaking the ground beneath his feet to bring him back to the moment. Brandon was waiting impatiently for *him* to roll. With a city man's aversion to weather, the newscaster hid beneath an oversized brolly, trying to make himself thin, so that the water sheeting from his personal canopy did not touch his suit.

Accidents happen. Sometimes innocent blood is spilt, and that is always to be regretted. However, occasionally, the blood of innocents is spilt with intent.

Scott's explanation for how Aleks was shot was feasible, in the heat of such an event. He almost believed it himself. They had both struggled for a weapon that went off – plausible. The argument would hardly exonerate him, but a good lawyer would certainly be able to blow subsequent holes in any future charges of murder. However, Scott also knew it was a lie.

As soon as the young man made a move to tackle him, he had fired deliberately and indiscriminately – knowing the consequences would be dire. He knew his intention and so did Rookstone.

The Hornèd One was not the only ancient spirit to inhabit those lands, latterly tamed by man – or so man thought. Herne was there first, but when man arrived, he brought *other* spirits with him. Most lived lightly alongside the natural world, barely leaving their mark, but one knew only darkness.

As Aleks Kaminski bled into the stones of Rookstone's oldest tower, something awoke.

The torturer, John Sage, dwelt in the obscurity of centuries. Almost forgotten. Once a man, he was imbued with light and darkness, wit and idiocy, like all his kind – and like all his kind, he made choices, too – choices that allowed the ancient evil to claim him, tying him to that place as an ambassador, his chamber of horrors an enclave of Hell. He now endured as little more than a shadow, a memory recorded in stone, his power owing more to the strengths and weaknesses of those he wished to affect, than any strength he now possessed... However, occasionally, the blood of innocents was spilt with intent.

Neither Jerry nor Floating George had any medical training, so they just lifted Aleks' unconscious body gingerly, moving him as slowly and gently as they could, terrified of doing further harm. No mean feat with a gun at their backs, and in the hands of a man who had proven time and again that he was willing to use it.

The small pool of blood left behind was swallowed instantly by the ancient stones. Fearing for their own lives, and the life of their charge, the bearers never even looked down. Even if they had, they would have probably attributed the phenomenon to the lashing rain.

Rookstone Castle was not fooled, however. The blood ran deep, the ancient stones carrying it like a high-speed conduit to draw John Sage right back to his happy place. He smiled.

"What's happening?" Sir Edward's spirit demanded, fear of events superseding his fearful respect for the forest god.

Herne reached out a massive arm, extending a long, claw-like finger to touch the nobleman's temple. Terrified, Sir Edward knew better than to resist. Either he was being honoured in a way none of his companion spirits had experienced before, or he was in real trouble – and having survived King Henry VIII's court, he knew it was entirely possible for both states to exist at once.

A vision jolted through his consciousness. Sir Edward had lived, and not lived, long enough to see much evil in the world, but never had he experienced such fear and despair. He looked up at the ancient spirit before him with new respect, as he realised for the first time the true extent of all that Herne did for Rookstone. The simple forest spirit was nothing of the sort; he was the balance, the counterweight that held the evil trapped within the ring of stone that was Rookstone. In life, Sir Edward existed in a state of happy ignorance of the forces battling around him, each constantly grappling for advantage. In the afterlife, he had gained some measure of peripheral understanding, but now he saw it all – a window into hell.

After centuries of balance, the evil beneath the castle had broken free again, to flex its muscles.

A hundred-mile-an-hour gust tore through the tents and vehicles ranged before the castle, flattening some and tearing awnings away from others. People were blown off their feet, reaching for something to hang on to.

Stan held on to his TV camera with every ounce of strength he could muster as he was pressed against the side of his own van, rocking on its suspension. Facing into the wind, he kept rolling, as the forest shed leaves and other detritus in his direction. Through his fear, he focused on the award such photography could win for a steely-eyed cameraman, able to keep his nerve against the elements, and who knew what other forces, ranged against them.

With the unconscious Worzel well secured in the castle's dungeon, Gary also made his way towards the gunshot at the top of the tower. Running up the spiral stair, he stopped when he heard voices.

Controlling his breathing as best he could, he listened hard. The conversation was less chilling than he had expected. More along the lines of 'to me, to you' than some kind of ongoing altercation. He recognised the mismatched plummy accent of Jerry against the Geordie dialect of Floating George. He closed his eyes, offering up a silent prayer of thanks, when his hopes were dashed by a third voice.

"Hurry up, ye damned Sassenachs. Ah'm getting drenched, ye hear?"

Gary's instincts told him to run back down the stairs, so that his presence remained hidden from their enemies for as long as possible, when he heard the men on the floor above enter his suite. Their footsteps vanished from the stairwell, so he risked climbing further up, to listen at his own door. What he heard made his blood run cold. His nephew was in serious trouble, literally fighting for his life.

"*You must hide.*"

"What the—" The voice was like an icy blast into his ear that made him stumble against the stone wall and bang his head. "*Jesus!* Will you stop doing that!"

"*You must hide, now! Quickly, up to the roof – and don't let Sister Beatrice hear you curse like that or she'll flat refuse to ever help us again.*"

"Inga?"

"*Obviously. How many other spirits do you know?*"

"Quite a few, actually."

"*Will you move, you stupid lump!*"

Gary's body caught on quicker than his wits and his legs propelled him up the last flight and through the door that led onto the roof. Closing it behind him, he was instantly soaked to the skin and sagged, miserably, as he hunkered down behind the battlements. The wind was so strong that he feared going over *again*.

"What the hell is going on?" he hissed, barely able to hear his own voice above the wind. However, he suspected it would not prevent Inga from making herself understood. He was right.

"*I've told you about using that wor—*"

"At the risk of playing into an idiom – go and suck an egg! Why have you brought me up here? Other than for the climate!"

"*Wait.*"

He waited, stewing as his anger and fear for his nephew coiled like a snake in his gut.

"*Now! They've gone down the stairs. Quickly, back into the rooms where we first met.*"

Wasting no further time, he ran down the stairs as instructed. Closing the door behind him, he burst into the bedroom where Aleks lay on Gary's own bed. Looking younger than ever, his face had taken on a grey, bloodless pallor.

"Oh, no."

"*He's not dead. Not yet. I can help him, if you help me.*"

"Of course. Anything, anything. What can I do?"

"*Hold out your cross.*"

Confused, Gary opened his fleece. He had learned not to leave the silver Saxon cross against his skin in that place. Even now, it was freezing to the touch, and as he held it, Inga appeared before him. He never doubted she was there, but jumped anyway. "I can see you!"

"Yeees," she drawled, ironically.

He could hear her clearly now, too. "But... but..."

"Yes?" she asked, sweetly.

"The last time I could see you, I was about to..."

"Die?"

He nodded.

"Our connection was made stronger once you *eventually* worked out our relationship, but what really made everything we have experienced together possible was that cross... *my* cross."

"Huh?"

Inga sighed. "Place it around your nephew's neck. Quickly. He grows weaker."

Again, Gary followed her instructions, this time without question.

Inga vanished.

"You're leaving me? *Now?*"

"*Touch the cross.*"

He did as instructed and she appeared once more before him.

He released.

She vanished.

He touched it.

She reappeared.

"Enjoying yourself?" she queried, sternly.

"Sorry. How can the cross help Aleks?"

"You don't think this is an opportune moment for the sign of the cross?"

He gave her a doubtful look.

"Oh, very well. I am now connected with Aleks, too. After all, he is also my many-times-removed grandson."

Gary's mind caught up. "*Your* cross?"

"Did all the brains go to the women in our family?"

"Not in the mood!" he bit out, angrily.

Inga softened. "I'm sorry. When you've been dead as long as I have, it holds very little fear. Yes, that was my cross. I was wearing it when I was killed."

"Killed?"

"Murdered," she elucidated.

"Oh, my God. I'm sorry. What happened?"

"A Dane. He stole the cross, because it was made of silver, and my cloak – which was a really nice one, too – the swine! In my fifties, he wasn't interested in anything else from me, so that was the price of my life – that silver cross and a woman's cloak."

Gary was appalled.

She gave a sympathetic half-smile. "That was how it was in those days. The younger women and the slaves had it far worse."

He gulped. "You had slaves?"

"Of course. We treated ours well. Many didn't. Our people have always been slaves, or masters – sometimes both. Death spared me that experience. For thousands of years it was normal. I understand it still happens now."

Gary gaped, equally disgusted by what had happened to his ancestor and amazed by how she took it in her stride.

Inga smiled patiently. "Though many great and wonderful things have been achieved during my time on Earth, yours is the best time any of us have so far witnessed, but it seems you have short memories. Our past could be brutal – vicious. It should be remembered but never revisited. And you should be more vigilant, for there is always someone who wants to take away the freedoms you inherited."

"Not in Britain, surely?" he answered, sceptically.

Inga raised an eyebrow. "We shall see. I never thought to see my cross again, though." She gazed down fondly at the small article of jewellery at the young man's throat, watching it move up and down as his chest rose and fell, almost indiscernibly.

"The cross..." Gary spoke his thoughts aloud. "Sir Edward said you all had a totem. That was – *is* – yours?"

She nodded, pulling a spiritual facsimile from within the folds of her frock. "I loved that cross. It was a gift from my father. I, too, wore it on a leather lace, just as you do."

A chill ran down Gary's spine. It was as though history was unfolding before him, *through* him.

"The pig who stole it from me took it to Mercia."

"Mercia?"

She nodded again.

"*I* live in Mercia. I mean, Worcestershire. It's part of the Mercian district, but..." He tailed off, astonished by the revelation. "I found it in an old house we recently renovated. Still, it wasn't *that* old – three centuries, maybe. It certainly didn't go back to the ninth century. I wonder how your cross ended up there?"

Inga was smiling. "You found it?"

"Yes. The house's owner didn't want it."

Her smile grew wider. "Because that so-called owner was never meant to have it. I suggest it found *you*. I also suspect that part, or parts, of that house might go back much further. It will have been found and lost again many times, I'm sure, before it came to you."

Aleks coughed and opened his eyes. "Uncle Gaz? What happened?"

"Keep still, lad. You've been shot."

Aleks groaned. "Oh, yeah... Wicked."

"No, it's not..."

"Yes, it was..."

Gary and Inga spoke simultaneously, not for the first time separated by a shared language.

They looked at each other, but before either could explain, the castle trembled again.

Gary saw fear in Inga's eyes.

Unable to stop himself, he span around in alarm, pointlessly seeking out danger that was hidden from mortal eyes. "What's going on?"

She turned his face back towards her, holding his cheek. Somehow, he felt her touch. "If I leave the boy, he will die. *You* must stop this."

Gary's alarm inflated to full blown panic. "What? What can *I* do?"

"At least warn your people. Sage will be powerful again."

"Who?"

"Sage. He's... different. Not like us – the other spirits, I mean. He was Rookstone's torturer, ooh, must be seven hundred years ago. We despised the Danes – thieves, murderers and slavers. *You* would have hated them! But Sage was worse than any Viking I ever met. This has happened before and there's only one who can stop him."

"Again, *who?*"

"No time to explain. Simply know this – under the old great hall—"

Gary was growing frantic. "*Old* great hall? You mean before the current one?"

"Yes. Before the south range was built."

Gary marvelled, despite his growing fear. "You remember that?"

"I do."

"But where's the original great hall?"

"Where Sir Henry's staff now serve up food and drink to Rookstone's visitors."

"The café?"

"Yes."

"But that's where my men are!"

"*Yes.* Will you listen? Beneath the..." she spoke the unfamiliar noun carefully, "*caffay,* is the old torture chamber. Where those dreadful acts actually took place. It's home to an ancient evil. The other is just a... a..."

"Façade? A fake?"

"If you like. There was something wrong with the ground there, long before the castle was built. We used to avoid that part of the woods when I was a girl, but it became far worse in Sage's day." She looked around, as though seeing through the mighty stone walls to the forest below. "*He* is coming."

"The one you won't tell me about?"

She leaned forward impetuously, to kiss Gary on the cheek. "Courage, my son. Now, go. Quickly!"

Chapter 19

Sabotage

John Sage could feel a stirring. Power was building in a way he had not felt in centuries. It was time to play, but first, an hors d'oeuvre...

The man was slumped on the cold, broken stones of the dungeon floor, also stirring. Sage grinned, showing broken teeth.

Worzel sat up, blinking into the total darkness. Suddenly panicked, he jumped to his feet and span around, arms outstretched to feel his environment. Eventually, he found the iron-strapped, oak door that completed his tomb. Scrabbling for a handle, he found none. Having no idea that he was in the castle dungeon, he cursed the stupidity of a door without so much as a latch.

However, Worzel was no stranger to the inside of a cell, and eventually it dawned on him where he might be. "Hammer!" he shouted, banging on the door. "HAAAM!"

Silence.

John Sage watched, gleefully, soaking up the man's growing fear.

This was by far the worst prison Worzel had ever seen – or not seen, for that matter. He was completely blind and there was no bed, nor even a toilet. He stopped banging. It was doing nothing more than damaging his hands. Eventually, he stopped shouting, too. Either no one heard, or no one cared.

The malignant spirit dragged his leg, cackling his choking, coughing laugh.

Worzel puffed out his cheeks, turned his back to the door and slid down to sit on the floor, as Jerry had. So many years had passed since Sage was allowed to toy with a victim, and yet, within the space of just a few hours, fate had handed him two. The power running through Rookstone was growing slowly, but there was still time for a little diversion before he would be summoned to play his part.

He dragged his leg again. Nicknamed John Dragfoot, he always enjoyed the terror his victims experienced when they heard that sound in the darkness.

Worzel sat looking forward, eyes unseeing, ears unhearing.

Sage dragged his leg again, cackling loudly, to make a point.

Nothing.

He tried choking the man on the floor before him.

Worzel rubbed the enormous egg-shaped bruise on his brow, left by Gary's improvised crossbow bolt.

Sage gathered all his limited might to strangle the oblivious oaf caught in his clutches.

Worzel yawned. The darkness was making him sleepy. He reasoned that, until Hammer realised he was missing, and went looking for him, he might as well make himself as comfortable as possible and try to sleep off the massive headache he was developing.

Lieutenant John 'Dragfoot' Sage raged. He could hardly believe how insensitive the man was. Even as he felt his power growing, he could not make Worzel aware of his presence. Did he not even have the imagination to be afraid? Not even when locked away, alone in the dark within a castle dungeon?

Sage swore. That was when an idea struck. There was more than one way he could use this unfeeling wretch. After all, his power *was* growing. Perhaps he could add to the chaos by just...

Worzel heard the drop bar slide out of its keeps on the outside of his cell door. He smiled. "Ham? How did you find... me?"

Shielding his eyes against the dim light from the antechamber, he could not see a soul. Checking the locking bar, now in its vertical position, he blinked in confusion. Shrugging it off, Worzel turned and walked straight through Sage, leaving the medieval torturer cursing furiously and jumping up and down painfully on his gammy leg.

The door to the tea rooms opened and Jerry was shoved in, roughly, followed immediately by Floating George.

Hammer waited for Scott to enter behind them. Closing the door, Hammer demanded, "Where's Wor—" Remembering his own embargo on namedropping, he changed tack. "Where's our teammate?"

Scott shrugged. "He wasnae with me."

Hammer glared at Floating George and Jerry. "What's goin' on 'ere?"

Both men looked baffled.

He looked to Scott again.

"These two jessies *were* with me."

Another rumble shook the earth. They could feel it through the café's flagstone floor. In possession of the only firearm, Scott shoved Jerry and George over with the other builders, grouping them together once more.

While Hammer pulled Scott to the side to interrogate him further about what might have happened to their colleague, Serj watched Jimmy and his boys closely, halberd still in his hands to hold them at a distance.

"Did you ever replace that nail in the fuse box with fuse wire?" Floating George whispered to Blackout Barnes, his back to their captors.

The electrician shook his head, almost imperceptibly. He had not had the chance. "Planning a bit of sabotage, like?"

"Thinking about it, bonnie lad. Follow my lead."

"Hey!" Serj grunted, separating the two men.

"Can I get a drink of water?" George asked, innocently.

Serj glowered at him, looking for a hidden threat. Eventually, he nodded towards the small Belfast sink behind the counter near the master fireplace.

As a plumber, George could not help but note any taps, fittings or associated pipework whenever he entered a room. The Belfast boasted a smart, new, brass pre-rinse tap, with a detachable nozzle ideal for swilling around such a large sink. He ran the ordinary nozzle until the water came out cold, taking as much time as he could. The pressure was good. Eventually, he poured himself a glass of water. Just as he lifted it to his lips, the door to the tea rooms burst open and Worzel stormed in.

"Where the 'ell 've you been?" Hammer challenged.

"That bloke with the crossbow locked me up, Ham."

"You wha'? What bloke? What crossbow?"

"The one who ain't 'ere. Their gaffer!" Worzel spat the accusation at Gary's men.

Hammer's eyes narrowed. "I thought he was dead! And what the 'ell 'appened to your 'ead?"

"He *shot* me, before he locked me up!"

"With a *crossbow?*"

"Look, let's not get bogged down, Ham. Where is he?"

The gang all turned to Scott. Hammer stated what they were all thinking. "You told us he was brown bread."

Scott looked mystified, moving to stand behind Serj, who still held the builders at bay. "He did a five-storey swan dive affa that tower. That'd normally dae tha trick, aye!"

"What's goin' on 'ere?" Hammer growled.

Floating George caught Blackout's eye and winked. Maxing the tap's hot and cold feed, he tore the pre-rinse nozzle from its holder and blasted lukewarm water across the tea rooms to hit Serj in the face. He grimaced, bringing the halberd round instinctually to face the stream of water.

Blackout Barnes took advantage of the commotion to snatch a small lamp from the nearest table. He looked to Floating George, who ripped the pipe from the tap and threw it to the floor. Once the plumber was clear, Blackout smashed the lamp's clay body on the flagstones and into the puddle rapidly expanding around Serj and Scott.

Eyes blurred by the initial assault, the Eastern European went down immediately, convulsing as mains electricity created a power-*Serj* he would never forget.

Vision unimpaired, Scott was quicker to react and dove as the first shock hit his system. He landed on the stone floor to roll away from the water. Groaning, he stood up – his hair was way ahead of him – and turned to face Floating George with murderous intent.

The floor shook again, even more violently that time, and everyone looked around fearfully. Everyone but Serj, who still kicked and spasmed on the wet floor.

"Get 'im out of that puddle!" Hammer bellowed.

Blackout stared at him incredulously. "You're having a giggle, aren't you, boy? There's two hundred and forty volts and thirteen amps running through that water, isn'it?"

Hammer reached for Serj's fallen halberd, but the long wooden stave was soaked.

There was a loud *crack,* and the cockney villain jumped back, sucking his fingers, while trying to swear at the top of his voice.

Andy Wilson reached up to take one of the myriad weapons from the wall.

"Drop it, kid!" Scott bawled, pointing his gun at the plasterer – the shock and tumble having completely removed any sense of humour he might have had.

"No! Let him!" Hammer intervened.

The socket the lamp was plugged into caught fire. "Better make it quick!" Blackout shouted. "The wiring's ancient in this place. It'll all go up in flames, isn'it?"

Nodding, Andy selected a billhook polearm and, taking it by its dry and immensely long wooden shaft, used the hook to yank the cable still attached to the broken lamp, pulling the plug out of the wall socket.

Serj went limp.

Hammer moved in, gingerly. "He ain't breathin'."

Sir Kenneth acknowledged Detective Inspector Mellow, calling him over as he spoke quietly with one of his aides. "Get Clarence here, immediately."

The man saluted and left, while Sir Kenneth returned his headphones to one ear. Sharing them with the detective, they listened to the fracas kicking off in the castle's tea rooms.

"That's sounds like our cue to go in, sir," Mellow suggested.

"I agree, before that Scotsman starts shooting again."

"He will if you burst in with guns," Emma barged into their conversation. "My family's in there!"

Sir Kenneth considered her point, while Mellow glared at her, pointedly. "Why is she here, sir?"

"Mrs Stone knows the men in there, better than anyone – knows how they are likely to behave and react."

Mellow continued to glare at her. "So, we're going with the idea that those brickies aren't the firm holding Grey hostage."

"No. It appears they, too, are hostages – my son among them. I very much doubted they had anything to do with this, other than on the periphery, but we had to let things play out. Now my son has brought us this audio evidence, we need to bring the situation to a close, before we run out of excuses about why we haven't secured a second helicopter. The strong winds are working in our favour for now, but they weren't forecast. We can't rely on them continuing and should proceed immediately."

"No!" Emma cried.

"Mrs Stone, you must understand that things have changed. The criminals know your husband is alive now. He, on the other hand, believes that, if he escapes the castle, he will be arrested. That may sound preferable to being shot, but we dare not rely on him making the correct choice. We're trying to save everyone's lives, here."

Gary sneaked around the back of the tea rooms, making his way to the sallyport they used as their tradesman's entrance. The drawbar was on the floor. Someone must have entered. Might they be hiding somewhere in the castle, waiting to move in? The thought gave him hope, but also concern. Though desperate to get help for his nephew, he did not want his men, or his brother, caught up in the middle of a firefight.

He was passing one of the small offices behind the kitchens on his way to the door, when an idea struck him. Making a quick search for some paper and a pen, he hastily scribbled a note.

Checking both ways, he left the office and returned to the door that led out to where his vans were still parked. He slipped outside.

It was good to be free of the oppressive walls of their prison, if only briefly. Unfortunately, knowing that a considerable portion of the Northumberland police force was waiting for him, almost certainly including a highly trained armed response contingent, took the edge off any jubilation he might have felt.

Hiding behind his van, he stole a look towards the outer courtyard's arched stone gateway. At first there was no one there, when, as luck would have it, Sergeant Gripper appeared. An old man was with him, almost dragging Gripper back towards the side entrance to the castle, gesticulating wildly. Gary recognised Albert, the Greys' family retainer and ticket vendor. He could not hear what they were saying properly over the ferocious wind, but the odd word or two he did catch led him to believe that the argument had been going for some time.

Gary smiled as the rest of his plan practically wrote itself. Taking one of the quadrant bolts from his side pocket, he pushed it through the note he had just written and rolled it around the shaft. Pulling back on his bow, he placed the bolt into the v-groove as previously. His smile wound up to a grin as he aimed and loosed.

Shielded from the worst of the wind by the courtyard's high stone walls, the bolt flew perfectly true, closing the twenty metres between Gary and his target in an instant.

Gripper jumped up in the air. His scream, Gary *did* hear, as the quarter dowel hit him squarely in the rump.

Hiding back behind his van, Gary stifled his laughter as he watched the old man ignore the police sergeant, still jumping around cursing, to pick up the bolt and its message. Albert looked up and saw him.

Gary showed himself clearly, waving for them to follow – hopefully heeding his written request to bring many armed and burly police officers to the castle tea rooms with them. He dashed back inside. As he passed the door to the café, he stopped to listen, hoping to hear anything that might signal that his men were all right. Another tremor shook the floor, tipping him into the wall. The door swung open.

Gary leapt out of sight.

"Hey!" Worzel cried. "There's someone out there."

Hammer snapped round to look. "You'd better go after him, then. If that's the geezer who's supposed to be dead, he must be on his last life by now!"

Worzel took a vicious-looking axe from the cafeteria wall[1] and ran from the room to make it so.

Gary dared not trap himself down in the cellar and so ran out to hide in the fake torture chamber that housed some of John Sage's many, and very genuine, toys. Long, narrow and windowless, it was lit only by shafts of grey daylight from the open doors at each end. Gary's foot caught something in the darkness – something metallic that scraped. Having no time to load and aim his crossbow, nor the room to really use it, he cast it aside and reached down to pick up the item he recognised and knew so well.

He hid to the side of the door and waited.

He did not have to wait long.

Worzel barrelled into the chamber, axe in hand, only to receive a shovel in the face, delivered with the practised strength of a man who worked with tools every day of his life. That would normally have offered offence enough, but Gary also made maximum use of what was on the shovel, something Poppy 'dumped' in

---

1. Only in a medieval castle!

the centre courtyard on a moonlit night several days earlier. He never had gotten round to disposing of it – and its scent had not improved with age.

Fortunately for Worzel, he was unable to smell what Gary had just pounded into his nose as he was completely spark-out, flat on his back for the second time.

Holding the shovel ready, just in case he needed it again, Gary peeked around the corner. He was alone. "Where are those coppers?" he fretted.

Chapter 20

I've Got the Power!

We've got big problems here!" Hammer shouted as he slapped Serj about the face, trying to bring him round.

"What the hell are you doing?" Jimmy demanded, incredulously.

Hammer turned, red-faced and angry. "I would have thought even a thick brickie could work that out. He ain't breathin'!"

James-the-Mason bridled at being called a brickie. Realising it was a pointless distinction at that moment, he shook his head instead. "As a thick brickie, I can tell you that it's not his face that's stopped working. Get out of the *way*." He knelt and flopped Serj fully onto his back. Hammer was right about one thing; he was not breathing. Jimmy wiped the spittle from the man's face after his convulsions, pinched his nose and blew a controlled breath into the gangster's lungs. Nothing. He linked his fingers to make a single fist and leaned hard on Serj's chest at the solar plexus, making a repetitive pumping action. After thirty seconds of muscular labour, he bent down to listen, but Serj was still not breathing. Three more controlled breaths and Jimmy raised his fist to pound the man's chest, when Serj began to cough, naturally rolling over onto his side as he fought to breathe on his own.

Jimmy wiped his own mouth disgustedly, glaring at Hammer accusingly. "A thick brickie, eh? Maybe, if you'd worked for a living, instead of trying to steal *other* people's livelihoods, you might have picked up a few skills yourself – other than nicking stuff and hurting folks. No need to thank me!"

"I weren't gonna. All you did was save your own lads from going down on a murder charge."

Jimmy squared up to the gangster, temper getting the better of him as he explained, using some very off-colour language, that Hammer was probably right about the state of British justice. "At least I won't now feel a fool for saving that toerag!" Turning his back on the villain, he stormed away.

Liam-the-leaver, For Keeps' joiner, kicked out a seat at the table where he sat, for Jimmy to join him. Such a small gesture, but Hammer could see bonds of fellowship in everything they did. They were a team. They were good mates. They were everything his gang was not.

The floor shook again as tremors became more noticeable, even through such a heavily built structure. They were coming closer together, too.

The Hornèd One swept through the woods and out across the lawns laid to the castle's north face. The wind rushed before him, whipping up leaves and bits of broken tree limbs as he glided up the small bank onto the driveway.

Completely jammed with vehicles and the wreckage of various tents, he drifted through them as though they were not there. However, he did not pass without trace, for though he avoided the people staggering about, bent double against the ferocious gusts, their equipment froze at his touch.

A police car bore a strip of ice diagonally across its bonnet. Its headlamp bulbs exploded, though the sudden gale-force winds masked the effects, almost immediately melting the ice as he moved on.

The forest god floated up the grand stone staircase to the main castle gates to bang on them, twice.

Gary heard a colossal *boom* on Rookstone's main gate, followed immediately by another. He remained in darkness, hiding just inside the doorway to the fake torture chamber and gripping a shovel smeared with days-old dog excrement like his life depended on it.

Another *boom* shook the gates. Even over the howl of the wind, he heard the crossbar Liam rigged to seal the entrance creak ominously. He looked around, frantically. Why would the police make such an obvious and clumsy attempt after he had shown them a quiet way in?

Boom!

"Stop it!" Instantly regretting his outburst, he hid further back in the shadows. *If they keep it up, that madman will start shooting people – my people!* "Ah, crap!" he snarled, and ran across the open courtyard to the main gates. Having no idea whether he had been spotted, he wasted no time in using his shovel to prise the heavy timber joist away from the gates. With the lock already broken in the robbery, the gates flew open, flinging Gary down the passageway.

Rolling to a stop, he leaned on his shovel to get up. The pressure of such a sudden, explosive gale, intensified by the narrow coachway, made it difficult for him to stand against it.

Staggering backwards towards Rookstone's centre courtyard and shielding his eyes against flying debris, he spotted a figure in the gateway. It was no policeman. The giant antlers scraping the vaulted ceiling of the passageway were his first clue. The second was the way the immense, black-cowled figure drifted above the ground, completely unaffected by the hurricane forcing its way through the narrow channel.

"Aaaaarrrgghh!" Gary screamed, all pretence at stealth long driven from his mind.

Flattening himself against the wall, he allowed the huge spirit to pass – it was not as though he could have stopped him. However, when Herne reached out to touch Gary, he almost collapsed. The touch on his forehead was fleeting, but icy cold. Even weirder, he clearly heard the words '*Thank you*' inside his head.

Terrified beyond rational thought, Gary's new gift of seeing and hearing spirits was really starting to play havoc with his inner calm. Worse, he got the impression he had just taken responsibility for letting something in, with no idea what that might mean.

Sir Kenneth was about to order an armed response team to storm the castle via the side door when, for no obvious reason, the front doors blew in. He gaped, half expecting the criminal gang to run out shooting, but there was no sign of life at all.

Putting it down to the high winds, he ordered a pincer movement – two teams, front and side doors.

Howling around the courtyard within the castle's massive walls, the wind and accompanying sounds of destruction caught everyone's attention. Liam and Willy Mammoth ran to the windows to see what was happening.

Scott fired a shot through the window above their heads, smashing one of the small Georgian panes. "Get away from tha windows! Ah want a clear field o' fire."

The tradies backed away, when something caught Willy's eye. Movement over the Scotsman's head, up in the minstrels' gallery above. Whatever it was flew down to strike the gunman on the back of the head, causing him to cry out and stagger.

Andy Wilson jumped to his feet. "Hey, that's my missing boot!"

It was, too.

"*I say, good shot, old chap, what?*" Enthusiastic Geoff congratulated Sir Edward, completely unheard by the living gathered below.

Scott picked it up and threw it at Andy. "Then ye'll be wanting it back, Cinderella!"

Andy raised his arms to block and the boot bounced off him. It landed on the flagstones for the merest moment before the floor began collapsing beneath their feet. Massive stones fell into a void below, into the torture chamber – Rookstone's *real* torture chamber – sealed off years earlier, following a séance that went horribly wrong.

Soon, everyone was edging back to the walls as the floor continued to fall away. Willy helped Sir Henry to his feet, drawing the injured man to safety. However, what they saw below was no mere vaulted room under the castle; it was a portal, where the falling masonry was torn away to oblivion.

Hanging on to anything secured to the walls, the men stared down in horror to a hell of torment and butchery, and standing at its heart, grinning up at them, was John Sage. He crooked a finger, beckoning them to him.

With so much power in the room, even the least sensitive among them could suddenly see everything. Hell's doorway was open, its tongues of fire and darkness reaching for them.

Stan the cameraman saw his chance and went for it. Legal or not, no one won awards for playing it safe. He charged after the armed police and special services operatives, camera perched on his shoulder, ignoring the bleating complaints of his reporter. As a professional visionary, he knew that when it was going down, people wanted to *see* it going down, not sit through the second-hand, warmed-up opinions of the commentariat after the fact.

The wind and rain tore at him, ripping away his camera's protective sheet – what he called, its shower cap – to vanish into the woods. He had to move quickly; the electronics would not stand such a battering from the elements for long.

Hanging back, he let the armed forces lead the way. Their focus all ahead, they barely noticed him file in after them, bringing up the rear. He ran through a twisting maze of corridors before arriving at a short passage that led from the kitchens through a massively built, early Tudor wall and out into the medieval – the original great hall that was modern Rookstone's cafeteria. At least, it used to be.

The officers in front pulled up sharply. Unsurprising. The floor was gone.

Police officers, builders and criminals were suddenly all in it together, all outdoing one another, as everyone screamed louder than everyone else.

The flying boot, whilst unnerving, was nothing compared with the floor falling away, and though that was terrifying, it was the view into Hell that really stole the show – until a monstrous, twelve-foot-tall, stag-headed spirit, draped in black reaper's rags, drifted through the wall.

Stan pushed his camera lens between armed responders too petrified to stop him or even notice as the horned god moved forward. Arms wide, reaching, bony fingers clawing, booming bark deafening; Herne's cry shook the ancient stones.

Ball in his court, John Sage waited for him to come on, red-hot poker in hand, a broken-toothed sneer on his face.

The forces of order and chaos met with a blinding flash and a sonic boom that rattled the teeth of the spectators in the terraces – or more precisely, those hanging from any hook or protrusion they could reach to avoid falling into the pit.

Herne drove Sage before him, while mankind's representatives wailed in terror – more discomposed than if they were forced to watch the supernatural slam dunk from inside the ball. He seemed unstoppable, until Sage focused the hellfire burning through him to push back. Flames engulfed the forest god, setting his robes alight as they came to grips.

Deadlock.

Nature and *un*nature, balanced.

Innocent blood had been spilt with intent and now there would be consequences.

Outside, Gary ran back to the relative safety of the tourist-friendly torture chamber – it was becoming that sort of day. Hiding in darkness, he could see armed police staggering through the main gateway as a freakish gale tore around the inner courtyard, toppling plant pots and knocking over benches. Bent double and recoiling from the elements, some doggedly headed for the entrance to the cafeteria, while others took up supporting positions.

To Gary, it looked like all hell was breaking loose – an easy metaphor to throw around when one was safely outside what used to be Rookstone's quaint little tearoom. Were he able to communicate with his men inside, they would certainly have straightened him on that score.

His thoughts strayed to Emma – thoughts of love immediately doused with a bucket of cold water, as he pictured himself trying to explain how much trouble he was in. Instantly, his mind flitted to the other prominent female in his life. Where was Poppy? Was she safe?

From somewhere at ankle height, almost lost amongst the monstrous din of the maelstrom erupting all around him, there came a determined snarl.

He looked down. "Poppy?" He could hardly believe it. She had already escaped from his apartment before he left Aleks with Inga. With everyone's lives on the line, there had been no time nor safe opportunity to search for her. Fortunately, man's best friend had found him. He guessed she must have trailed in after the police, but however she came to be there, he was indescribably glad to see her.

As he reached down to stroke his beloved pet, he noticed something less welcome – the flash of a blade. Worzel got to his feet in the shadows, pulling a second knife from somewhere hidden about him. Swapping it from one hand to the other, he leapt for Gary with murder in his eyes.

Stooped, Gary jumped sideways and fell into a stack of horrifying memorabilia, knocking timber staves and rusted blades all over the floor with a clatter.

Worzel followed, thrusting the blade forward, but Gary was just out of reach, so he took a step and slipped because Poppy had his ankle in her jaws. She snarled, her sharp little canines making short work of his trouser leg to bite into flesh. Worzel cried out, furiously shaking his foot to throw her off.

While his opponent was distracted, Gary got to his feet and caught Worzel with a powerful roundhouse punch to the side of his head. He would have gone down but for John Sage's favourite invention – a barrel with hundreds of rusty iron nails sticking through its sides. He fell onto it, causing it to wobble but neither it nor Worzel went down. He span instantly, swinging his knife in a vicious arc to keep Gary at bay.

Gary looked around for his shovel. Backing away, he reached down quickly to retrieve his faithful tool, holding it ready. In the low light, he could see Poppy poised to leap again for their enemy and that he was ready for her. "Poppy, no!"

Unsure what was expected, she hung back, and Gary moved forward.

Fear crossed Worzel's face. He had the knife, but with the shovel, Gary had the reach – the strapping, six-foot tradesman had the power, too. He flipped the knife over, to throw it again.

Gary had seen him try that last time and he, too, was ready for it. He brought the shovel down in a brutal sideswipe, carrying all his prodigious strength, born of years on the tools, to strike Worzel's right arm.

The thief screamed as the knife flew from his grasp. Grabbing his damaged arm with his left, he stepped back and stumbled once more against the spiked barrel.

Nearer the exit, Gary could see his face clearly. The expression of a beaten man. On any other day of his life, the builder's sense of moral decency would have made him withdraw, but all he could see that day was his nephew bleeding to death on his own bed, up in the north tower. Without stopping to think, he brought the shovel back round on the upswing with a roar of fury to chop into Worzel's side, giving him two broken ribs to go with his broken arm. Worse yet for the knifeman, he fell headfirst into John Sage's barrel. His clothing took the brunt of the damage, but his arms and face were shredded by the vicious, rusty nails all around the inside of the cask.

He screamed again, but Gary brought the shovel down on his backside, forcing him further in. Raising the shovel again for another, *final* blow, Gary shook with incandescent rage, his every sinew screaming at him to make the world a better place by ending this creature. Perhaps not the worst of their captors, he was, nevertheless, the one he had his hands on. Almost hyperventilating, he could barely see through his fury, when thoughts of Emma returned, and what might happen to her and their home, and those who relied on him, if he went to jail for administering the justice this animal so richly deserved. Twice he had tried to throw a knife at Gary, not caring about the outcome.

So stressed that his teeth chattered, Gary raised the shovel higher, his inner struggle, terrible, unbearable, when Poppy brushed against his leg. She was also shaking. As he looked down, eyes wild, she backed away, terrified, reminding Gary who he truly was. Throwing the shovel aside, he cast about, saw the barrel's lid and flipped it into place, banging the barrel head down with his fist.

Worzel was bawling for all he was worth, not daring to beat on the sides. He was folded up and trapped inside a cylinder of spikes, his broken bones setting the pain receptors in his brain on fire.

"Shut up!" Gary hollered back. "Now you listen to me! *Any* more trouble from you, and I'll roll you out of here, understand?"

A muffled, whimpered, "*Yes.*"

"If you struggle and this thing goes over, they won't be able to put you back together with superglue, got it?"

"*Yes.*"

Gary shook his head with contempt as he leaned on the barrel for support, releasing a long, slow breath.

Poppy whined.

He reached down and lifted her into his arms, kissing the top of her little head as he held her tight. "I'm sorry I frightened you, girl." It was the best he could do, for there was no time to lose. Aleks needed urgent help, so he ran to the doorway, not trusting himself to look back.

He burst out into what little daylight filtered through the growing storm. Pressing himself against the substantial walls of the south tower, he called out to the armed police officers hunkered down into their defensive positions opposite. Holding Poppy close to his chest, he waved his free arm to show that he was neither armed, nor dangerous. He had no wish to be shot by their rescuers, and for once, Poppy made no complaint.

They summoned him in turn, and he ran towards them, pathetically grateful for the chance to join hands with the real world.

Fire swirled, its roar deafening as it completely encompassed the once dainty tearoom, and at its heart, John Sage and the Hornèd One circled, each looking for advantage. The forest god hoped never to set foot inside the ring of stone, but there was always someone willing to draw evil to them, and he was now locked in single combat with no guarantee that he would win.

In contrast, and charged by blood and hellfire, Sage could not remember when he last felt so strong. Maybe this time he would break free to run amok far outside the stone walls of his prison.

Another item flew down from the minstrels' gallery. Unlike the work boot, this one carried meaning. The crucifix from the chapel's altar bounced off Sage's head and he cried out as it burned him.

"Have that, you blighter!" the Honourable Geoffrey hollered.

"Marvellous shot, fellow," Sir Edward applauded, returning his earlier compliment. "Remarkable how much easier it is to move things that are already spiritually charged, isn't it? I found that boot in the chapel, too."

"I say, one of the old ones must have left it there for dear old Beatie to bless by accident. You know how they love moving things around. The chap will have one foot that smells of flowers from now on, what? Wish we could get her to bless a flagon of ale, eh? Eh?"

"Capital suggestion!" Sir Edward enthused. "We'll see to it, right after our bully rook friend puts that churl back in his box. Incredible, how the old chap hid his true purpose from us all these years. At him, fellow – we're all behind you!"

In the crucible beneath the gallery, and with his adversary's concentration momentarily broken, Herne pushed his advantage, thrusting Sage down, but with the power of Hell at his back, Sage again recovered quickly to launch a counter-attack.

Sister Beatrice knelt before the altar in her chapel, just above the minstrels' gallery. Every moment she spent on the earthly plane was spent in prayer. However, the horrendous din from the next room below was becoming so all-encompassing that she could no longer hear herself think.

She prayed for patience. It was not forthcoming. No one had presumed to make such an almighty racket outside her chapel in centuries. She turned to the door and glowered, her anger growing by the second. *How dare they? Have they* no *respect?* Twice she had stirred, intending to go down and shut them up, and twice she had stopped herself, for they never heard her – and if they did, they never listened – but this really was too much.

She redoubled her efforts to concentrate on her prayers, when she noticed her crucifix was missing from the altar. Someone had stolen it while her back was turned. A bang rattled the chapel's door behind her. "Right, that does it! Play knock and run on God's house, would you? Steal his things? I'll show you!"

She shot through the door – in her temper, not bothering to open it – and flew down the short flight of stone steps that cut through the mighty wall of the south tower. Drifting out onto the minstrels' gallery that, just minutes before, had overlooked Rookstone's tearoom, Beatrice stopped mid-bluster. Flabbergasted, she had never seen the 'old problem' get so far out of control before – and right outside her chapel, no less. She could hardly believe the temerity; they had even filched her crucifix! Filled with a fierce, heavenly wrath, never experienced before in her death, her rage bubbled forth like an exploding kettle. "Forsooth, WHAT THE BLOODY HELL IS GOING ON HERE?"

The combatants released and backed away, each dumbstruck as they looked up at Sister Beatrice along with everyone else.

The torture chamber, the original great hall and subsequent quaint little tearoom all fell silent. Even the flames of hellfire banked, for the nun's spirit was no longer alone. Completely eclipsed by brilliant white light, she was thrown into silhouette. Behind her, the short stair up to the chapel morphed into a gleaming, pearlescent stairway that wound upwards, seemingly forever.

Herne bowed and stood aside as the Wrath tore through Sage, white hot, burning him back to a human shadow, etched in stone.

Beatrice turned to look up in beatific ecstasy, falling to her knees in abasement. Answering a call only she could hear, she stood and began to climb. Everyone watched in awe until she vanished, taking the stairway with her.

Chapter 21

The Size of a Crown

The builders, criminals, and men and women of the constabulary all fell onto a remarkably solid flagstone floor.

Still holding Poppy close to his chest, Gary burst into the room with another half-dozen officers, only to skid to a halt in the sudden silence. However, not all was returned to normal. Sir Edward and Enthusiastic Geoff floated down to stand by him.

"Better late than never, young man." Sir Edward winked. "Clever dog, that. Splendid little chap—" *Woof!* "Girl."

"Wha'?" Gary barely enunciated as the others picked themselves up from the tearoom floor.

"Looks like old Beatie got a ticket back upstairs, what?" Geoff noted, looking back up to the minstrels' gallery.

"She'll be pleased about that," Sir Edward agreed. "Looks like they've forgiven her, now she can no longer cast the first stone."

Gary slowly began to realise that everyone in the room could also see the ghosts.

"Residual energy." Sir Edward guessed his thoughts. "It'll pass."

"But I never got to thank Sister Beatrice for saving my life," Gary mumbled, not wanting to be overheard.

Sir Edward smiled. "She'll hear you. They'll be able to cope with her up there, now she's no longer perfect. 'What the bloody hell's going on here?' indeed," he chuckled. "That'll keep me warm on cold nights. Her stairway to Heaven began with a minor sin, you see?"

"I knew it began with A-minor," Willy Mammoth muttered, distractedly, as he sidled up to Gary and the talking spirits. He waved a hand through them.

Even Enthusiastic Geoff managed a look of disapproval.

"Sorry, I just wondered... never mind..." The giant tailed off.

Materialising from a darkened corner, a truly giant shadow drifted towards the centre of the room to loom over them.

Suddenly reunited with the Hornèd One, Gary dropped Poppy and jumped a foot in the air. "Holy s—"

"*Don't you dare!*" Sister Beatrice's voice boomed, as though through a PA system.

"Sorry," Gary called. "Oh, and thank you!"

Poppy *yipped* at him for dropping her.

"I told you, fellow," Sir Edward noted, smugly. "Knew she wouldn't be far away."

Enthusiastic Geoff grinned. "At least she'll be far enough that I can do this without having to sneak off to the *Stag's Head* all the time, what?" He took a pull from his hip flask.

"*Wastrel! Profligate boy!*" Sister Beatrice's voice boomed again, making him choke and cough.

Ignoring them, Herne glided across the room to float in front of the main fireplace before turning to face them all. He looked down, almost dotingly.

The criminals were too scared to run away and no longer sure enough of their legs to try.

The forest god rose up to the enormous elk crown that spanned the wall, high above the great fireplace. Perhaps half a million years old and the largest yet found, its antlers measured eighteen feet, tip to tip, dwarfing even the spirit himself. Arms wide, he became one with the remnant of that majestic beast, eyes filling empty sockets only briefly before vanishing, seemingly absorbed by the ancient horn and bone.

"I'm amazed," Sir Edward admitted.

"You're not the only one!" Gary retorted.

"No. I mean, with so much power channelled through that rogue, Sage, I thought it would take a sacrifice at the very least, to bring the darkness back under control."

Gary turned to him. "Well, wasn't that heavenly light sort of, you know, the power of... of *Him?* Upstairs, I mean?"

The Tudor spirit frowned in puzzlement and then shrugged. "Perhaps. Don't know anyone who's actually met Him. Not sure He likes us very much. We're considered something of a flop in Heaven, after the big launch He gave us and everything. Caused a bit of a family rift, too – I'm sure you've heard the stories – very nasty. Anyway, that aside, we won't see our hornèd friend again for a while."

"Dear old Ernie," Enthusiastic Geoff noted, gently. "Or should I say, deer old, eh? Eh? *Deer* old – get it? What?"

"Stupid boy! I've told you not to call him that."

Geoff sighed, contentedly. "Still, first rate performance. Certainly showed that rotter, Sage. Total collapse of stout party, what?"

Sir Henry hobbled over on his crutches. "Great-Uncle *Geoffrey?*"

"Hello, old man," the youthful spirit greeted. "Harry sends his best. Often pops in now and again, to keep an eye on you and dear old Rookstone, what?"

Sir Henry smiled, a tear in the corner of his eye. "Grandpapa Harry..."

"Here, have a snifter." Geoff offered his flask to Sir Henry.

The baronet tried to take it, but his hand grasped nothing but air.

"Allow me, old chap." Geoff poured the gin into Sir Henry's mouth.

Sir Henry's eyes widened in astonishment as his long-dead relative became solid before his very eyes.

"Not really meant to do that, but it might help the next time we need to send you a warning, what?"

Sir Edward frowned, but what was done was done. "I do wish you'd stop saying that," he deflected.

"What?"

"What!"

"What?"

"No, I mean I wish you'd stop saying wha..."

Sir Edward and the Honourable Geoffrey Grey faded, yet somehow Gary knew their bickering continued, right by his side.

Their final disappearance led to a certain amount of clearing of throats and checking of shoelaces from all who remained. No one wanted to be the first to admit to *anything* they had just seen or heard.

Only one man moved. Scott took the forgotten pistol, hidden in his jacket, and grabbed Gary around the throat, pulling him off balance to take him hostage in one final bid to escape, when the gunman's eyes crossed and he fell backwards.

Hammer stood behind him, hand still raised, having brought it down on the back of his ex-known associate's head, right at the crown. He took the gun from him and, lifting it carefully, barrel first, handed it to the nearest police officer.

"That's the second time Rookstone's played host to the Hammer of the Scot!" Sir Henry noted, drolly.

Gary groaned, massaging his throat, but grudgingly thanked the gang's leader, before throwing his arms around his brother, Jimmy.

"I thought we'd lost you," Jimmy admitted, with a manly sniffle, whilst removing some dust from his eye.

"I thought I'd lost me, as well. From now on, we only renovate bungalows – deal?"

The For Keeps team laughed and gathered around, boisterously congratulating each other on their survival, when an urgent thought struck Jimmy. "Aleks! Where is he? Is he OK?"

Before Gary could allay his concerns, DI Mellow spoke. "Don't worry about the lad. A medical team already have him in an ambulance outside. I hear they've stabilised him and he'll make a full recovery, given time and rest."

"That was the first thing I took care of, when I made it to the police," Gary explained. "That's why I wasn't here. You won't believe what happened to me out there."

His men looked at one another, and as one, burst out laughing.

"Yes," Mellow continued. "This is likely to be a very, *very* long debriefing. Come on, you lot. Let's be about it. Sergeant." He summoned one of his officers and gestured to Scott. "Pick that rubbish up off the floor, would you?"

Turning away to carry out the order, the officer cried out in alarm.

Everyone looked round urgently.

Scott's unconscious form was no longer there. In his place, there lay a wrought-iron poker with a rag wrapped around one end for a handle, red tip smouldering as it cooled.

Everyone froze in shocked silence. Everyone but Hammer. "Looks like there'll be a new face in Hell tonight." Never given to any such beliefs, he surprised even himself.

"What was it the spirit of Sir Edward said?" Gary mused.

Sir Henry nodded, catching on. "Something about being surprised that no sacrifice had been necessary."

A chill ran through the room, making them shudder.

"Aaarrghhh, *noooooo!*"

Again, every person in the room jumped, dreading what might be coming next.

Stan the cameraman was on his knees, hands in the air, screaming at the heavens, like an iconic scene from *Platoon*.

"What's the matter with him?" Mellow demanded. "And what the bloody hell's the press doing in here?"

Two officers tried to help the distraught cameraman to his feet, but Stan just hung between them, shaking his head miserably. "My rig got wet and didn't record any of it. Not a damned thing. Oh, *noooo,*" he groaned. "I'm gonna be the punchline to a joke – doomed to film talking heads for the rest of my natural."

Chapter 22

Bird Up

Sir Kenneth entered the tearooms, greeting his son with an awkward handshake. Weirdly, given the extraordinary events of the last few minutes, nothing in the room was awry – not so much as a wrinkled tablecloth – further mystifying the witnesses and leading them to question whether any of it happened at all.

All Gary knew was that he was grateful, because two others entered the now-calm, pretty little café with Sir Kenneth. Richard Clarence, Sir Henry's secretary, and even more welcome, his wife, Emma. Had she witnessed the recent insanity, she would never have let him out of the house again.

She ran to his arms. He lifted and span her round unashamedly. Poppy *yipped* at their feet to be included.

Emma kissed him. "I checked on Aleks. He's conscious and doing well. He gave me this."

She held out Gary's silver Saxon cross. He bowed his head for her to place it around his neck. "Should be a gold medal, really." She smiled proudly and kissed him again.

He smiled back. "I'm happy with silver." It felt cold, so he pulled it out, over the top of his T-shirt, half expecting a word in his ear, but none came.

Henry's reunion with Richard was less enthusiastic. The baronet eyed the man who betrayed him and his family, balefully. "Why?" he asked, simply.

Before Richard could answer, Sir Henry held up a hand. "Who's the senior police officer here?"

Mellow approached him. "I'm Detective Inspector Mellow. You'd be Sir Henry Grey?"

Henry nodded. "Inspector, I have documentary evidence that I believe will help you convict *everyone* involved in this fiasco. When the original robbery took place, the police asked me how the criminals gained access to the security codes for my new alarm system. I can now answer that. I found a set of photographic negatives in my secretary's desk, showing every blueprint and code for the entire system. When I questioned the head ruffian," he gestured to Hammer, "he confirmed that Richard was their inside man. He photographed all the information they needed and must have forwarded it to them."

Mellow turned to Richard. "How do you answer this?"

"Actually," Sir Kenneth intervened, "*I* can answer your questions, gentlemen. While the drama of this situation has distracted the nation, MI5 has been running a covert mission to arrest the people behind this and several similar, high-value crimes across Europe. Mr Richard Clarence was approached by Security Services as soon as Interpol informed us of the possibility that the Grey Emeralds might be the next target." He eyed Sir Henry directly. "You understand that, until the crime was in motion, all we had were a few meetings with various proxies. Easily deniable, a good legal team would have shredded our case. Now all we need to complete our investigation is to get full statements from the thieves themselves, but whether they cooperate or not, we have enough, now the crime has taken place."

"I'm sorry, Henry," Richard apologised. "I'll, of course, tender my resignation with immediate effect. Wanted to tell you, but I would have been in contravention of the Official Secrets Act."

"They were coming for you, anyway, Sir Henry," Sir Kenneth explained, "but Mr Clarence's assistance allowed us to get those *truly* responsible."

"You were meant to be absent when the crime happened – away with Eleanor and the children, down in Yorkshire. When I saw what they did to you..." He faltered.

"I seem to recall it was no picnic for you, either," Sir Henry allowed.

Richard smiled, ruefully. "No. Being beaten half to death wasn't part of my plan, but I'm sorry, Henry. Truly. I would never have kept silent if I'd known you planned to return and confront them – whether it meant prison for me or not. You see, I *did* know that the emeralds in the alarmed display cabinet were fake, so I believed there was nothing to lose. I would never have put the real emeralds at risk, either."

Henry nodded, digesting all he had learned. "How did you know they were fake? I never told you."

Richard nodded to Sir Kenneth. "MI5 seem to know more about our lives than we know ourselves," he explained, sardonically. "I couldn't have borne it, had the real ones been stolen."

Henry scrutinised his secretary, wondering why he felt such a strong attachment to the Grey family heirlooms. Gripper, of the local constabulary, moved into his peripheral vision. When he focused on him, and when the sergeant thought no one was looking, his expression was furious as DI Mellow arrested the miscreants. Henry had no idea about the man's scheme to acquire a new extension to his home, but he certainly had no wish to see him promoted. He was equally certain that Gary would tell him where to go, should he be asked to quote for the work.

Mellow began with Hammer. "Jack Clarence, also known as Hammer, I am arresting you—"

"Jack *Clarence?*" Gary could barely stop himself from laughing.

Hammer glared, murderously. "You got a problem with that?"

Trying unsuccessfully to wipe the grin off his face, Gary replied, "Sorry, *Jack,* but you're no angel, are you?"

The builders laughed.

Gary turned to the arresting officer. "By the way, if you haven't found him already, their fourth man is in the touristy torture chamber room, over there." He waved, vaguely. "He's the one in the barrel with a face covered in s—" he glanced nervously up at Beatrice's chapel, "—omething awful."

Sir Henry could not help noting Richard's surprise at Hammer's real name, too. Sharing a surname was nothing unusual, but MI5 obviously had not informed him of the fact.

"You do not have to say anything," Mellow continued, "but it may harm your defence if you do not mention when questioned something which you later rely on in court. Anything you do say may be given in evidence—"

"Hang on," Hammer forestalled him. "I'd like to return these." Before a constable put him in handcuffs, he took out a black felt bag and offered it to Sir Henry. "These ain't real, are they?"

Sir Henry gave just a hint of a wry smile. "Afraid not, old chap. It was all for nothing."

"I'd like to see the real ones... just once."

Mellow barked a laugh. "No problem, we'll have Sir Henry run out and get them for you!"

Hammer locked an earnest gaze with Sir Henry. "Please?"

Despite himself, Sir Henry had to ask why.

"I dunno. Don't think I could have sold 'em on, you know?"

"Really?"

Hammer shook his head as the officer cuffed him. "As soon as I saw them in the photograph I was shown, I knew I wanted 'em. Not to sell, but to keep 'em safe, like."

"Oh, my... He's one of them."

Gary jumped again, placing a hand over his complaining heart. His cross was *freezing.* He almost called out for Inga, but realised in time that he would look like a man in need of psychological evaluation if he did. Perhaps he was.

"Remember the vision I showed you." Inga went on to explain what she knew and what she believed, and Gary's whole body went cold.

Once the criminals were removed, Sir Henry was questioned about what lay beneath Rookstone's tearooms. He explained what little was known about the castle's original torture chamber and some of the atrocities that took place there. Mellow was not given to flights of fancy. The Scottish villain had clearly gone somewhere, and he intended to find him. He ordered men to search the chamber beneath the cafeteria.

"You can't. It was blocked up years ago," Sir Henry explained.

Mellow turned a baleful eye towards Gary's men. "You lot! You can start helping the police with their enquiries by grabbing your tools. I've got a job for you."

Within minutes, the blocked-up entrance was open again. Torches were shone into the dark space beneath the castle, though they mostly just reflected the dust caused by falling masonry. Eventually, it cleared enough for Mellow to step inside.

The ceiling was of vaulted stone – no surprise, given the flagstoned floor above – but more disconcerting was the way the floor sloped. It created a dizzying effect.

Sir Henry hobbled his way in after him, crutches *ticking* on the stones. "It was sloped for the blood to run away," he stated, reading the policeman's mind.

Mellow stared at him. "And you *live* here?" he asked with morbid incredulity.

"Of course. Well, not in *here,* obviously."

Mellow shook his head as he shone the torch around. "Love what you've done with the place." It was obvious that no one had been in the empty chamber for some time. There was certainly no evidence that the floor above had ever fallen into it – and none that a Scottish villain had, either.

"Alright, I've seen enough. You can rebuild that wall now, bonnie lads."

"We'll get right on it," Gary replied in a tone that might have been courteous, but might just as easily have been narky. Realising he could not prove it either way, Mellow simply walked out, leaving dusty footprints in the corridor outside.

It occurred to Gary that, just because they saw nothing of interest with the naked eye, it did not necessarily mean the chamber contained nothing of interest. Jerry flat refused to go near the place, which concerned him. Of all his men, he was the most unswervingly enthusiastic and willing. Gary would make it his business to find out what happened during Jerry's short incarceration and how he acquired the burn on his arm – neither of which he seemed willing to discuss – at least, not yet. He would give the young man time.

Andy knocked up some mortar while Jimmy cleaned old mortar from the stones they had removed, readying them to be relaid.

As the wall grew back, shutting out what little light there was, two pairs of eyes watched from the shadows. Invisible to all, they missed nothing as they were sealed back within the absolute darkness of their tomb.

Six weeks later
"That's the last of the masonry in place to the south range, and the cellar and vault room are ready for your valuables as soon as the paint's dry." Gary held out his hand to Sir Henry. "It's been quite a ride."

Henry shook the hand and laughed; his strength was returning. "Haven't been able to do that for a while."

"Shake hands?"

"No. Laugh. Not without literally splitting my sides, anyhow."

Gary grinned broadly.

"Look, I know this job has been hell for you chaps," Henry continued, "and I'll understand if you never want to set foot in the place again, but if you do find yourselves in the north again, you'll be most welcome guests at Rookstone. I'm extremely grateful to you for finishing the job, after everything." He handed Gary an envelope. "Just a small drink for your lads, with my compliments."

"Thank you. Most kind, and I'll bear that in mind, Sir—"

"Henry. Just Henry. You're family now, remember?"

Gary smiled again. "Yes, that was quite a shock, I don't mind admitting. As for finishing the job – it's what we do. Even if we had a huge win on the Pools, we'd make sure of our commitments before retiring to Barbados."

Sir Henry studied him. "Yes, I believe you would. And I'm sorry I ever suspected you. Didn't know who to trust."

"With good reason."

"Yes, well... All that's behind us now. By the way, you'll never guess who called me this morning. Remember that cameraman chappie? I think his name was Stan."

Gary nodded.

"Apparently, he's not willing to give up on collecting evidence about the supernatural occurrences at dear old Rookstone. He's put a team together to come back and carry out a paranormal study – for television, no less. That should round up a few tourists." He smiled. "Might get my money back on all this wretched security equipment yet!"

Gary grinned. "That's great. I'll look forward to watching it, although, for their sakes, I hope they don't find much."

"Quite," Sir Henry agreed, ruefully. "Ooh, I almost forgot. Come, let me take you back to where all this began."

Gary followed Sir Henry into Albert's ticket office, where the old man was reaching up onto a shelf to bring down a lollipop for the little girl buying a ticket.

"Morning, Albert."

"Good morning, Gary. You lads gannin' hjem[1]?"

"Yes, we're off shortly." He shook the old man's hand, while Sir Henry went through his old retainer's desk for the Grey family album.

"You might be interested to see this."

Gary was intrigued.

"Gary?"

He turned to see Jerry at the door. "I say, good morning, chaps. Just wanted to let you know the vans are loaded and the men are ready for the off."

Gary called him in. "Come and see. This is the photo that started all this – sixty years ago."

Jerry frowned and leaned in with interest as Sir Henry thumbed through various pictures of his ancestors until he reached the photograph of a man who looked not unlike him, leaning proudly against what must have been a brand-new Bentley at the time. In the background was Gary's out-of-context Transit van, with For Keeps Ltd livery emblazoned along its side. Gary had seen that before. What was new, was the hand reaching out from the driver's window giving a middle-finger salute known as 'the bird'.

He looked up in astonishment, but Sir Henry was already rocking with laughter. "I can't possibly let you leave before you explain how *that* happened."

During their subsequent weeks at Rookstone, Gary had told his team about the existence of the photograph, but Jerry had never seen it before, so failed to get the reference. He was more interested in the photograph beneath it. "I *say*, it couldn't be, could it?"

Gary, Albert and Sir Henry looked at him, quizzically.

By way of explanation, Jerry took out his wallet from a trouser pocket, opened it, and pulled out a photograph of his own. He placed it on the table. It matched the one in the album exactly – clearly a second print from the same negative.

"I *say*," Sir Henry echoed in his identical public-school manner. "That's Grandpa Harry – Henry Grey the first – and that's his best friend, Dodgy."

Jeremy Horatio Jarvis stood open-mouthed. "You recognise him? He was my grandfather, Roger Jarvis. He served with the Royal Northumberland Fusiliers. I knew he was barracked up here somewhere. Sadly, the old chap was lost on the beaches in Normandy, in '44. My father was just a baby, but he gave me this photo when I was a child, so that I would never forget him, nor his sacrifice for our country."

Sir Henry's jaw dropped, too. "Roger was Grandpa Harry's closest friend. He spoke of him often, forever telling me stories about him and his mate, Dodgy, and all they got up to – and you're his *grandson?*" He stood, no longer requiring the aid of crutches, and reached out his hand. "My dear fellow. I had no idea."

---

1. 'Going home'. As well as many place names, some dialects in the north-east of England still retain Norse and Danish expressions from the centuries of Viking invasion that ended almost a millennium ago – just one more drop in the bucket of Britain's unique history and heritage (no endorsement from the tourist board yet, but I'll keep writing).

Gary was bemused. The upper echelons of society were by their very nature a select group, so it came as no great surprise when so many of them knew one another or were related in some way. Despite rubbing along together in Rookstone for several weeks, they shook hands like long-lost friends. Gary studied Jerry in particular; no longer the callow youth of just six weeks ago, his experiences had indeed made a man of him. About that, at least, his father seemed to have been right, and when Jerry extended his hand, Gary could clearly see the livid scar left on the young man's arm by the torturer's poker.

He stood back, taking them both in. "Well, hasn't *this* been a family affair?"

"It certainly has," Sir Henry agreed, shaking his head in bemusement. "But the one thing it has not been, is a coincidence. I'm convinced of it. It seems that when our ancient home was threatened, we were called – all of us."

Gary nodded. "And we answered."

"And that's as it should be," Jerry conceded.

"Come on, Poppy, hup!" After her last comfort break on the D-shaped lawn – exactly where her first had been – the little dog jumped happily up into Gary's van. Emma was still wrangling with the insurance over the one Hammer had stolen and Serj had burned out. *That* would be an incidental, tacked onto the end of the gang's long list of crimes, but it would all sort itself out in due course.

Jerry sat in one of the two passenger seats, gazing down lovingly at the Kodak Six-16 Junior camera Sir Henry gifted to him – the one that belonged to Roger, Jerry's grandfather, and which shot that very photograph so many years ago.

Gary looked back at Rookstone with mixed feelings. Within her walls, he had suffered the worst and most terrifying time of his life, but also discovered family he never knew he had, and made many lifelong friends – who would probably remain friends long after that life drew to a close. While in no hurry to cross over, at least he was assured of a warm welcome when the time came. A great comfort.

One hand on his Saxon cross, he raised the other to shield his eyes from the sun and smiled. Inga, Sir Edward and Enthusiastic Geoffrey all stood in Rookstone's mighty shadow, ready to wave him off. It occurred to Gary that he had seen something very similar somewhere before. When a giant, black-caped figure materialised to stand behind them, he snorted and raised his hand in farewell. "May the force be with you!"

Sir Edward's smile froze. He leaned in close to Inga. "What did he say?"

"Don't know. Something about gravy sauce with stew?"

Sir Edward shook his head, sadly. "Still not sure your fellow's playing with a full deck o' cards."

"How dare you, after all he's done here!"

"Come back soon, what?" Geoff called, raising his gin flask.

"I *do* wish you would stop saying what all the time," Sir Edward scolded.

Gary laughed and climbed into his van. Turning the vehicle around, he waved again and drove away, leaving them bickering, quite possibly forever.

After a long day at the wheel, Gary delivered his men home safely and finally crunched up the gravel of his own driveway.

Poppy yapped, spinning excited circles on the passenger seat.

They disembarked together to enter their very own castle like conquering heroes, complete with damsel-in-a-dress and dinner on the table. Gary was indeed a lucky man.

Later that evening, he sat on the sofa in front of the television, Poppy on his lap, arm around his beloved. Everything seemed perfect, but Emma had something she needed to get off her chest.

"Before we switch the TV on," she began, "there's a couple of things I want to tell you."

"Oh?"

"Mmm. Firstly, I think I've found our next project. I'm sure you've had enough of medieval castles for a bit – how would you feel about an old railway station?"

"Is it single storey?"

"Not sure, why?"

"No reason. Carry on."

"OK. I saw an article in the paper a few days ago, about a man who's bought a station in North Wales. It was once part of a narrow-gauge railway that delivered slate down from the mountains."

"Sounds intriguing," Gary allowed.

"I thought so. Anyway, I contacted the new owner. He'd heard all about the famous, heroic builders who defended a castle and saved its owner from violent criminals, so it was no great sell on my part. He wants to meet us – *you*. It's a beautiful part of the world and you need a break, so I've booked us a cottage nearby. Thought we could make it a busman's holiday?"

Gary nodded, approving. "Sounds great."

"Well, there's more."

"'Course there is," he muttered, tiredly.

"What?"

"Nothing, darling. Carry on."

"Well, it's just that the station is called *Gorsaf Hen Garreg* – not sure I pronounced that correctly. It means Old Stone Station."

"You trying to say I'm past it?"

She grinned. "No, silly, but let's just say the name *called* to me," she explained, wryly.

Gary's expression clouded. He had had just about as much destiny as he could handle for a while. "Which railway is it?"

"Actually, the railway no longer connects to the station any more. It was a branch line, built later, to transport workers to the slate mines, but the lines were taken up years ago. The owner wants to turn the building into a home for himself, with tearooms on the side, for the tourists."

Gary's enthusiasm dropped another notch. "Tearooms? Why am I already getting a bad feeling about this project?"

"Don't be silly. It'll be lovely, just what you need after... well, everything. The owner is in talks with the railway to reconnect *Hen Garreg* back onto the line. Again, as part of a mutual scheme to capture tourism. The railway is called... oh, dear me, I don't how to say that, either."

"Give it a go," he encouraged.

"*Dim Ffordd Heulog Siamus.* Apparently, it's ironic."

"What's it mean?"

"Couldn't find that one out. Chap said they don't talk about it. Maybe we can ask the locals when we get there? Or perhaps we could ask Blackout – he speaks Welsh, doesn't he?"

"I suppose."

"What's wrong?"

"Oh, nothing."

She threw her arms around him and kissed his cheek. "A week in the gorgeous mountains of Snowdonia, long walks on the beach and—"

Woof!

"See? Poppy's excited about it already – aren't you, darling? Yes, you are." She tickled the little dog under her chin.

"Great. She gets doted on, and *I* get outvoted on."

"Oh, don't be such a grouch. We're going on holiday!"

Gary brightened. "You're right, I'm being silly." He sighed contentedly and reached for the remote control. "Let's see what's on."

The TV came to life with a new show titled *The Villain Next Door*. "One for the neighbours," he commented, drily, immediately switching channels. Next up was *Ghostbusters*. He groaned and tried again. *The News*. "Nope." He switched it off. "I'm not even going to try Channel 4. It'll probably be a show about health and safety on building sites with endless clips of people falling off buildings! You know what, Em? I fancy a nice quiet evening with no telly. What do you say?"

Emma smiled but seemed troubled. Having sedated her husband with a hearty meal, a pretty dress and some positive news, the moment she had been dreading could not be put off any longer. "Remember I told you I had a *couple* of things to tell you?"

Gary sensed her reservation and braced himself, holding his Saxon cross nervously – a recent habit he had fallen into. After all, it had certainly brought him luck when he needed it most. Thankfully, it remained metal-cool, rather than frigid cold. Cautiously, he asked, "What now?"

Awkwardly, she explained about his winning ticket. The one she forgot to pass on to the Pools man when she rushed out to see Sir Kenneth, all those weeks ago. The one with a dozen Score Draws that were never entered into that week's competition.

He blinked, instantly taking in the full ramifications of her news and almost as quickly passing from fury, at the injustice of it, to collapsing into fits of laughter. Poppy jumped down to the carpet and yapped excitedly as Gary kept on laughing until his sides hurt and tears came. Eventually, he managed to speak. "That was the day I fell from the roof of Rookstone Castle." He kissed her, to set her mind at rest.

Emma had been so upset when she found his slip, staring accusingly up at her from the kitchen table. Worth a small fortune, it was now just a piece of paper, and bringing such news after everything he had endured was awful, but she could never have hidden it from him.

Gary continued to laugh. "Listen, why don't you get that ticket framed, because I tell you sincerely, I regret *nothing!*" Nor did he, because they were alive, and life was good, and about to get even better.

He produced three Polaroid photographs from his pocket. Still chuckling, he showed them to Emma. "In the morning, I'd like you to lodge an official complaint with Northumberland Police, please. I wrote the location, date, the officer's name and collar number on the back for everyone's convenience – not that you'll forget our friend, here. See? He even, very kindly, provided me with his fax number! Sergeant Gripper is a very naughty boy, driving a police vehicle with bald tyres like that. Someone should do something."

Emma burst out laughing. "Don't worry, *someone* will!"

The Interview: part VII, August 1994

Brandon burst out laughing. "No!"

"Yes," Gary confirmed with a smirk. "Earned him three points on his driving licence. I had the recently promoted Sergeant Josh Charlton send me confirmation that he'd paid the fixed penalty notice, too."

"Excellent." The interviewer clapped his hands together, still chuckling in high spirits. "So, what's next for Gary Stone and the For Keeps team?"

"Exciting times. We're about to begin a project in the mountains of North Wales, but we've also had some interest from a celebrity I can't name at this point, who wants to make a documentary about the restoration work we do and the importance of saving our historic structures. Touch wood, things are going to get better than I could have hoped just a couple of months ago."

"Wow. Well, I'm sure everyone at home will look forward to hearing more about that. And to finish off, have you seen any more ghosts lately?"

Gary rubbed the Saxon cross at his throat between his forefinger and thumb with a faraway look in his eye. "They're never far away from us."

Brandon frowned, turning to see what Gary was looking at.

Drawn to the cross, Inga moved in to gently stroke his cheek. "*Well done, my son.*" It was a proud moment for Gary Stone, and she would not spoil it. The warning she carried could wait.

Hammer lay on his upper bunk, reading a fortnight-old newspaper. He looked up as one of the screws dropped an envelope onto the small table in his cell.

"Clarence. Post," the guard stated.

"Thanks, Mr Hives. Mr Hives?"

The guard stopped midway to the heavy steel door and turned. "Yes?"

"Couldn't pass it up here, could you? I've just gotten myself comfortable."

Hives treated him to a wry smile. "You're getting fat, Clarence. Need to move around a bit more. I'd be doing you a disservice. Enjoy your letter." He left to continue his mail run along the mezzanine where Hammer was stored at Her Majesty's pleasure.

The morose safecracker who shared his cell was out in the yard, making the most of the time he was allowed to spend away from Hammer.

Listlessly and with a great sigh, the prisoner slid off the side of his bunk to take the envelope from the table. It was postmarked Northumberland. He turned it back over and studied the handwriting – a neat cursive.

Opening the letter, he flicked his kettle on and sat at the table to read something, hopefully, *less* than a fortnight old. The letter was written on two sheets of heavy grade, high quality notepaper and looked like it had been written with a fountain pen. Rather different from the missives received from those who occasionally remembered him, but what really caught his attention was the Grey family seal at the top, addressed Rookstone Castle.

He read the letter in growing confusion, not at all sure what to make of it. When finished, he read it again, more slowly. It did not help.

A week later...
Another letter. Hammer had never been so popular. The new letter, also postmarked Northumberland, was thicker and heavier. Bemused, he tore it open and began to read. Now he was really confused.

Getting to his feet, he tucked the papers into a pocket and walked out of his cell, down the steel steps from the mezzanine to the concrete floor at ground level. A guard sat by the door reading a paper. He looked up, questioning.

"Library, sir."

The guard looked genuinely surprised but nodded, before turning to the sports page at the back.

Hammer entered the prison library and searched for what he was after. Perhaps unsurprisingly, it was not there, so he approached the man Her Majesty's Prison Service laughingly referred to as the librarian.

Hardly a connoisseur of literary endeavour, he was nevertheless helpful, and, once certain Hammer was not there to prank him, promised to order the books he requested.

Three years, one month later...
Hammer stepped outside the gates of Wormwood Scrubs Prison. It was a fine day in October, with clear blue skies carrying sparse puffs of white cloud that occasionally crossed the sun. The temperature was cool, but he did not care. He was outside. The very air seemed different this side of those great and awful walls. He breathed deeply, holding his face up to the sun and closing his eyes contentedly.

He had experienced the joy of release more times than he cared to admit. It had never stuck. Invariably, he had gotten into a car – quite often stolen – to begin his cycle of crime and punishment all over again. It was not as though anyone would have offered a man with his record a job. At least, not until now.

Hammer was about to go and work for quite possibly the only man in Britain who would ever trust him. There was a reason for that.

The gentleman in question had also been kind enough to advance him some cash against his first month's salary, so he hailed a black cab and asked the driver to take him to London's Victoria Station.

Ten hours later...

Rookstone Castle cast long shadows across its driveway and lawns. The taxi crunched the gravel as it pulled up in front of the main gates. Hammer paid the driver and stepped out with his suitcase.

With a toot of the horn, the cabbie drove away, leaving him alone.

He looked up into black windows that gave nothing away. The last time he stood there, he had also taken a moment to look around, before being bundled into a waiting police van and taken to the nearest station to be held overnight, while overlapping jurisdictions decided what to do with him.

He puffed out his cheeks, struggling to believe where he was or what he was proposing to do. His life, as he had known it, was over. Nothing was yet written about what came next.

A bolt slid noisily across the inside of the gates and one of them creaked open. Hammer remembered that sound. It had not changed. As far as he could tell, *nothing* had changed – perhaps it never would and, just maybe, he might find contentment in that.

Two men stepped out of the shadows within the gateway. He recognised them both.

Sir Henry Grey walked down the stone steps to greet him. "Hello again, Jack."

Hammer... no, that name was dead to him now. *Jack* shook the proffered hand awkwardly. "Sir Henry."

Henry smiled disarmingly. "Just Henry will do fine. You remember Richard, of course, don't you?"

Richard Clarence also held out a hand to him. "This time, we both know who we are. Better that way, don't you think?"

Jack Clarence nodded awkwardly. "I..." He tailed off, not sure how to express himself.

"Go on, old chap," Sir Henry encouraged. "We understand this is... an *adjustment* for you, but please, speak your mind."

Jack nodded. "It's just that I wanted to thank you, both of you, for speaking for me, before the beak – I mean, in the court."

"Let's say no more about it," Henry assured. "We knew you were unaware of your colleague's murderous intentions. When you biffed him on the head, you saved yourself, too, don't you know."

The ex-con frowned. "My first step to redemption?"

"Yes, that, too. Moreover, he was hired separately to take the emeralds to Europe and dispose of the rest of your chaps – you included."

High above, up on the battlements of the north tower, Scott observed Hammer's return. Unexpected as it was delicious, he saw an opportunity for revenge. A dragging sound made him turn.

John Sage approached. He sneered nastily. "The game begins again." His laughter became a hacking cough.

Scott's lip twisted in amusement but also anticipation.

"Come." Sage pulled him away from the battlements.

"Wha'?"

Sage pointed out to the woodland's edge, north of Rookstone. Both dark spirits saw the giant, black figure of the Hornèd One.

"Never let him come near you," Sage advised. "And never let anybody find your bones."

Scott nodded and backed away, following Dragfoot back inside their domain that was also their prison.

Sir Henry and his secretary, Richard, showed Jack to his new quarters within the castle. As head of security, his duties would now include safeguarding the very emeralds he came to steal – who could know better how that might be done?

Sir Henry allowed him to put down his bags before speaking. "I'm sure you'd like to settle in, but before you do, we'd like to show you something."

The three men left the west tower where the Greys and their staff lived, and crossed the courtyard to the vertically opposite east tower.

Jack could hardly suppress a shudder as he walked past the tearooms where he witnessed the opening of a gateway to another world, or some kind of meta reality that existed above the one he had always known. He had no idea what happened to Scott and hoped never to find out.

They walked down a vaulted corridor to a heavy steel door. Sir Henry operated the keypad to disable the alarm and then typed a separate code to open the door. Wrenching the steel handle, he pulled it open. Lights came on automatically in the room beyond. Unlike the damp, flooded cellar it used to be, the room was now brightly lit, its temperature and humidity moderate.

Against the southern wall was a set of built-in, heavy steel cabinets, each locked separately. Sir Henry took a key from his pocket and opened one of them, seemingly at random, for none were marked.

He slid a box out and placed it on the small table in the centre of the room, lit by a spotlight directly above. Taking yet another key, Sir Henry unlocked the box. He took a moment to study the men in his most secure inner sanctum. Both eyed the box keenly, hungrily. One knew what lay within and the other had clearly guessed. He smiled and opened the box.

Jack's sharp intake of breath spoke volumes. For the first time, he truly saw with his own eyes – *Hammer* was no longer anywhere to be found.

Scott's shade drifted towards the cellar, Sage dragging his leg right behind him. He had no need to drag it, not for nearly seven hundred years, but he enjoyed the effect it had on any who heard it.

Within, Sir Henry, Richard and Jack looked round at the sound. When it stopped abruptly, they simply put it down to Rookstone Castle just being Rookstone Castle, and returned their focus to the table and its small box.

Inga appeared in the doorway, blocking Sage's path. "Out of my way, wench!"

"I was just about to say the same to you."

Sage sneered, but before he could answer, Sir Edward spoke from behind him. "Get out, vermin!"

Scott and Sage turned to see the Tudor noble, not in his customary finery, but dressed in his best armour.

"I say, Beatie's chapel's right upstairs," the Honourable Geoffrey reminded them, gently. "One would hate to have to cry out, what?"

Sage tapped Scott on the shoulder. "There will be other times. They'll let their guard down sooner or later. They always do." The dark spirits faded through the wall into the old torture chamber.

"Need a bally lock on that place," Sir Edward chuntered, irritably.

"We'll keep them in check," Inga asserted. "And well done, Geoff. The Wrath terrifies Sage. He almost got himself trapped in Hell the last time it burned him. That was quick thinking."

Always enthusiastic, Geoff almost floated away with pride, because for him, praise was *rare*.

Jack's eyes glistened in the green light reflected from the emeralds – the *real* emeralds. They were like nothing he had ever seen before, like nothing he would have believed possible, growing up among villains in London's East End.

"You can hold them," Sir Henry broke into his reverie.

Shocked and delighted, he took them, one at a time, holding them to the light.

"And now it's your job to protect them," Sir Henry continued.

"I will." Jack spoke hoarsely.

"*We* will," Richard seconded.

"I *know* you will." Sir Henry smiled, for a spirit had explained to a builder friend of his who these two men were, so that he finally understood their fierce love of the gems on the table before them. There was even a moderate resemblance between them. Both were illegitimate, but nevertheless genetic descendants of George, Duke of Clarence, brother to Richard II, the last Plantagenet and heirs direct of Edward I – the original owner of the emeralds, who placed them into the safekeeping of the Greys once and for all time.

So not the end...
Gary and his lads will return for more ghostly goings-on in
For Keeps | The Railway Papers.

I hope *For Keeps | Rookstone* made you smile. Rookstone itself is inspired by one of Northumberland's many gems, the beautiful Chillingham Castle, owned by Sir Humphry Wakefield. I heartily recommend a visit to anyone travelling that part of the world.

Readers of my stories will have spotted that I love castles and ancient places, I'm sure, but Chillingham will always be one of my favourites. Stuffed with memorabilia from all over the world, there's always something you didn't notice the last time you visited, but my personal fascination is with the castle itself. So many of its rooms feel like its ancient owners have just popped out for something and might return at any minute. Perhaps I'm being fanciful, but it's almost as though they're still there, in the air.

Its place in British border history cannot be doubted, but Chillingham is also a favourite haunt for ghost hunters, no pun intended, and people interested in the supernatural. *Most Haunted* visited there on their first investigation (after the pilot episode). That was also the first time I saw Chillingham, and I just had to visit. In this story, Stan the cameraman's idea to ditch Brandon Porkpie and move into paranormal investigations, while fictitious, is my little homage to Karl Beattie and the *Most Haunted* team who brought ghost hunting to the mainstream. Regardless of any controversy, I thought they were great shows and perfect Halloween fare. You have to love anyone willing to terrify themselves witless, while you sit in a comfy chair in front of the television with the lights low, eating pizza.

Obviously, this story is a work of fiction, and all the characters within it are also purely fictitious, but I did borrow some of the history from Chillingham Castle's long heritage to flesh out the plot – dates of construction, crenellation, etc. Needless to say, my Greys of Rookstone bear no factual resemblance to Chillingham's residents, other than by name. Although Chillingham does have spiral stairs, as I described in the story, some of the towers' main staircases are in straight flights with a quarter-turn at each corner. They're beautifully constructed and impressive. I made them all spirals in the story to reduce confusion with the already complex layout of the castle. The south tower may actually be the oldest – and possibly most haunted – the one named for Edward I. Again, I changed the oldest part of the castle to the north tower within my story to better fit the plot, and to give Gary's accommodation a spookier history. Although the existing castle has a decidedly square stance on the ground, it was built on a more or less north-north-westerly heading, giving it a rhomboid layout when viewed on a map. The west tower, where Sir Henry lives in my story, was converted to holiday suites some years ago by the current owner, Sir Humphry Wakefield. I once stayed there myself during the Christmas period, in the early 00s – a proper winter wonderland under its blanket of snow! The castle only became the four-tower construction we now see, many decades after Edward I's visit, under the reign of his grandson, Edward III. The decorative mullioned window I mentioned in the story is real and was installed specifically for Edward's visit, and is to this day an oddity in that austere elevation (to my eyes, at least) – the other windows on that side being a later addition when the castle became a grand home. Despite being the King of England, Edward, like many of the aristocracy, spoke mostly Norman French, though he could speak and read English and Latin, too. Inga's reaction to hearing it spoken aloud would probably have been natural to anyone walking the Earth during the Harrying of the North, AD1069-70 (even in spirit). That awful event in English history, and what the Normans did to the Saxon people, from York up to Durham, would almost certainly be considered genocide now, as Gary noted. However, back then, it was simply how war was done – although a particularly vicious and egregious example, even by the standards of the day. The risings in the north threatened William I (the Conqueror)'s grip on England, possibly even threatening to reverse his conquest, so there was almost certainly an element of vengeance driving his actions, over and above his desire to quell the insurrection.

Spinning forward to Edward I's reign again (1272-1307), I also borrowed the reprehensible torturer, John Sage, from Chillingham's lengthy and fascinating story. It's quite difficult to find detailed history about the real John Sage, (*soap box alert*) but I believe it's important to remember that such monsters existed and continue to exist to this day. Many physical descriptions of the locations within the story are also based around the castle and grounds. Chillingham is a truly beautiful and intriguing place. I hope my attempts to describe it will inspire readers to visit.

The second worst man in my story was Scott – of no surname. I hope my Scottish friends will forgive me here, but after writing for years about the heroic exploits of Captain James Douglas from Hawick in my New World series, it was time for balance :o)

Most of the measurements used in this book are imperial and this was deliberate. Feet and inches have always been used widely in the British construction industry and only very recently have they begun to fade out with the latest generation of builders. I grew up with metric but the generation before me used imperial, so knowledge of both was essential. Personally, I found metric better for critical accuracy, but in most instances imperial measurement was easier for construction. For example, you *could* ask for a piece of timber stud to be cut to 2133mm or you could simply request 84", so imperial died hard, regardless of legislation on the sales of materials. I mention this because some readers will rightly note that Britain was metric by 1994. However, I wanted this story to better reflect the time, when the older men would have used, almost exclusively, good old imperial feet and inches.

I set the story in the '90s purely for the sentimental value; after all, what's wrong with a little nostalgia? To many of us, we look back to the '80s and '90s as a golden age now, when things were taken so much less seriously – and arguably for granted. Certainly, no one was above being mocked. I've heard those times described as the apex of western civilisation and culture (though others hold that the apex was actually a century earlier). Whatever your views, it could be argued that we enjoyed optimum levels of freedom, but still largely within a framework of respect, and with just enough tech and cool stuff to be interesting, but not so much that it enslaved or stifled us, as some feel that it does today. Although I hope anyone might enjoy these stories for their entertainment value alone, my upcoming FOR KEEPS series is dedicated to any who remember those times fondly. To help further foster memories of that time, I chose chapter titles that were corruptions of songs from popular culture between 1980 and 1994 – recent history when the book was set. Obviously, there was an exhaustive list to choose from and some were more famous than others, but I simply chose titles for no other reason than they fitted with each chapter's theme. You may have guessed a few of them, but here's a list for anyone who's interested:

1 | Smells Like Mean Spirits – a fairly obvious take on Nirvana's 1991 hit, *Smells Like Teen Spirit.* This story was set in late spring of 1994, just after Kurt Cobain's passing.

2 | Sweet Dreams (Aren't Made of This) – again, an obvious one. The 1983 Eurythmics hit, *Sweet Dreams (Are Made of This).*

3 | Dead of the Night – less obvious, perhaps, and deliberately so. Given the theme and the location of the story, it would have been all too predictable to go with Thin Lizzy's *The Boys Are Back in Town,* so I went with another Newcastle band instead, and with Venom's 1985 single, *Dead of the Night.* It fitted the scary goings-on in that part of the story far better.

4 | Boredinary World – my title is a damning indictment on the humdrum day-to-day of working life, perhaps, and a play on Duran Duran's 1992 classic, *Ordinary World.* It's always difficult to write about the ordinary, though often important, tasks we all undertake each day and make them interesting. I try to throw in a few of those 'ordinary world' touches, here and there, to make the characters feel real. Whenever I visit an ancient building or monument, I always place a hand to an ordinary block of stone, or piece of timber. Once a builder myself, I know that the man who laid them was unlikely to be thinking about all the visitors that would admire his work over many centuries to come – he was more likely thinking 'Is it time for dinner yet?' I love that connection to a real person, so long ago.

5 | Hollow Man – Entombed's 1993 classic. I kept the original title, *Hollow Man,* as its meaning – someone with no morals or values – fitted well with the apparent treachery taking place in the chapter and Richard's introspective feelings of guilt.

6 | From Out of Nowhere – Faith No More's first single from their 1989 *The Real Thing* album. Again, I kept the original title, *From Out of Nowhere,* because it fitted exactly with the catastrophe about to strike Gary Stone's life.

7 | Cashes to Ashes – a corruption of David Bowie's 1980 number one single, *Ashes to Ashes.* I'm sure you guessed that one, but Hammer certainly didn't see what was coming when he opened the bag to find fake emeralds!

8 | What's Up – the 1993 hit single by 4 Non Blondes. Again, I kept the original title, *What's Up.* Considering Worzel's run-in with a wild bull during that chapter, and what followed, it would have been rude not to.

9 | 999 Emergency! – based on Motörhead's 1980 belter, *Emergency.* 999 is the British number for the emergency services, equivalent to America's 911. I was quite pleased it landed on chapter 9, too. God bless Lemmy!

10 | Under Siege (Regnum Trullae) – based on Sepultura's 1991 single, *Under Siege (Regnum Irae),* meaning Under Siege (Kingdom of Wrath). My version means Under Siege (Kingdom of the Shovel) – or possibly the trowel; translations vary, but I think both work. I felt very smug about that one.

11 | When Will I Be Famous? – the 1987 hit from Bros. *When Will I Be Famous?* seemed the perfect chapter title to herald the arrival of Brandon Porkpie, of *Whopper TV,* to chronicle Gary Stone's ever-worsening predicament for mass consumption.

12 | Things Can Only Get Better? – D:Ream's 1993 hit single, *Things Can Only Get Better,* made UK number one in early 1994. Recycled by one of our political parties, it's viewed with some irony by many in Britain thirty years later, at the time of writing in 2024. Perhaps the question mark on the end is surplus, and might just as easily have been implied, or dare I say it, inferred, but it fitted with the decline in fortunes of my characters.

13 | What a Fall – borrowed from the widely regarded Stone Roses single, *Waterfall,* from 1991. Needless to say, that chapter charted Gary's swan dive from Rookstone's north tower and his unlikely salvation.

14 | Losing My Derision – as that chapter took place in Rookstone's chapel and was probably the most serious part of the book, I took inspiration for the title from REM's *Losing My Religion.* No surprise, I'm sure.

15 | Cars (and Vans) – title inspired by Gary Numan's classic, *Cars.* Technically, the song was released in 1979, but the song and video in so many ways set the tone for the early '80s that I had to cheat.

16 | My Friend of Misery – from the mighty Metallica, back in 1991. Originally written as an instrumental, *My Friend of Misery* was never a single, but it fitted nicely with the direction of travel the story was taking at that point.

17 | Always the Son – original named *Always the Sun,* by The Stranglers, released in 1986. It marked a point in the story where the younger members of the For Keeps team played more prominent roles.

18 | Barklife – inspired by the title of Blur's hit single, *Parklife.* Certainly iconic of the early '90s Britpop sound, the name was a gift for Poppy's adventure outside to call in the big guns. Although my in-head OCD companion forces me to 'fess up and admit that it wasn't released until August 1994 – after the setting for this story. What a cheat I am!

19 | Sabotage – The Beastie Boys' 1994 *Sabotage* has made its way into films and all sorts of popular culture – even *Star Trek,* somewhat bizarrely – and this one was out in January '94, so I can relax! It fitted with the wilful damage our heroes inflicted when they weaponised Rookstone's fragile electrics and plumbing.

20 | I've Got the Power! – inspired by the well-known chorus to 1990's *The Power,* by Snap!

21 | The Size of a Crown – not sure if this one made it across the pond, but the chapter title was inspired by *The Size of a Cow,* a 1991 hit by The Wonder Stuff. The characters within this story were certainly 'building up their problems' by that point.

22 | Bird Up – a take on *Word Up,* popular again in 1994 after the cover by Gun in July, the track hit the airwaves just in time for the end of this story. An iconic song of the period, the gag in the title made me chuckle, especially after Gary's unintended 'alteration' to the photograph that began our story, so I used it.

To expand on the subject of popular culture, I have to mention another timeline cheat, and make a shout-out to the 2011 internet sensation, and modern-day deer stalker, Fenton the dog – can't remember how many times I watched that hilarious clip, back in the day. He may have been a naughty boy that afternoon, but what a legend!

Thank you for reading. Until the next time...
Stephen Llewelyn

THE NEW WORLD AUDIO SERIES

100 MILLION YEARS OF ADVENTURE

STEPHEN LLEWELYN
DINOSAUR
PERFORMED BY
CHRIS BARRIE
THE NEW WORLD SERIES BOOK 1

STEPHEN LLEWELYN
REVENGE
CHRIS BARRIE
THE NEW WORLD SERIES BOOK 2

"You'll relish this series."
NIGEL MARVEN
WALKING WITH DINOSAURS

NARRATED BY
CHRIS BARRIE
RED DWARF, TOMB RAIDER